BITING BACK

Crowe & Thistle Books

More by the Author

THE POTATOES OF DEFIANCE

A collection of satire and political commentary

BLOOD WILL OUT
(With the Proper Solvent)

A satirical fantasy

A MOST PECULIAR CHRISTMAS
Songs of [J]Oy or Mirth

Christmas carol parodies for our time

(Dedicated to the late, beloved Tom Lehrer
and written under Laurie Hall)

www.LaurenHStoker.com

Biting Back

Unsterbliche Wölfe, Vereint in Adel, Reinheit und Blut

Lauren Stoker

BITING BACK

A Crowe & Thistle Book

For permissions contact:

Crowe & Thistle Books
99 Rocky Hill Road
Plymouth, Massachusetts 02360

ISBN: 979-8-234-01238-8

Library of Congress Control Number: 2026905077

Interior and cover design: Laurie Hall
Moon-phase chapter ornaments (modified): Bianca VanDijk
Wolf's head image (modified): Freepik
All images are license-free.

Dedications

To the late, great Kathryn Robinson,
my old partner in mischief.
I miss your gleeful wit and husky chuckle.

And to Bill Moore, who gave me such fabulous
material to work with.

And to Augustine Dionysius (Tommy) Ready,
my favorite skateboarding ninja.

Also, to Joanne Cavatorta and her husband, the late Gene Cavatorta—
the funniest husband-and-wife writer team I've known.
Miss you, Gene, but thank God that you left me Joanne.

Bet you guys never imagined you'd make it into a book.
(Hope you don't mind that it was mine.)

ONE

SAINT AND SINNER

I didn't choose this life, it chose me. Bit me on the ass, in actual fact. Embarrassing, especially as my underwear was already holey. And now I'm unholy. I really should have listened to my mom—the thing about not going out unless you're wearing good underwear, because you just never know. . . .

You sure don't, Mom. If only I'd stayed home and done laundry. But it was summer, and Friday night, and this girl needed to party.

That bite has really messed up my social life, not to mention giving me bad-hair days for life. And, from what I've read, hairy shape-shifters like me have a long, long life. Unless somebody comes after them with a silver bullet, and I'm not talking about a Coors Light.

It would be nice if I at least matched the description in that song, "Werewolves of London." But my hair is never perfect. And the London part sounds so much classier than "Werewolf of Revere."

Not as in some deranged pet of Paul Revere, the dude who spurred his trusty steed to alert us to the Redcoats' arrival. *That* Revere is commemorated, permanently astride a big bronze horse in Boston's North End. But wouldn't that have been a surprise for the Brits? Talk about making mincemeat of the enemy—steak-and-kidney pie!

But I'm getting off point.

The Revere I'm referring to is the beach town north of Boston, where big hair on women and honkin' gold chains on dudes are still cool. Kinda like the Massachusetts version of the Jersey Shore, only with better roast beef (thanks to Kelly's of roast beef fame). At night, it's not so bad, mixing with the zonked-out drunks and druggies when you're doing your damnedest to walk upright on only two legs and keep your doggy breath to yourself. They're trying their damnedest to walk on two legs, too. See, we have something in common, once a month.

I vividly remember the beautiful full moon shining on the ocean the July night it happened. And still clearly see the guy who bit me. He had a hefty, bearded overbite and a massive mane of hair like an 80s rock star.

"Tell me, darlin', are you a saint or a sinner?" he asked me, bouncing bushy eyebrows. His s's came out like z's: "zaint" and "zinner."

Like a campy Mata Hari, I batted my false eyelashes and replied, "Yes," making him grin wolfishly.

"My, what big teeth you have!" I exclaimed.

"All the better to eat you up with, my lovely!" he replied, long tongue hanging out.

That should have been my clue.

From my somewhat cross-eyed standpoint, I thought he was sort of cute, if a little kinky, when he got down on all fours on the dance floor and bit my butt. I giggled at first, then smacked him a good one when I noticed the blood dribbling down his jaws and the back of my jeans, along with the largish hole that now gaped in both the jeans and me, the iffy panty elastic now dangling out. I don't mind a bad boy now and then, but removing a chunk of my anatomy went a little too far.

And that's when I noticed a disturbing change in him. His amber eyes were glowing and he was growling, and *not* in a sexy way.

The band crashing its way through hard rock covers that night was so loud, no one heard his howl when I kicked him in the *huevos* raunch*eros* and booked it out to my Kia in the parking lot.

But the damage was done, as I found out when the next full moon rolled around.

———

So, yeah, I'm a werewolf now. Lucky me. At least I know better how to handle the losers that hit on me in bars.

But I hate being a bad guy! If I were some sort of Jennifer Dahmer, instead of a reasonably kind person, at least I'd be conforming to type while getting my monthly quota of gore.

That whole thing about ripping people's throats out just because you have a biological urge is crap. I've never liked my meat rare. It makes me gag. But now, thanks to Lon Chaney III (or whoever the hell he was), I have no choice. Or at least I thought I hadn't one.

Eventually, I found out I could make do by pounding espresso shots. (Only during the daytime, obviously. I would *not* want someone like me even wider awake at night at that time of the month.) Slurping blood from Styrofoam butchers' trays helped, too, as well as forcing myself not to cook the meat that day. It did save the landlord a bit on utilities. And I made sure to stay home during the full moon, double-locking the doors and giving the keys for safekeeping to my best friend, Kate Harris, who lives in the apartment across the hall and is the only other one who knew what I was going through. I'd sworn her to secrecy. She also bought me a set of handcuffs and keeps the keys hidden at her place.

But there was this one time, last January, she had to be out of town during the Big Lunar Bloat. Her grandma in Iowa had gotten COVID or RSV, something bad anyway, and the whole family had rushed to Gramma's side. Thankfully, her grandma made it.

But meanwhile, I was stuck.

Despite the below-freezing temps, the lunar pull was so strong I just couldn't help myself. Slinking down the stairs in my XXL-sized parka (you have to allow for expansion) and letting myself out onto the sidewalk, I breathed in the smells of the night. Then gagged and nearly vomited.

By then, I was used to smelling stuff regular people don't. Stuff like three-day-old underwear (like from a block away), a lack of soap or deodorant, a fart that they *thought* was contained, and the scent of fear. This was way worse. It was the stench of sickness and dying.

In the dim lamplight from an apartment across the street, I strained my eyes to see what direction the smell was coming from. Two doors down, by the entrance to another apartment building, a figure was curled up like a decaying fetus. I crept up to it, my unavoidable sinner instincts directing me to take an easy bite. Hit-and-run take away.

But as I got close, my saint side gave that bitch a vicious slap and took over.

Huddled up under the building's heat exhaust vents and wrapped in a single, grey, shelter-approved blanket was a scruffy young man with long, dirty-blond hair and a beautiful face. So beautiful it made me cry.

Gusts from the louvered vents were billowing the thin blanket away from his thin frame. Mouth-breathing, I squatted down to his level and put a hand (that wasn't yet a paw) on him, checking to see if he was still alive. He was, and his clear, green eyes opened, his beard parted, and he gave me a smile. He looked like an angel, his smile like a benediction. Then he reached out a hand and brushed my tears away.

"So have you come for me finally? I was wonderin' when you'd get here."

I didn't know what to say to that. Could he smell that I was a werewolf on the point of change? Or was he mixing me up with some other sinner?

So I shrugged, ashamed of what it looked like I was about to do. "Guess so."

"Don't fret, sweetheart. I've been bad sick a long, damned time. I'm ready. You'll be doin' me a favor, and that's a fact."

Gulping, I nodded, pulling my parka's sleeve across my running nose.

"Will it hurt?" he asked.

I shook my head. "Not much. I'll be gentle. You want some of this first?" I asked, holding out a joint. I always kept one in my jeans pocket for when bad smells and life got too overpowering.

"That sounds just dandy."

No one was around to notice, it was so freaking cold, so I tugged out my lighter and lit up, gave him a hit and took one myself. Then curled up next to him on the cold, cold ground. We passed it back and forth like lovers after loving, watching the stars come out.

He took another long hit and exhaled. Sparks flew into the icy air, then extinguished. "What a beautiful night to join the heavens," he sighed, gazing clear-sighted at the constellations above and the growing, golden moon. "And an angel to help me."

Me, the angel? The irony slammed into me and I burst out sobbing. "I'm sorry!"

"Now, now! No tears for this sinner," he said, smoothing back my dark hair. Then he took my hand in his. He had lovely hands, despite the grubby fingernails. Looked like hands Michelangelo could have carved: holy hands accustomed to prayer.

As if he'd read my thoughts, he said, "Don't be sorry. You're the answer to my prayer."

Then he pulled down the blanket from his neck.

He did know what I was, after all. And didn't despise me.

My tears were soaking my fleece collar, flash-freezing to a rim of ice as he said, eyes crinkled, "Give me a one helluva hickey, woman!"

So I did.

"Wow!" he wheezed. "What a ride!"

Then, still smiling up at me and the stars, I saw the little puff of his soul sail up and away. I licked the tears and blood off my growing incisors, closed those green eyes and swaddled his body inside his blanket, my chest heaving from inexplicable loss.

"Bye," I whispered, to no one present.

A light wind had come up. I was getting hairier by the moment, so needed to hurry back home to make an anonymous call to the police while I could still speak. As I stood to go, the risen moon high above shrugged off a passing banner of cloud and illuminated the man lying still on the sidewalk. I was left in shadow. Some mother's son was gone from the world because of me. At least I'd released him from pain. Kissing the pads of my fingers, I stooped and laid them across his lips, adding my benediction to the moon's purifying light.

I wondered if I'd found my new calling: Angel of Death. A weird, hairy one, if so. I would have to have a spare key made for the handcuffs and hide it from Kate. But maybe this would be a way to make some sense of my life as it now was, and only for those who desperately need helping along. It's not hard to smell the difference.

I think often of what the shifty guy who turned me asked back in that bar: "Are you a saint or a sinner?" Though I'm grasping at the first, I'm stuck lapsing toward the latter. So I guess I'd have to give the same answer: "Yes."

TWO

A MOON FOR HARVESTING

August, the previous year

A slaughter moon was rising red from the sea, and it was making my jaws ache. It was also making my clothes get suddenly tight, which was weird—I was wearing a beach caftan. Lotta room in those, normally.

My buddy, Randy Brewster, and I had come out to hang at the beach for the afternoon and ogle the hot guys with their glistening, bronze bods. We were both between boyfriends.

We'd shared some gummies earlier, but now that it was getting dark and most of the beach partyers had packed up and left, we'd stayed to watch the moon rise and smoke some doobies.

We were lying back on the sand, getting mellow. Exhaling, he raised his joint hand at the August sky and said, "Look at that goddamned Harvest Moon!"

I was trying to match his enthusiasm, but at that moment I was too busy freaking out at the stuff that was happening to my body. It felt like my teeth were growing, especially the dog teeth. And my entire dental bite seemed to be shifting like tectonic plates set on time lapse. When I'd passed him back the joint, I could've sworn my hand was growing fur and long nails. I sat up, heart racing. "What the *fuck* is in this stuff! LSD or something?"

Still gazing at the moon, he laughed lazily. "Pretty good shit, isn't it, Alice?"

"Seriously, Randy, what in unholy hell is going on? Do you see what I'm seeing?"

At this he looked around, then sat up fast. "Oh, Christ. Oh, no. I don't believe this!" Then he backed away a foot or three. He held up a hand, palm out. "Just . . . stay calm, okay?" I think I harshed his buzz. He looked stone cold sober all of a sudden.

"I'm trying to, but you're scaring the crap out of me even more than I was."

"How do I look to you?" he asked.

"Like you always do, when you're stoned."

He nodded. "Well, you sure as shit don't. Now, don't bite my head off—we need to leave. *Now.* I need to get you back to my car and out of here."

By this time I was trembling. "Randy, what's happening? You're scaring me."

"Not nearly as much as you're scaring me," he answered, dousing the joint, grabbing our towels and gear fast, then pulling me upright. "I do believe you've gone down the rabbit hole, Alice. Come on!"

I staggered after him, blubbering in fright. The most hideous noises were happening inside my skull, noises like tendons stretching to snapping tension, molars grinding like glaciers. The hairs were standing up on the back of my neck . . . and all over, and they looked pretty lush.

At the parking lot, he beeped open his black Ford Bronco and threw our stuff onto the passenger seat.

"Where am I going to sit?" I asked, my voice small.

"In the back." He hauled me by the arm around to the back, opened the cargo door. There was a grille between the back seat and the cargo area for the strays and wildlife he rescued in his spare time. "Get in and lie down, Al. There's a blanket you can cover yourself with. I'll get you home. You just need to keep out of sight right now."

"'Kay." I lay down on the rubber mat and pulled the doggy blanket over me.

Randy's a nurse practitioner at Beverly Hospital's ER and was the one who stitched me up after I was bitten on the butt by that overly enthusiastic and hairy admirer at Bill's Surfside on Revere Beach a month back. I was embarrassed to show up at the ER for such a dumb reason, but I'd lost a surprising amount of flesh and was oozing blood. When I came in, explaining diffidently what I needed, the triage nurse smirked and said, pointing down the hall, "Just ask for Randy."

Noting the tall, blond, not bad-looking guy with a brush cut and white coat, I limped down to him. He was the only one around at that time of night, but I still asked, "Are you Randy?"

He grinned and replied, "Often."

I did an eye roll and handed him my triage form.

He looked me up and down with a doubtful smile. "Is Alice Cooper really your name?"

I huffed out a sigh. "Yeah, like the hard rocker, only he does better makeup." My parents had been big fans of his, so choosing my first name must have been irresistible. Then I gave him my story, about the bite.

"Well, *that's* different. Come into my parlor. I'll fix you up." He beckoned me into a curtained examining area and told me to drop my drawers. I gingerly eased them down, what was left of them.

"Didn't your mother ever tell you never to go out wearing holey underwear?"

I groaned. "Hey, they weren't that bad when I started out."

"Yeah, these are pretty shredded. This may sting a bit." He started swabbing my butt cheek down with antibiotic disinfectant.

I yelped. *Understatement of the year!*

"Jeez," he said as he worked. "This guy have braces or something? I've never seen this much damage to underwear or flesh just from a bite, except maybe from a dog."

"No braces, but 'dog' is a good way to describe him," I muttered.

Six stitches later, he told me I could pull my panties back up, if they'd stay up, or just leave the "sad remnants" in the trash can.

"Funny." I scowled at him. "It hurts, you know."

"Yeah, sorry." He grimaced sympathetically. "I'm sure it does. I'll give you something for the pain and some antibiotics. You'll probably want to use a soft pillow for a while to sit on while it heals."

While he was getting my meds, I peeled off my ruined knickers, which parted like bloodied pages from a rejected bodice-ripping romance novel, and tossed them in the trash. When he got back, he caught me gazing at them mournfully.

"They were my favorite pair, damnit, just a tad worn." They had little red apples and a caption running around the band that read, "Bite Me."

He snorted. "I can see why. But it looks like the message was taken literally."

"Hey, it's not like I dropped my jeans in front of him! You think he had X-ray vision or something?"

He backed up, waving his palms at me. "Peace. I'm just funning you." Randy handed me a glass of water and two different pills. "Take these four times a day. And here's the scrip for more." I gulped them down, then he walked me down the hall toward the entrance, matching his stride to my slow limp. "You okay to drive home by yourself?"

"I got here that way," I pointed out.

"Yes, but now you've got meds in you, and you're probably hitting your trauma slump about now."

"Trauma slump, huh?" I smirked at him. "Is that a 'thing'—the technical scientific term?"

"Sure, 'cause I said so."

I nodded an "unh *hunh*" back. "I'll be okay driving home, but thanks for worrying." As I reached the door I looked back. "That was funny, what you said back there."

"What was that?"

"When I asked if you were 'Randy,' " I said with finger quotes. "I'll bet that's a favorite comeback."

He laughed. "Busted. Sometimes I vary it with 'yes.' Or even 'whenever you want.' "

"I'll bet you say *that* to all the girls."

Randy quirked his mouth and said evenly, "Actually, no."

"Ah. Pity. Why do guys always get the good ones, guys I mean?"

He shrugged. "Why not?"

I smiled and gave him a half-shrug back. "Do I need a follow-up or anything?"

"That wouldn't be a bad idea. That was a pretty serious bite. Why don't you come back in a week to let me see how it's healing? Here's my card. If you have any reactions, either to the drugs or the bite, give me a call. Sooner rather than later, okay?"

I took his card and put it and the scrip in my back pants pocket, the one that was still intact, giving it a pat. "I will."

We both hesitated at the door. "Hey, you ever want to hang out with the opposition, look me up." I added, with a wink, "I appreciate randy guys, too, and can always use a good laugh."

Randy had long-lidded blues eyes, expressive sandy eyebrows and a low, dry chuckle. When he was amused, he had a habit of looking down his high-bridged nose, eyebrows raised in the middle and mouth crimped at the corners. He was doing that now.

Smirking, he tutted at me. "Be careful what you ask for."

So, both of us being at loose ends, we started hanging out now and then. It was sort of fun sharing the same romantic tastes and exchanging critiques of the men passing by. We shared the same wicked sense of humor, too. It was also nice, for a change, to be with a guy who wasn't trying to maul me, any way you want to take that.

Which is how we ended up on the beach when the change happened. Rolling around the back of his SUV, I was trying not to scream from the building, tearing pain. "It's bad, Randy! I mean really, *really* bad!" I was starting to froth at the mouth. "Do something!"

Randy pulled over on a dark side street and reached for the med kit he kept behind his seat for the rescues. "I'm coming. Just stay flat and try to relax."

Right. Like *that* could happen.

A moment later, he came around to the back wearing thick leather gloves and holding a syringe. I'd begun bucking and barking. Pinning my legs down with his knees, he gave me a quick jab in the thigh.

A blessed calm washed over me as the tranquilizer took effect. "Sweet Jesus! Thank you." As I started to fade out, I asked him, "Do you think this has anything to do with that bite, Randy?"

His fearful blue eyes confirmed what I dreaded. "Yep. I do."

I used to love watching a Harvest Moon rise. It conjured up warm autumn images: sheaves of corn being gathered in, Halloween night skies crackling with stars, the shriek and giggle of kids dressed up as spooks and monsters, hot cider with maybe a little rum tipped in, candied apples sticking to your teeth. But now . . . Whatever you cared to call it—Harvest Moon, Blood Moon, Slaughter Moon, or even Sturgeon Moon (for you fishy folk)—from here on out, any of its monikers would all bear for me the same shuddering implications.

THREE

SHARING AND SCARING

A Tuesday night in October

I was standing in a gymnasium, with my plastic nametag on, in front of a sea of strange faces and my knees were knocking.

Okay, maybe not so much a sea. More like a murky puddle.

I took a big breath. "Hi, I'm Alice," I began. "And I'm a werewolf."

The last word bounced off the walls, "wolf, wolf, wolf," and I almost snickered.

A wash of "Hello, Alice" came back to me, mixed with some alarmed shushing. I'd forgotten I wasn't supposed to actually say the word, merely mouth it.

Whenever I'd read that clichéd phrase about a person's knees knocking together, I used to guffaw.

"Guffaw" is such a great word, isn't it? Kind of a barked laugh of derision, like that dude on top of the French castle in the *Holy Grail* shouting down at Arthur, "I fart in your general direction!" Substitute "guffaw" for "fart" and you've got the art of guffawing down pat.

And, lord knows, I was good at barking laughter these days. I just wasn't mentally prepared to meet a whole bunch of others who were, too, ones who normally walked on only two legs until a full moon came out.

Hence, the knocking knees. Thankfully, my stripey, wool, thigh-high socks dampened the sound.

I reddened as I saw the leader's warning finger across her lips. They knew what I was anyway, because we were all in the same, hairy fix.

It was my first meeting of the W.A. (Werewolves Anonymous). A month or two ago, I had no idea there were more than two of us, let alone that a whole bunch met monthly in the local high school gym, which doubled as an auditorium.

When I first learned about the group and was told the venue, I'd asked the group leader how in holy hell had they gotten permission to hold their meetings there. She'd said, "Well, we don't call it that, obviously, to the public. We use the name Wise Asses."

I'd done a Scooby Doo *Arruh*? "There's got to be some backstory to that name, right?"

"Sure. We describe ourselves as a sort of toastmaster's group, working on our comedic repertoire for roasting people. Only," she paused, "we don't describe the types of roasts we've taken part in. If you know what I mean."

Eeeeuuuw. But this was my first inkling that others *had* actually done hit-and-run take aways. And apparently even, um, cooked the leftovers. I shuddered.

With her frosted blond, medium-length hair perfectly coiffed and her smart navy suit with its pencil-thin skirt, Sheila, our moderator, could have been anyone's soccer mom. Except she wasn't. Unless she'd had to give up her kids to her ex in the divorce. I didn't like to ask, but that would suck, maybe even more than her life sucked now.

She had looked at me to see if I'd gotten the joke, as well as the warning. I had.

"And why a high school gym?" I'd asked.

She'd lifted an eyebrow. "What are my other choices? Libraries, conference rooms, *churches*?" She had a point. Finding discreet venues for howling fiends would pose a problem.

We were set up at the far end of the gym against the stage, with three rows of folding chairs in a rough semi-circle. I noted all the attendees except one were female and that the women all had on their nametags, but I couldn't read them from up here. The font used on the labels was a bit too fancy. And only about half the seats were filled, which was worrying. Was the leader expecting more? I mean, how far had this wolf man spread his joy? Was there some kind of epidemic of wolf people now?

Anyhow, there I stood, on that October Tuesday night, upfront in the middle, fiddling with my dark, spiky hair, willing my knees to cut it the hell out, and going through the whole saga about how I got this way and why I was sharing it all.

When I finished, a hand shot up from the second row.

"Alice, is it?" the woman asked.

I hate my name, both parts, but especially the first. It's so sweet and old-fashioned, and so not me, even before I changed. Doesn't even suit a dog, unless she were a Golden Retriever. But, hey, I'm stuck with it. With no middle name, and shackled with Cooper, it's a lose-lose.

"Yep, that's me," I said, trying for a sappy, ingratiating smile.

"Can you describe that jerk who bit you again and where it was?" China Doll do in burgundy, she looked mid-thirties or a young 40. Could have been older, of course.

We wear well, I'm told.

"Sure. Hard to forget." I described him and the bar where it happened in detail.

"Was his hair sort of a golden mane, like—"

"An 80s rock star?" I finished.

"Yeah! Like maybe Motley Crue or something?"

"Not that wild. More like David Coverdale. You know, Whitesnake? Only not as frizzy and with a neat Van Dyke."

"Exactly!" Her black yoga pants were bouncing in her seat. "And did he have an intricate gold chain around his throat?" she asked.

I snorted. "Babe, *all* the guys at that bar wear gold chains." This earned some laughter.

"Yeah, been there. But was there this sort of antique-looking pendant of a wolf's head on a shield hanging from it?" she persisted.

I thought about it, running the familiar tape backwards in my mind, hearing the godawful band, seeing the bar, the dancers, the PBR in my hand and the spiked Red Bull in his hairy one . . . then the gleam of gold around his neck . . . and that pendant. I recalled now boozily peering at it and asking if it was an heirloom. He'd laughed at that. "Could be . . . a hairloom," pronouncing the "h" with exaggeration, but not sharing the spelling. I thought he was correcting my pronunciation, or it might have been his accent, and chuckled. That's when he bit me.

"Now that you mention it," I replied, "yes. That pendant was super unusual. The shield looked like some kind of family crest. It had a motto or something beneath the wolf's head in, like, Gothic lettering, and some kind of red cross. Maltese, maybe? Couldn't tell you what it said, though." *Even if I'd been sober*, I added to myself. "And he seemed to have some kind of accent sometimes. Kinda switched on and off."

There was a growing murmur mumbling up, echoing off the basketball court walls. Like a bubble, it burst. "That's the same damned guy who bit me!" China Doll cried. Maybe from Charlestown?

"Me, as well!" an older woman chimed in. She had silver curls and a brogue. "Only I was over to the Porthole in Lynn. The fecker was hitting on me like I was some cougar! I knocked him arseways and he bit me."

A third spoke up—attractive brunette with a swept-back Jackie-O coif, only mildly Stepford Wife-ish: "I was at Maddie's in Marblehead. There was a Halloween contest going on, so I never suspected a thing!"

"Same here, only in Salem!" a fourth exclaimed. Knowing the usual witchy crowd, I tried picturing her with kohled eyes, in a hooded robe, and sporting a pentacle, but failed. Her apple cheeks and golden carrot curls looked more like Anne of Green Gables.

"Damn!" the women chorused.

My eyes went wide, like a rogue linebacker. I probably put my fists on my hips, one of them cocked. Sorry. But canid response can't override the wiring of female attitude.

"So, ladies," Sheila asked, "what do we want to do about it?"

"Get him!" we shouted, fists punching air.

"And you, sir, the gentleman" ("We assume," she murmured) "there in the back row, do you also want to take this creep off the grid? Or would that be letting the brotherhood down?" She arched a plucked eyebrow at him.

The guy slouching in the back looked about 17, high-school age. He had the 'tude down: scowl, shrug, crossed arms, ratty man bun up in a rubber band. Went well with the Ferdinand bull ring in his nose and porthole earlobes. I couldn't help feel sorry for him—to be so young and have his life messed up so badly. Teenhood's bad enough without *this*.

But what did I know? Maybe it gave him a rush and a sense of power—a way to get back at the kids who'd made him miserable. He certainly looked miserable, but then didn't all of us here? Still, if you had massive, flesh-ripping jaws and claws, who needed an AR-15?

I shuddered again. Doing my best to ignore his camo hunting jacket, I prayed I was wrong about him—benefit-of-the-doubt kinda thing.

"Not sure, yet," he drawled at Sheila, with a lip curl. "Need more data about the dude."

"Like what, *dude*?" Maddie's Meagan challenged.

Here, he sat more upright. "*You* know, like a definite I.D., photo, name, something. And, like, what's his story?"

"His 'story'?" she snarled, eyes slitty.

Sheila broke in. "I realize this is your first session with us, sir. As you're new to the group, why don't you introduce yourself?"

She tipped her head, crossed her arms. "I'm sure we'd like to hear *your* story."

"Yeah. He's not even wearing his name tag," objected Salem Suzy.

"Nametags are stupid," he responded.

"In this group, we require nametags to be worn by everyone at each meeting." Sheila pointed to her own. "It's not such a stupid requirement, actually. It helps protect the group from outsiders, as they're printed and issued in advance only by me, upon registration. That, and keeping the keys to the gym on my person while we're here. Luckily, I knew who you were when you came in, or I wouldn't have let you join us. So please, Jared, put your nametag on."

With a grumpy, predictable grimace, Jared yanked his nametag out of one of 20 or so jacket pockets and skewered it onto a lapel. "How didya know who I am?"

Sheila smiled from the cheekbones down. "I know your parents. You look just like your dad did at your age."

This, apparently, was a touché he wasn't expecting. He slid back down in a furious pout. "Keep my parents out of this!"

"As long as you mind your manners, and, shall we say, your menu, that won't be a problem."

His chin made a sharp, challenging up-jab.

Sheila walked up to the front, high heels clicking on the hardwood floor. "You all remember our program's twelve steps, right? For the benefit of our new members, why don't we re-familiarize ourselves with the steps? If you haven't already done so, please pick up a pamphlet from the table, then open it to the outline on page one."

Jared shuffled forward and snatched a pamphlet, then flopped back down in his chair, scuffing the professionally polished court floor. Sheila rolled her eyes but said nothing. Not her budget.

I sat back down in my seat and we opened our pamphlets.

"Now, what's the first step? Sally, will you read it for us, please?" She pointed to the apple-cheeked carrot-top who'd got tagged in Salem.

I wasn't far off, then: Salem *Sally*, not Suzy. It's a little name game I play.

Sally read out, "'Step 1. We admit we are flawed but we are not powerless over our condition.'"

Not? "Is that right? We're all ears," someone harrumphed.

"All the better to hear you with," a woman growled, accompanied by titters.

"And fangs. Don't forget the fangs and large slavering jaws," another wiseass added.

Sheila gestured to Sally "keep going," and walked off to the side.

"Um, 'Step 2. Came to believe that a power greater than ourselves could restore us to sanity.'"

The grey-hair bridled. "And who or what, pray tell, might do the job? It's not batty I've become. I've still got all me wits, thanks very much. And don't you be puttin' this nightmare onto the Blessed Savior."

That was Connie O'Mara, with the brogue, from over in Chelsea. Had a sister in Lynn. I'd met Connie coming in. She's 70 and Irish Catholic. Reformed, she said.

"Some vet with a silver bullet, I'd say," the Maddie's woman whispered back.

"Got that right," someone muttered.

Ignoring them, Sheila asked the woman who'd been duped at Maddie's Sail Loft, "Martha, why don't you read the next couple?"

Martha, huh? Damn, I'm good. Martha is as good as Meagan, right?

Martha mumbled, clearly mortified, "'Step 3. Made a decision to turn our will and our lives over to the care of God as we understood Him.'"

Somebody snorted. I had a hard time avoiding it myself. Like that would fix everything.

"And . . . ?" Sheila prompted.

Breathy sigh. "'Step 4. Made a searching and fearless moral inventory of ourselves.'"

Ouch! Who wanted an inventory? Like a body count? And was this saying this was supposed to *our* faults?

"Emma, would you care to read the next couple?"

Young Emma (from Everett I hoped—I was on a roll) responded, "Not really, if it's all the same to you, Sheila."

Emma looked to be about 18, maybe 19, at least in body language and neon hair tints on her shoulder-length, black hair. Sheila waited, peering down her nose.

"Ah, go on, Emma," Connie hissed. "You'll only have to do it in the end. You know how she is."

Emma snatched Connie's pamphlet, and read in a sullen monotone: "'Step 5. Admitted to God, to ourselves, and to another human being the exact nature of our wrongs.'"

Well, our butts were here in the seats, weren't they? Check that one off, anyway. Emma looked up at Sheila, who was waiting for a further installment.

Heavy sigh. " 'Step 6." Emma rolled her green eyes and droned on, "'Were entirely ready to have God remove all these defects of character.' Happy?" She passed the pamphlet back to Connie, her metal chair whanging as she slumped down. "Yeah, right. God to the rescue!"

At this Jared was huffing and bouncing in his chair, hand upraised.

"Yes, Jared?" Sheila forebear to ask him.

"How is getting turned into a werew—"

Connie shushed him, under lowered brows, nodding sharply up toward Sheila. "You're not supposed to say the 'W' word here, in case, *you* know . . ." Here, she head-gestured around the ceiling at the security cameras.

Jared smirked. "They're just cameras. They can't *listen*."

"You're sure about that now, are ye? Well, I always say, where there's eyes, there's sure to be ears."

Emma, who was closest to Jared's age, leaned back and muttered to Jared, "It's one of Sheila's rules, so just go with it."

"You were saying, Jared?" Sheila skewered him with a look.

"Yeah, I was, wasn't I? So, how is getting changed into . . . what we are . . . a 'defect of character'? And who wrote this crap? Except for the altered first step, it's a total rip-off the AA's steps."

All eyes were on Sheila's red face, followed by dead silence, apart from coughing and squirming butts squeaking on metal. I was beginning to like this kid.

Jared scowled down at his pamphlet, reading, then stood up and stared Sheila right in the eye. “It is, by God! It’s the stupid AA 12 steps all over again.” He read in a mocking falsetto, “‘Step 7. Humbly asked Him to remove our shortcomings.’

“Well, that’s all fine and good, but my ‘shortcomings’ weren’t what got me this way. Anyone else?” His daggered gaze swept the room. “Anybody have, I don’t know, a childhood yearning to rip out people’s throats for a giggle? Maybe you followed the bastard who turned you back to his lair, begging him, ‘Please sir, set me free to be with thee!’” Jared’s hands were clasped like Oliver Twist’s in supplication. “‘All I’ve ever wanted to do is maul and murder.’ Anyone?”

Sheila opened her mouth to object, but before she could get a word in, Maddie’s Martha stood up, and stabbed her pamphlet. “Oh, this one’s rich: ‘Step 8. Made a list of all persons we had harmed, and became willing to make amends to them all.’”

Fuck’s sake, again with the inventory! So did Miz Sheila keep a spreadsheet or something?

Martha must have had the same thought and asked her, “When you were roaming the streets, did you keep a little black book or collect their business cards, perhaps? You know, the ones you nibbled on?”

(Grisly thought.) And no answer.

Like a Tiananmen tank, Martha rolled on. “‘Step 9. Made direct amends to such people wherever possible, except when to do so would injure them or others.’ Now, I’m more than willing to apologize to them, although it might be tough for them to hear *six feet under*. And you’re making us out like we’re trying for sainthood. Yay, Team Saints!”

Sheila’s mouth gaped open again like a guppy’s, attempting to speak.

Martha waved it shut. “And I’m willing to bet, if we just strolled up on a full moon to their heirs’ homes, begging forgiveness, there’d be even more to apologize for.”

Agreement muttered the room, punctuated by more butt squeaks.

Connie flipped open her own pamphlet and pronged on her bifocals, head shaking. “I *knew* I should have put me specs on when I was goin’ over this.” She sighed and set it down on her lap. “Sheila, love, I know ye meant well . . . but seriously?” She read, ‘Step 10. Continued to take personal inventory and when we were wrong promptly admitted it.’

"I think you're just a wee bit hung up on this inventory stuff, Sheila, love. Or was it just laziness, an easy cut-and-paste and ye didn't have yer readers on? Do ye make up spreadsheets of them all?"

I fiddled with my Goth-black gelled spikes. Great minds were thinking alike.

Shoulders hovering under my ears, I stood. "Look, I know this is my first time and all, but most of these steps don't really apply to our actual . . . situation. Like these two, for instance." I read, "'Step 11. Sought through prayer and meditation to improve our conscious contact with God as we understood Him, praying only for knowledge of His will for us and the power to carry that out.'"

I sighed. "If it only was a matter of prayer and meditation—"

"Or medication," some joker interrupted.

"—I'd be over the moon, um, I mean thrilled. I used to be all about the meditation thing, mantras and the rest. But I'm pretty sure all the conscious contact with the supreme being won't fix this. And I just can't get my head around believing our curse is His will. Sorry."

I referred back to my pamphlet. "Or the last one: 'Step 12. Having had a spiritual awakening as the result of these steps, we tried to carry this message to others like us, and to practice these principles in all our affairs.'"

Sheila threw her shoulder pads back and thrust up her trembling chin. "The last one works, at least. That's why I set up this group, after all."

There was a general nodding of heads, affronts simmering off the boil.

Connie stood. "And it was right and brave of you to do so." Sheila's face was turning puce again. "There now, Sheila. You've done a good thing, indeed ye have. We could all try better to be saintly. It's just . . ."

Half turned away, Sheila asked sharply, "Just . . . what?"

"Look, what about this? Why don't we make up our own steps, ye know, to fit *us*, help this group here and the awful thing that's been imposed upon us? Wouldn't that be a good approach, a better way to go about it all?" Connie asked, appealing to the room. A susurration of yesses spread.

"Right then. And it would likely be a fair bit shorter, cheaper to print, ye know." Connie seemed to have the business head in the group, as well as being the den mother. "Let's you and me put our heads together on this, shall we, Sheila?"

Sheila tipped an "Okay" with her head.

Connie twisted back in her seat, facing the rest of us. "But just because the pamphlet is a bit off, it doesn't take away the sound mission of the group. None of us, I feel quite certain, wants to harm another."

"Unless, like, the guy really, really deserves it." That was Jared, grousing in back. So maybe my suspicions were right about him.

"Not even then, young man. Sure, didn't Christ say to turn the other cheek?" Connie lobbed back. I reddened, thinking of my *un*bitten one. I was glad I hadn't offered it up and still had an intact one to sit on.

"Revenge is never the way, Jared, and ye know I'm right. Think of what yer poor father went through."

Tight little community, this. Now it was Jared's turn for red-face.

Sheila glanced at the big clock on the gym's wall and clapped: half-time. "Okay, people, let's form groups and do some brainstorming about ways we can cure the urge and turn our disability into a plus for our communities!" Jared's story would have to wait.

I was thinking sharing my own "solution" had better take a pass, too.

I caught Jared and Emma banking eye rolls off each other at Sheila's psychobabble. Still, I was up for living and learning, and vice versa.

Sheila passed around a sign-in sheet, asking only for our names, phone numbers and email addresses. "I'll email you all the list when it's completed. And I'll assign buddies for the ones who don't yet have them. It's important that you all have a buddy to turn to when things get scary."

"How's that gonna work," Emma muttered, "when we're all getting 'scary' at the same time?" I shrugged. Guess I'd find out. Maybe we could work out a relay system. "Clean-up in aisle—." Never mind.

An hour later, at 10 p.m., just as we were all getting stiff and brain-dead from numbing input/output, Sheila took pity on us and let us out of school. No brain-storming light bulbs had gone off anyway. We gathered up our notes, shrugged on coats, and headed for the parking lot.

As soon as we got outside, we all did a quick neck crane to check the moon and remind ourselves of its current stage: waning crescent. It was like we were doing a choreographed "wave," only with heads. Would have been funny, if you didn't share our paranoia. Naturally, meetings were scheduled when the moon wasn't remotely close to full, which must have taken some jockeying, considering all the school's night games and social activities. But our knee-jerk (or neck-jerk) habit was hard to quell, especially for the ones who'd been cursed the longest.

I found myself wondering about that, about how long each group member had been struggling with the change. Connie had mentioned getting bitten at the Porthole in Lynn, the town her sister lived in. As a hang-out, it was an icon in its day, but after 51 years closed shop in 2018.

Doing the math made me sick, thinking of my own future.

And I also was wondering about Jared and what the whole thing about his dad was about. It was odd he was the only male in the group. I tried to picture his getting hit on by the guy who chomped on me, and failed. Wolfman could have been bi-, I suppose. Or just had too much of an urge for a fresh throat to be fussy about whose it was. But something wasn't quite adding up.

As I reached my Kia, I saw Emma and Jared talking together. He looked extra bummed and furious. She had a sisterly hand on his shoulder, as if she was trying to talk him off the ledge. I threw my bag in my car and walked over.

"You okay, Jared?"

"Just peachy," he jeered.

I put my palms up. "Sorry! I just meant . . ."

"Nah, I'm sorry. I'm just so pissed at Sheila's veiled threats. And I don't know what in fucking hell I'm going to do! Right now, the thought of ripping someone's throat out has big appeal, full moon or not. Know what I mean?"

"I do. . . ." Trailing off, I looked hard at him. "But I'm doing my damnedest not to give in to that. Look, you want to go for a coffee? There's gotta be a Starbucks somewhere close by. There always is."

He hesitated. "Does coffee actually help, or is that just some bullshit the others handed you?"

"I find it does, especially the closer I get to being mooned. Come on. I'll buy."

"Okay if I tag along?" Emma asked.

“Why not? The more, the loonier.”

I actually got a chuckle out of Jared. “That was good, actually. You know—the connection of ‘looney’ with ‘lunar’?”

I smiled back. “I try.”

“So, there’s a Starbucks just a couple of blocks away,” Jared said.

“We’ll follow you, then.”

We saddled up in our cars and headed off after his rusted-red banger.

FOUR

TRE, UP FRONT AND CAFFEINATED

Grouped together inside the coffee shop, we picked up our overpriced, frou-frou coffees (mine was a cappuccino with a double espresso shot) in laughably-named sizes. "Tall" was a small, in actual fact; then they went all Italian: medium = "*grande*," large = "*venti*," extra-large = "*trenta*." I couldn't think why they switched to Italian, except to disguise the fact that a large was about 20 times more expensive, and so on. Or maybe it was a measurement thing. But judging by the bill I got for three coffees, my bet was on the first guess.

Scraping our Euro-trendy chairs up to a tiny, round table in the farthest corner, we sat and sugared up. This late on a school night, we were the only ones there, besides the zombie-eyed staff, longing to close.

Stirring my coffee thoughtfully, I was racking my brain how best to approach a touchy subject. "So, is this your first time, Jared? Were you a werewolf virgin?" didn't seem to be the best to go with.

It was Jared who took the plunge. "You're probably wondering about my family, right? The 'goods' Sheila and Connie have on them."

"It crossed my mind. Would they, like, ground you forever if they knew? I mean it's not like it's your fault." I paused. "*Is* it?"

"*No*, it's not my fault! Why would you even think that?" Jared jammed his straw into the bubble top of his caramel *macchiato grande*.

"Of course we don't, Jared," Emma put in. "I can't imagine anyone asking for this, like, knowingly bringing this on themselves."

Actually, I could, if someone were wickedly wired that way or too angry and stupid to work out the consequences—that old-time lure of immortality, plus getting your own back.

Emma forged ahead. "So did someone else in your family, um, go that way and you don't want to add to their worries by letting them know about yourself . . . or something?" Her voice dwindled.

"I guess you could say that, yeah. Someone else in my family 'went that way,' as you put it."

Jeez, so maybe Lon III was bi-. Or was it trans? I gave up jumping over both sides of the gender fence. Cartoon bubbles with giant question marks were figuratively popping up over our heads. Emma and I sipped and waited.

"It's my dad," Jared mumbled, finally. Four eyebrows shot up and two chairs scooted back, fast.

"No! He's not the one that's out there turning people. Honest! He's a good guy."

Emma and I scooted back in, prodding him with beetled brows.

"It's hereditary for us, our family, anyway. Only hits the males and skips a bunch of generations, showing up again just when it finally seems safe, like it's used up its evolutionary whatsit. Lucky us."

Emma and I slid suspicious eyeballs toward each other.

"So, how does that work, exactly?" I asked.

"I don't *know*, 'exactly.' It's like some recessive gene or screwed-up chromosome, or something."

"Sucks to be you, then," Emma said.

"Oh, ha ha. You're in the same boat," Jared pointed out.

"You're right. All three of us are. It's just you've had a lot longer to get used to the idea, as it's in your history and DNA."

"Which actually makes it worse. Why do you think I don't want my dad to know? He's been struggling my whole life to keep me safe from it. We had special tests done, and it looked like I'd be okay."

"You can get tested for this?! By whom? Or what?" Emma demanded.

"By a friend of our family, a scientist. Works on some really twisted things, shit like hypertrichosis."

"*Gesundheit!*" I responded. "What's this 'hyper-tricky . . . ?' I give up. What you said."

Jared graced us with a smile, albeit a smug, attempt-at-omnipotence, 17-year-old smile. "Hypertrichosis is just the fancy word for 'werewolf syndrome.' It causes excessive hair growth basically anywhere on a person's body, and it's not always the same with each person. The abnormal hair growth can cover the whole face and body, or just show up in small patches."

"Terrific. Doggy alopecia." I snorted. "So each victim looks different under the change, then?"

"Pretty much. Haven't you ever looked in the mirror during . . . ?"

"No! I think I would have lost my mind," I said. "It was bad enough just seeing my limbs grow fur and sprout claws!"

"Yeah, well, you're still new to this. I've had to witness my dad when he was starting the change since I was a kid. Not a pretty sight. Mom always whisked him away, of course, to the basement. Or the dungeon, as she calls it. We've got shackles down there and everything. And, yep, he goes the whole way, full wolf." He shook his head, sorrowfully.

"God, it must be so hard on you and your mom. So what about you? Do you look the same as your dad when you turn?"

"Not so much." Jared looked away. We waited. "Okay, I look more like an Airedale. Happy?"

"Oh, man." Emma and I had clapped hands over our mouths, busting not to laugh.

"Well, it could have been worse, I suppose. Like a Chihuahua or a Bichon Frisé," Emma said, then thrust her nose into her latte.

"A what?" Jared screwed up his face. "What's a 'bitchin' frisbee'?"

Trying my damnedest not to guffaw, I enunciated, "*Bichon Frisé*," in my prissiest Poirot French. "It's a small, white, fluff-ball lapdog. They're very cute."

Jared glared at us. "It's not funny!"

At this, she and I both writhed in mirth. "Yes, it is!" we chorused.

Finally getting the picture, Jared started laughing. "Yeah, it is."

"I mean, can you imagine?" Hiccupping, I leaned forward, eyes wide in mock terror. "The moon's full, you smell the scent of blood, and there's your prey, right ahead. You race up and . . . yap?"

"Scary," said Emma, lips trembling.

"And with my luck," snorted Jared, "my target would just call the dog catcher to haul my ass away, thinking it's a simple case of rabies. Fat chance I'd have then of striking the fear of *dog* into the rat bastards at school." Nice use of anadrome. Kid was smart.

"Ah, I did wonder if the scare factor might be a plus for you, in your situation. You get a lot of bullying at school, do you?" I asked.

He shrugged. "The usual. Science geeks aren't on the popularity list, not at my school. It's like those bozos are still locked in the 60s, all sports and babes with big tits but no brains."

"I have heard the kids here can be pretty rough at this high school."

"I don't go here. We live in Salem and I go to the high school there. But school bullies are pretty much the same everywhere."

I nodded, processing that, and turned to Emma. "How about you, Emma. You live close by?"

"Lynn, like Connie."

Well, there went my name/town match mojo, unless maybe Emma lived on Elliot Street or something. Back to Jared. "You said you're a science geek."

"Kinda had to go that way, on account of my dad."

"Your dad is a scientist?"

"No, on account of his *condition*," he replied with an implied "duh."

When he still saw the disconnects in our faces, he said, "Look, the caring and worrying part goes both ways, at least if you have a dad as kind and cool as mine. He's been bending over backwards to keep me from becoming like him, which is why he'd be devastated if he found out. And I'm trying to figure out a way, scientifically, to fix *him*."

Jared's face was red again. Emma and I had both expelled an "Awwww."

She leaned over and put her hand over his. "We shouldn't have teased. This stuff is really tough, Jared, on everyone."

"You can say that again!" Jared mumbled.

Emma swivelled in her seat fast, spearing me with a "Don't go there!" just as my mouth opened to do just that—say it again. It had been a long night and hysterical laughter was overdue, all things considered.

I stood up and collected my trash. "Maybe you'll find a way, Jared. You're smart and you care."

He shrugged.

Emma was studying him thoughtfully, like maybe he was just bullshitting us. "So," she asked him, "you've never been tempted to get your own back at these 'rat bastards,' as you call them? You know, besides scare the bejesus out of them?"

"Of course I have. And I did once. Thought I'd never get the taste out of my mouth." He made a gagging gesture, one finger down his throat. "The kid got whisked away to the ER, but lived. Kind of a shame. He's one nasty piece of work. The world would do just fine without him.

"But it scared me, *bad.* So I'm done with that shit. My buddy, Dion, talked me down, too. That helped."

"Don't tell me he's another one!" I whimpered.

"Nah, he's just a regular dude. Well, an outsider like me, just— He stays in the same form. But he can kick ass when he needs to. He's the one that got the assholes to back off."

"I would have thought your attack would have achieved that. Don't those kids know it was you?"

"Nope. I was in full, you know, Airedale, at the time."

"Good thing. Otherwise, they would definitely have thought you were barking mad."

Laughing, we all high-fived, then got up and slam dunked our coffee cups into the gleaming, chrome trashcan.

"So, if your parents don't know about your change, how'd you hear about the group?" Emma asked. "Sheila contact you?"

"Nah. Dion saw that 3x5 card in the convenience store and told me I should come. You?"

"Same. The card, not Dion," she smirked. "Plus junk mail."

"See you in a month?" I smiled at him encouragingly.

"Sure," Jared said. "And, guys, um, thanks for listening."

We gave him another "Awwww" and a hug.

As I reached the door, I turned back as something occurred to me. "Wait! Have you seen any of the others' transformations?" I asked Jared.

"Uh huh: Connie. She looks like one of those Bitchin' Frisbees."

FIVE

PRIVATE EYES ARE WATCHING YOU

Hugging my bag to my chest, I crossed the parking lot, heading to my car. Starbucks turned off its lights. In the dark customer lot, our cars were the only ones left. Jared's old banger rattled off in a tattoo of backfires. I smiled at his ratty ride, recalling my own starving student days, then gave Emma a wave as she took off in her tan Hyundai.

I checked the sky again. The night was black and still and getting chilly. Just three strides from my car door I heard a whistle, a long, rather musical one. You know that eerie, three-note whistle in *West Side Story*, when the Jets are on the prowl? Like that. I felt the hairs on my neck and arms stand to attention, despite the absence of moonlight. Shivering, I whipped my head around, peering into the dark to see who or what had whistled. Not another soul moved, as far as I could see. But I felt eyes watching me—a psychic pressure that made me jam my key into the lock, jump inside, and lock the doors. Without the pull of a full moon on my anatomy, I was as vulnerable and weaponless as any other female.

I forced myself to resist burning rubber out of the lot. Predators love a chase. My eyes kept jerking up to my rear-view and side mirrors, half-expecting a set of amber eyes and snarling maw to spring into view.

"Alice, honey, get a goddamned grip!" I scolded myself. "He can't be everywhere." Assuming there's only one of him. And, of course, there wasn't, was there? There was a whole group of us I'd just met, all trying to figure out a way to foil the curse and be good citizens. So we said. I had to admit to myself that a twelve-step (well, make that a TBD number of steps) self-help group, would offer a perfect opportunity for a shape-shifter to size up the competition, and maybe eliminate it.

But it wouldn't do to go all paranoid about my new buds at this stage, not without more data, as Jared said. "And anyhow, it's not even the new moon so Lonnie boy would be in normal human form," I told myself. As normal as he ever got, that is. "Still, let's not just hand him our address on a platter," I told myselves (the human and un-). So I kept checking for a tail, as in a car, not one connected to a four-legged body hanging its head out a window.

I made some clever twists and turns and block-circling, just to throw a would-be pursuer off the scent. Then felt like a double ass, and not a wise one.

Didn't see a single headlight following me so, dousing my lights, I eased into our communal apartment lot, shared with two other buildings, parking in the shadows and hoping my Hyper Red Kia would somehow melt into them. Yes, that is the actual name of the color and not a comment on its owner, thank you very much. I thought it was funny when I'd bought the car off the local, no-money-down automart a couple of years ago. Matched my partying personality, Kate had joked. Now, I wished I'd gone for the Steel Gray.

Walking quickly to our building's back security door, I let myself in via the keypad. At my unlit landing, just as I was releasing the tumblers of my deadbolt, I heard a sound behind me and jumped a foot.

Kate was standing by the hall window, cracked open to let the smoke from her cigarette out. "You're home late," she commented through a smoke ring.

"Jesus! Will you cut that out? You nearly gave me a heart attack!"

"You still nagging me to stop smoking?" she asked, peeved. "I thought we'd been over this 'heeding one's health' thing a million times. My lungs, my life."

"No, not that. Cut out the lurking in dark hallways thing."

She laughed.

Kate had the best laugh. You could never stay annoyed at anyone with that laugh—low, throaty, sexy. A smoky, whisky voice, although a six-pack of Mich Ultra was more her thing.

"And just what are you doing, lurking in the dark, Katie dearest?"

"The Sandersons next door were having another holy holler. I was listening in to try and calculate how many more place settings of the wedding set got bashed and whether or not to call the cops this time."

Amused, I cocked my head, and squinted sideways at her. "Uh *hunh*. You were also waiting for the howls of make-up sex. Am I right?"

Another chortle followed, along with a choking cough as she fanned away the fumes. "Jeez, I really got to stop sucking these things."

I threw up my hands in defeat. "I'm not saying one more word, missy, about that!" I turned my key in the lock. "Want a nightcap?"

"Sure." Kate stubbed out her Marlboro on the sill, adding a blackened mark to the dozens of others, and followed me inside. "Killing my kidneys is just as good as killing my lungs."

I turned on her and made a "zip-it!" gesture across my lips.

She loved winding me up, tempting me to trot out my "evil nicotine" lecture. I'd shown her full-color photos of what her addiction did to lungs, telling her how they turned hard like tough plastic and couldn't expand. All righteous and mom-like. She'd just give me that look, the one that said, "Oh yes? And how are you handling *your* addiction, the one where you can barely stay away from fresh flesh, especially when it's still on a body with a beating heart?"

She had me there. "But," I would harrumph to myself, "at least I didn't choose it." The end result, I had to admit, was just as killing.

I dumped my bag on the table and grabbed a couple of beers from the fridge. "Sorry, I've only got Rolling Rock."

She scraped up a chair and waved away the apology. "Still gets the job done." The chair jostled my bag, which vomited out half its contents. As we chased the lipsticks, eyeliners and ballpoint pens out from under the table, Kate pounced on the W.A. pamphlet which had joined them.

"W.A., huh?" She was skimming down the 12 steps of the program. "Jeez, this sounds just like AA, except, I'm guessing it's not."

I sighed. "Yeah, it is, but only for . . . you know."

"Werewolves?"

"Yep. Anonymous."

Kate's eyebrows rose. "Christ! There's a group of you?!"

"Sick, right?"

"Silly old me thought, no, make that *hoped*, it was only the two of you, the biter and the bitee. Sounds like this dude gets around."

"It certainly does. Most of the group is female. There's just one guy, and it turns out with him it's genetic, passed down from his dear papá."

"You sure he's not the actual biter?"

"Oh, I'm sure!" I laughed. "One, not enough hair and gold jewelry. And two, way younger." I gave her a description of Jared, and how he became wolfish through the family curse, and she seemed satisfied.

"But do you truly think everyone there is on the up-and-up, trying to overcome the urge, instead of just going with the flow. Pardon the pun."

"Pardoned. It seems so, but it's early days. I've only met a few, but I'm keeping vigilant."

"Good girl!" Kate took a swig from her Rolling Rock and belched. "So, tell me about the meeting."

I gave her the sad, sordid details.

At length, she sat back and expelled an amazed whoosh of air. "Man, I need another smoke." I gestured grumpily toward the hall landing.

She shook her head. "Nah. I'll be good. Got another rock-and-roller in there?"

"I do, in fact." I grinned, grabbing two more cold ones from the fridge, and passed one to her.

"Good." We twisted the tops off and swallowed, mired in thought.

Kate banged her half-empty bottle down and leaned forward. "You know what we need to do?"

"We?"

"Well, yeah. I mean what's a friend for, if not for . . ." She waited for me to finish the cliché.

I knew her sense of humor, so finished it with: "For holding the fur out of your eyes while you're wolfing someone down?"

There came that laugh again. "Exactly!" We bumped bottles and drank. "Although, you do know, Al, I wouldn't joke about it if I didn't know what a good person you are and that you genuinely hate this . . . this situation."

"Yeah, I know, Kate, I know."

We both sobered.

"What a foul, crap thing to happen—to anyone, let alone the person I care most about in the whole world. Well, besides Reggie, of course, but he's no longer in it." Reggie was her sweet, black lab, who'd gone to doggie heaven. Now we were sniveling and hugging.

My chin wobbled as I nodded. "Oh, Kate! What am I going to do?" I wailed.

"Well, as I was about to say, before I so rudely interrupted myself, what we need to do is form a posse."

"A posse, huh?" I sniffed then snickered.

Images from *Blazing Saddles* were sprinting through my mind, Harvey Korman swearing in a bunch of rejects, too stupid to replace "your name" with their own. And Gabby Hayes hobbling up to warn the good townspeople, "The sheriff is a werew—" as the church bell gonged him out.

My chest was heaving again and beer was spurting out my nose as I cracked up.

Kate pursed her lips and gave me the hairy eyeball, although that was more my thing than hers. "What?" she demanded.

I repeated the swear-in and gonging Gabby Hayes parts, then sang a suggestive stanza from the "Darkie" railroad scene: "I get no kick from champagne. . . ."

She rolled her eyes, then broke up, singing back, "Mere alcohol doesn't thrill me at all, but I'll get a bite out of you!"

"No, but seriously!" And we busted up again, spewing beery suds over the table. Our laughter ran its course and I put my head in my hands and groaned.

"It could work, you know. Maybe," she said.

"I'm all—"

I was about to say "ears," but caught the mischief leap in her eyes again. "I'm listening."

She waggled her head sadly at the ceiling over the lost comedic opportunity. "Okay, for starters, you've got me, right?"

"Oh, Kate. I don't want to put your life in peril, as well as others'. I could never live with myself if something bad happened to you because of me."

"It won't. I have a lot of silver," she replied inscrutably.

"I honestly don't think your silverware will do a lot of damage, even if it is sterling. Bread knives are pretty dull. And that armful full of silver bangles you wear, bonging away, might hurt his eardrums but surely that would only make him lunge for you just to stop the blasted clanging."

Her bottom lip stuck out and her upper lip trembled. Oops.

"You said they looked cool. You said I sparkled like a sexy gipsy."

With narrowed eyes, she got back to business. "*Anyway*, who's talking about bread knives or bracelets?" She waited.

So did I.

Huffing, she gave in. "I happen to own a gun."

Yikes! "A gun?" I asked in fright.

"A gun," she pronounced, nodding owlishly and peering over her uptilted nose.

"Um. Do you know how to use it?" Picturing poor aim and bloody mayhem, I had to ask.

"I do. 'And I'm a dead eye shot, shooting.' "

Right outa the script of *Help!* I had to smile. It was one of our favorite films.

"Good to know. So I'm assuming you also have silver bullets?"

"That would be affirmative, pardner."

"How?" I asked limply.

"I called in a favor from a pawnbroker friend. He has a little side biz melting down what doesn't move. *Sell*, I mean," she amended quickly, knowing I'd imagine some old guy on a bad day, torching rats and recumbent druggies behind his shop with his flame thrower.

Then the penny dropped. Tails up. "Were you planning on, um, using it on me?" I asked, shrinking into my chair.

She came around and hugged me. "Oh, Al. Of course not. Unless I had to. *Absolutely* had to."

Some comfort there. Not much, but some.

"But a girl has to look after herself. With at least one other of you guys out there, I wanted to be ready for him, if it came to that."

"Yeah, I get that." And I did. I still scooted my chair away, just a teensy bit.

She paid no attention. "So, back to the posse."

I put a crossing guard palm out. "Hang on. So far, there's only the two of us. How are we going to round up more? Pardner. You and Randy are the only ones who know about my predicament and I really would like to keep it that way."

Her eyes slid over to the W.A. pamphlet. An auburn eyebrow raised. "Have you forgotten something, Sherlock?"

I did a head slap. "By Jove, Watson, it appears I have," and groaned again. I thought, *This is really getting out of hand*, and said so.

"Well, it's too late to worry about that, wouldn't you say?"

I grimaced, nodded, and pulled my beer forward.

"But it's all good, actually. Al, it sounds like you've got a ready-made posse with your wolfy group, and from what you told me, the women at least are raring to take the fricker down."

Kate may sound like a female trucker with a 10-packs-per-day and a fifth of Jack Daniels habit, but she's too lady-like to cuss. "We've just got to come up with a plan."

"Oh, that."

We raised our bottles and drank.

SIX

VANITY, THY NAME IS WOLF

Wednesday morning, as I dragged my hangover out of bed, my cell was pinging. And pinging. I squinted at it, but the bathroom had more urgent calls. The messages would have to wait.

Relieved, I started the coffee and rummaged for the Pop-Tarts. Stuffed one in the toaster and waited for the java to brew. I worked from home, mostly doing data entry and transcribing medical records and white papers for some local docs, so my hours were pretty flexible.

Back in bed, cradling my Pop-Tart and coffee, I checked my texts. The first was from Randy. So were the second and third.

WTF? I tapped the first one.

"Got another patient in last night in ER. Same MO as you. Call me."

This was followed by: "Al? Did u get my text? Kinda urgent. Call me, OK?"

Then, "Alice where the F R U? Call me ASAP. I'm home. Randy."

I checked the time. I dialed his cell, hoping he hadn't had to do the graveyard shift again. He had said it was urgent.

A coughing, froggy voice croaked, "Hello?"

"It's me, Randy. Alice. You said to call you ASAP."

He groaned. "That was last night. It's now the crack of godawful. Had to pull another late shift in the ER last night."

"Sorry, but I had a meeting, so didn't see your texts until this morning. What's up?"

I could hear the strike and flare of a match. He'd be coming to any time now.

He exhaled a grateful puff. "Last night there was another woman who came in with a humongous bite on her derriere. You were lucky you were wearing jeans. She'd only had on a pair of Pilates pants, so the damage was worse. A whole lot worse. Had to give her a rabies shot, just in case."

"You never gave *me* a rabies shot," I harrumphed, rubbing the sizeable divot in *my* derriere.

"Early days, Al." He took another deep inhale. "Her undies looked like they'd gone through a shredder. Fell off her like bloody tickertape. And this time, I kept them as evidence. Did some DNA swabs, too."

"Smart. Where'd she been?"

"Same place you were, that bar in Revere with the tone-deaf hard rockers."

"She describe the guy?" I asked.

"Yes ma'am."

"You think it was the same dude?"

"From what she said, yes. Same hair and beard, height, and square-jawed toothy grin. Even asked her the same question. Oh, and he was wearing this weird pendant with a wolf's head. Was your guy wearing one of those?"

I shuddered. "Yep. He was." I told him then about the W.A. meeting the night before and how one of the women had asked about that, among other things, and how at least four of them confirmed that the guy who'd done the tag-and-turn on them matched the same description.

"No shit," he commented.

"No shit," I confirmed.

"Well, this is a major CF. Not that it wasn't already. So this asshole is just spreading his bullshit as fast as he can."

"Sounds that way."

"We gotta do something, Al."

Here was that problematic "we" again. I told him my reservations.

"I appreciate it, honey buns, but I can kick butt pretty well, too, you know." I imagined he could. Randy was 6-foot-2 and pretty buff, the gym being one of his favorite "markets," as he put it.

I rolled my eyes at his "honey buns." Seemed like my friends just couldn't resist punning on my predicament, but I forgave him, too. "I'm sure you can, but all he has to do is give you one quick bite and you're screwed. And not in a nice way."

"Don't forget I have my wildlife tranquilizers." A fireman buddy and wildlife co-rescuer had set him up with the kit.

"You'd probably need a big dose like for big game, like maybe an elephant. That and a dart-gun or something. You wouldn't want to risk getting up close and personal."

"No worries. I don't do dudes with big hair. Kind of a turn-off when it gets caught in my nipple ring."

"TMI!" I yelped. "But seriously, he's strong and, depending on the moon's phase, he might have the advantage of having two more legs. He could spring on you pretty fast."

"Well, you'd have the same advantage on him, wouldn't you?"

"I suppose. It's not always easy to control or predict. I'm finding. I wouldn't want to, you know, get confused about who not to bite."

"I'd hope you wouldn't be biting anyone! We talked about that."

Jeez, was I supposed to fend off Wolf Man with only a bark? "Not even someone who really needed it?" I hadn't shared my Death Angel epiphany with him.

He took it the way I hoped he would. "That *would* be rather fitting, but you could also get hurt. Best to stay well back, both of us."

"So that brings us back to the problem of a dart gun or rifle."

"Lemme make some calls. I just might be able to rustle up a dart gun, actually, and maybe a rifle, too."

"I'm impressed. First the fireman, now a . . . what? Big game hunter? You do get around, don't you?"

"I do what I can," he smiled into the phone.

"Oh! And how 'bout a pith helmet? Then I could call you Bwana."

"Alice! I would *never* use a helmet to pith in! That's why God made Go Cups."

Ick, but I still snorted. "But even if we could tranquilize him, we could maybe chain him up but where'd we stash him? And how long could we stash him? Because you know . . . he'd still be a werewolf."

I heard him taking a pondering drag.

"Look, Randy, I'm sure you could kick his butt, normally, but I also know you pride yourself on being a pacifist, and you're especially soft-hearted when it comes to 'wildlife.' So, my worry is that you might end up feeling conflicted, when push came to shove." Or bite to bullet.

"Al, we both know this guy needs taking down. He's a serial killer, the worst kind: he's making his own army of serial killers."

"Yeah, but they're all or mostly women." Sexist me.

"They'd be lethal against straight men. Poor slobs would never see it coming," he pointed out.

"I didn't either," I pointed back, "and the roles were reversed."

"True. In any case, rabid wildlife still should be taken down. He's not an endangered species. Okay, say we get ourselves a proper, long-range weapon. I hear silver bullets are the way to go, or silver darts."

"About that . . ."

I told him about Kate's suggestion of forming a posse and her just happening to have both a gun and said bullets.

"Hunh. Well, that's mighty handy. But first we have to find the ass-bite. Any thoughts on that?"

I was about to give him some, when someone pounded on my door.

"It's me! Let me in quick!"

It was Kate, and her blue eyes were popping. She gave a whiplash peek down the hall, then turned and bolted the door.

"Nice jim-jams," Randy commented. I'd put us on teleconference.

Kate looked down at her Mr. Spock pajamas and reddened. "Oh. Thanks. Didn't know you had company, Al."

"It's only Randy. So . . . ?" I prodded, doing a two-hand, move-forward roll.

"Oh, right. So, guess who I just saw out the window just now?"

"The Easter Bunny."

"It's not spring yet, so no." We waited.

"Mona! Mona Abbott. In her long black cloak."

"Thought she always wore her cloak. She's a cloak kinda gal," I said.

"We're both that kind of gal, actually," Kate said, lips pursed.

Kate was liberal about her infatuations and saw no conflict in mixing *Star Trek* with Conan Doyle and the Brontës. "I'm very fond of my grey cloak. And it's a sight more practical when it's sub-zero. You can layer so much under them."

Good point. Note to self.

"Not judging, Kate honey, but you're more *Wuthering Heights*, whereas Mona is *Addams Family.*"

She chuckled. "Yeah, she kinda is."

Randy waved at the screen, "Ladies, while you're discussing literary matters, I really have to take a leak. I'll be right back."

We were treated to a backside view of white boxers with red, humping bunnies disappearing into the distance.

"*He* has some nerve—making fun of my Spocks!" Kate tapped her foot.

"Well?"

"Might as well wait for Randy to get back, so I don't have to tell it all twice." She flopped down on an arm of my sofa, kicking her heels against the side. Thunder had been stolen.

"Here. Spock's shivering." I handed her my guest robe.

"Okay, I'm back." Randy was wearing a bunny-fluffy white bathrobe, to go with the boxers' theme, I assumed.

"So anyway, Mona was sashaying down the street—"

"Oh, it's 'sashaying' now, is it?" Randy asked. We exchanged a smirk.

"Do you want to listen or not?"

I sat on the couch next to her. "Sorry! Go on."

"She was sashaying down the street—"

"In her long, black cloak," Randy finished.

"Yes!" Her eyes narrowed. "In her long, black, hooded cloak that she only wears to the Goth Book Club nights. Usually, anyway. Apart from some frat parties she's crashed. Well, and Halloween, of course."

I did the two-handed roll thing again.

"Well, I *would* get on with it if you two would bloody well let me!"

"Yep, definitely *Wuthering Heights*," Randy commented.

Kate's upper lip began its signature tremble, indicating she was feeling put upon.

"Sorry, sorry! But what is such a big deal about her wearing her cloak outside of book clubs, or whenever she chooses?" I pressed. "Is there some, oh I don't know, significance to this?"

Making a gesture of tearing out her auburn hair (which would have been difficult, as it was braided) she stood up, hands on hips. "There certainly is some significance, on account of who she was walking *with*."

"And . . . who was it?"

I beat a drum roll on the sofa's arm. Randy sing-songed the *Jeopardy* timer tune.

"Your dude!"

"*My* dude?"

"The one who customized your right butt cheek?"

My pulse accelerated. "You sure? I mean, how do you know it was him? You never saw him."

"Jeez, Al, you described him enough times to me, I'm pretty damned sure: a shaggy mane like a rock-star, gold pendant, beard, and strong jaw with an overbite? Anyhow, I grabbed a shot of him with my cell.

"Here." She pulled her phone out of her Spock command-center pajama pocket and thrust it at me.

It was a little blurry, but when I finger-spread it larger, it sure as hell looked like it could be him. I said as much to Kate.

"Yeah, it's a bit blurry, but I was in a hurry to snap them before they got away."

I studied the shot some more. His outfit looked very like the one my wolf man was wearing that night, although there was now an expensive suit jacket over it. "It's definitely Mona, anyway."

I'd hung out with them on a few Halloween nights. Even tried the Goth Book Club once, but they were too Anne Rice for me. So, yeah, I knew Mona.

"I wonder what they were doing in our neck of the woods."

"My guess would be they were coming back from that new Italian bistro at the end of the block. Spaz's?"

"Spazza's," Randy replied, spitting the z's out correctly like t's.

It sounded reasonable; Spazza's was all the rage with foodies and phonies. And parking on our street was tight. We lived in a mixed neighborhood of vinyl-sided three-deckers and 80s-modern, red-brick rows of one- and two-bedroom apartments. The addition of trendy businesses was an unwelcome attempt to gentrify what was comfortably going to seed. I hoped he got a blister tramping back to his stupid car.

"Any chance you saw where they went?" I asked.

"No."

I huffed out a lost-hope sigh.

Kate, on the other hand, looked like the cat that had filleted, marinated and sautéed the canary and was now poised for a bite. "But I got a shot of the car they got into. Scroll down."

I scrolled. I was looking at the rear end of a shiny, new, steel grey Rolls-Royce, and the vanity plate was quite visible: "RCH FKR."

SEVEN

BALANCED ON A PLATE

"Either of you know any cops? Somebody who could run that plate?" I asked the two of them.

My phone screen showed a blissful smile of reminiscence spreading over Randy's face. "I do know that gorgeous fireman who could get the job done. He certainly did for me," he sighed.

Kate and I looked at the ceiling. "Honestly!"

"The question is, Randy, could he do this *totally different* job for us?"

"I imagine so. Fire and police share the same database. And I'd love the chance to get back in touch with him. I hear he's between honeys."

"Great! When will you call him?" I pressed.

Randy consulted his bedside clock. "Last I heard he was still on the day shift, so I'll call him as soon as I have my shower."

"Wonderful! We owe you!" Kate and I sang out.

"Oh, no. I rather think in this case, I'll be owing *you*." His eyebrows waggled at the screen.

Kate put her fingers in her ears, sing-songing, "La la la la!"

Randy stubbed out his morning cigarette. "I'll be back to you in an hour, one way or another. Okay?"

"Perfect. And thanks, Randy."

"Oh, don't thank me . . ." he persisted.

"Got it! Signing off now."

I ended the call and turned to Kate. "Well, that was a bit of luck."

"Sure was. You got any coffee?"

I was the one with a coffee machine, so Kate provided me with the good stuff. Reasonable trade-off.

"Coming right up." I shuffled into the kitchen and came back with two steaming mugs a couple of minutes later. "So, what do you think Mona was doing with this guy?"

Kate looked worried. "I honestly don't know. I wouldn't have said he was her type, but they looked pretty cozy together."

"And she did have her cloak on."

"Yeah. I guess if I'm honest, she does tend to wear it when she's, you know, on the prowl and interested. Sort of her mysterious come-hither thing. I still can't see it—her with him."

Mona had shoulder-length, dark hair, big brown eyes, a smirking kitten mouth, and a turned-up nose like Liz Montgomery from *Bewitched.* She had no trouble at all in the come-hither department.

"Well, if it's any consolation, *I* thought he was sort of cute at first. Of course, I was judgement-impaired at the time. But he could be charming, in a predictable, chauvinistic way."

"You suppose he's involved in the Goth stuff? Maybe a new member of that book club?"

I shrugged. "Who knows?" The club was mostly women, so I'm sure they would have welcomed a new male, whatever his hairstyle.

"I think I need to call Jared and maybe Emma, too," I told her. "Let them know what's come up."

"Who are they?"

"They're the two youngest members of the W.A. group. I had coffee with them after the meeting last night. Jared's the one whose dad passed the curse on genetically. He might be able to fill us in more while we're waiting for the plate to be run. A vanity plate like that has surely been noted in this area. Maybe his dad even knows the guy."

"Good thought. But what about Emma? You don't think she could be a cohort of the wolf man, like an infiltrator?"

I'd considered this and shook my head. "I don't think so, but what do I know? I just met these people. She just doesn't come off that way."

Kate gave me her Ducky look, the one he does, peering up from the autopsy table at somebody who's just said something really stupid.

"Yeah, I know. But I'm really pretty good at reading body language. These days. And before you say it, no, not just rigid fright. Besides, she's young like Jared, and not prone to buying crap off adults like Sheila."

"Sheila's the leader?"

"Right."

"So you don't think it would be better just to take the intel to Sheila?"

"I don't, though I can't say why, at least not until we know more. She sort of puts my hackles up." The punning thing was contagious.

"Interesting. But she put the group together, right? That sounds encouraging."

"That's what she said. Connie, the Irish lady, also confirmed it. So Sheila's probably okay. But if she blabbed to the wrong people, it could really screw things up. I don't have a lot of confidence in her judgement, to be honest. Like that stupid pamphlet."

"Yeah, I noticed it was basically a brainless AA cut-and-paste with one alteration."

"*Yes*. The part of *not* being 'powerless over our condition.' I can't help wondering what she knows that she's not sharing."

"And I would like to know what Mona knows about this guy," Kate said. "I think I'll give her a call from work on my break and tease her about the company she's keeping. She always gets on her high horse whenever I question her taste in men and goes to great lengths to defend them, alas, with lots of details, many of which I *really* don't want to know. I just hope it's really not a romantic thing she's got for this guy."

"Me, too. The wolf harem is already big enough without Morticia's joining the forces."

Kate gave a half-hearted chuckle. "Whatever her weird penchants, she's my friend and I need to warn her off this man, if it's not too late."

She shot up. "And speaking of that, I'm about to be late for work! Gotta shower and suit up! Thanks for the coffee."

"Any time. I'll call you when I know something."

"Okay, bye!"

Watching Kate's Spock PJs disappear out my front door recalled the *Star Trek* infatuation of our youth and made me yearn to be beamed up somewhere. Somewhere like a parallel universe, where there weren't any nightmarish predators like werewolves. Like me.

Damn! Where was a magic wand when you needed one?

EIGHT

Wake Up Calls

I pulled out the member sheet Sheila had emailed me with all the other W.A. members' contact info. Scanning the list, I saw that Jared's was the only name missing. Well, of course it was. I shook my head. *Teenagers!* At least Emma's was there. I dialed her number, figuring she'd be at work so I'd just leave her a voice message.

A groggy female voice answered, "This better be good."

I seemed to have developed a new, insensitive skill: waking people up at bad times.

"Um, hi! Emma?"

"No. I'll get her." I heard a disgruntled huff and a pair of bare heels stomping off.

"Hi," another grumpy voice answered. "And who exactly is calling me this freakin' early? You'd better not be a telemarketer!" That was definitely Emma's voice.

"It's Alice." Silence. "From the group last night? And coffee afterwards?"

"Oh. Right. Alice. Sorry, I'm just waking up. My roommate and I work in the evenings, so sleep in most mornings, when we can." She must have sensed my puzzled silence. "We're both bartenders," she clarified, a tad sternly.

"Ah!" I laughed. "It was just the way you put it, that—"

"It's okay. I should have worded it differently. But I haven't had my coffee yet. Brain's not up to speed."

"I'm sorry I woke you guys up. I figured I'd just leave you voice mail.

Another huff. "'S okay. So what's up? I mean, since last night?"

Her irritation was loud and clear.

"I really should have waited to call. It's just that, well, I got a big breakthrough this morning on Wolf Man, the one that's been tagging us. And I, um, thought you'd want to know."

Emma immediately sounded more awake. “You did?”

“Yeah. My friend who lives next door saw him sauntering down the sidewalk less than an hour ago in front of our building, arm in arm with a mutual friend.”

“Seriously?”

“Seriously. She took some quick pix of them and it sure does look like him. And it was definitely our friend with him, so she’s going to check with her on that, about who her companion was. But she also grabbed a shot of his car and license plate. They’re pretty unusual so I was wondering if you or Jared had seen the car driving around the area. I’ve got a buddy working on getting the plate run to get an address.”

“I’m assuming it’s a vanity plate.”

“And how!” I cackled.

“So what’s the plate number?” I spelled it out for her then heard her wiping down her phone from her guffaw.

“I know, right? And it was a Rolls.”

“Well, *of course* it was!”

“I tried to call Jared first, but his name’s not on the list. Was kinda hoping his dad might recognize the car and plate. I don’t suppose you would have Jared’s phone number?”

There was an embarrassed silence. “Actually, I do. Hang on.”

She came back. “Here it is. Got a pen?”

She gave me the number and I read it back. “That was quick work, Emma,” I commented, endeavoring to keep the smirk out of my voice.

“Look, it’s not what you think. I was just trying to be, like, a big sis to him, since he’s new to the group . . . and everything.”

“None of my business,” I replied breezily, smiling to myself. “Although, I’m sure he does have his charms.”

“He actually is sort of sweet, once you get past the prickles.”

“I can imagine. Do you know what his schedule is? I don’t want to be three-for-three and wake up yet another poor soul.”

“Well, he’s still in high school, remember,” she began.

“That’s assuming he actually shows up,” I countered.

She laughed. “Good point. But I think he actually does, at least to his science courses. But, why are you contacting us with this? Why not just call Sheila?”

It was my turn to huff. "I don't know. I'm just feeling my way, I suppose, and I'm not sure yet of who I can trust."

"But you called me."

"Yes, but I had actual one-on-one face time with you and Jared afterwards, away from the structure of the group. Neither of you impress me as being phonies or of having ulterior motives. I could be totally wrong, of course." I hoped she wouldn't take the last part as a threat.

"Yeah, I know what you mean. And I don't think you are either. But you're worrying about Sheila—the woman who put the group together?" Emma sounded worried herself now.

"Maybe 'worrying' is too strong a word. I'm just being careful. And I absolutely trust my two friends who 'have my back,' as you might say. I don't know what I would have done without their help, as well as hindrance, since . . . you know." Reliving the last nightmarish months, I sincerely didn't. "And they're completely discreet," I assured her.

"My roomie's the same. I mean, she'd have to be eventually, right?"

I thought about the implications of that, wondering how her roommate managed, living in the same apartment when Emma dropped to all fours at that time of the month. "About that—"

"How do I or we manage?"

Were we all becoming telepathic?

"Our duplex has a full basement, not just a laundry room," Emma said. "It's an old building. Really soundproof. My roomie June's boyfriend is the super and a locksmith, so he got us past the locked door into the storage area the landlord keeps for himself. The landlord stays in Florida, so is never around to check on 'alterations.' " I could hear the finger quotes.

"So it's just June and her boyfriend—"

"Mike," she finished.

"Right. June and Mike," I repeated, depositing the names into the old memory bank. "So it's just June and Mike who know about your condition?"

"And . . . ?" She paused, telepathing her mental drum roll. ". . . the entire W.A. group, now."

Man, that was *twice* I'd completely forgotten that the secret about me was out and spreading like a virus. Another head-slap moment.

"Is it just me," I ventured, "or are you also just a little uncomfortable about this group knowledge aspect?"

"It's not just you," Emma replied. "But what choices do we have? I mean, if we want to find a way to manage this thing without turning into mass murderers?"

"How long have you been with the group, Emma?"

"Coupla months, maybe three. Why?"

"Have you found it beneficial?"

I heard her sigh. "I guess. It's nice just knowing that I'm not alone, I suppose, and feeling some sense of 'community,' as Sheila likes to say."

"About the management—has Sheila actually come up with ways in which we can manage our urges and situation?"

Emma took some time thinking about that. "It's funny, now you mention it. So far, it's just prayers and coffee. I guess I was just assuming that was something that would evolve as we worked on the program's steps."

"Like even the steps that don't actually apply to us?" I pressed.

"Hunh. Yeah." I felt there'd be more coming. And there was.

"You know," she continued, "I actually got more ideas and help just talking with you and Jared last night. From the group—not so much."

"I wonder if Jared's feeling the same, since he didn't add his name and contact info to the list."

"Maybe he's not comfortable with Sheila either," Emma ventured.

"Well, that was pretty obvious, what with his family history and her knowing about it and all. Or do you think there's more to it than that?"

"I just don't know. I'm like you: call it a gut feeling or something."

Time to change the subject. I told her about Kate's idea of forming a posse and running the creep to ground. She significantly brightened at the idea. "That would be fun! Count me in!"

"So, shall I call you when we have an ID on the plate?"

"Definitely!"

"And should I call Jared or would you rather do it?"

"Maybe I should do that," she said. "We're closer in age, after all."

I resisted a wisecrack about the inference that I was a dinosaur.

Hmmmm: a werewolf dinosaur. How would *that* work? It would certainly surprise some paleontologists, exhuming from the Jurassic goo a giant lizard's carcass with fangs and fur.

I also smiled at the coy way Emma dodged the real reason for "reaching out" to Jared. "By the way, Emma, have you been assigned a buddy?"

"Sure. Weeks ago. It's Connie."

"The Bichon Frisé!" I yapped. "Sorry! She seems very nice and reliable, though," I commented, smoothing feathers, or fur, as it were.

Emma barked back a laugh. "I *know!* I'll never get that image out of my head now. But honestly, I think she *is* reliable and rather sweet. And motherly, of course. So who's your buddy?"

"Sheila." From her long pause, I sensed her mental "Oh." So I asked, "Does that make me special or something?"

"I'd say! But not necessarily in a good way."

"And why's that?"

"Well . . . for one, it's become her policy *not* to be anyone's buddy. Sheila wants the group to learn to trust and rely on each other."

"And for the other?"

"Um, last time she buddied someone, I heard the girl disappeared."

"Like, permanently?"

"Yep. Like that."

"Oh."

"Listen. Do you mind if I put the phone down a moment? I just got up, so . . . you know how it is." I did and knew that nature was calling Emma in its bathroom voice.

"That was it anyway for now. You don't need to cross your legs. I'll call you later when I know something."

I could practically hear her bladder thanking me. You get that way after being wolfish a while. All the natural processes are so much more . . . urgent.

"*Thanks!* I was about to burst. Talk to you later!"

"You bet," I said to a silent line.

I muttered to myself, "Well, Alice, this rabbit hole is looking curiouser and curiouser."

NINE

CONNECTIONS

There seemed nothing to do right now but wait for my buds to get back to me. Might as well log in and see what the docs had sent me. But first, I'd better get another cup of Joe. Data entry and transcription can put you in a coma fast, so you need plenty of caffeine to avoid editorial wrath from the bosses for typos and mixed-up entries. At least I could do both in my sweats, slobbing at home.

I fired up the laptop and signed in. Pulled up my company's time clock software and logged on for work. My email inbox had 52 new emails, most marked urgent. That's doctors for you. Ditto academics. I switch-hit for them, too, typing up and proofing patent applications to send to their patent lawyers. It was actually interesting stuff and broke the boredom of data entry. But, jeez, you'd think the sky was falling if you didn't answer them within a minute or two.

Turning on Outlook's reading pane, I scanned through the earliest urgent emails for frequent nags. Just as I thought: big whoop. They'd have to wait. Then I went back to the oldest emails and started triage and fire-fighting. Yes sir, no sir, three bags full—mostly of pompous shit.

An hour or so later, I saved the file I'd been working on, rolled my neck and shoulders, and got up to get another cup of coffee. Outside, the sky glowered and it had begun to rain. Nice to be inside instead of in rush-hour traffic. As I was stirring in the sugar, my cell rang. I peered at the number—Randy.

"Hey. Any luck with your fireman hottie?"

"Yes, indeed," Randy said. I could hear the smirk in his voice.

"I guess I should have clarified that. I meant with running the plate."

"That would also be a 'yes.' Which do you want to hear about first?"

"Oh, let's just stick with the info on the plate, shall we?"

He chuckled. "Hank really came through." The double-entendre was still dangling.

Okay, I'd play. "That fast? Thought he worked the day shift!"

"He does get a break now and then." The mind boggled. "Ahem. Here's the data."

"Wait!" I grabbed a notepad and a pen. "Okay, shoot."

Scribbling fast, I jotted down all the details.

"You know, Alice, I could have just emailed you the stuff. Would have saved you from carpal tunnel."

"True," I said, "except I'm logged in right now for work, and I don't want this to be traceable from the company's server."

"I wouldn't send it to your *work* address, Alice." I could hear the "duh" in his voice.

"I would hope not! But one of the big wigs' private emails to his current naughty lust interest recently got seen by IT and shared. With his wife. Not good. So I'm not taking any chances."

"You must have some sneaky IT people with a whole lot of time on their hands, then. But okay. We'll do it your way."

I'd pretty much screened out most of the last part he said. It was just background noise to what I was reading on the paper. "Shit, Randy, the dude lives up on Dexter Lane! I think I know that house!"

"Not ringing a bell."

"I wouldn't expect it to. It's in the hoity-toity heights of Manchester."

"Address was in Massachusetts, Al, not New Hampshire."

"Manchester-*by-the-Sea*," I clarified. "That's up in Cape Ann."

"Aha, where the rich people live. Fits with his vanity plate."

"Not all the residents are filthy rich. It's actually a very nice town, for the most part. But, yeah, there are quite a number of insanely rich folk there. If it's the house I'm thinking of, it's this amazing faux Victorian red-brick mansion on oodles of acres on the top of a hill. Very secluded and chock full of antiques, naturally. There's even a brick and stone cellar with huge, black iron doors. Got a custom-made wine cellar, down there, too. Among other things . . ."

I was thinking about what other things might be hidden down there when Randy interrupted my thought. "And how do you know about this place? Doesn't exactly seem like your usual hang-out."

"I can clean up sometimes!" I objected. "But, yeah. I used to do catering gigs to make some extra dough. And the owner was throwing a gigantic party there a few years back. Bunch of us gals in our black-and-whites passed around silver platters of canapés and things on sticks and poured the pinot noir. That kind of thing."

"Nice gig. Man, I sure would have loved to have been a guest there. Hope they paid you well."

"Oh, they did!" I'd considered framing the check I got (a copy, of course). "It was pretty amazing, especially the basement where the wine cellar was. I couldn't begin to calculate the cost of that wine. Some of it was ancient."

"Like how old? More than 50 years?"

I remembered peering at some of the dusty labels. "More than 100, some of it."

"Really? I've always heard most wines don't age well after 50 years, 100 at the most," Randy said, "and only for really superb vintages."

"The over-100 lot was under lock and key. I had to squint through the glass doors to read the labels."

"Can't really blame the guy. I'd love to see his selection." Randy sounded wistful.

"Well, that was the odd thing. With all his money, he only had red."

"He didn't serve white wine at all?"

"I mean the wine down in the cellar. The catering owner had to order the whites. We brought them with us. They were decent, but no match for the old reds, so they said. And some of the reds we brought up from the cellar were only served to a select group in a separate room."

"Did you get to try any?" I could practically hear him salivating.

"A few, but not from the select group. But what we had was still extremely tasty. Very good legs."

He sighed. "How the other half lives."

"I wouldn't say 'other half.' More like the top two percent. Seems like I saw Elon Musk's name on the guest list."

"Seriously?"

"Also some spiky initials: 'DJT.' Looked like a psychopath's scrawl. Well, I suppose somebody could have written those names in as a gag. But the owner certainly seemed well-connected." *Like, with the rotten rich* was our unspoken sentiment.

Our brains were digesting the significance of that connection and how far it could spread.

“And this is the guy—” We both started talking at once.

“Go ahead, Randy.”

“Well, I was just thinking that if this really is our guy, the ‘Wolf Man,’ then . . .”

My shivers were making it hard to finish that thought, too. “Are you worrying about what I’m worrying about? Like how big *is* his bloody circle of influence?”

A shaky exhale reached me over the phone. “Pretty much, yeah.”

“Good God! It could be some, I don’t know, giant secret society of werewolves!” Dan Brown would love that.

“Lord, let’s hope not, Al. If they’re all as rich as this guy supposedly is, then they could be running the world and we’d never know it.”

I nodded at my phone screen. “One bite at a time. And they’d be in a position to ‘cull’ the pack of undesirables all by themselves.”

He was silent, thinking. “Was it mostly men or women at the party? Do you remember?”

“I’d have to say more men than women, maybe by two thirds?”

“So, his tagging mostly women now could be to fill out the pack, get breeders in, maybe.”

My stomach flipped. “But Connie, the older lady I told you about? She’s a grey-haired senior.”

“Someone’s got to mind the pups, Alice.”

Wow. “But maybe the party guests are just business connections?”

“They’re definitely connections of some type.”

My coffee had gone as stone cold as my blood.

I needed to mull this over. “I’d better get back to the grindstone and make the bosses think I’m earning my keep.”

“Yeah, me, too. Call me tonight after my shift is over with whatever you find out from Kate et al., okay? I’m back on the day shift.”

“’Kay.” I paused. “Man, this whole thing, Randy . . . ,” I began.

“I *know*. Talk at ya later.”

TEN

ONE RICH MF

Friday the Thirteenth

Couple days later, hunched at my laptop, I noticed Mickey's hands pointing to just past 5:00 p.m. Quitting time. Rescued by a rodent! I saved the transcription I'd been working on, sent an email to my bosses, updating them with my progress, and clocked out. Checked my personal emails. Still nothing yet from Kate, Emma, or Jared.

By now, I was basically chewing what nails I had left, worrying about the implications of what Randy and I'd discussed. I never had good nails anyway, except, you know, during *that* time. In which case it was probably a good thing I was gnawing them away now.

Next, I checked my texts. Bingo! Jared had finally texted me back. I made a note of his cell number in all my contacts, then read the text:

"Hi Al. Emma got in touch & I know the dude. Sorry for the delay. Had to wait to talk to m&d. Call me, DO NOT text. -J."

I glanced at my calendar: Friday the 13th. I dialed his cell fast.

"Yo. Who's this?"

"It's Alice, Jared."

"Oh, right! Lemme just store your number, okay?"

"Sure." I waited.

"Okay, got it."

"So is this a good time to talk, Jared?"

"Yeah. It's Friday night. My parents are out, so I'm on my own."

"You said you knew who the guy was."

"Boy, do we! My dad and I. I can't believe I didn't think of him. 'Course, last time I saw him I was like maybe seven. He is one rich mutha, that's for sure."

"I got that much when we got the plate run. Lives up in Manchester in a Victorian mansion in quite an elite neck of the woods, with a whole lot of those woods, if I remember the house correctly. Am I right?"

"That's the guy. How do *you* know the place?"

"Used to do some catering work on the side years ago. He threw a big party there. I was one of the servers."

"Then you've seen the dungeons."

"Well, he referred to them as the wine cellar, the gym, and all that."

"But I'm willing to bet you didn't get to see the whole layout in the basement. Like behind the big, iron doors."

"True. Those were locked, so off-limits."

"The guy's a serious creep, besides super rich. Obviously."

"Obviously."

"And that cellar's the perfect set-up for a serial killer."

"That's what I'm worrying about, too, Jared. He also has quite a network. Definitely well-connected. When I was there, his guest list was basically a short Who's Who of the filthy rich and influential, at least from what I saw. My friend Randy and I are wondering if he's enlarging his pack through his contacts and now by his tag-and-turns on women.

"Was he active back when your dad knew him? Oh, and I hate to ask, but . . . um, why exactly did or does your dad know him? Sorry."

"Well, the obvious, the wolf thing. Dad told me they both showed up at the same time going after a victim—"

"You said your dad was a good guy!" I interrupted.

"He is. He saw the other wolf man leaping for the chump, then jumped on the wolf dude to keep him from hurting the guy. Dad wrestled him to the ground and subdued him so the victim could get away. Then they both started changing back and, after the snarling was over, had a wolf-to-wolf talk. Dad like counseled him that there was a better way, and murdering folks wasn't it. They exchanged business cards. Dude invited Dad over to his place, they had drinks and talked until the wee hours over some really fine wine and, you know, did some male bonding.

"Dad finally became convinced the guy wanted to reform. That's why the dude set up that 'gym,' as he calls it. It was to work out his aggressions. Or so he said. Plus, he told Dad that he added the same set-up we had, with the shackles and all. Dad had showed him some plans at some point. He even gave Dad a tour, just to lay his worries to rest."

"And then what?"

"Oh, you know. They got busy with their lives and work stuff. Sort of lost touch."

"On the info we got from the plate, his name is Rolf. Is that right?"

"Rolf! Yeah, Uncle Rolfie! Rolf Wolfgang, to be exact, von Something Something."

"That's too rich! *Wolf*gang?"

"I know, right? And too fucking obvious, you'd think, wouldn't you?"

"Certainly arrogant and self-entitled: 'I'm so stinking rich I don't have to worry about your rules, world, any more than I need to hide, because *I've* got people.' "

"Uh huh!"

I looked at my notes. "I'm not sure I spelled his last name right." I stumbled over the pronunciation, "*von Wildlebend Herunterschlingen*?"

"That's right!" Jared pronounced it back to me in perfect, heel-clicking German.

"What's it mean? Since you're so good with German, apparently."

"I'm not that great, but Dad translated it to me back then and I used to practice saying it because it sounded so, you know, cool und zo Churman, exotically European anyhow. If I remember right, it means something like 'from the devouring wolves in the wild.' "

"Seriously? Pays to advertise, I guess. So his lycanthropy is genetic like yours, it sounds."

"Hey, you know that word! Cool. But yeah, it must be. In the old country, there are apparently several old noble families of us types."

"Your own being one?" I asked.

"Yeah. Only we're from Poland."

"And that brings up another issue I've been mulling over."

"What's that?"

"Well, according to legend and fairy tales, for what that's worth, vampires are the ones who can bite and turn their victims into one of themselves."

"Yeah. So?"

"It's just that I've never heard of werewolves being able to do that. Yet, here we all are, except for you, of course, miserable living proof that it's so. What do you make of it?"

"You just didn't read the right fairy tales. There's plenty of stuff saying the same thing can happen from werewolves' bites."

"Hunh. You suppose it's like a virus or something that's mutated over time?"

"That's a damned good question, a super interesting one."

I could practically hear his mental cogs cogitating.

"You know, I just might run that by Dad's scientist friend."

"I was hoping you would. In the meantime, we need to come up with a plan. You any good at surveillance?"

"Not bad. I've done a bit. But my friend, Dion, is practically a ninja."

I laughed. "A *ninja*?"

"You laugh now. Wait 'til you meet him."

"Looking forward to it. Oh, and I totally forgot to tell you that Randy, my ER nurse friend? He told me another bite victim came in not long ago, with even worse damage than I had, and yep, right on the butt. Rolf must have a fetish for booty."

Jared howled. "He's certainly invested in getting into women's panties!"

"True. And this poor gal's were toast, just so much cotton confetti. But this time, Randy was smart and saved them as evidence and took some saliva swabs from them. He's going to send the swabs to some medico connection to sample the DNA."

"Good going! Will you let me know what he finds out?"

"Of course. So, be thinking about how we can approach this guy, okay?"

"You know I will. Okay if I share this with Emma?"

"Sure. She seems straight up. But . . ."

"But?"

"I was just wondering about the advisability of sharing it with Sheila," I replied, letting that thought dangle just a tad.

Jared hesitated. "I don't think I would, actually, Alice."

Aha! I pounced. "Why?"

"I dunno. Just a gut thing."

Hunh. Guys got gut hunches, too. I nodded at my phone. "Yeah, mine too. Okay, bye for now."

"Yeah. Later, Al."

ELEVEN

STRANGE DAYS IN ADVERTISING

My stomach was getting its own gut hunch: "Food!" I tend to hyper focus, so I forget about the basics.

Opened my fridge to confirm its sad contents: half a quart of iffy milk, some cheese no longer recognizable, due to the blue mold flourishing on it, some shriveled apples, and a plastic container of fizzing mango salsa. No chips to even go with that.

Rats. I'd have to put on some form of clothes that could be viewed in public. Dragging on sweats over my pajama bottoms, adding clean socks (surely the undies were good enough for going to the store), then stuffing my feet in my old loafers, I started to head out.

Then I stopped, remembering the last time I hadn't bothered to change to better underwear. . . . Nah, that couldn't happen twice. Could it? You could only be turned into a werewolf once, right? And I was only going to the corner store. Shaking my head, I finally gave in, went back and exchanged them for spanking new bikini briefs. And hoped there would be no spanking to follow.

There's this little convenience store not far from me that's in the most improbable spot, right on busy Route 1A at a four-way intersection. I decided to head for that, thinking it would be the least likely place on a Friday night to run into anyone I knew, or wanted to know. People with a life would be hitting the bars and restaurants.

Sadly, the more progressive Brazilian family who ran it now had replaced the friendly, tinkly bell at the entrance with an electronic security beep. Still, it was a good place to get in and out fast with your short list, with only a 20% markup.

I grabbed more milk, some chips to go with the aging salsa, and a carton of eggs. Then added a block of cheddar and a marked-down "Manager's Special" pound of hamburger. It looked okay. No green showing.

Back at my car with the bag of groceries, fumbling in my pocket for my key fob, I felt again a frisson of fear, a sense that I was once more being watched by someone or something.

I tossed the bag onto the front passenger's seat, closed the door then fobbed the car locked again, scanning the nearly empty lot and all four streets at the intersection. Nothing. I still couldn't shake off the creepy being-watched feeling. So I strolled back inside.

"Forget something, honey?" the nice woman at the check-out asked.

I laughed ruefully. "Yeah. Always seem to." Then, stalling, I headed over to the small bulletin board they kept for local businesses to advertise their services. Don't know why I hadn't thought of that bulletin board the whole the time I was telling Kate and Randy about the group. I guess we'd gotten wound up in other more pressing matters. But it came back to me now. It was how I'd first found out about that W.A. group. I walked up to the board to see if the notice was still there.

It was: a single, typed index card, now curling at the corners. *Who advertises on an index card these days*? I'd thought then and again now. All around it were glossy, laser-printed business cards with snazzy logos and photos, and color-copied flyers offering pet sitting, math tutoring, house cleaning. Which is why the index card had stood out. The card read:

> Having Bad Hair Days?
> Especially at a certain time of the month?
> I can help!
> Call to make a private appointment today. 100% discreet.
> Dr. S. Armstrong.

A phone number followed. I'd been intrigued, especially combining the "certain time of the month" with hair problems. But the first time I saw it, I still didn't know the outcome of the butt bite.

This September, after over a year's anguish had left me with no doubt, I'd gone back to see if the card was still there, wondering if I were actually putting two and two together, but coming up with five. I felt foolish, but I still had to check; I was desperate. I jotted down the number and took it home, mulled it over a few more days, then called.

That's how I came to meet Dr. Sheila Armstrong. Over the phone I was cagey and she was careful. She merely set up an appointment, a free initial exam to see if she'd be able to assess my problem and help.

Her office was in her home, a tidy house up in the hilly residential area of Lynn, close to Route 129. Split-level with oatmeal wall-to-wall, dated 90s window and door trim, chrome coffee table, kitchen papered with flowers. A family home, clean and pleasant throughout. Her office was downstairs in the well-lit basement. Walls lined with lots of what looked like deep, built-in closet space, maybe a Murphy bed.

She sat me on the leather couch facing her desk and we talked. At first, she questioned me about the frequency of hair growth and when it typically occurred, taking careful notes. I wasn't giving *anything* away, as far as I knew. After a bit, she took off her readers, put down her pad and leaned forward.

"I know what you are, Alice."

My heart rate spiked. "What I am? You mean like a nut case or something? I'm *not* imagining this." I began to rise, grabbing for my purse and keys.

"Please. Sit, Alice, and hear me out."

I sat. An obedient, petulant puppy.

"I know because . . ." Here she closed her eyes, like it was costing her to say it. She looked up at me. "Because I'm one, too."

"One *what*?" I challenged, pissily. "You've got a stubborn moustache and are addicted to depilatories?"

She laughed. "Got me! Busted." I didn't see even the slightest evidence of a moustache or even hairy arms. "Just not at the moment. Not at this time of the month," she added.

"So is your moustache a hormonal thing, like tied to your period?"

"No, it's not. Is yours?"

I'd originally hoped it was, back when it didn't seem too bad yet. I knew better now. "No."

"Can you or will you tell me about the other changes you experience at the same time?" she pressed.

"Why do you think there *are* any other changes?" I bridled.

"Because, as I said, I already know. I know what you are because it's what I am. I can smell it on you."

I resisted an armpit whiff test. Pretty sure I'd used deodorant that morning.

"I wasn't always what we are, though. I went through the same horrendous nightmare you must be going through."

My arms crossed. "Go ahead. Spell it out. Tell me what I, *we* are."

"Werewolves."

I barked a guffaw, going for the now-this-is-*really*-ridiculous angle. She was still peering kindly at me. Whereupon I broke out sobbing.

We probably talked about an hour. Sheila sat patting me and murmuring soothing responses, sharing bits of her own nightmare over the last decade or so. Then she told me what she'd done about it, the research she was doing on the "disability," as she called it, and the support group she'd formed for others like us.

My eyes dried up. "Shit!" I clapped a hand over my mouth. "Sorry. But how many of us *are* there?"

"In this area? Quite a number, unfortunately."

"So there could be even more, like nationwide?"

She raised her shoulders.

Wow.

She handed me her card for the W.A. group, told me where it met. There was a discreet website, encrypted and all that, where you could check the meeting schedule. "Will you come?"

I'd grabbed a tissue from her desk-top Kleenex box and dabbed at my running mascara. I nodded. "Sure. I'll give it a try."

She stood and held out her hand. "It *can* get better. Honest."

Struggling into my leather jacket, I stood, too, and hoped she wouldn't try to hug me. I'd only blubber more and I'd just mopped up.

She didn't.

"Oh, before you go, let me give you this." Sheila handed me a plastic bottle of what looked like a hair product.

"Hair conditioner?" I burst out laughing.

"It works really well. Makes that fur glossy and sleek. During and after." The doctor had a sense of humor? That was a relief to know.

"What do I owe you, Dr. Armstrong?"

"Nothing. I told you the visit would be free."

"Okay, um. Thanks. But going forward, surely . . ."

"Going forward, we'll work through the group, if you'll come, that is. If you should find you need special counselling, I can see you again privately. My hourly rate is $30."

"Thirty bucks!"

"I hope that's not too much," Sheila frowned, worrying a lip.

"No, that's fine, but—"

"But you know that most people charge a lot more?"

I didn't want to ruin the deal, but I couldn't help but nod.

"Alice, what I'm trying to do is provide a service that no other agency—scientific, medical or governmental—would provide, because we're not supposed to exist, and *also* because we have the potential for causing great harm. I wouldn't charge anything, except I occasionally need some extra cash for the research I'm doing on lycanthropy."

"Oh. Well then, thanks. Time's up, I'm sure. I'd better get going."

"I'm not actually that strict about the hourly thing. Anyway, I hope to see you at our next meeting. Just don't share any of the details about our group, please."

"Sure thing." I didn't see how I could. Until later I did. Hey, I could be 100% discreet, too, or close to that percentage. I believed.

Much later, when talking to Emma, Jared and, even later, Martha, I discovered they'd responded to the same index card. And that it had been up there for years.

Now, returning to the convenience store's parking lot, I beeped open my Kia again, got in, locked the doors and scanned the streets once more. No sign of watchers and my goosebumps had gone home to roost or nest—or whatever geese and their bumps do. I checked the sky, as always. The moon was waning to barely a crescent.

Putting the car in drive, I headed home. Something still wasn't adding up.

TWELVE

A Tail with a Tail

Driving home, I was lost in thought, but my inner radar was always in service. Just before I turned the corner onto my street, I picked up an unusual set of headlights in my rear-view mirror. They were up high and horizontally squinty separated by a massive, shiny grille with a silver hood ornament, both of which only showed when I passed under street lights. Before I could check the plate, it sailed on past my corner. I couldn't be positive, but it sure looked like it could be a Rolls. Not a lot of those in my neighborhood, which tended to older Japanese imports and rusted pick-ups.

I waited a few minutes before pulling into my parking space. When I couldn't hear the sound of a single engine, I grabbed the groceries, power-walked to my back entrance, sprinted upstairs and let myself into my apartment. Didn't breathe until I heard the solid snick of the deadbolt.

Stood to reason: if somebody like Randy had connections to run Wolf Man's plate, with all Wolf Man's entitled connections, finding me would be easy-peasy. I drew my shades, closed my curtains. Only then did I turn on my lights. I was seriously creeped out now.

My stomach rumbled and told me to snap out of it: "Eat! *Now!*"

Stowing the comestibles, I took out the fizzy salsa and sniffed. How much worse could it get? Couldn't kill me—I was supposed to be immortal now. Tore open the tortilla chip bag and took it and the suspect salsa to the living room to watch the news.

House fire, water main break, the Red Line was broken. Like *that* was news? Then came a follow-up on a special investigation into a body, White female in her teens, found in Lynn with her throat brutally torn. The discovery had occurred a couple of weeks ago, but I'd missed it. I'd had my own problems to deal with.

But now I shot out of my couch slouch and turned up the sound. The video re-run avoided the gory shots, but the sound bites spelled out what I'd feared.

Wolf Man, or one of his pack, had been at it again. Musta been.

That cast my mind painfully back to the beautiful, terminally ill homeless man I'd helped shuffle off his mortal coil.

Then I re-remembered a completely stupid thing to forget: only a day or two after that, I'd gotten a flyer in my mail box. Something about hair problems. Junk mail. I tossed it. But in my mind, I saw it again: it referred to *cyclical* bad hair days. *Just like the bulletin board index card.*

After I'd left the homeless man, I'd made the anonymous call to the police from my home's landline. Could that have been traceable? I didn't see how. I wasn't on the line more than a minute, two tops. And by that time my voice had changed and deepened, my diction only slightly impeded by overhanging fangs.

And that returned my fuddled brain to exactly what I'd been mulling on the way home tonight, what wasn't adding up about the junk mail. To wit—you couldn't possibly locate and contact each of us wolf people solely through an index card in a small, local convenience store. Didn't make sense. So Sheila must have also had some way of connecting the bite incidents to the perpetrators.

If not Sheila, someone had. I was going round in circles, ending up with Wolf Man. And Sheila. Wolf Man and Sheila. A twosome? Crazed canids in cahoots? She'd seemed so genuine, so earnest. And yet . . .

And yet you don't totally trust her, do you, Alice? Nor do Emma and Jared. And Emma had mentioned that the only other group member Sheila had buddied had gone missing, apparently permanently.

Hell, even the pamphlet and its ersatz 12 steps seemed like a sham or a cover. For?

Whichever way I looked at it, the unavoidable conclusion was that one or both of them knew where I lived. And could be watching.

The TV news had moved on to a car crash in Saugus. I switched it off and trod back to the kitchen.

I'd never bothered to hang curtains in my kitchen. The windows were small and only faced the parking lot in the back. What was to see—me at the sink in my pajama top? Big whoop.

I stood next to the stove whisking eggs and fresh milk in a bowl for an omelet, when a pair of headlights slid into my peripheral vision through the windows over the sink. It was 8 p.m. By now, most of the residents would have long been home. As the car backed out, I saw that the headlights were up high, horizontal and squinty.

I wondered if fizzy, hot mango salsa could be classed as a projectile weapon, if need be.

Setting the bowl down, I dialed Randy. He'd be home by now.

"Hi, Alice." Caller ID still startled me. Kind of a Big Brother thing.

Had to smooth the jitters out of my voice. "Have you heard anything back from whoever is checking the DNA on the 'evidence' you have?"

"Not yet, but I think I'll know something soon."

"Can you divulge the name of the person who's doing the research?"

"Sure, but we should still keep it amongst ourselves. Let me get her card, so I don't get the last name wrong."

There was a pause, then, "Here it is: it's Dr. Armstrong. But we just call her Sheila."

Oh boy. My stomach was telling me: *Maybe pass on the omelet. How 'bout some beer? That's filling, right?*

"Al? Alice? You still there?"

"Something's come up, Randy. Sorry. I'll get back to you." I hung up and grabbed a trembling Rolling Rock from the fridge.

There was a knock on the door.

I jumped two feet and wasted good beer spraying it down my front. Something *had* come up or was about to. I grabbed a paper towel and sponged down my sweatshirt.

The knock came again. I didn't answer it.

Heart pounding, I eased off my plastic-soled slippers and padded over to the peephole in my socks. A big blue, Kate-shaped eye was staring back, bulging like a goldfish's from the fisheye lens. Heart rate simmering down, I whispered through the door, "Who is it?"

"It's the plumber!" Kate sang out, followed by, "Landshark!" when I didn't respond right away.

"Is anybody with you, Kate?"

"Just Mr. Spock. You gonna let me in or what?"

I turned the deadbolt, snatched her in by Spock's flannel arm, and slammed the deadbolt back into place.

"Okaaay. Something's up," she said, noting the freaking obvious.

The jitters had come back. "Something definitely is."

She waited, shivering, like me.

"Jeez, Kate, don't you own a bathrobe?" I grabbed my loaner and shoved it at her again.

"You're only across the hall, Al. Should I have worn my cloak?"

"No! Sorry, sorry. Been a long strange trip today. Beer?"

"That would appear to be appropriate."

THIRTEEN

BEAUTY AND THE BEAST

Kate screeched a chair up to my kitchen table. As I pulled two beers from the fridge, I couldn't help craning my neck toward the window. Kate noticed and said, "You look spooked. What's up?"

I set our beers down and popped the tops off. "You first."

Kate nodded, taking a swig. "Well, it's about Mona."

"Figured. You talked to her?"

"I sure did. Lost a long lunch hour on it. And she's smitten."

"But not bitten?"

Kate smiled wanly at my humor. I resisted tearing at my cuticles. "Not yet. But." Her eyebrows peaked in worry. "Oh, Al, I think it's just a matter of time."

"Whadya tell her about him?"

"Just stuff she could believe, if she would. Not the werewolf part, obviously. Although, if she did believe it, she might think that was cool, knowing her and knowing she bloody well wouldn't think that through. She never does. Thinks she's invincible."

Didn't we all, once upon a time?

"So I told her about all the womanizing he's done, yadda, yadda. And I think I mentioned that a few went missing afterwards, when that didn't take effect."

"Jeez, what'd she say to *that*?"

"Oh, she waved it away—fake news, jealous slanderers, whatever."

"And *why* is she smitten?" My lip curled in disgusted hindsight. "I know he can be kinkily charming, but . . ."

Kate laughed out loud and shook her head. "It's just so typical of her. You know she works for Disney Vacations, right?"

I waved the non-sequitur on. "Sure. So?"

"Well . . ." Kate stifled a snort, wiped the beer off her nose, and continued, "You do know how she is about her passion for costumes and looking impeccably comely in them."

"Boy, do I."

"She told me she's always had a hankering to leave the boring desk job and become one of the costumed characters at Disney World."

I snorted. "I can totally imagine that." But, wow, Disney? Nature's happiest despoiler. Florida's anyway.

She held up a hand. "I know, I know. We both adored dressing up at Halloween. But Mona always had to be the queen, better, fancier than everyone else. You remember how flamboyant her getups were, right?"

I nodded. They'd have had the men of Provincetown in tears of envy. "Go on."

"This wolf man dude, she gushed, is filthy rich and fabulously connected. On their last date—"

Uh oh. "They're actually dating, as in a plural episode sense? It's not just a one-off, hope-he-calls-again thing?"

"No. I mean, yes, they're dating. No, it's not a one-off."

I gulped. Kate gulped. We drank again. "How long?"

"Couple of months."

"Shit! Well, then she's gotta know about him by now!"

"I thought the same, so I asked her about the whens, as casually as I could. He was away on a 'business meeting' (finger quotes) over the first full moon, and she was out of town on the second. Neat timing, huh?"

"Quite tidy. So, going back to the Disney thing?"

"Well, on one of their dates (more finger quotes), in the throes of intimacy (and more 'uh oh'), she tells him her dream. And he up and says, 'Babe, I've got people. I can fix that easy!' or words to that effect.

"Anyhow, he says he's lined up a gig for both of them. He knows the Disney CEO personally, who owes him a favor, blah, blah, blah, and they could be cast as a couple."

I groaned. "Don't tell me. Beauty and Beast?"

"Knew you'd get it." Kate grimaced.

I wished I'd bought beer by the case.

"But, the sad, rock star hair thing. Mona likes that, *our* Mona?"

"I asked her about that, doing my best to dampen the infatuation. She said he doesn't look a bit like David Coverdale, even if Coverdale had sported a beard back in the day."

I reared back with a "Huh?"

"She said he looked 'adorably intellectual.' More like Ernie Boch Jr. Even wears the doofy glasses, when she's with him."

"Does he wear the looped scarf, too?"

Kate chortled. "I did actually ask her about that. And he does!"

Kate and I felt the same about that scarf bit. I'd had to be shown how to loop my scarves the trendy way, but I seldom bothered. And looking like Dickens carolers didn't faze us.

Head in my left hand, I bottle gestured with my right. "You know what this means. What it probably means, anyway."

"He wants her as his forever she-wolf?"

I snorted again. "I'll bet that's what he's *saying*, but not in those terms." My stomach flip-flopped again. Rolling Rock was doing nothing to help. "Kate, Mona's right on the money. This dude *is* filthy rich and fabulously connected. I think he's doing just exactly what Randy and I have been talking about: building a larger pack. I mean, can you even fathom the victim count from all those tourists just strolling around all day and night, every day at fucking *Disney World?* Even just keeping to a single full moon night a month, the probable statistics are terrifying!"

Kate's blue eyes mirrored that terror.

"But Mona would see what he was up to, wouldn't she?" My bleak look answered her.

"Maybe she wouldn't know," I offered, being kind. I didn't know Mona as well as Kate did, but I couldn't honestly see Mona going for bling and glory, despite what harm she'd do, just to achieve immortality, not if she were truly apprised of the facts. And I said something like that.

"No, I can't see it either, Al, despite her love of being in the center spotlight."

A new thought came to Kate and she brightened in defense. "And the Disney couples don't always stay together, you know, side-by-side, as they're working the crowd."

"Still doesn't lessen his threat."

"No." She slumped. "It doesn't."

"Want another?" I offered, going automatically to Dr. Fridge, the solver of all problems.

"No, thanks. I need a smoke," Kate said, getting up and heading for the door.

"Wait! Stop!"

"Oh, I forgot your bathrobe. Sorry." She started disrobing.

"Forget the bathrobe, Kate."

"'Kay. I'm stopped," Kate said, beneath worried brows.

"Just . . . don't go outside, okay? And don't smoke in the landing, either!" Our landing's tall hall window, where she smoked, overlooked the parking lot.

"Look, Katie, sit back down. I need to tell you my news. It might even cure your nicotine addiction."

We screeched back to the table. She peered at me through narrowed eyes. "About time you filled me in."

"So much has been going on, I tend to lose track."

"Just since this morning?"

"Yeah, things are kinda moving at warp speed, Scottie."

There was so much stuff to process, I wished I'd kept notes. I promised myself in future, I would. Maybe. I gave Kate my memory bank's Cliff Notes on the most recent developments.

"Mein Gott in Himmel!" Kate mirrored me: head in hands.

I was desperate to lighten the mood, despite urgently needing to figure out the timeframe we were working against. "Zo, ven ees dees new gig goink to begin, *meine liebchen*?"

She screeched backward and walked over to the counter where I kept my coffee machine. "You mind?"

"Help yourself. You know where everything is."

Pouring herself a cup of cold Joe, Kate shoved it in the microwave. While she was waiting for the ping, she peered out the window, as I had, hand shading her eyes against the overhead glare.

Scooching back up to my table with her hot coffee, she pulled my robe tight around her neck. "I didn't see anything, Al. No UFVs in the parking lot, as far as I could tell." It was our shorthand for unidentified vehicles. (I'll let you extrapolate the F.)

"Doesn't mean anything, Kate."

"True. Ow! This is f— frigging hot!"

Kate always forgot I had a full-powered microwave; hers was thrift-store and wimpy. I passed her the cream. Nuked myself a cup as well.

"Christ, Al. We're going to have to move!" she wailed. "Where are we going to find new apartments? With utilities included?"

"I hope it won't come to that, Kate." Rent control and decent landlords were going extinct like dodos. "We just have to be super careful and more vigilant than ever. And we no longer have the luxury of waiting and seeing. Time is *not* on our side."

"You're right there, Ollie."

"You and Spock still up for posse partners?"

"I don't know about Spock. He'd probably snipe about Earthlings and their weird subspecies. But I'm still up for it."

"You sure? I won't feel bad if you run away screaming and diving for cover."

She smiled. "Yeah. I'm sure. But maybe I can snag some body armor."

"Not a bad idea."

FOURTEEN

CRUISIN'

Setting down her empty beer bottle, Kate rose and stretched. "I need some food in me. Wanna go for a pizza or something? It's 8 o'clock and Gino's is still open. And I'm still gasping for a smoke. If you drive, I could always smoke hanging my head out the window," she suggested, mimicking a happy dog with its tongue hanging out.

I looked at the sad bowl of eggs on the counter. An omelet no longer appealed. I needed carbs and grease. With more beer. But I was skittish about going out with who knew who or what possibly lurking in the parking lot.

"Yeah. A large pepperoni and mushroom would hit the spot." I got up and put some plastic wrap on the bowl and shoved it in the fridge. "But maybe we should take your car, instead. I'm worried he knows mine now. You can smoke outside while we're waiting for our order."

Kate's car was an older, silver Honda Civic. There were hundreds of them around and, without a vanity plate, it was about as anonymous as you could wish for.

"Sure. I'll just get my purse."

"Um . . . Aren't you going to change? Spock might get you some looks in the pizza place."

"We're only going to Gino's. I'll just cover him up."

"Not with my bathrobe, I hope!"

"Surely you jest. I'll throw my cloak over Mr. Spock," she said. "He'll enjoy the disguise."

"Whatever. I'll phone Gino's and see you in 10, but wait inside before going to the parking lot, okay? Safety in numbers."

"Aye, aye, Kirk!" She saluted then left. I phoned in our order, then had to think up a disguise for myself.

After pulling on a pair of Levis and cowboy boots, I swathed myself in a brightly striped Mexican poncho and crammed my Indiana Jones hat on my head. That would have to do. I was starving and half in the bag.

When I got downstairs, Kate batted away the cigarette smoke through the open back door, took one look at me and one at herself, and busted up. "Jesus! Look at us: Jane Eyre and Miz Temple of Doom."

"When worlds collide." I hoped the doom part wasn't prophetic and we weren't about to collide with it.

Outside, I scanned the lot from end to end as Kate unlocked the Honda. No UFVs as far as I could tell. With her hood up and my hat on my short hair, I hoped we looked like a heterosexual couple. I still scooted down on the seat and donned a pair of Ray-Bans. *Cruisin'*. All we needed now was a pair of fuzzy dice on the rear-view mirror.

My head was swivelling like a tennis spectator checking for squinty headlights in my side-view mirror as Kate eased out of the lot. The shades presented a bit of a problem with checking for a tail in the dark. I was just easing them below my eyes, when a car pulled up in the lane next to us on Route 1A.

I jumped in surprise and gasped. At my gasp, Kate swerved reflexively toward the curb. We hadn't heard its approach at all. And I hadn't seen any headlights behind us, but I'd been busy checking the side roads on the right before it showed up. The streets had been pretty empty for a Friday night. But then, we weren't near any bars.

As I turned my head towards the car next to us, a dark, tinted window slid down and I heard a very familiar voice: "Good evening, gorgeous."

I shot my Ray-Bans up and yanked my hat down, heart rate ramping.

Kate donned her granny glasses, turned her head toward the man in the driver's seat and peered coolly over her specs. "Do I know you, sir?"

We were stopped at a light, so I shrank back, slouching against the passenger's side window. I could see him stretching across the seat to see Kate more clearly.

"My mistake. I thought you were a lady I knew."

The window slid back up and the light changed. He drove off. We puttered behind a block, then took the next right and circled around.

"Jesus, Mary and Joseph and all the disbarred saints, that was close!"

"Christ, the way you gasped," Kate hissed, "I thought we were about to be side-swiped!"

"Sorry! But did you see him?"

"Quite well and too close for comfort."

Even in the dark, I could see her tremble. Her voice was quiet. "Al, that was the guy, wasn't it? Mr. Wolf Man, right?"

"Oh, yeah, that was the guy. He looked a bit different, though, from my encounter. More like Ernie Boch, Jr., though blonder, just as Mona described him. You suppose he has a collection of wigs or something?"

"Peculiar, but possible," Kate answered. "Unless, he's gay. But Mona's lusty report seemed to indicate he's not."

"He sure didn't seem gay to me!" I confirmed, remembering his sexy, predatory grin. "That car is still bothering me. I'm pretty sure it wasn't a Rolls. Looked more like a Lexus. Think I saw that boomerang L in a circle on it. And why didn't we hear his approach?"

"Electric?"

"I didn't know Lexus made electric cars."

"They do now. Hybrids, too. Saw the ads."

"Damned electric cars! You never hear them coming."

"But they're good for the planet," Kate pointed out.

Sullenly, I said, "Not so much for the critters. They can't hear them coming either. Think of the poor squirrels and skunks that get run over."

I was still freaked about the guy's just showing up out of nowhere. It was damned inconsiderate of him.

Kate sighed. "I know. I try not to think about that. They should have a law requiring those cars to have some kind of whistle or noise-making thingy installed to alert wildlife." We both loved the creatures, but I knew she was mollifying me.

Changing the subject back, she echoed my thoughts, "Weird how he just popped up like that, like someone beamed him down. Or over." She figured she'd get a smile at the Trekkie reference. And she did.

"So why was he driving a hybrid or whatever instead of his Rolls?"

"Guy's got plenty of money. Probably's got a buncha cars."

I sat back. "Makes sense. But how and why would he switch cars so quickly? Because I can almost swear the UFV lurking earlier in our lot was a Rolls. I Googled them and they have very distinctive headlights. The grille, too.

"So who . . . ?"

We were pulling up to Gino's. Kate got out. "Hold that thought. Roni-and-shrooms help is on its way."

Gino himself was behind the counter, a big grin on his face. His wife, Joanne, waved from the kitchen. "Hey, girls! Is it Halloween already?" he called out. Then he peered at me. "It *is* still 'girls,' isn't it? Don't want to offend if . . . you know." He rubbed his balding, grey head.

"Yeah, it is, but keep it to yourself for tonight, okay?"

"Got it." He nodded, knowingly. "You're in disguise."

I put a finger across my lips and checked for eavesdroppers.

Looking around, I saw that all the booths were empty. It was late enough we were the only customers.

Gino handed us our pizza. "Well, then, 'Trick or Treat!' "

Grabbing a couple of cold Miller High Lifes from the reach-in fridge, we paid, lifted our box up and reverently inhaled. There's nothing like the smell of hot, fresh pizza to drive all bad thoughts away. We nabbed our favorite booth at the far end, the one under the big poster of Napoli, I put my hat on the seat, and we tore into our pie right there, even though it was so molten it scorched the roofs of our mouths off. Not a fan of cold, limp pizza.

That was another thing we loved about Gino's (besides the fabulous pizza and subs)—the homey, old-fashioned décor: red leatherette, high-backed booths, red-and-white checked tablecloths and curtains, Italian travel posters.

Gino and his white-haired wife, Joanne, took the place over back when they were hippie newlyweds and had stuck with what worked. They'd even kept the tinkly bell at the entrance. And it was in a little, three-business strip: laundry, package store, and Gino's—talk about all the best conveniences in a single stop.

Three slices in, each, we slowed our snarf attack, blotted lips with paper napkins, and sat back, drinking our beer.

"All better," Kate pronounced.

"Yeah." I took a pull on my Miller. "Except for one thing."

"What? Did you want the Parmesan shaker?"

"No, not that. The guy in the car."

"Oh. That." Kate had beamed back down to earth. "But which car?"

"Yeah, which?"

She leaned forward, beer in hand. "Do you think it was an accident he showed up when he did?"

"Nope. And I don't think it was an accident that a Rolls resembling the one in that photo you took showed up in our parking lot either, Watson." I took another swallow.

"Well, Holmes, it would appear, would it not, he's got henchmen enlisted in the chase."

"It would, indeed. And he's stinking rich, so he could have several of them stalking us and who knows who else. He has a six-car garage, I remember. It was the old stables, back in the day."

"So we don't even know how many cars to watch out for or what type, besides the Rolls." Kate pulled her cloak tighter.

"Right."

"It's okay for *you*. You work from home, so you can stay put. I'm slogging to the store every day," Kate pointed out. She worked as assistant manager at the Whole Foods in Swampscott. It was a waste of her anthropology B.A., but paid the bills and came with some nice perks: great bread and top-shelf coffee.

"True. But I don't think he'd recognize your car again. He took off ahead us so couldn't have noted your license plate."

Here came the "but" clause. "Yes, but . . ." I could virtually hear Kate's synapses snapping. "He came from behind and since we didn't hear him, who knows how long he was back of us."

"Too bad we couldn't have gotten *his* license plate," I grumped, that barn door firmly shut behind a horse long gone.

"I thought it prudent to keep our distance," she remarked.

"Yeah. You did well." Kate had certainly kept her cool and I didn't want her to lose it, so I added, "Obviously he thought you were Mona, so he probably didn't think to check your plate, just followed your hood, expecting her."

Kate turned to me anxious eyes. "But next time he sees her, wouldn't he just ask her if there was anybody else she knew who wore a hooded cloak?" Two beats. "And then find *me*?" she whispered.

Oops. *Damn.* "Good point."

"I think I'd better call Mona when we get back."

"And tell her what, Kate?"

"I don't know! I'll think of something."

Gino's entrance bell tinkled. I put back on Indiana and Ray-Ban and kept my head down.

Two dudes in hoodies came in for their pizza, paid and left. After they'd gone, Kate leaned over and said, "Let's go."

She grabbed our leftover pizza, her purse, and inched toward the glass door, looking out.

"Clear!"

I sidled up alongside her.

"Clear!" I echoed, and we sprinted for the Honda.

It was starting to sprinkle and the warm pizza box was fogging up the Honda's windshield. Kate turned on the wipers and defroster.

We rode in silence. Not another soul was on the road, as far as we could tell.

Entering our long back street, I had a small brainwave.

"Any chance there are more folks in your Goth Book Club who are fond of hoods and cloaks?"

"By golly, you're right! Yes, to both!"

"To both?" I crooked my head.

Kate gave a saucy chuckle. "Besides vintage outerwear, some of the gals like their guys greased up and naughty—you know switchblades, black leather and pompadours."

"Oh! *That* kind of 'hood'! You mean like the Jets and Sharks?"

"Uh huh. It's the New Goth." My mind boggled. The Everly Brothers come to *Twilight.*

"So Mona might not *automatically* think of you. . . ."

I swivelled toward her. "I know! Maybe call her and say you saw this guy tonight chatting with a woman wearing a hooded cloak in the car next to his while they were stopped at a red light. And at first you thought it might be her and were about to say 'Hi,' but then when you got close you saw it wasn't her car. Then you can suggest maybe it was one of the other book club women."

"That might work! And next to her was some doofy guy in a Harrison Ford hat and sunglasses."

I forgave the "doofy" inference; after all, I always made fun of her Spock pajamas (and socks). Each to her own cinematographic trope. Besides, she'd kindly kept quiet about the Butch Cassidy poncho.

Relieved by our solution, she turned on the radio, then laughed out loud at the familiar, creepy opening bars, and started singing along, paraphrasing tunefully:

> She wears her sunglasses at night, so she can, so she can
> Watch him weave his wicked story lines.

Kate grabbed my hand and gave it a squeeze.

"Speaking of 'doofy,' " I began, still feeling a bit rankled, "did you catch the stupid, fuzzy scarf he had on, tied like a Möbius strip?"

Nodding vigorously, Kate guffawed. "Probably had Martha Stewart knit it for him from her own Alpaca wool. In apricot, no less. Carly Simon would love *that*. Like it makes him look harmless."

We both broke out in song, paraphrasing happily:

> Don't switch the blade on this girl in shades, oh no.
> Don't masquerade for this girl in shades, oh no!

That deserved and got a high five.

FIFTEEN

FANS AND FOLLOWERS

When we got back to our building, Kate parked her Honda and I walked over to my Kia to get a library book I'd left on the seat. There was a note under a windshield wiper. Puzzled and a little worried, I pulled it out then smiled in relief to see Randy's slap-dash print: "Came by, but guess you were out. Sorry I missed you. R."

I opened my car and grabbed the library book, forgetting to take Randy's message with me.

When I got inside, my message machine light was blinking. I was still old-tech, partly because I was too stingy to pay the phone company the extra charges for voice mail and Caller ID. I pressed the button.

"Al, you there?" Randy again. "Give me a call when you get back from wherever you are, okay?"

Kate was holding our pizza box up. "You want to divvy this up?"

I shook my head. "No, you take it. You've got the toaster oven."

"I could always heat it for you, if you want some tomorrow."

"Nah. Knock yourself out. I need to call Randy back."

"Okey dokey. See you tomorrow."

"Yeah, bye." The tone of Randy's voice was troubling. I dialed his number.

"Hey, Alice. I drove over to your apartment tonight to check on you. I was kinda concerned after you hung up so fast, saying that something had come up. Came in the back and saw your car in the lot, so thought you were home. When you didn't answer your door, I left, then decided I'd leave a note on your windshield."

Randy was the only man I'd given our keypad code to, besides the ex, and I'd changed the code after Asshole moved out. "Yeah, I saw your note. Thanks for having my back, Randy. And I'm sorry I kept you hanging. Kate and I went out for a pizza and took her car."

He went very quiet. Then: "Where'd you go—for pizza, I mean?"

"Gino's. Where else?" It was the best in the North Shore. "Why?"

"You alone?"

"Yes. Kate just went beddy-bye."

I could hear him exhaling worried smoke. "Because when I went back to your car to leave the note, someone had beat me to it."

"They did? What did it say?"

"You'd better read it yourself, Al. I took it off your windshield and shoved it under your doormat. I replaced it with mine so someone might think you were still out."

"Okaaay," I said, feeling far from it. "Hang on while I get it."

I put the phone down and opened my front door, checked the hallway for lurkers, then bent up a corner of my doormat. A sliver of white paper peeked out. I picked it up, closed my door and locked it, then brought it over to the phone, holding it under my lamp. My hands started trembling. I could hear Randy's muted inquiry from the phone I'd laid on the table.

"Alice? You there?"

I picked the phone back up. "Yeah, I'm here."

"You read it?"

"Oh, my God," I said, feeling like any moment I was going to get an unhappy re-visitation of pepperoni. I was staring at a Gino's receipt for a large pepperoni and mushroom pizza dated that night at 8:43 p.m. I turned it over and read the note scrawled in a spiky hand: "Pepperoni goes better with onions, darlin'. It masks the stink of blood on your breath."

"Oh. My. *God*, Randy!" I repeated, my voice quaking like my limbs.

"You want me to come over?"

Sniffling back snot and tears, I said, "Yes, please."

"Sit tight. I should be there in half an hour. And tell Kate not to go for a ciggy break until I get there."

"'Kay."

I went to the kitchen, turned off the lights, then looked out the windows. All quiet, if you disregarded the booming tom-tomming of my heart. I dialed Kate.

"*Al*ice! You coulda just knocked on my door." *She* had Caller ID.

"I didn't want to open my door right now," I whispered. "Katie, Randy's coming over and said to tell you that if you have an urge for a smoke, *to wait until he gets here*."

"Randy's coming over? At this hour?"

"Yes. When he's here, I'll knock on your door and you can smoke then. Just . . . stay inside for now." *And safe*, I prayed.

"Dear God. What fresh horror has transpired?"

"I'll tell you when he gets here." I hung up, then sprinted to my toilet.

Thirty-five minutes later, as I sat mourning the loss of the world's best pepperoni and mushrooms down my toilet, my door buzzer buzzed. I peeped through the peephole.

"It's okay, I'm alone. And armed," Randy added, in a slightly louder voice.

I opened the door and wrapped my arms around him like an octopus. "Thank Christ! The cavalry has arrived!"

He *was* carrying a gun of some kind and had odd-looking binoculars around his neck. "You want me to check the premises, ma'am?" he asked in a butch cop drawl. He two-handed his gun in a partial crouch.

"I *think* it's okay, but be my guest. Maybe you'll see something I missed."

My place is a small one-bedroom and I'd changed into my pajamas, robe, and slippers in the meantime. I hang my PJs and robe on the back of my bedroom door and leave the slippers sprawled on the floor. They'd been still there. So, unless someone was still in the closet (which left Randy out), my place appeared to be intruder free.

But despite my bathrobe and the old afghan I'd wrapped myself in, I couldn't stave off the shivers.

He checked my bedroom closet and under the bed, then came back, laying the mystery gun on my coffee table. Pulling me to the interior of the room, Randy sidled up to the windows, holding up the binoculars.

"What kind are those?" I asked.

"Infrared. Use 'em for locating injured wildlife at night."

Impressed, I nodded. He stepped back. "Can't see anything unusual out front. I'll check out back."

As he went into the kitchen, there was a deafening, explosive bang. He ducked then slid down the front of my under-sink cabinets, slapping his heart. "Shit!"

"Jesus! Randy, are you hit?"

Hyperventilating, I crawled gingerly over to him on all fours, expecting the crunch of broken glass.

"I'm okay, if you don't count a heart attack. Scared the hell out me!"

The floor was as clean as it ever was.

"The fuck was that? A rifle?"

"No. A goddamned backfire. The asshole should get a tune-up."

I was now slapping my own heart. "Christ, I think I just peed my pants." Another sprint down the hall. My bathroom was getting a lot of action tonight.

Through the closed door I heard, "You want to hurry up in there?"

Finished, I called out, "It's all yours. Hope you don't mind that I didn't flush. Didn't want to take the time."

"Just let me in and go away!"

While Randy was in the john, I got out sheets and blankets and made up the sofa for him. He looked calmer when he emerged and drier.

"I found some old ratty towels—" he began, wearing one.

"Use any you like. What are friends for?"

"Hope you don't mind I hung my jeans, etc. over your tub to dry."

"Not at all. It's been a long time since a man's pants adorned my apartment." I winked.

"Just don't get any ideas, lady."

From the now-lit kitchen, I called out, "Spoilsport! Beer?"

"Now *that* I'll take you up on!"

I'd had hops aplenty so nuked myself some coffee. When I heard the ping, I poured and brought my cup in, plopped myself down on the made-up couch and handed Randy his beer. We took some sober swallows.

"Hey, I don't suppose you have anything like an old pair of boxers?"

"You didn't bring an overnight bag with you?"

"I was sort of in a hurry, Al." I gave him a shoulder hug.

"I actually might have a pair or two left behind by He Who Must Not Be Named."

Randy chuckled. Doug, my last boyfriend was a nightmare, just the normal kind—control freak with self-image issues. Aggravating, but not life threatening. I didn't know then how bad a nightmare a guy could be.

"So if the sudden urge for pizza wasn't what came up, what was it?" he asked, pulling his towel tighter.

"About that . . . ," I began, then slapped my forehead. "I forgot to tell Kate you're here! Let me go get her. Then we can tell you together."

"Um, let me do that. Can you lead me to those boxers first? Don't want her to get the wrong impression."

I looked down at the frayed, purple towel around him and laughed out loud.

"That *would* be a surprise. Walk this way." I headed off to my bedroom.

"I'm not sure I *can* walk that way," he answered, in falsetto.

From my bureau, I pulled out two pair of boxers, one in pink paisley, the other purple with tropical fish on them. "He was kinda chunky, so they might be a little big on you."

Randy bobbed his eyebrows. "That's what *you* think." He grabbed the boxers and closed the door on me. Emerging from my bedroom, he swivelled, showing off the pink paisleys. "How do I look?"

With an eye roll, I handed him the ex-boyfriend's pilly, plaid robe he'd also left behind.

"Jesus, what else did he leave? Anything good?"

"You mean besides a broken heart?"

"Ah, honey." He put an arm around me. "You know you dodged a bullet with that one." Randy and I had shared our war stories.

Doug had dumped me right after my 30th birthday. "I do. And I got over it." I raised my mug and clinked his bottle in a toast. "To the asshole. May he never return, because I'm damned well keeping his CDs!"

Tying the robe, Randy walked to the door to get Kate, thought better of it, and came back for his gun. "Better safe than sorry."

He bent his tall frame to look through the peephole, then turned the deadbolt, finger on the gun's trigger. There went the lightened mood.

A moment later, he came back with Kate, her own bathrobe on her for once and a smirk on her face. "Well, don't you two look cozy?"

Randy responded, "Woman, you're lucky I'm not still in my towel."

Kate's eyes popped open. Mine narrowed at him and I did a game-show side wave to the made-up sofa.

"Just funnin' ya," Randy said to her.

I told Kate about the backfire to explain Randy's nightwear situation.

"Hunh. So what's with the gun?" she asked, stepping back.

I turned on Randy. "Yeah, where *did* you get that gun?"

"It's a dart gun, broken down for short range, that I borrowed from a guy I know. Works with animal control."

His fireman buddy, I was betting. "Looks pretty intimidating, like the real thing."

"It *is* the real thing. Used right, it can take down a bear."

"Or a wolf?"

"Hope so—the Big Bad kind."

Nothing like a man around the house, one with gonads *and* a gun.

"I think I have another beer in the fridge," I suggested to Kate.

She sat on the rug by the coffee table, tucking her legs under her. "Nah. I'm all beered out for the night. But I'll take some of that coffee. And maybe a smoke later, if your bodyguard will join me."

Randy bowed. "Glad to oblige, ma'am. So . . . fill me in, girls."

When I came back with Kate's coffee, we did.

Randy sat back, and rubbed his brush cut into a Pee Wee Herman point. "Your turn, Alice. Show Kate that note someone left."

I handed it over. This time her signature lip tremble was for real.

Scooching over to her across the carpet, I hugged her. "I know, love. I know."

"Maybe I will take that beer after all," she whispered back.

I stroked her hair. "I've got some Jamison's if you'd prefer. Want a shot instead? Hair of the dog."

She nodded unhappily. "Hair of the dog."

SIXTEEN

Tag, You're It!

I awoke Saturday morning to sounds of snoring—in stereo. Shooting upright, I woozily tried to sort out why I would hear even one set of snores. Then remembered and flopped back down, wheezing off my fright. Not only had Randy stayed the night, but Kate had, too. She'd been too freaked to go back to her own apartment. Couldn't blame her.

So we'd had a little sleepover. Kinda nice. But her ladylike snorts and whistles on my queen bed next to me, added to Randy's more *profundo* contributions, were too much cacophony to ignore, and my dream fled in startled confusion. Which was a good thing, actually, because the dream was badass awful.

Because it was Saturday, and all of us had the day off, even Randy whose schedule had rotated, I let them both sleep. I eased out of the bed, tucking the covers back over Kate, wriggled into my robe, and padded out to the kitchen. I needn't have worried about waking them. Both slept like the dead, something I envied or used to.

After last night's damp and dolor, it was good to see sun streaming in my windows again. Something to brighten my spirits. But in the daylight, I could clearly see Randy's note, abandoned under the wiper blade of my bright red Kia. Recalling the other note, my spirits took another nosedive. Yet Randy's note *appeared* undisturbed, just soggy.

Coffee! my brain demanded. Maybe that would wipe the cobwebs away so I could get a grasp on a game plan.

I filled a filter with grounds, poured in the water, hit Mr. Coffee's bellybutton. Shuffled over to the cupboard and grabbed three mugs. Kate's favorite was my Captain Picard, Randy's was the one from *Rumpole of the Bailey* that read, "She Who Must Be Obeyed." My new fav was "Talk to Me Before My Coffee and I'll Bite Your Head Off."

Dark humor for dark times.

I remembered the bowl of eggs I'd put away and took it out. Cracked four more into the bowl, added more milk, and re-whisked them.

Exhumed some un-moldy cheddar and a wizened but still serviceable poblano pepper. Popped the cover off the mango salsa. Slapped the cover back on fast and tossed it. It had progressed from fizzy to fuzzy. I'd wait until the others came to before I started cooking.

As the coffee perked, I checked my emails. One from Dr. Gupta, complaining about some typos in my latest transcription. "Well, if any of you docs would *write* legibly, I might be able to figure out what the fuck you were saying!" I huffed to myself. They'd never had it so good until I came along: I was the only one in the typing pool who could (and *would*) actually spellcheck their blasted bio-chemical terms. I'd let His Highness cool his heels and get back to him Monday.

The next was from Sheila. That made me sit up and pay attention! We were only at the new moon, so I hadn't expected to hear from her so soon after her email telling me that she'd assigned herself to me as my buddy. Following on the weirdness of last night, the timing seemed way too coincidental.

"Hi, Alice!" I read. "I wanted to reach out to you again to see how you're coping." She was the sort who "reached out." I scrolled down. "How did the conditioner work out? Would love your input. Keep safe. Only 2 weeks before . . ."

As if I could forget. As if I didn't mark all the moon's stages in my calendars, *all* of them: wall, cell, Outlook. And added numerous reminders, stuff like "New moon, 14 days to go before showtime."

Thanks for the reminder, Sheila, I bitched to myself. *I'm just a silly little airhead, obviously, and couldn't have figured it out by myself.*

And why had she mentioned the hair product she'd given me? It was nice, actually, despite an earthy scent I couldn't identify. And, yeah, it made my hair glossy and more manageable, at least in human form. I had no idea what it did in my other form, as I tended to stay home then and out of sight (others' and mine), unless I got a tip-off of some terminally-ill homeless person. And they didn't mind bad hairdos.

By now, I knew all the regular homeless in my town, even some in Boston. A lot of them hung out in South Station at night, to keep out of the cold. There was a sort of network of them and we'd gotten onto first-name basis. They kept me up-to-date on who was still around (or wasn't), and where they hung out. They thought I was just asking to be kind.

I still didn't make a point of seeking them out unless somebody told me the poor souls were definitely on their last legs, on a one-way trip to the Big Kind Shelter in the Sky. Even then, I tried to get them help if they'd take it, which was almost never. People who've been on the streets a long time are stubborn and suspicious of almost everything. They'll freeze under some cardboard before they'll go into shelters with all their rules and recriminations. But their freedom doesn't keep them well.

It was a logistical nightmare, though, timing it right and getting away quickly and unnoticed. I'd worked out a few places I could hide safely while the effects were wearing off. And I always brought some pot to help them along, and flowers . . . you know, for afterwards. Don't know what the cops made of that, but the media kept whinnying it was some sort of twisted vigilante assault on the homeless.

Funny how the reporters cared so much about the homeless that they never bothered to get people's stories or even their names. Wasn't that hard to find out. You can easily talk to the grimy folk slumped nightly on metal chairs in South Station. Jeez, just bring your wet-wipes, Prissy Pants.

Anyhow, it wasn't something I did often or felt that good about, even though those I helped all seemed grateful. Which made me feel so sad.

That was the hardest part: being *thanked*. I kept picturing them as little kids, fresh-faced with lives still ahead of them, full of hope and wonder. Some mother had loved them once. Or should have.

Mine had loved me. But Mom had been gone for ten years—lung cancer (which was why I was sometimes on Kate's and Randy's cases). I still missed her, desperately at times, but was glad now Mom wasn't alive to know what had become of me.

That made me think of Sheila again, how she looked so much like a mom, albeit a soccer one. Her three-bedroom house looked like such a nice family home. I remembered some framed photos of young people on her desk. I'd assumed they were nieces and nephews. But maybe not.

And now I knew she was the Dr. Armstrong who was doing the DNA testing on Wolf Man's bite victims. I really needed to find out what her story was.

I was about to email her back when I heard the sounds of my slumber party waking up.

"I smell coffee!" Randy rasped. He hadn't had his first smoke yet. Padding into the kitchen, he cried, "Oooh! And what's this? Are you actually going to cook for us?" Then he peered closer. "Seriously? What *is* that?" He pointed to the suggestively misshapen pepper.

"It's still good!" I frowned. "See, no mold, just a bit limp."

"Said the priest to the hooker," he deadpanned.

"You'll never notice once it's diced," I assured him.

He shuddered, crouching and covering his man parts, earning an eye roll.

Kate next scuffed into the kitchen, pouncing on Picard. Holding the captain up in both paws like a beseeching squirrel doing its own Oliver Twist impression, she inquired, "Please, miss, may I have some coffee?"

I poured the fresh brew into their mugs, and pushed a spoon and the sugar over to them and sat. Randy got up with his mug and went to the fridge. "Got any cream?"

I shook my head. "Just milk now. Sorry." They both shuddered. "I've got non-dairy creamer, though. It's in the cupboard to the left."

Randy reached in and grabbed it. "Hazelnut!" His butt sashayed. "That'll do just fine, thanks." Standing by the window stirring it in, he commented, "My note's still there, I see."

"Yes. I saw. Guess I ought to go retrieve it."

He put a hand out as I rose. "Maybe just leave it a while longer. Might make someone think you still weren't home."

"Oh." I sat back down.

"So," he persisted, "you feeding us or not? I'm famished."

"Jeez! Can I just have my own coffee first?"

"If you must," he smirked. "Although *most* chefs are capable of drinking while cooking." Randy was an expert at that.

Kate was still eyeing the pepper. "Alice, you really don't have to go to the trouble for me."

"Be not afraid!" I threw back a gulp of coffee and started heating oil in the skillet. Chopped up the geriatric pepper and some garlic. Fished around for my bread in the fridge, which emerged mostly blue. "Sorry. Guess there won't be any toast to go with that."

Harrumphing, Kate got up. "I've got some. I'll be right back."

"Holly Homemaker, huh?" Randy snarked.

I pursed my lips. "When I feel like it."

"I'm going out to the landing for a smoke."

"If you must," I replied.

Five minutes later, Randy came back in, waving off a haze of nicotine. Stirring the eggs, I heard the door open again. Kate had an artisan loaf of Tuscan bread in her hands and a look of fright on her face.

"What now?" Randy and I demanded.

"I got a note, too."

I turned the heat off under the eggs. At this rate, we might never eat that omelet.

She set the loaf down, fished in her bathrobe pocket and handed the note over. It was soggy but still quite legible. "It was on my car windshield. I saw it through my kitchen window. I'd parked next to yours last night, remember?"

It too was written on the back of a Gino's receipt, but for a large pepperoni and onion pizza: "Be careful of the company you keep."

Damn.

Her windshield had been bare when I looked out last night. And that meant Randy's replacement note trick most likely failed.

SEVENTEEN

We Need to Move It, Move it, Move it!

"What say we take a little drive in the country?" Randy said. "It's Saturday. You guys up for it?"

"Where are you suggesting?"

"I think it's time we did some reconnaissance—check this guy's lair out."

"During daylight? Won't he see us coming?" I asked. "He knows our cars now."

Randy's left eyebrow arched. "He doesn't know mine."

Kate and I looked at each other. "If we're taking yours, then okay."

"But first, we need fuel," Randy said. "We can't go off with stomachs running on empty and I'm starving. Might as well put this chow to use."

I sighed and got up from the table.

He held up a palm. "Step aside, woman. I'll show you how it's done."

Randy was by far the best cook I knew. "I guess I can handle the toast, at least," I pouted.

"Sure," he said. Not a whole lot of confidence in *that* reply.

I sawed some thick slices off Kate's loaf. Plopped them in my toaster, buttering them as they came out, and put them on our plates. Randy came over and slid out a superb, fluffy omelet onto one of the plates, cutting it in thirds and divvying it around. "Salsa?" he asked.

"Not anymore," I said, pointing to the trash. He bent over and scrutinized it.

"Ah. Science experiment, I see."

"There's some tabasco sauce on the counter. Grab that and bring it over with the salt and pepper."

"Some utensils might help, too," Kate added.

"Yeah, those, too." I flung an arm toward the utensil drawer.

As we were digging into our breakfast, I said, between bites, "Speaking of science experiments . . ."

"Don't blame *me* for that pepper!" Randy said.

"It's not that. The omelet is quite tasty, thanks. But your remark jogged my memory about something I wanted to tell you."

"About?"

"About the name of the doctor who does your hospital's forensic testing."

He circled his fork to go on.

"It's Sheila."

"I *know* it's Sheila. Dr. Sheila Armstrong. I told you."

"It's *our* Sheila, Randy, the woman who heads the W.A. group."

He put his fork down. "Well, I'll be damned!"

I sighed and shook my head. "I already am."

"I just got a bad taste in my mouth. Pass me the hot sauce, Al."

"Rotten pepper?" I winced. I felt sure I'd cut out the bad bits.

He grimaced. "The pepper's fine, surprisingly. It's all the rotten coincidences."

I nodded morosely and forked in a mouthful of eggs.

When we finished, I gathered the plates and took them to the sink to soak.

Randy scraped back his chair. "I'm just going to check on my jeans and the et cetera. See if they're dry."

Kate stifled a snort and took a slurp from her mug.

I turned on her. "That backfire was scarier than hell, Kate. Didn't you hear it?"

We'd told her how we both dove for cover. Seemed like she wasn't totally buying it.

"No, but I'd turned on my stereo by then."

"What the hell were you playing, Motörhead? It would have had to been something really loud, if you didn't hear *that*."

"Really? Then why didn't you pee *your* pants?"

"Who says I didn't?"

"Wow." She went quiet, then, "And you're sure it was a backfire?"

"Randy said so. I would have said it was more like a cherry bomb, but he'd know better than I."

"Weird coincidence that it went off just then."

"One of many recent weirdnesses."

"And we don't believe in coincidences," we added in stereo.

"Except that some unconnected events do coincide," Kate said. "You do know that not everything is a harbinger sent from the cosmos, right?"

"Of course I do, although lately . . ."

"I know. Them harbingers been gangin' up on us."

We heard the shower shutting off. A few moments later, we heard Randy calling, "I'm coming out!"

"What, again?" we called back.

"And I'm *sans* towel and bathrobe."

Kate and I ducked down, covering our eyes. But it was okay; he was back in his jeans.

"Such naughty minds you two have!" he tsked. "Hope you don't mind that I switched to the fish. I washed out the paisleys and hung those up to dry."

Kate shot me a screwed-up *Huh?* look.

"I let him borrow Balding Wart's boxers he left behind." That was Randy's nickname for my last ex.

"*Eeeuww*. Did they stink like fish or something?"

I LOL'd. "Nah. One pair was purple with tropical fish on it," I explained. "The other was pink paisley."

Kate gawped. "Seriously? *Doug?* Hidden depths. Or should that be shallows? I'm guessing that's where the sad, plaid robe came from, too."

"You guessed right. But *I* didn't give them to him!"

"Well, at least they came in handy, unlike his lifetime supply of dental floss he left you. Such a caring man."

Hopefully, toothless soon. "The CDs are pretty good," I admitted.

"Fluke."

"Agreed. Definite fluke."

The ex was about as boring a guy as I'd ever known, once I'd gotten to really know him, you know, after our abbreviated period of crazy monkey sex. He had nice brown eyes, but he was totally obsessed with his hair loss and flab (yet unwilling to do a thing about them)—and happy to transfer that angst onto any of my imperfections, constantly telling me to quit the beer and go to the gym, get a better hairdo, stop biting my nails, blah, blah, blah. Nothing I did was right. But he did have excellent taste in jazz.

"So you guys going to suit up?" Randy prodded.

"Sure. Kate, you want to shower here or at your place?"

"It makes more sense if I go home, I guess. I don't want to go out wearing something else Asshole left behind. Just . . . Can you go to my door with me?"

Randy shrugged back on his jacket and grabbed his gun. "I'll be right behind you, babe." He stooped to look through the peephole, then slid back the deadbolt. "Looks okay."

I'd fished the fizzy, fuzzy salsa out of the trash, pried off the lid, and held it ready to aim. The hall was empty. Our trio of relieved sighs sounded like a pool toy losing air.

"Gimme your key, Kate." Randy held out his left hand, pedaling his fingers. Turning her key quietly in her lock, he eased open the door, gun ready. Did that back-to-door swivel thing they do in all the cop shows, crouched in a two-handed gun-holding position. We heard a voice inside and froze. "Sorry I'm not home right now to get your call . . ." Kate's voice spoke from her answering machine.

All of us slumped back against the hall wall. "You need to wash those jeans again?" I asked him.

"I'm good, this time," Randy laughed weakly. "But thanks for asking. I'll still go in first, so wait a bit, okay?" He crept in.

I was kinda enjoying this manly man side of him.

Kate must be, too. "In the immortal words of Lili Von Shtüpp, 'Gee, what a nice guy!' " she said in that husky voice of hers. We cracked up.

Randy came back. "All clear, sweetums." We hugged him. He fanned away the toxic fumes from my re-opened salsa container. "You can disarm your salsa bomb, now, ma'am. Whew! Makes your eyes water!"

"That was kinda the idea besides, hopefully, a toxic burn." I snapped the lid back on.

"Okay, 10 minutes do you two? I'd like to get on the road."

We tipped our heads and squint-eyed him with eyebrows raised.

He rocked on his heels. "Okey dokey. How 'bout 15, then?"

EIGHTEEN

SPY GLASSES

Twenty-five minutes later, showered, blown dry, faces on, and dressed in jeans and hoodies, Kate and I emerged from our apartments. Randy'd said he'd be waiting for us downstairs in his car.

Men always do that. They think it'll hurry us along.

But when we went out the back, we saw no sign of his car. Before my heart could leap out my throat like a bullfrog fleeing a big-mouth bass, my cell pinged with a text. "In front, ladies. R."

We turned around and went out the front door where his Bronco was idling at the curb. The frog got away.

"Did you really think I would park out back near your cars?" He'd even parked a few doors down in front. Smart guy.

We buckled up and he pulled away. I'd left Indiana behind, but brought the Ray-Bans. You know—gotta change it up.

All of us were watching for signs of a tail, but gave it up once we turned left onto Route 127 in Beverly, following the coast north. Pretty pointless, watching for tails when it's a twisty, two-lane road: everybody's close behind or in front.

That's one of the prettiest stretches of road in New England, IMHO. The views of the rocky coves and old houses as the road winds past Landmark School and Endicott College are stunning. Next comes the quaint train stop of Prides Crossing, followed by exclusive (and smugly entitled) Beverly Farms with its private West Beach. Then it crosses the tracks onto the straightaway toward Manchester past Boardman Avenue, with its graceful enclave of moneyed old homes and the tiny yacht club's gazebo on the inner harbor. On a normal day, we would have gone past Crosby's on Beach Street in the town center to check out Singing Beach.

When I first heard about that beach, I'd jibed, "Is that the beach where opera stars go to sunbathe?" Turns out, it got the name from the squeaky sand and the noise it makes as you cross it, "singing" in C flat.

But this was no normal day.

Randy handed me his cell. "Give Siri the guy's address."

I spoke into the phone and robot woman began her GPS instructions: "Turn right in 100 yards, turn left in 50 feet," and so on.

"I know where I am now," I said, shutting the bitch up. "There's the gate." I pointed to a huge, wrought-iron, double gate with gilded curlicues in front of a long, winding drive bordered by giant hemlocks. There was a key-pad and a speaker on the left-hand side.

"Now what?" Randy asked.

"You didn't really think we'd just ring his doorbell, did you?"

He shrugged.

"And do we really want him to know we're here?"

"So, what's our plan?" Kate asked.

"Keep going. Down there," I ordered, pointing. "Park near the next mansion." There were a bunch of cars already lined up down the street. Judging by the big marquee erected on the lawn, looked like a party was being set up. We'd blend right in, unnoticed.

We got out. "There's a back entrance to his place. You know, for the help. It's got a separate gate, but it's never locked. Or never used to be. Let's check it out." I turned to Randy. "You still have those binoculars with you?"

He reached back into the Bronco for them, then beeped it locked.

"If anybody challenges us, just say we're on a bird-watching hike," I said. "The place is lousy with egrets and great blue herons." Indiana Jones would be impressed by my cunning.

"Ospreys, too, on occasion, and great horned owls," Randy added. Mr. Wildlife Rescuer ought to know, especially about anything horny.

The place was as magnificent as I remembered. Looked like a National Trust stately home you'd find in Jolly Olde England. Except there was nothing jolly about its owner. But the views were amazing. Rounding the curve of the back lane, we came out on a sprawling expanse of parklands, studded by still more ancient trees, gently sloping away from the back of the mansion to display a 180º expanse of sea view, only a few acres away.

"Wow. I think I just came." Randy lit up a cigarette, blew out some smoke.

"Is that like a post coitus smoke?" Kate cracked.

Randy laughed. "Close to it."

Kate gestured a "Gimme." Randy passed her his ciggy.

When he stubbed out their butt, I motioned to some shrubs near the house, with my finger across my lips. "Let's stick to the tree cover until we get up close."

Creeping under shaggy branches, we came to the back drive where the six-car garage was. Five of the doors were closed. The open one's bay was empty. No cars on the drive.

I sidled up to the house's back door, beyond the garage. So far, no sign of life through its reinforced glass window.

I gestured for them to join me. "That's the basement hall you're looking at down there," I whispered. "The house is like one in Europe, where the 'first floor' living areas are actually on the second storey."

I went through the layout with them—the wine cellar at the back, then the so-called gym, and nearest us, the two off-limits iron doors, then pointing out the stairs to the kitchen above, beyond the wine cellar.

"Randy, you and Kate check out the garage and see if the Rolls or the Lexus are there. I'll stay here and keep a lookout."

They tiptoed inside the open bay door.

"The Rolls is there, but the Lexus is out," Kate murmured a sec later.

"Shit. It'll be harder to hear him when he drives up." Figures it'd be the electric car that was missing. We couldn't seem to get a break.

Then we heard a dog start barking down the hall. "Get ready to run!" The barks were joined by the click of steel-toed boots on tile, then the crackle of a walkie-talkie. A henchman cometh.

We dove under the azaleas.

As his boots tapped up and down the hall, we heard his voice loud and clear. It was obvious whose voice was on the other end. "Yes, sir. I'm down in the basement now. Over."

"No, everything's quiet. Just fed and walked the dog. Over."

Laughter.

"Understood. Over."

"She's still sleeping it off. Over." More laughter.

"So when shall we expect you? Over."

"Okay, I'll see you in an hour or so, then. Over and out."

The boots and dog paws clicked away and up the wooden stairs.

Finally, we'd gotten a break.

Crawling out from the shrubs and picking off leaves and mulch, I whispered, "We have an hour, possibly less, so let's make the most of it."

Now that the coast was clear, I led them around the side of the house, past the bunker-style barred windows, obscured by shrubs, of the front two basement rooms, giving them a virtual tour. On the backside of the house, facing the ocean, I pointed up to the row of tall windows above.

"That bank of five windows on the right, above the kitchen, is his dining room. Seats 30, 40 at a pinch.

"Then the next room is his library, Command Central." I pointed up to a bank of three windows.

"Why's there a big space of brick between them?" Randy asked.

I pointed higher to the ornate chimneys on the roof. "There are two enormous stone fireplaces in each room, back-to-back. They share that middle chimney."

"All that masonry between the rooms should damp the sound from the party-goers next door, I imagine," Randy said.

"It must. The library was surprisingly quiet, when I served in there."

"And what's next to that chimney stack on the basement level?"

"Just the kitchen stairs. The kitchen is ground floor, mostly on the side, away from the view."

Kate murmured snidely, crooking a pinky, "One mustn't have one's help enjoying the amenities."

I chuckled. "The stairs come up next to the walk-in pantry actually, at the back of the kitchen."

"Even more sound-proofing," Randy noted. I nodded. "So, what's on the other side of that brick basement wall on the right?" he asked.

"Just the boiler room and laundry. Oh, and, the billiards room."

Randy crooked *his* pinky. "By Jove, yes! Must have a billiards room!"

"Bedrooms are on the floors above the second storey?" Kate asked.

"Yes. There are two sets of stairs to get to them, the grand staircase from the front hall entrance, and the servants' stairs in back, which correspond to the ones down here going up to the kitchen. And there's a dumbwaiter, too, on the right side of the kitchen stairs, there." I pointed to its door recessed into the basement's right-hand brick wall.

"It goes to the top floors?" Kate asked.

"I think so, although I heard some complaints from some overnight guests about getting cold eggs on their breakfast trays. The few times we used it, we just helped load it and pushed the button."

"So staff might have had to bring their trays up," Kate pointed out.

"True." Something was scratching at my memory. "You know, I think the dumbwaiter must go all the way up to the attic."

"That's odd. Why would that be?"

"Dunno. I just remembered one of his staff grousing about its getting stuck again at the attic when they wanted it back down in the kitchen. He had to trudge all the way up to the top to get it to go back down." To myself I mused, *What might be up there that would need lift access?*

Kate smiled at us. "A handy factoid, indeed."

"Would you remember how to work it? You know, if need be," Randy asked.

"Like riding a bicycle." I grinned.

Randy peered at his fancy fit-bit watch. It told him everything except where he'd left his stash. "I think we'd better skedaddle, girls."

We tiptoed back across to the back lane, then out onto the road. Randy, the expert birdwatcher, panned the skies through his binoculars, keeping up the ruse.

As we got to the Bronco, we heard the thwap-thwap-thwap of copter blades. He trained his binocs on the spec approaching us.

"Guy have a helipad, too?"

"I don't remember one." I frowned, thinking. "Wait! There's that second terrace, off the other side! The one without the balustrade. Do you suppose . . . ?"

Kate and Randy shot me daggers under crimped brows.

"Sorry," I muttered. "We never had to serve anybody over there, so I kinda forgot about it." Damn. Did Rolf have eyes in the sky, too?

"Incoming!" Randy hissed.

The chopper was getting close and definitely descending to Wolf House. We scrambled inside the car, but were careful to set off at a sedate pace, until we rejoined 127.

NINETEEN

OFF DUTY

"Quite informative, as surveillance goes, Alice. And it's still a beautiful Saturday," Randy said. "Shame to waste it. Either of you up for some fried seafood? We could hit Woodman's."

Kate brightened at the thought. "Oh, let's!"

"Sure, I'm in."

So we headed back into downtown Manchester and took School Street over to Essex. Another gorgeous drive. I always loved going past the old farm on the right.

It was just noon, so Woodman's wasn't too packed yet. We ordered our fried clams and fish and chips, grabbed three singles of white wine, paid, and found a table out in the sun. Nobody'd sat at the next table yet, so we did some brainstorming on a plan of attack.

"What we need," Randy began, liberally dousing his chips with malt vinegar, "is a hacker. Somebody who can get inside the guy's security system, maybe even his phone calls and emails. Know anyone like that?"

"No." I swallowed. "I thought you were the one with cop connections."

"Yeah, but no cop I know would jeopardize his pension for doing that. Kate, you know anyone with that skill set?"

She shook her head, her mouth being currently occupied.

"I wonder if Jared would know of someone," I mused. "Seems like it's usually kids like him that get into that."

"You said he's kind of a science geek, didn't you?" Kate asked me.

"Yeah."

"So he'd be the likeliest to know a hacker, I would think."

"Damn good thought, Katie. He did mention his buddy, Dion, was good at surveillance. I'll give Jared a call." I went to pull out my phone, but Randy put a hand over mine. "Not here."

"Oh. Right." More people were pouring in for fried fish. The table next to us would soon be filled. "Anyway, I need to get back to Sheila, and see what she wanted." I'd told them about Sheila's unexpected email.

Kate held up a finger. "Which reminds me, I need to call Mona again. She still hasn't given me a start date for the Disney gig."

"I doubt it'll happen before the next full moon," Randy said.

"Why do you think that?" I asked.

"Those things take a while to set in place, I'd assume. Signing contracts, sending out W-4s, making up costumes. I doubt Rolf would want to mess things up by turning bestial in the middle of the set-up."

"Maybe not. But he does have all sorts of powerful connections, don't forget. They might expedite the thing."

Randy waggled his head. "Possible. But there's nothing we can do about it at this exact point in time, so let's enjoy the rest of the day. Besides, sometimes great minds like ours need a break so solutions can simmer in the background.

"Do you want your tartar sauce?" he asked me.

"No. Go ahead." I shoved it across. "I'm a lemon girl."

"Thanks, Sourpuss!" Randy winked.

"And I prefer tabasco. So what does that make me?" Kate asked.

"Hot Stuff!" we shouted, clacking our plastic cups of wine.

"If only." Kate shook her head.

We tossed our trash in the outdoor cans and climbed back in Randy's Bronco. It *was* a glorious fall day. The Essex River shimmered in the sun, ducks and kayaks leaving Vs behind as they took to the outgoing tide, the big gumdrop of Hog Island looming over the marsh. An afternoon like this made it easy to put our troubles aside for a while.

Randy took the right turn and pulled into the lot at the White Elephant, a favorite haunt of ours. We got out and poked through all the cool, old stuff. I found a signed, hand-colored woodprint of antique sailboats, docked at Rockport's Bradley Wharf (the famed "Motif #1").

"Twenty-five bucks!" Randy exclaimed. "If you don't buy it, I will."

It was even beautifully framed. I happily forked over the $25.

While I was stowing it carefully in Randy's Bronco, a band of clouds slid over the sun, lowering the temperature instantly. I shivered.

"Want to go over to Ipswich?" Randy asked. We loved the Choate Bridge Pub and he so seldom got a weekend free. "I think those clouds will pass." But the sky was getting darker by the moment.

Kate scanned the sky. "I don't know. Looks like a big system's coming in." She was like a cat—hated getting wet.

"Oh, come on, Mabel. I'll buy." He always called women Mabel or Edna when they were being fuddy-duddy.

I checked the time. "It's only two o'clock, Kate. I can loan you my umbrella if you want to keep your coiffure dry."

"Oh, all right. I'll just pull my hood up if I have to," she capitulated.

"Ooh! There's a thought!" She gave me the stink-eye and yanked my hood over my eyes.

The Choate Bridge is sort of like the Cheers of Ipswich. The same regulars seem to be there every time, perched on their usual stools. A comforting consistency, seeing faces we knew or at least could recognize. A threesome at the bar were just paying their tab, so we soon grabbed their stools.

Sharon was behind the bar. She came over, a big grin on her face. "Hey! It's been a while, guys. What'll you have?"

"As if you have to ask," I smirked, tilting my head toward Randy.

"Three Buds coming right up!"

"No!" we yelled in tandem. (We'd rather drink horse piss.)

"Just yankin' your chains," she tossed back at us from the taps where she stood pouring three lovely Ipswich Ales.

"Madam, you frightened me!" Randy fanned himself. "I thought I was about to swoon and would have to ask for smelling salts."

We all took grateful swallows. "Mother's milk," Randy declared.

Sharon beamed at us and poured out some bar mix into a paper boat for us. "Wanna hear the specials?"

"Sorry, Sharon. We just ate at Woodman's."

"No problem. If you change your minds, just let me know."

It was great to be out, just us three Musketeers.

After two more lingering rounds, Randy checked his bionic watch. "Probably should get back. I don't think I could stand if I keep this up."

"Come back soon!" Sharon called. "I can always use the laughs."

Everybody loves Randy, on both sides of the fence.

TWENTY

STORM'S A-BREWIN'

The sky had been getting ominously darker, another reason to get a move on. But we'd left it a tad late; no sooner had we stepped outside than the heavens opened up. "Run for it!" Randy yelled.

We jerked up our hoods and bolted down the sidewalk to his car, and jumped inside, laughing. "See, you're not melting, Kate."

She bounced her eyebrows and smirked her kitten smile. "That's because I'm wearing the Ruby Sneakers!" I coveted those vintage, high-top, red sneakers. They were so cool. She clicked her rubber heels, intoning, "There's no place like home, there's no place like home."

The sky was now so dark, I wouldn't have been a bit surprised to see a broom-riding witch in a pointy hat sailing past.

Despite the downpour, we took the same, scenic way through Essex, now heading towards Gloucester, a nostalgic tour of good times past.

As we were coming abreast of Tom Shea's (now *très* upscale and refashioned into Shea's Riverside Restaurant and Bar), we saw a familiar Rolls pull up to the front and park . . . in the handicapped spot. The long-haired driver put a blue, handicapped tag on his rearview mirror and sprang out, hale and hearty, and with apparent impunity. Popping open the rolled umbrella he carried, he opened the passenger door with a bow to a simpering brunette.

Randy noticed Kate and I had immediately slid down in our seats, pulling our soggy hoods up. There went the hairdos. I was glad I hadn't wasted any of Sheila's special conditioner on mine that morning.

"Quick! Pull in there!" I pointed to the gravel lot across the street.

He did and parked facing out at Shea's, keeping the wipers going. I was glad to be in the back seat.

"That the guy?" he asked.

I leaned forward. "Yep. That's Rolf."

"Who's that with him?"

Kate groaned. "It's Mona."

As we watched them saunter in, another car eased up to the curb on our side: a big white SUV, the kind of whale soccer moms favor. It idled across from the Rolls, then pulled away. But not before I caught a glimpse of the driver. I'd know that blond-streaked bob anywhere, even through a rain-smeared windshield. It was Sheila.

"Follow that car!" I shouted.

"Bet you always wanted to say that," Randy said.

"And you didn't?"

As we drove along Main Street, two or three cars pulled out between us and Sheila from the various businesses.

"Rats, I'd hoped we could get her license plate."

"Why? You know where she lives, Al," Kate said.

"I know, but it would be handy to have the plate number to compare next time we see a white SUV like that parked somewhere."

"You can always cruise by her place and check it out," Randy said.

I shook my head. "She must park in her garage, or I'd at least have seen what model it was when I went for my consultation."

"Then at the next meeting, copy it down from the parking lot."

"That'll be after the full moon," I pointed out. "It's only monthly."

He shrugged. "Maybe one of the others will know what it is."

"Or maybe we'll get lucky and catch it when we turn back toward Manchester," Kate said.

So we decided to stay put in the conga line. As long as no delivery trucks got in between, her SUV was high enough we'd be able to see which way she turned.

Not the way I'd assumed, however. At the split, instead of turning right onto Southern Ave., heading back to Manchester, she kept going on Essex Ave. toward Gloucester. Our luck ran out; we lost her at Blackburn Circle when we got cut off by a refrigerated truck as it merged from the right, probably doing the rounds of the waterside restaurants with fish from the Gorton's.

We gave it up and headed back to Revere.

TWENTY-ONE

HANGING OUT TO DRY

The wipers were on high all the way back to my apartment, slapping furiously like hooked two trout. Randy let us out at the curb.

"Aren't you coming in?" I yelled over the tempest.

"I need to go home and take care of some things. I'll call you later."

"Bye, then!" I waved him off and dashed for the door. Kate was holding it open, bless her. We were dripping like colanders.

"Sometimes I wish I were a dog so I could just shake the wet off," she laughed, wringing out her hair. She turned, caught my look and blanched.

"No, you don't, Kate."

We trudged up the stairs. I waited as she unlocked her door. "I'll come in with you, Katie, just, you know, to make sure. . . ."

"Thanks, Al." She eased the door open and we peered in. All we could hear were the drip of the faucet and the tick of her kitchen clock. She tiptoed in, Pink Panther style, peering around the hall corner into the living room. Nothing out of place. Ditto the bedroom, closets, and bathroom, but we were ready to spring back and aim an indelicate kick.

Kate dumped her purse by her bed. "Okay. Now you."

Relocking her door, we went softly across to my place. Did the same routine, then heaved two sighs of relief. I'd had the strap of my bag wrapped around my hand, prepared to wallop, and unwound it. As I threw it on a chair and stood empty-handed, I realized I was missing something. "Damn. I left my picture in Randy's car!"

"Randy will take good care of it, Al. In any case, dashing through a downpour with it wouldn't have done it any good." She was right. When he called, I'd remind him.

"I do believe we've had enough excitement for one day and I am dying for a hot shower!" Kate blew me a kiss and went back to her place.

That made two of us. She was also probably making her excuses so she could sneak a smoke.

Turning the shower on full blast, I wriggled out of my wet things, dropped them on the tiled floor, and climbed into steamy bliss—one of the best mood improvers I knew of, aside from good beer and great pizza. Well, and sometimes sex.

As I massaged shampoo over my head, I recalled the steamy showers another ex (two previous) and I used to have. There is absolutely nothing more erotic than a man shampooing your hair. Manny was the only man who'd done that. Sometimes I still missed his unreliable ass. What a wild ride he'd been, anyway you want to take that. He was my sexy bad boy, bad in all the good ways. A fast car running all the stops. Every woman needs one of those once in her life, even though you know it won't last.

For years, he'd call me up from California at Christmas to shoot the shit and reminisce. Hadn't heard from him in a few years now, though. No point getting in touch anymore, being what I was now. My sex life was now terminally in the crapper, forever and ever, amen. And I was staring down a long tunnel of forever.

I turned off the shower, pulled a fluffy bath sheet around me and towel-dried my hair. Wiped the steam off the mirror and looked at my reflection. "You need to stop with this morose shit, Alice!" I scolded my image. "Won't do you or anyone else any damned good."

I still had clear skin, now glowing pink from the steam, my dark hair was smooth and strong, and my punk pixie cut framed my face perfectly. My best feature is probably my eyes, which are grey, or sometimes blue or green, depending on what I wear, and rimmed with thick, dark lashes, thanks to my Black-Irish grandmother. I didn't really need mascara, and I certainly didn't need false eyelashes. They were simply fun to bat.

I wondered how long my looks would last. Would I be like a bug in amber, preserved in perpetual youth? If I had to be on this earth forever, that would be *some* compensation. But if I kept thinking about that—the forever part, the way I was now—I'd get morose again.

I brought Sheila's conditioner over to the sink and squeezed out a dollop into my palm and rubbed it through my hair. "Snap out of it, kiddo. A pity party's not gonna help."

I bared my teeth at the mirror.

That conditioner did do wonders for my hair. I was even getting to like the odd, rather come-hither smell. Wasted on me now.

Which reminded me: I should get back to my "buddy." See what Sheila had to say for herself (and where she'd been today). I'd keep mum for now that we saw her outside Shea's. I just couldn't shake the feeling that she wasn't being completely up front with me, maybe any of us.

Connie had known her longest. Tomorrow was Sunday. I wondered which mass she'd go to. Maybe I'd give the old girl a call, compare notes.

Back in my jammies and robe, I flopped on the sofa and grabbed the remote, pulling a blanket around me. My sofa was still made up for sleeping, in case Randy returned. I punched the channel guide and switched to the news.

There was a break in a case where a young woman had disappeared five years ago. The TV showed a photo of her, taken right before she went missing: dark pixie haircut, gamine face with expressive grey eyes and sooty lashes, slim, five-feet-four.

I swallowed hard. My doppelganger.

A couple who used to raise Shetland cattle had found her corpse in their pasture in Manchester-by-the-Sea. Like the kid in Lynn, her throat had been torn out.

I dialed Randy with a trembling hand.

"I was just about to call you," he answered. "You forgot your picture."

"I know, but I'm not calling about that. Did you see the news, the special they ran on that girl who disappeared up here five years ago?"

"No, I was in the kitchen doing a stir-fry."

"Well, they found her—Dee Dee Thornton. Her body anyway. It was found in Manchester-by-the-Freaking-Sea, throat torn out."

I could hear the clatter of a spatula hitting a wok.

"Dear God," he breathed out.

If there is a God, I thought to myself.

"There should be a rerun later at 11. WBZ. Check it out and tell me what you think."

"I feel sure I already know what I'm going to think."

"Yeah, well, you'll think it even more when you see the photo of her. Unless I've gone absolutely bat shit."

I heard his long exhale as he connected the dots.

"That sofa still made up?"

"Yes, but Randy, you don't have to—" I began, trying for bravery. "I haven't seen any UFVs in the parking lot. Except, I guess maybe we can't call them that anymore, can we? Seeing as how we know who they belong to."

"True. But if they didn't turn on their headlights, would you know they were there, Al?"

I had actually thought about that, but didn't see how anyone could drive with no lights in the dark and said so to Randy. "Are there, like, infrared headlights or something?"

Randy sighed. "I'm sure someone that rich could probably find some genius inventor to whip some up for him, although I doubt any mechanic would risk his job to install them.

"But, Alice, you wouldn't need the *headlights* to be infrared, just what you were looking *through* as you drove."

Duh. Like his special binoculars. I always found Randy to be a wealth of information, some of it humiliatingly unwelcome.

"Okay, Einstein, but would they be clear enough to keep you from sideswiping other cars as you passed them? And what about cops? They'd be on you like flies on shit, the minute you went by."

"Or . . . ?" he prompted. I knew his hand was circling forward.

"Or," I mumbled in embarrassment, "if they saw cops, they'd just turn their headlights back on and either wait or clear out."

"Atta girl! Got there at last."

"I am *so* screwed," I moaned. "Although Wolf Man and I never did the 'beast with two backs,' har-har, so no joy there," I added, grasping at a laugh.

"You already were screwed, honey, even though you didn't. But, cheer up, you're not alone, Alice. We're all screwed now."

"God, Randy, this is *awful* and it's all my fault! Bad enough *my* life's in the shitter. Now I've gotten my best friends involved and the doggy do smeared all over you, too. You could both *die* because of me!"

I could hear the pop of hot oil and a spatula stirring again.

"First," he said, "you didn't get us involved, we volunteered, honey. Second, you didn't bring this on. It started long ago with Rich Fucker and his whole ancestral line of hairy assholes.

"So lemme just store my stir-fry in the fridge—I'll heat it up tomorrow—and pack some overnight things and I'll be over, okay?"

When I didn't answer right away, he repeated, "*Okay?*"

"Okay, thanks," I breathed out with a delayed hiccupped whimper.

"And I'll bring your lovely print with me. It's not raining anymore, so it'll stay dry."

"Thanks. Oh, and can you pick up some wine or something on the way, Randy? I'll pay you back."

"Don't worry about that. I've got some white in the fridge I've been meaning to share. See you in a bit."

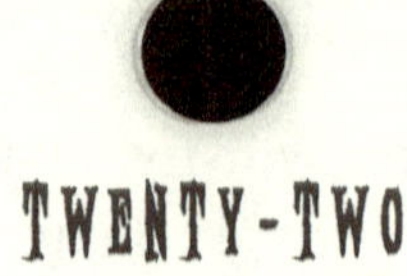

TWENTY-TWO

TIME TO WINE

As I held the door open for Randy and his overnight bag, he sniffed my hair. "What's that smell?"

I shrugged. "It's that special conditioner Sheila gave me when I went to her for my private consultation." I'd told him about the index card ad and the junk mail that followed.

He sniffed again. "Weird, but not bad. Although it makes me a little horny."

I backed up from him. He put out a spread-fingered palm, the other over his heart. "Don't worry, my testosterone is spoken for. I only go for Girrls with more than one R."

"Just so we're straight on that," I scowled.

"Oh honey, I was never straight." I chuckled and socked his arm.

"Ow! She hit me!" he said to the room. "And it was my bottle arm!"

He held out a bottle of Bread & Butter chardonnay. Nice!

I put his bag down by the sofa. "Lordy, did you bring your anvil collection?" I asked.

"Just the usual: clean drawers and socks, my own pill-*free* bathrobe and a change of shirts. Oh, and the hardware." I got it. As he unpacked the infrared binocs and dart gun, I started for the kitchen to get a couple of glasses and a corkscrew.

"Wait a bit, Al. Why don't we get cozy? You know, turn the lights down low."

I got that, too. If we were an actual romantic couple, we wouldn't have all the lights blazing like a goldfish bowl under a spotlight. I turned off all but a couple of lamps and let him do his thing with the binoculars. He motioned me over and handed them to me, pointing. "See that guy crossing the street?"

"Looks like a ghost, but yeah, I see him. Doesn't look like Wolf Man, though. But that might not mean anything, having henchmen."

"I'm just showing you how things look through them. What else?"

I adjusted the optics. "There's a car idling across the street. I can tell by the exhaust. The guy's walking towards it. Now he's opening the passenger side door."

"Can you make out the license plate or car brand?"

"Yes, I can!" Reading the plate, I slumped. "But it's not our guys, as far as I know." I passed them back to him.

"Older Toyota Corolla, maybe 2010, blue, big dent on the rear left side, and the license plate is . . ." He made a scribbling gesture. I grabbed a pen and an old envelope and he read it out to me. The Corolla drove away with its bass notched up high, booming rap down the street. "Probably not connected. But it's always good to have data to compare."

"Shall I get the wine glasses now?"

He hesitated. "Yeah. Do that. And keep the lights on bright in the kitchen. While you're getting the glasses, I'll make a sweep of the lot through the landing window, with the hall light off, naturally. Any stalker out there watching you will be focusing on your kitchen."

"God, I love it when you talk butch." He flapped a limp hand at me. It's not that Randy is ever truly swish; we just love teasing each other.

Two minutes later there was a knock on my door. I looked through the peephole, then seeing Randy's wide-angled schnozz, sang out in an old lady tremolo, "Who is it?"

"It's the plumber!" he sang back. "And the plumber's friend."

It was Kate, not a rubber sucker on a stick. "I'll get another glass."

Curtains drawn, we sipped Randy's chardonnay. At 11, we lumped together on my couch, like those three monkeys that never see, hear or say a damned thing. Wistful thinking. I clicked on the TV opposite.

More car crashes and house fires, and updates on when the Red Line was ever going to run again. We were almost to the sports highlights, on the point of despair that they wouldn't rerun the piece about the dead girl, when they finally did.

"We might want to set our glasses down before this part," I cautioned. "They're my good ones."

When they saw the girl's photo, their jaws dropped to the collars of their pill-free robes and they whipped their heads toward me.

"Oh. My. Great. Aunt. Fannie!" Randy breathed.

I nodded, breathed out slowly, and held out the bottle. "More wine?"

TWENTY-THREE

SOY SAUCE, NO CATCH-UP

"Did you ever email Sheila back?" Kate asked me, after inhaling a slug of wine and resuming her perch on the arm of the couch.

"No. Just as well, I guess. I've got more ammo now to question her with. Subtly, of course. How 'bout you? You talk to Mona again?"

"I missed my 'window of opportunity.' And I very much doubt she'll be home tonight. I just pray she gets home at all." Her blue eyes teared. "God, that poor girl they found. And she looked so much like you, Al!"

I clicked off the TV. "She sure did. He does seem to favor brunettes." I thought about the women at the W.A. meeting. Hard to tell what Connie originally was but Emma, Marblehead Martha, and I were all brunettes. But then there was strawberry-blond Sally from Salem. And what was the burgundy-haired gal's name again, the one with the China Doll do? I'd look her up later on the group list. Now Sheila, with her frosted hair and dark roots, could certainly have been a brunette once upon a time.

But it might mean nothing; maybe creeps like him like to mix it up.

I turned to Randy. "Can you describe that new bite victim you patched up?"

"I really wish you hadn't asked."

I worried a chapped lip. "Like me? And that dead girl?"

"As close as makes no difference, except for size."

I inhaled some chardonnay to cover the bad taste in my mouth. "And now that we know that it's Sheila who'll be studying the sample you sent, we have every reason to expect the results to be skewed."

"Bingo!" Randy spat through crimped lips. "Or incomplete."

"Crikey! I could use a fag," Kate said, in Brit mode.

"One always strives to be useful. Right behind you, my lady."

"Just keep the hall light off and the window cracked, okay?" I called through the open door.

"Yes, Mother!"

While they were poisoning their lungs, I ordered us some Chinese takeout, then cranked up my laptop and scrolled down to Sheila's email.

It was sent at 9:23 that morning. An early riser on a Saturday. We'd left for Manchester around 10:00. The email said, "Sent from my iPhone." I wondered where she'd been when she emailed me and even if she'd been behind us at some point. If only I'd known what she drove, I might have spotted her earlier, but glossy white SUVs were practically ubiquitous, especially ones driven by blond soccer mom types. And she did drive by Shea's just after we had, coming from the same direction—Ipswich. I was liking my "buddy" less and less.

"I ordered Chinese, the usual. Hope that's okay," I announced when they came back inside. "I know you never got to eat your lovely stir-fry, Randy." They gave me a thumbs up. "So, how should I respond to Sheila when I email her back?"

"Just do a hit-and-run, say 'Hi' back and ask what she wanted," Kate said. "You know, 'Tag, you're it!' "

"Or," Randy said, "you could apologize for not replying sooner but you were out, saying it was such a nice morning you went for a drive."

"But if she was stalking me, too, she'll have seen my Kia in the lot."

"Okay, then just add that you went for a drive with a friend."

I composed a reply. "How's this? Should I mention where we went?"

Randy toggled his head. "I'd just see what she says back first."

"And what about Mona?" Kate asked. "I still need to call her—tell her about the long-haired guy we saw that night chatting with a woman in a hooded cape in the car next to his, someone I mistook for Mona at first before I saw the car wasn't her VW. Then add the possible book club connection or whatever."

"Okay, but don't mention the guy next to her in a hat and sunglasses."

"No?" Kate asked me.

"Not unless she asks. Let her work up some jealous doubts about the creep. If he told her about the encounter and threw off her suspicions by mentioning a man in a hat sitting next to her, then we'll know for sure he or one of his guys followed us to Gino's."

"We will?"

"Remember? When we walked in, I had my hat on. But there was no one else there, besides Gino and Joanne. I only took my hat off when we sat down. Then two guys in hoodies came in for their pizza and left. They could have been watching us from outside when I didn't have it on."

"They could have ID'd you, then, Al. And followed us back home."

"And you left the receipt on the counter, didn't you?" Kate shrugged. I shook my head. I frequently nagged her about not doing that. "So they could be the ones who planted the notes on the backs of Gino's receipts."

Randy had a way of pooching his lips in and out when he was cogitating. They were going like a bellows now. "Those receipts, you've still got them?"

"I do." I got them from my bedroom. "I dried them out. Here."

"Good." He took some photos with his cell. "The handwriting on each is different so it might help later if we have something to compare them with. Save these. And not in your underwear drawer!" he called to me as I went back to the bedroom. "It's the first place people look!"

"They were in my *sock* drawer."

"Same thing, too close. Put them separately between the pages of a book, something you never use, like a cookbook."

"Ha. Ha. Oh! There's the buzzer." Randy went to the door with me, we came back with the takeout, spread it on the coffee table.

Randy extracted a spring roll. "So maybe his henchmen were in the Rolls, scouting things out back, possibly also listening in. Then they called Rolf, who just happened to cruise by on 1A in his Lexus."

Kate gasped. "Listening *in*? Like they planted a bug?" Randy shrugged at me. "That would mean he knew it wasn't Mona all along! The sneaky bastard!"

I nodded, looking at her. "Kate, don't tell me this was your first clue."

"It was probably the rock star hair and gold chains that threw you off, right, Katie?" Randy said, kindly. "Flashy, macho and dumb stereotype."

"Also vicious," Kate said. "But, I admit I was figuring on dumb."

Maybe not so dumb. "Go ahead," I told her. "Call Mona. See what she says."

"I just hope she picks up," she replied, echoing my worry.

We'd hoovered the Chinese and had been talking for hours, so I added, "But wait until tomorrow. It's late." Kate was quiet.

"Honey, you want to stay here again?"

She shook her head. "I want to go home."

TWENTY-FOUR

¡ÁNDALE!

Sunday morning. Randy had pulled the curtains back. Last night's deluge had passed. The sun was back, streaming in my front windows, spotlighting the burgeoning generations of dust bunnies and all the popcorn and broken tortilla chips colonizing the cracks of the sofa.

That's the problem when you work from home: you lose structure. With all that time to organize as you wish, it's easy to put lesser things off, like housecleaning. And anyway, what's the point? It just gets dirty again. Maybe I'd vacuum later.

Randy had tidied the sofa's bedding and had his feet up on my coffee table, perusing the Sunday *Globe*.

"You got a paper?"

He looked up. "And some bagels and cream cheese. Coffee's ready in the kitchen, the good stuff."

I sighed. "How much do you charge per hour?" There went those eyebrows.

"I assume you're referring to butler service. You can't afford me." He snapped the paper to the sports section, going over the football coverage. "Yum. Don't you just love all those tight ends?"

I dragged my butt into the kitchen and poured myself a cup of Pete's dark roast. Popped a bagel into the toaster, got out the cream cheese: jalapeño chive and "everything" bagels. Perfect.

Shuffling back out with my bagel and mug, I plopped down in my armchair and bit in. "Mmmmph! Wonderful. Fanks. Any sounds from next door?"

"Yep. She lives. I could pick her froggy cough out from a crowd of TB patients, even from her bathroom with the door closed."

"You could hear her that far away, through her fire door? You must have ears like a bat."

"Stethoscope," he replied, hoisting same. The man came prepared.

A moment later, we heard her familiar nicotine cough outside. I went over, checked the peephole, and let Kate in.

"Coffee!" she demanded hoarsely.

"Coming up, madam!"

I came back with a steaming cup and a plate.

"Who got the bagels? And jalapeño chive cream cheese!"

Randy raised his hand. Kate flashed him a thumbs up, too busy scarfing cheese-spread bagel to speak. Our mom-and-pop corner deli made up the cream cheese specially and made the world's best kosher dill pickles. Thankfully, the chi-chi new bistro hadn't edged them out.

When Kate could talk again, she asked him, "So how come you're so bright and frisky this morning?"

"I figured, since I woke early, I might as well scout for stalkers, check on my car, and grab a paper and some bagels on the way back. Women aren't the only ones who can multi-task."

"So . . . ?"

He put the paper down and sipped his coffee. "Car's okay, far as I can tell. And I didn't see any sign of them, but then I wouldn't expect to see their vehicles around here in daylight."

I set down my mug and licked the cream cheese from my fingers. "So what's on the agenda today?"

Randy's cell was playing the beginning bars of Bizet's Toreador march from *Carmen*. His mouth quirked and he held up a finger to shush. "Hello there! Was just thinking about you." As he was listening, he mouthed to us, "It's Hank." Kate and I did the Oooh! squirm.

"Not much. A late brunch sounds peachy. Where and what time?"

I passed him some paper and a pen. He scribbled, then rang off with a cheery, "See you then!"

He grinned at us. "Well, that was a pleasant upturn of events."

"We could tell," Kate smirked. "So I guess you're ditching us today."

"You guys can do without me for a *few* hours, right?"

We mumped a bit, then said, "Yeah, sure."

"You should be okay during the day. Just keep a sharp eye out. I'll leave you my dart-gun. It's loaded."

"I'm afraid I'd shoot somebody, the wrong somebody. I'm not great with guns. You keep it with you. But in case you're having too much fun to come back tonight, I wouldn't mind holding on to the infrared binocs." He handed them over. "Thanks."

"So what were your plans for today, girls?" He got tandem shrugs. "There's that new Mexican place in Beverly you could try. They do the authentic stuff, cooked by actual Mexicans, not like that expensive gringo crap from *Su Dinero, Mi Dinero*." We all had a loathing for mediocre, overpriced Mexican food, especially as it was originally poor folks' food: rice, beans and corn.

"We could do that. You up for it, Kate?"

"Sure. And I'll even let you wear your Butch Cassidy poncho and cowboy boots." I thwacked her with the *Globe*.

"Well, I won't let you wear your cloak."

"Awww," she pouted. "I thought I could be Catherine Zeta-Jones to your Zorro."

Randy howled. "Al's right, though. Probably better not to wear the cloak. *Or* the poncho," he added, turning to me. "Just try to look like two normal, unnoticeable women out for salsa and margaritas. If you can."

Repacked overnight bag in hand, he stood at the door, doing his surveillance routine.

Our building was one of the red-brick 80s ones, a four-plex, listed as secure: two up, two down, stainless steel and glass front door with electronic keypad, panel of buzzers, squawk box, mailboxes on the left. The occupants of the downstairs apartments were both senior citizens. Bud Kazinsky, on the right side, was 87 and deaf as a post, which should have been a security plus, except in case of a fire. But if he was fiddling with his hearing aids, the squealing could confuse him into thinking it was the buzzer and he'd buzz the place open, without checking out any callers. Mrs. Chang on the other side was just as bad. Her hearing was okay, but she had difficulty with English. Plus, her hips were shot, so she mostly stayed put in her Barcalounger by the door watching her soaps, and just buzzed anyone in by hitting her button with the tip of her cane.

So, security? Not so good, at any time. But a date is a date.

As Randy closed the door, I remembered I still hadn't gotten my print from him. I threw on a coat and ran down to the street to him in his car.

"Wait! You forgot your paper," I said.

"Keep it. I can grab it later. For now, I've got better fish to fry."

"And you still have my print." I saw it was still nested on blankets.

"Crap!" He opened his car door to go to the back for my print, then looked at his watch. "I'll bring it back later, Al, I promise. I really don't want to be late for my date. You keep a guy waiting, he might get lured by someone with better abs."

"Okay, go! Go! Just don't get rear-ended and break the glass."

There went the eyebrows again. "I promise not to break any glass."

As I watched him pull away, it dawned on me that I should have scanned the street before running out like a fool to the only friend's car left that Rolf and his minions hadn't yet connected to me.

It was a Sunday morning. Maybe they were sleeping in.

In my hurry, I'd forgotten my key so buzzed my own apartment, hoping Kate was still there. I blew out a sigh as I was answered by three corresponding buzzes. The buzzers were so loud, you could hear them in the lobby. At the top of the stairs, Kate opened my door. "I saw it was you from the street. Glad I was still here to hear your buzz. I was about to go back and shower."

"Wouldn't have been a problem. Our ever-vigilant guards, Chang and Kazinsky, buzzed me in, too."

She grimaced. "We do keep a tight ship, don't we?"

Showered, hair-gelled and dressed as uncharacteristically girly as I could, Kate and I met by the backdoor to the lot. She was wearing an off-the-shoulder, floaty ankle-length dress in blue, which matched her eyes, and had combed out her braids into long curls. She'd borrowed my conditioner, as she was out. Her Spock socks and fuzzy slippers had been replaced by honest-to-God Mary Janes. I know, but the look worked for her. The effect was spoiled somewhat by the old, brown raincoat over it all. She must have seen my wince at the raincoat. "You *said* not to wear the cloak," she pointed out. I had to admit the cloak would have been better for the look she was going for.

"I know. And Randy agreed, under the present circumstances." I'd gone for a knee-length black skirt, red Mexican blouse embroidered with flowers around the neck, and strappy low heels. They would have gone great with the poncho, but I'd made the same sacrifice, and hitched my thrift-store Burberry over my shoulder.

The restaurant we were going to was in Beverly on Cabot, thankfully across town from the hideous new high-rise apartments that had gone up on Rantoul. They were erupting like toadstools all over the North Shore, effacing lovely neighborhoods of older homes and businesses from the Revolutionary War to the Victorian. Greed had no taste.

We'd taken my Kia; being daytime, I couldn't think of a reason not to. Nevertheless, before Kate and I got in, we made sure it was still locked with no foreign objects that we could see inside, then walked around its perimeter. Everything looked normal so I dinked it open. But Kate came up to the driver's door with something in her hand.

"I just found this on the ground beneath your car. What is it?" She held out a black, rubber disk with a lip around on it.

"Can you show me where it came from?" I followed her to the back and looked underneath, but couldn't see anything wrong or missing. "I see those things all the time on the road. Seem to pop off of cars easily, but I don't know what they belong to. Can't be anything vital."

"I guess so." Kate stowed it in her bag. "Maybe we'll show Randy if he comes back tonight."

La Cantina was packed and Mariachi music was blaring from the wall speakers. Stools upholstered in *sarape* fabric lined the long bar. The booths were upholstered the same way. The walls were covered with colorful Mexican tiles, and wrought-iron and glass lamps hung over carved, wooden tables—the perfect antidote to the new black, grey and stainless-steel horrors infesting New England towns. The best part was the smell. If you've never had real Mexican food, you probably wouldn't know the difference. But we had; we'd been to Mexico, bought the T-shirts, the chiles and the *guacamole*. We were in heaven.

A toffee-skinned, dark-eyed girl in a white, flower-embroidered blouse approached us, adjusting the hibiscus in her black hair. "How many?"

"Two. And can we get a booth?" There were also some tables out in the open next to the bar, but we might require more privacy.

"It might be a while, but if you want to wait at the bar, I'll let you know the minute one opens up."

We found a couple stools at the far end and settled in. Our bartender came over with complimentary chips and salsa. "What would jou like, *mis hermosas*?" He was dark and gorgeous and obviously working on a good tip. It was working.

Kate cocked her head at him, coquettishly. *"¿Somos hermosas? ¿No somos simplemente lindas?"* ("Cute.")

He smiled in delight. "No, no! *¡De vera, hermosas!*" ("Gorgeous.")

"Well, in that case, I'd like one of your La Cantina margaritas, on the rocks, *por favor*."

"Salt and lime?" he asked.

"*¡Por supuesto!*" She dimpled at him.

"Make that two!" I added before he was too dazzled to remember me. Kate could really do gorgeous. Now that the raincoat was shed, she looked *muy hermosa*. But I was getting looks too from all the men in the place. Our hair did look especially nice. And on the way over, Kate had remarked on how good the conditioner was, despite its odd, earthy smell.

"I think I like this place," she commented, swivelling her stool as he mixed our drinks. Nice décor." She wasn't referring to the *sarapes*.

Fifteen minutes later, the hostess came over. "I'll have a booth ready for you in a few minutes." Perfect timing. We'd be sorry to leave Chuy, but we were starving.

We poured over the *combinaciones* and taco selections on the fold-out menus. "They even have *tacos al pastor!*" I crowed. They were my taco favorite and made *properly* in corn tortillas. "And *carnitas* and *chiles rellenos*!" When a hunky new guy came over with fresh bowls of homemade chips and salsa, I thought we'd died and gone to heaven.

"Jou ladies need a few minutes to decide?" We nodded dumbly. Kate was fanning herself. "I hope that salsa is not too hot for jou," he said, pouring it on. "I can bring jou some that's milder if jou like."

"No, no. Everything is just dandy, *gracias*." We ordered another round of margaritas. When Ricardo left, Kate moaned. "It just keeps getting better and better."

"The décor?" I winked.

"The tequila's not bad, either."

This place had me missing Manny. Like the Rose Café on Haley Street back in Santa Barbara always did.

Ricardo came back with our margaritas and took our orders. As we were waiting for our food, I heard my name called across the dining room. Looking up, I saw Jared and Emma waving at me. "Hey guys!" They came over and I introduced them to Kate. "So, what's up?"

"We heard how good the food was here and thought we might give it a try," Emma said. "Only there's quite a wait for a table."

It seemed like my hunch about those two had panned out and they were an item now. An age difference of one or two years was *nada*.

"Why don't you join us?" I offered. "We've got plenty of room." They slid in next to us. "I only hope you don't mind our drooling."

Emma took a sidelong glance at Jared. "I did hear that the tacos are pretty amazing," she offered.

I leaned over to her and whispered, "We wouldn't know yet. We're just appreciating the view." I jerked my head toward Chuy and Ricardo at the bar. Emma took a quick glance, and stifled a snort behind her hand.

"I see chust what jou mean. *¡Caramba!*"

Jared brought his head up from his menu. "What?"

"Nothing!" we said. He turned back to his menu.

An hour and half later, when the last refried bean had been hoovered off my plate, I sat back, groaning. "Stick a *tenedor* in me, I'm done."

Except for the obligatory patch of shredded lettuce, Jared's plate was also astonishingly clean. I was impressed. He'd had the *combinacione grande:* taco, enchilada and relleno, and *dos* of each.

Ricardo came over for our plates. "Everything hokay?"

We raised our glasses to him and the chef. "*¡Fantastico!*"

He beamed. "Can I interest jou in dessert? Our chef, he makes a wonderful flan." We'd seen him coming in and out of the kitchen, in his white hat, chatting with customers, and giving the wait staff instructions. Salt-and-pepper hair, a natty mustache, and a well-earned bay window, he was the only pudgy one of the crew.

I pointed him out and asked, "Is that the chef?"

"*¡Sí, sí! Mi papá,*" Ricardo said proudly, "Chef Felipe Montoya-Gonzalez, a most famous chef back in Guadalajara."

"Do you call him 'chef' or what?"

" '*Flaco.*' "

Kate and I burst out laughing.

Ricardo grinned at us. "Jou know this word?"

"*Sí,*" I answered. (It means "skinny.")

"Jou guys are all right. I get my papa to comp jou some flan."

I thanked him. "That's so nice, but I don't see where we could possibly put it. I do love flan, though, so maybe a rain check?"

"Jou got it, *chica.*"

While we were waiting for the check, my cell pinged. It was Sheila again. I still hadn't gotten back to her. That was a buzz killer. Then there was a text from Randy.

"Why don't u 2 swing by my place? I'd like u to meet Hank."

I texted back, "Met up w/ E & J from W.A. OK if we bring them too?"

I could see his typing dots as he was taking a moment to respond. "Sure, bring E & J."

I turned to Emma and Jared. "Randy invited us over to his place. Wanna come?"

"Okay with me," Jared shrugged. "Emma?"

"Sure."

I texted Randy back, "C u in 15 or so."

TWENTY-FIVE

Pow Wow with Bow Wows

They followed my Kia over to Randy's. His place was in Beverly, just a block off Cabot, so it was close. His neighborhood was way nicer than mine. The condo he rented was in one of the refurbished Federal homes. It even had a garden, and no alleys or parking lots behind the house.

Randy met us at the door and ushered us up the porch steps into his place. Looked like he was alone. "What happened to Hank?" I asked.

"He's on call and, sadly, had to go in to the station."

"But you two had a good time, right?"

"A very, very good time." Randy was grinning from ear to ear. "Anyhow, it's a school night for me. I have to be back in ER bright and early." Randy turned to my friends. "So this is Emma and, was it Jared? Did I get that right?" He held out a hand, shaking theirs in turn.

"Yep, it's Jared," he replied. "Like the jewelry store."

Emma scooted a sly smile his way. "As in 'she went to Jared'?"

Jared turned red and mumbled, laughingly, "Something like that."

Yep, definitely an item.

Kate and I did an "Awwww."

Randy rubbed his hands. "So! I've got beer, wine, gummies, maybe even some Bombay Sapphire. What's your pleasure?"

Jared replied, regretfully, "I'm not old enough to drink, actually."

Randy turned to Emma, "How about you? Are we the only old farts here?"

"Technically, I'm not either," she answered. "Maybe just some coffee if you have it." She didn't want to one-up her honey.

"Technically?" he smiled and she blushed. "Fine then! Gummies it is! I hear they mix really well with coffee."

"I'll take a low-test beer, if you've got one." I was driving.

"I believe I would quite like a G&T, if you can scare up that Bombay and you have any T to go with it," Kate said. "And perhaps some lime?"

He bustled off to the kitchen and we flopped down on the couch and floor.

"Randy loves playing host," I told the kids. "You can't not partake of something in his place, but you can skip the gummies if you want."

"Hell, no!" they replied. Clearly, they weren't newbies around CBD.

Randy called out, "Found the gin, Kate, and some tonic *and* a lime! Put on some music, Al, while I'm getting stuff."

He came back with a tray of drinks, followed by a burlwood platter of nibbles: an assortment of olives and cheeses, some crackers fanned around the edge. A ceramic dish of gummies sat coyly to one side.

"You play butler so well!" I raised my beer bottle, "Here's to the butler!" We tapped glasses, cups, and bottles. "To the butler!"

When we were sufficiently mellow, Randy sat forward. "I just want you to know that Alice told me about you guys and you have no worries from me. Long as you don't go on the rampage or something."

"And I told them about you and Kate," I said to Randy, "so I think they're cool with it, right?" I queried Jared and Emma.

"You're the ER nurse who patched Alice up, aren't you?" Jared asked. Randy nodded. "And weren't you the one with her the first time she turned?" He nodded again. "So what did she look like when she . . . you know, changed?"

The eyebrows went up. "Besides hairy, with claws and bad doggy breath?" Randy asked.

Emma snorted.

"Did she go full wolf? 'Cause not everybody does."

Randy turned to me, tapping his lips, eyes half-closed. "Maybe a Schipperke mixed with a Scottie dog, only not the short legs."

"So . . . kinda cute and friendly?" I ventured.

"Sure. Right up until you tried to bite my hand off." I winced in shame. He patted my head, "Who's a good girl? You are! Aren't you?"

Randy could always get me out of a funk.

"Alice mentioned back at the restaurant that you have some new leads on our wolf man," Jared said. "On good ol' Uncle Rolfie."

"Uncle, huh? Now *there's* a relative who should be kicked to the curb."

"He's not a real uncle. It's just what I called him as a kid."

"Jared's dad has the same affliction, though not the same intent," I explained. "During the change, he discovered Rolfie about to pounce on some poor guy and fended him off, then gave him a good barking-to about being a bad doggy."

Jared snorted. "That's one way to put it. But yeah, Dad counseled Rolf, showed him how to deal with the urge instead of going for the kill, and Dad really thought it had worked. Rolf seemed to do a full turnaround. He even showed Dad around his lock-down area in the cellar, where he'd go during a full moon. Dad felt so pleased with Rolf's progress, they sort of bonded. Rolf even donated a bunch of money to St. Jude's and set up a fund for blood donation."

"The blood donation bit must have been a nice sideline for him," Randy commented dryly.

"I'm sure it helped with managing the urge," Jared admitted, "but it was another reason Dad stopped worrying about Rolf and just got on with things. Plus, it was years ago."

Emma put a hand on Jared's. "It wasn't until Jared came into his—you might say genetic inheritance—that Rolf came to mind again."

"And even then, I didn't put two and two together until after the W.A. meeting," Jared said.

Randy sat forward. "So, here's what we've found out so far. . . ."

When everyone was up to speed, and no longer buzzing on gummies, we sprawled back, each of us pondering our next move.

Randy sat forward again. "When's the next full moon?"

Emma reached to check the organizer on her phone, but I beat her to it. "Thirteen days away. Right, Emma?"

She nodded. "The 28th." Just three days before Halloween.

"We don't have much time to organize people," Randy pointed out.

I didn't want to think of all the ways Rolf and his ilk could disappear among a group of costumed merry-makers, either here or at Disney World during Halloween. "But you said you didn't think the Disney thing would happen that soon," I responded with alarm.

"Yes, but do we want him still at large here a moment longer on our turf, if we can prevent it?"

The ghost of Dee Dee Thornton was nudging me. "You're thinking of Dee Dee, aren't you?"

"And that new girl in Lynn who was torn to pieces. Then there's Mona and who knows how many others. And you."

"But I'm already turned. That horse has already left the barn."

"Yes, but you're still alive to tell the tale."

"A tale no one would believe if I did."

"Depends on who you told it to," Jared put in.

"Like that scientist your dad knows?" I asked. Jared nodded. "Do you think Rolf knows about the guy?"

He shrugged. "It's possible. In any case, Rolf's stalking you so he probably thinks you're trouble and know too much."

"Or wants to head Alice off from interfering with his thing with Mona," Kate said. She turned to me, lips sucked in. "Or maybe he's hung up on you still."

"Maybe he's hoping for a threesome," Randy raised an eyebrow.

All three of us gals went, "EEEeeeeeeeeuuuuuuuuw!"

Randy shrugged.

"About that new victim in the ER—when do you get the results back from Sheila?" I asked him.

"From Sheila?!" Jared exploded.

I turned to him, wincing. "Sorry. I keep forgetting to tell you. She's the doctor who processes the lab results for Beverly Hospital."

"*Our* Sheila?"

"The one and the same. Dr. S. Armstrong."

"Man! This is messed up." Jared dove his fingers into his scalp, stirring the grey matter in his database. "But, it kinda makes sense."

"How so?"

"Until now, I'd forgotten the last name of my dad's scientist friend. I'm pretty sure it was Armstrong, too. I never actually met him. He could be Sheila's hubby, well, ex by now. I do know she's divorced. She and my dad went to school together, so he's known her from way back. Of course, her last name wasn't Armstrong, then." Jared cinched up his man bun. "So, okay, she and her ex are both doctors, right? And after she changed, they broke up. . . . Hey, maybe they're *both* working on a cure!"

I was practically bouncing in my chair. "But she had to keep a low profile, on account of—"

"Exactly!" Emma chimed in. "What about kids? Do you know if they had any?"

Christ! There could be little Armstrong wolfies running amok.

Jared scrunched up his face. "Seems like Dad did mention something about the husband likely getting custody of the kids."

Which *could* mean they were still unchanged.

"Where's her husband these days?" I asked.

"Somewhere in L.A., I think."

So the kids, whatever shape they were in, were far away, presumably safe from their mom's bite.

"That DNA sample . . . ," Jared began, fiddling with his nose ring. "Did you give the entire thing to her, Randy?"

"You know, Jared, I don't know why, but I did not. I still have some bits of the victim's bloody panties in safekeeping. I suppose I worried that if the sample got lost or misplaced, we'd be up a creek."

"Do you have enough to send another sample out and still have some left?" Jared asked him.

Randy smiled. "I do. Three bags full. She was not a slim woman and should *never* have been wearing Pilates pants."

"Then here's what we should do." Hands joined, Jared leaned forward. "After you get the sample to me, I'll get in touch with her ex, send it to him, and ask him to expedite it."

"How will you explain it—getting the sample?" Randy asked.

"Because of our family connection to Sheila, he'll probably think it was passed on to us by his ex-wife for verification. In any case, I'll say it'll be a favor to my dad and ask her hubby to remain discreet."

"How long will it take for him to get back to you?" I asked.

"If I send it Express Mail, that's two days, then a day or so to run the sample, another two days back. Six days at the most."

"Six days . . ." I raked a hand through my spikes. "That leaves us only seven days before the next full moon! If it gets delayed and she's turning, she'll be on the prowl and out for blood!"

"Well, then! Chop, chop!" Randy rubbed his palms together. "Time's a-wastin'. Be a good thing, though, to call his workplace first to make sure he's around to get the package. Do you remember where he works?"

"My dad will know."

"About your dad . . ." Randy hesitated. "You should probably keep my name out of it, and the hospital's as well, if you can."

"My dad's cool. But I don't think I'll give him all the details right now. Don't want to worry him too much."

"And," I said, filling in the blanks, "you don't want to add too many more players to the plot, either. Not until we need them and have a viable plan of action. Am I right?"

Jared nodded. "Right."

"So, Al, what do we do while we wait?" Emma asked.

"Well, I'll get back to Sheila and see what story she gives me, and Kate, you'll catch up with Mona, correct?"

"Correct."

"And Randy should have his results back from Sheila. So we'll know whether they're legit or not. If they're not, that'll be a big tip-off of where she stands."

"Unless she's trying to protect the evidence for personal reasons," Randy put in.

"Well, *of course* for personal reasons!" I said.

"No, I mean those reasons might not be totally bad. I'm wondering about those kids," Randy mused. "Anyhow, we need more data."

"Talking of data," I began, "I've been meaning to ask you, Jared, if you know anyone who's good at hacking. Maybe one of your high school buddies? We'd really like to be able to get in to Rolf's systems."

Jared smirked. "As a matter of fact, I do. I get what you said—about not adding more players right now—but he's definitely another player we *should* add, and right away."

"Who's that?" I asked.

"My buddy, Dion. Guy's an IT wizard *and* a badass ninja."

I laughed. "I remember you mentioned him before. So what makes him a ninja?"

"He's this strong, little Oriental dude. Dion Rikitake. Studied all kinds of martial arts shit and can kick some serious butt. He even works with throwing stars."

" 'Throwing stars'?" Kate asked, puzzled, putting the stress on the second word. Not many of those mentioned in 18th-century literature, 19th-century either.

"Yeah," Jared beamed. "They're these metal stars that you throw like a frisbee at an opponent."

Aghast, Kate pulled her chin in. "They must be sharp."

"Super sharp. They're lethal when you want them to be."

Randy pooched out his lips, eyelids at half-mast. "What sort of metal does he use?"

"Oh, any kind, anything that you can hone a good edge on. He forges them himself."

"So . . . could he make some out of silver?" Randy's Sherlockian, steepled hands tapped his lips.

Jared's face lit up with a grin. "I'll bet he could!"

"And he can be relied upon to keep quiet?"

"Definitely. He's one stand-up dude."

"Well, whadya know. A ninja hacker right in our very midst." Randy turned to us. "Ladies, I do believe we've found us a knight to aid us in our quest." He raised his wineglass. "Here's to Sir Dion!"

"To Sir Dion!" we echoed, raising ours.

"How soon can you enlist him?" Randy pressed.

"Tomorrow?"

Randy and Jared high-fived.

TWENTY-SIX

CELLULAR CENTRAL

As Jared was thumbing a text to Dion (I never could get the hang of that), my phone pinged, as did Kate's, only hers yodeled. Then Emma's chirped (her message tone is crickets). A moment later we heard the theme song from *Benny Hill* tootling out of Randy's iPhone.

"Jesus!" I griped. "It's like Central Communications all over again!"

I'd once worked swing-shift for a police department as a dispatcher and that's what they called our dispatch center. Some genius thought it'd be brilliant to put all the departments' dispatching in a single place—police, fire, and city hall. So while you were trying to dispatch guys to fight a fire or bust up a knifing, some doofus interrupted, calling about a lost dog or voting places. Talk about stressful. I only lasted ten months.

So there we were, a quintet of cellular dopes doing triage on our smartphones, much like dispatchers. Only instead of a chaotic cacophony of voices, the room was now silent as we peered and poked at our replies.

Kate was the first to sit back and give us an update. "That was Mona. She said she's free tomorrow night and can't wait to tell me her news."

I looked up from fiddling with my text reply, battling the autocorrect demon to the death. "She didn't give any hint what it was about? No mention of Florida and mouse ears?"

Kate shook her head. "No, but I can guess. Can't you?"

I certainly could but hoped I was wrong.

"What was your text?" she asked me.

"Sheila again. She wants to meet for coffee."

"When?"

"I'm just asking her that." I finished my reply and hit Send.

Emma looked up and frowned. "I just got the same text from her myself. She's never done that before."

"Well, three's a charm," Randy said. "I just got one from her office saying the results from the DNA sample are in."

"Sheila's been a busy girl."

Jared was oblivious, still texting. At last, he looked up. "Great news! Dion said he could meet up tomorrow. I was about to suggest a time and—" He finally logged our apprehensive faces. "I thought you'd be psyched. What did I miss?"

"Only that Emma, Alice and I just now got texts from Dr. Sheila Armstrong," Randy informed him.

"Weird." Jared set his phone down. "So, how do we play this?"

"Like, who talks to her first?" I asked.

"And should we talk to her separately or together?" Emma asked. "What do I say back to her now?"

"At this point, divide and conquer might be the better way to go," I suggested. "Maybe I should go first, since she's my 'buddy.' "

"I think you're right," Emma said. "If she realizes we've been working together, she might change her tactics and take evasive action."

"*Now* who's talking butch?" Randy winked at me.

"My schedule's pretty open," Emma said, "until my 5 p.m. shift. So let me know when you're meeting her, and I'll plan around that."

"Assuming she gets back to me first," I said. "If she gets back to you first, maybe we follow her lead and you go first, see what's she after.

"So . . ." I laid my phone on the coffee table and sat back.

Four others joined it. Thumb twiddling time. The top of the coffee table looked like a sports bar in miniature, all the screens playing different games.

After ten minutes of staring at our smartphones, Randy stood. "Well, to quote Great Aunt Edna, 'A watched kettle never boils.' Anyone care for another beverage?"

"Nah, I'm good, but thanks," Jared said, standing up and stretching. "Gettin' late. Need to take Emma back."

She rose and gathered her purse and jacket. "I guess I can stare at my phone just as easily at home. Thanks for your hospitality, Randy. It was great meeting you, and you, too, Kate. Good to have 'normal' people watching our backs."

"Normal? That's a bit of a stretch," Randy chortled. "But I know what you mean."

Kate gave Emma a little hug. "It was great meeting you, too. You'll let us know what you hear back from Sheila?"

"Of course. And you'll all do the same, right?" Emma's gaze swept the three of us.

"Absolutely," I said. "I'll forward her reply to you all immediately."

As we waved them off, Randy remarked, "Nice kids. I have a hard time, though, picturing them as werewolves. Wonder what he looks like, when he's changed. And Emma, too. Can't see it."

"Airedale, so Jared said. Don't know about Emma. Black lab?" He shrugged. "So what do you two make of the barrage of Sheila's texts?"

Kate plopped back down on Randy's sofa. "Feels like she's herding you all in."

Ever the voice of reason, Randy replied, "Well, she *has* been nagging Al to reply for a few days. Could be just general housekeeping, keeping things on track. She *is* a doctor, remember. They tend to be that way."

"Or keeping *people* on track?" I threw out.

"Could be. Could be making sure you're where she can find you."

"And finding out what we know," I said.

"And *who* you know," Kate added.

"Very possibly," Randy replied, "but we don't know yet what her game is. She could be as worried about you and the others in the group as you are about her, wondering if you're all you say you are. Can go both ways. She doesn't necessarily have to have her own evil agenda. She could just be extremely cautious."

"In any case, it's fairly obvious she's doing surveillance just as we are," I said. "I just hope it's *of* Rolf and his agenda, not *for* them."

Randy nodded. "Will you two be okay on your own tonight?" Translation: Hank might return. I gave two thumbs up. "So! Now that the kiddies are gone, I could crack out the Jameson's if you want."

"Tempting. Very tempting, but I sense Spock telepathing me to beam back home, so can I have a rain check?" Kate batted her baby blues at Randy. He batted his back. "Of course you can, fine lassie like you."

"Well, that was a waste of goo-goo eyes if I ever saw it!" I snarked.

Kate snickered. "At least it didn't get me bitten on the butt."

I hung my head. She'd never let me live down my fatal eyelash batting. Randy put a comforting arm around me. "There but for the grace of gender go I."

TWENTY-SEVEN

SHE WHO BITES

Randy walked Kate and me back to my Kia, and checked the street both ways, then did a circle around my car. "Looks okay." He shrugged. "Can't be too careful."

Kate and I gave him quick hugs. "Thanks for everything, Randy."

"You're welcome. And by the way, you two clean up really well. I'm sure the *muchachos* at the cantina really enjoyed the view."

"*Muchas gracias*, kind sir!" Kate dipped a curtsey.

"The view was pretty good from our standpoint too!" I laughed, eyelashes batting.

Randy batted his back. "Why do you think it's one of my favorite new restaurants? I wouldn't mind chewing on gorgeous Chuy!"

Kate was wistful. "He is an eyeful, isn't he?" We all sighed.

"I wonder what this ninja guy, Dion, is like," Randy mused. "You suppose he's all Jared cracks him up to be?"

"I guess we'll find out soon."

I frowned at my still-silent phone. "Speaking of non-boiling kettles, this one seems to have been tossed in the freezer." I checked my battery charge: 65% left. "I'm surprised I haven't heard back from her yet. What are her hours likely to be? Sheila's not a surgeon, right?"

"Nope. She's our head pathologist. Mostly stays in the lab. But they keep odd hours, depending on what they're working on. I'll let you know what her lab report says tomorrow."

"I'll check my emails when I get home. Maybe she switched modes and simply emailed back." It was way easier to type on a laptop.

"Don't you know how to email on a cell phone?" Randy asked.

"No. Do you?"

He chuckled and shook his head. "Hmph! Kate, how about you?"

"Um."

The Three Technically-Challenged Musketeers. But software was the least of our worries right now, and we'd gratefully leave that to Dion.

To save time, we took Route 128 back to pick up Route 1 toward our building. It had been a long and perturbing day, aside from the wonderful Mexican food and male eye candy. On the way, a white SUV blew past us in the fast lane and Kate and I laughed out loud when we saw the Massachusetts plate, red letters on white: "I BITE."

It was fully dark now, so we couldn't see the driver, but we couldn't help remarking, "That should be Sheila's car!"

Then Kate turned to me. "Do you suppose . . . ?"

"Nah." And we cracked up again.

Back home, I circled the lot slowly, headlights off, cruised by Kate's Honda. No notes on the windshield. Tires weren't flattened. Good so far. Then I parked as far away from it as I could.

I could feel the tension releasing from us both. We glanced up. The only light upstairs was on the landing. And then it wasn't. Our two apartments were the only ones on our floor. So imagine our surprise when we saw a light go on in my apartment.

Kate turned to me. "You didn't leave your kitchen light on, did you, like on a timer maybe?"

"No. And, actually, that's not my kitchen light. It's the bathroom's."

Kate peered upward. "You're right. Hard to tell with the landing light off. So what do we do?" she whispered.

"Watch and wait," I whispered back.

We shrank back into the shadows, letting our eyes get adjusted to the gloom. Presently, I saw my bathroom light go out, then the hall landing light go back on. We crept farther back to the far side of the line of shrubs by the back entry. Maybe two minutes later, we heard the back door ease open, then softly close. A figure speed-walked away on high heels toward a car on the street behind us. When she walked beneath an overhead light, I could easily ID that shoulder-length, blond-streaked do as she got into her white SUV.

Kate already had her cell phone out, camera positioned. As the woman pulled away, the parking lot's lights clearly revealed the license plate: "I BITE."

Click.

TWENTY-EIGHT

INTERLOPER

"Well, I'll be goddamned," I breathed out. "That really was Sheila with that vanity plate!"

"So . . . what, then? She's advertising her . . . her biteyness? The fact that's she's a freaking werewolf??" Kate hissed.

I was glad Kate had ignored the part about my being damned, its being a given. "Who'd believe it was advertising? All but the craziest don't believe in people like me. Not that *you're* crazy, Kate," I added.

"Thanks for *that*. Pretty damned cocky of her, anyway."

"Maybe it's just her sense of humor?" I suggested. I'd seen evidence of it before. Spending a decade or more stuck as a werewolf, maybe she needed something to laugh about—by startling others. I could relate.

"The real question, Kate, is: What the hell was she doing at my apartment? And how'd she get in?" She shrugged. "Well, time to find out."

"Should we call Randy first, Al?"

"I've bugged him enough. And he's got to be at the hospital early."

We trudged upstairs, flipping on the landing light from the bottom of the stairs first. I also had my cell out with its flashlight feature turned on. Getting to our landing, I shone it around my doorway, then the mat and underneath it. Looked clean.

Did the same around Kate's door. *Nada*.

"Hunh. She had to be actually inside my place. The bathroom light came on, then went out."

"I'm surprised she didn't turn the landing light off before she went upstairs," Kate said. "The light would have made her visible to someone in the parking lot."

"Probably just didn't know the layout, that the switch at the bottom of the stairs operated the one at the top as well."

"And maybe she wanted a brighter light to see how to get in without making it obvious by damaging stuff?"

I nodded. "Probably."

But Kate's remark about being visible to the parking lot worried me. Like what if she *wanted* someone out there, waiting for her, to know she was there, to confirm that she was following orders?

I checked my door's lower lock plate, saw some scuffing and pointed it out to Kate. "Used a flat-blade screwdriver, looks like."

"Okay, but how'd she get past your deadbolt?" Kate asked.

I raised my shoulders. "I have absolutely no idea." I turned the key in my locks, first the doorknob's then the deadbolt. The deadbolt turned smoothly. "You coming?"

Kate nodded, wincing. We scanned the living room, then went into the kitchen. Everything looked as I'd left it—a semi-organized mess with dirty dishes in the sink but nothing added to it. I even checked the fridge, the microwave and the oven.

"Well, the obvious place to check is the bathroom," Kate pointed out.

"I want to finish checking the rest of the place first." I headed to the bedroom to give my bureau and closet the once-over.

She followed. "Like underwear drawers or *sock* drawers?"

"You're thinking of those Gino's receipts?" She nodded.

"If they're missing, I still have two witnesses who saw them. But I moved them out of the sock drawer, plus Randy got shots of them." (Hopefully good ones.) I trotted back to the kitchen and pulled out my ancient copy of *Joy of Cooking.* "Receipts are still here," I called out.

"Where?"

"Never you mind. You'll only laugh."

From the bedroom she called back, "Be good to know if she's been in your drawers, though."

I laughed. "I think I'd remember *that!*"

"Ooh! Maybe she's a kinky, lesbian werewolf!"

"That'd be just my luck. But let's take a look."

My underwear, holey and un-, and socks looked undisturbed, likewise the bed, in and under it, and the closet.

"Time for a bathroom search, Sherlock?"

"So it would appear, Watson."

The bathroom looked okay, too, except the little throw rug was rucked up at one edge. Coulda been me, I guess, although I'm OCD about that, too. Like paintings hanging crooked.

"You should check the medicine cabinet," Kate suggested.

"I have no drugs worth taking. Unless you've got a thing for ibuprofen, iodine and eyedrops. Well, and dollar store make-up." I wasn't a brand name kinda girl. "Maybe she just needed to pee?"

"Unh *hunh*. Doing a B&E just 'cause you can't find a closer toilet?" Kate shook her head. "Maybe she wasn't taking something, but *leaving* something. Like, I don't know, switching your ibuprofen for something nasty, or putting arsenic in your foundation makeup or toothpaste?"

Frowning, I opened my economy-sized bottle of ibuprofen. The capsules were still their distinctive red. The bottle of foundation was undisturbed, still crusted around the top from long disuse. That left the toothpaste and deodorant. Neither had been touched. I was on the point of giving up when I remembered the shampoo and conditioners in the shower. I pulled aside the curtain. They were still there in the same order I'd left them.

"You've got two bottles of conditioner?" Kate asked.

"Yeah. The one I usually use plus the one Sheila gave me. I told you about it. You even used some today, because you were out."

"That's right, I did. Guess you don't use hers much, though."

"I've used it quite a few times, actually, especially around *that* time. It smells kinda funny but works really well."

"True, but this looks like a full bottle and brand new."

I turned back to the shower rack. By God, it did. Lifting one eyebrow, I stared back at Kate. "She broke in to give me more conditioner?"

"Alice, that is one weird werewoman." She unscrewed the cap, sniffed and her eyes widened. "Whoa! This one smells a lot stronger!"

I took a whiff and agreed. And the aroma was just slightly skewed.

Back in the living room, Kate pointed to my laptop on my old desk. "Did you leave the surge protector strip on?"

Now *my* eyes widened. Kate knew how OCD I was when it came to my computer. I never left it on or even connected to live current when I was out. The surge bar's light was on, showing me it was getting power.

"You use a password, right?" she asked.

"Of course. And it would be damned near impossible to figure out."

"Well, that's good. Doesn't mean someone wouldn't try, though."

"A very good point, indeed, Watson, and bears inspection."

I opened the laptop's lid and powered it up. At the sign-in screen I tried signing in without a password, just for yucks. It blocked me. Then I tried my own password, just changing one number. Still blocked me. *Whew!* Then I logged on correctly and checked my emails.

Three down there was one from Sheila. I looked at the time it was sent. "About what time did we pass Sheila on the road?"

Kate squinted. "Maybe 9:30, 9:45?"

"That was roughly 20 minutes before we pulled in, wouldn't you say?"

She nodded. "Around that time."

I swivelled the laptop around toward her. "Well, Sheila sent this email at 10:18 p.m., from her iPhone."

"So she sent it after she left here."

"Yep. Wants to get together tomorrow at noon for lunch now, at Spazza's, just down the street."

"Bloody foodie. Costs two arms and a leg to eat *there*."

I didn't care for *that* image, all things considered. And I wondered why Sheila didn't seem to be bothering to hide that she knew where I lived now, even though none of the group had supplied their addresses. Had she forgotten that, or was she in too much of a rush to think straight?

I was also worrying what would be happening to my Kia while we were lunching. She must know I wouldn't need to drive there.

I emailed her back that I was a little strapped for cash. Could we meet somewhere else? Her reply was immediate: "My treat!"

Didn't see how I could duck out of that. Might never have another chance to eat rich people's food. So I accepted.

I closed my email and put the laptop to sleep, locking its access. "Should we check your place?"

Kate put up a finger. "I'll be right back and let you know." In a minute she came back, smirking. "I'm good. I did that old James Bond trick, with the hair across the door jamb. Still there."

"Sure it was yours?"

"Yep. Long, red, and kinked from braiding." I gave her a thumbs up. Then, seeing her shudder and hunch her shoulders, I put an arm around her. She frowned. "But my doormat did seem skewed, like from a kick."

Kate was a person, like me, who straightened pictures. (Speaking of pictures, I still hadn't gotten mine back from Randy!)

"You checked under it, right, Katie?"

She nodded. "Yeah. Didn't see anything odd."

I could see she was worried now. "You okay here on your own, Katie?"

"I think so." She hesitated. "You wanna watch TV or something?"

"It's late, but sure. Maybe Jimmy Fallon?"

Her shoulders settled down. "I'll be back in 10 with the Vulcan!"

I had the coffee ready when she returned and had woken my laptop back up. Right now it was Googling "How to tell if someone has been hacking into your computer."

Kate poured herself a cup and looked over my shoulder, reading through a long string of inscrutable instructions and DOS commands. "Why the heck can't they just use English in these things? What the hell is your 'registry'? And where do you find your error logs? For that matter who puts things in them? Certainly not me!"

I shared her views. These techies were just chest-pounding, showing off to their mostly male IT audience, rather than giving the rest of us clear, layman's explanations. It was an inconstant hall of mirrors that stretched all the way to the next update. I shut down the laptop. Turned the surge strip back off. "I'd really like to understand this stuff. You suppose this Dion could explain it to me?"

Kate sipped, fanning steam and fogging up her glasses. "That's a thought. I'll bet he could."

"Remind me to ask him, okay?"

"Sure, if *I* remember. Time for Jimmy?"

"Might as well," I said, grabbing myself a full mug and heading for the living room.

Not too long after the monologue, with our eyes drooping closed, I turned off the TV. "School night. And my butt is dragging, Kate."

She came to, I walked her across the hall, and she shuffled inside. "Call me, if anything . . ." I head shrugged.

"I will." She raised a Vulcan salute. "May the farce be with us."

TWENTY-NINE

PASTA CON CONFESSIONI

I got to Spazza's early on Monday to grab a table where I could watch the street and see Sheila coming. Before I got there, of course, I'd texted everybody, telling them what was going down, when and where. Told them I'd send an update as soon as our bullshit "lunch" was over.

Randy confirmed he'd gotten Sheila's lab report but wouldn't divulge more over broadband. Jared said Dion and he were meeting after school; he'd let us know where and when so we could come meet him. Kate said she was meeting Mona sometime that night but would plan around the Dion meet-up. Emma said she was on board, just waiting to see when Sheila suggested meeting her.

Spazza's was just as you'd expect: trendy, slick and soulless. You'd think, serving Italian food, it would be at least a little colorful. But apparently that was sneeringly old-school. The décor was the regulation trend: grey, black and white, relieved minimally by some sepia-toned vintage photos of Mamma, Nonna and Papà back in Napoli, stirring vats of pasta and marinara, and posing with celebrities and Mafia dons in front of the original *ristorante*, each framed in thin black aluminum.

Before walking over, I'd moved my Kia even farther from Kate's into the middle of the practically empty lot, easily visible to passersby on the back street—no cars nearby to cover anyone who was up to no good with my ride. Made sure all the doors were locked, then walked to the end of the block on the back street. Anybody planning on trailing me from the front entrance would hopefully still be waiting and fuming.

At ten minutes past 12, Sheila rushed in, somewhat out of breath.

"Oh, good! You got us a table. Smart thinking. And before the noon rush!" She pulled forward her black, pleatherette menu folder. "Sorry I was a little late. Parking here is tough!"

I nodded. "Unless you're a resident. So where did you park?"

She looked up briefly. "Hm? Oh, on your lot. I hope you don't mind."

I waited, arms crossed, silent. Then saw the penny drop as her face reddened. She looked up, set the menu aside, knowing what was coming.

"Thought you didn't know where any of us lived," I said. "You know—the contact sheet. You'd made a point of asking only for our names, email addresses and phone numbers."

Sheila sighed and picked the menu back up. "Let's order first, shall we? I'll get to that. I hear the *cannelloni* is fabulous."

A sleek waiter, with his black hair combed straight back and his smarmy smile fastened straight, came over. She ordered the *antipasti per due*, the veal *cannelloni* for herself and a bottle of Montepulciano. I chose the *chicken cacciatore* on *pappardelle*. I removed my black napkin from the black tablecloth and unfolded it on my lap. They matched my mood.

Signor Smarm came back with our bottle of red wine, wrapped in a black napkin, and two long-stemmed, teetering wine glasses. They'd never last a second at my place. With a flourish, he poured their big balloons the regulation third full. Good thing Sheila'd gone for the whole bottle. I took a sip. Not bad. This was going to put some color back in my mood.

I raised my glass, arching an eyebrow over it at her. "So?"

She sipped from hers and looked away. "I'm sorry. I wasn't completely up front with you."

"Ya think, *'buddy'*?" I sipped some more. "Nice wine."

Sheila took a big breath, about to plow in to her narrative. But the antipasti arrived and we busied ourselves with divvying it up onto our salad plates. Taking a bite of a *peperoncino*, it squirted on her posh suit and in her eye. Blinking furiously, she scrubbed at the eye, then the suit, tsking at herself. The suit wasn't too bad; the eye was a mess, red and mostly devoid now of eye makeup. She looked like one of Ralph Steadman's crazed druggie cartoons. I smiled.

"Terrific!" she huffed. "Oh, well." She stuck her napkin in her water glass and dabbed her eye some more. "So, what was your first clue?"

I sat back, savoring the wine and the moment. "Oh, I don't know. Maybe your breaking into my apartment last night?"

Her head jerked up mid-dab. "What makes you think I broke into your apartment?"

"I saw you. And I was with a friend." Didn't want to mention who. "We saw the landing light go out and my bathroom light go on."

I could see her eyes racing back and forth like a tennis match, trying to find a way out of confessing. "Then," I tormented, "10 minutes later my john's light went back out and the landing light went back on, you came downstairs and out the back door and walked to your SUV. Nice vanity plate, by the way." At this, I couldn't help but laugh.

She knew I had her. Elbows on the table (Miss Manners would be horrified), she put her face in her hands and groaned. "I've made such a mess of this!"

I picked up my fork and leisurely tucked into the prosciutto and olives, cut *into* my pepperoncini (so they wouldn't squirt), paired one with a morsel of white mozzarella and bit daintily. "Yum!" Rich folks' food was great, when it wasn't you who were paying.

Sheila did the same, stalling for time. For all her expression of regret, the woman maintained a good appetite. Her plate was pretty much clean in record time. Seeing our vacant plates, the waiter came back. "*Tutto bene*?" Signor Smarm inquired.

"*Molto bene*," Sheila smiled up at him.

He frowned at her, waving at her smeary eye. "You've got something, just there. The ladies' room is on the right," he added, baldly, pointing to the back hall. Then whisked away the antipasti plates.

As Sheila hurried toward the ladies' room, he asked me, "Does *la signorina* wish me to serve *il secondo*?"

"You're talkin' about the main course, right?" I couldn't resist letting him know his smarm wasn't cutting it with me.

He gave me the stink eye. "Yeah. The pasta and gravy."

I smiled broadly. "Well, why didn't you say so? Sure, bring it on." Definitely not a guy from Napoli. Probably Chelsea.

In low dudgeon, he trudged back to the kitchen. Couple of minutes later, Sheila returned with two eyes the same size. Abashed, she sat down and smoothed her napkin back over her lap.

"Luigi's coming back with the pasta," I said, just to fill the awkward moment.

"Great."

"Yeah. Great." We both sipped our wine.

The waiter came back and placed our entrees in front of us.

"More wine?" He gestured with the bottle, hovering over our glasses.

"*Grazie*," Sheila responded, raising hers. Dark eyes smiling into hers, he put a polite hand over hers and the base of the glass, pinning it to the table as he poured. So that's how they kept those tall, double-wide glasses from tipping over and the clientele tipping well.

The dining room had been rapidly filling up and there was a convivial hubbub around us. In our cone of semi-privacy, Sheila dove into her *cannelloni* and her tale. It began predictably.

"It's not what you think," said Sheila.

I forked in some pasta and *cacciatore*. "Mmmm. Very good." I swallowed appreciatively. "So, what do I think?"

"What it looks like. What it *must* look like."

"And what is that? You tell me."

"A ruse, or a . . . a scam."

"Same thing."

She looked up. "What?"

"Synonyms."

"Oh, right. Look, I'm not working with Rolf. Honestly, I'm not."

My eyebrows went up. "So you know his name."

"Yes."

I shovelled in some more *cacciatore*, waiting. "*Cannelloni* okay?

Sheila nodded. "Delicious." She set her fork down. Gulped a giant, shaky breath. "Rolf's got my daughter. I don't know where, but I know he's got her." She teared up. "I'm just trying to get my daughter back any way I can."

I set my fork down. "I'm all *orecchiette.* Tell me about it." See, I knew my way around pasta, not just Prince's "spaghet" on Wednesdays.

"I will, I swear, when we're done. Just not here, okay?"

"Okay. My place? It's pretty private." I added, "Or used to be."

She bowed her head. "Yes. That would be fine. For now, let's just enjoy our overpriced meal. All right?"

"Sure. You said you were buying."

"Yep. I am."

"Then I'm a gonna enjoy." She sent me a weak smile and tipped her wineglass against mine.

THIRTY

AN AFFAIR *NOT* TO REMEMBER

From our waiter's renewed swagger, I knew Sheila had tipped him well. His smarmy smile was also back, Crest Strips-whitened teeth flashing at his new *patrona* with the generous wallet.

We walked back to my apartment and went upstairs. Opening my door, I ushered her in. "You know the layout. Make yourself at home. Coffee?"

She sighed. "If you're having some, that would be nice." Sheila shed her cashmere coat and flung it on a chair, then sat on one end of the sofa.

Coming back with the coffee in my two poshest mugs, I set them on the coffee table, then came back with two clean spoons, the sugar bowl and a plastic bottle of clumped-up, non-dairy creamer. "Sorry. I'm out of cream."

She waved my apology away. "It's fine."

"So, why did you leave me a new bottle of conditioner? Oh, and how did you get in?"

She stirred in some sugar, took a sip and didn't make a face. Kate brought me the good stuff. "Magnets."

"Sorry?"

"There's this magnet gizmo that you can place on the outside of the door that turns the deadbolt."

"No shit?"

"None. Been around for years. A friend got it for me. He knew I was desperate."

"A 'friend?' "

"Okay, my ex. He's invested in finding Patty, too."

"That's your daughter's name?"

"Yes. Patricia."

I figured. "And the new conditioner?"

"I'll get to that."

Sheila had been at a medical convention. Frank, her then husband, was supposed to have joined her, both of them being doctors. At the last minute, he made some lame excuse and bailed. "You go, honey. You'll enjoy it. There'll be a lot of famous speakers."

"Then why aren't *you* going? Thought you wanted to rub shoulders just as much as I with their imminences."

"Just got too much on my plate, babe."

Yeah, like that new lab assistant with the shortened lab coat and runway legs, thought Sheila. She'd make a tasty plateful. Tracy, was it? Elsa? Danielle? She'd lost track of the late-work-night babes.

So she'd gone to the convention alone. She could have cancelled their swanky room at the Boston Harbor Hotel but didn't, even though she could have driven in and saved a bundle. She'd been hoping the four-day convention, the king-sized bed with a harbor view, and the well-stocked mini-bar would be a romantic getaway from work and the kids, and help paste their crumbling marriage back together.

The speakers were good, and she got to meet some very well-connected people. Her purse was bulging with business cards. One of the most interesting was a rather handsome man who was introduced by a colleague as Dr. van Helsing. When the crowd laughed, the professor who introduced him said, "That's not his real name, of course. His work at the moment is rather 'classified,' as his paper is not yet published and the field he's working in is extremely unusual. But I can personally vouch for him and I think you'll find his research fascinating."

It was Rolf, of course, milking the audience for all it was worth with a charming German accent. And the subject, which drew some well-refined gasps, was lycanthropy. It was a fascinating lecture. He took pains to reassure everyone that actual werewolves didn't exist and then launched into a brief history of their legends through the ages, followed by explanations of why they persisted and what the science was behind the phenomena. He also gave documented examples of escalated psychotic episodes during the full moon—in the jails, hospitals, mental wards—as well as talking about heightened animal response and the use of pheromones.

Sheila was fascinated, as were they all, but she was the one he sought out at the hotel bar after that night's talks were over.

"You are alone?"

Sheila nodded, twiddling with her wineglass and checking for texts from Frank. There were none. She'd only hoped, not expected.

"No Dr. Armstrong with you?"

She bridled. "I'm Dr. Armstrong. Too," she added.

"Indeed, you are." He signaled to the bartender.

"How do you know us?"

"I haff been following your work on pheromones. It is very good."

Sheila blushed. That was a first.

"What'll you have, sir?" the bartender asked.

"Do you haff a pinot noir?"

"Certainly, sir. We have a very good one, The Corners, from Walt." He didn't mention the house brand. Dude looked like he had some dough.

"Ah, yes. I know it. From ze Anderson Valley, yes?"

Bingo. The bartender grinned. "It is, in fact. But I'm afraid we only sell it by the bottle." At $85 a bottle, there was no way he was gonna pour it by the glass.

Rolf turned to Sheila. "In zat case, perhaps ze lovely doctor vill choin me? It vould be a shame to drink it alone." He raised an eyebrow at Sheila's house white. "You really should taste zis most rare and toothsome vintage."

Laughing at his use of "toothsome," Sheila said, "Oh, why not? It'll give us something to chew over."

Rolf laughed back. He appreciated women with brains *and* wit. And lovely, long necks.

Of course, he had asked to walk her back to her room. But she declined. The first night. And the second. The third, furious at not being able to reach Frank, she accepted.

The sex had been phenomenal—wild, almost bestial in the most tantalizing way, and very . . . thorough. There was no part of Sheila that did not feel well attended.

When they left the hotel, he had her phone number and business card.

She had a bemused smile and a sore neck with a humongous hickey, now swathed in a scarf.

"He didn't give you *his* business card?" I asked.

"No. Probably the only one I didn't get."

"And that's when he bit you? In the hotel?"

"I'm not sure. That could have been just foreplay."

"*Sheila*, don't tell me—! You didn't keep seeing the guy, did you?"

Sheila hung her head. "Yes." She took a small sip of her stone-cold coffee and set the mug back down.

I grabbed it from her. "Let me get you some fresh," and hustled into my kitchen. This story was getting good.

I handed her the freshened mug and my bottle of cooking brandy. "Something to go with that?" I didn't want her to leave anything out.

"Thanks." She poured in a slug, sipped, and relaxed a bit.

Great. Girl party! *In vino veritas*, and all that.

"So . . . then what?" I prompted.

"So, Frank continued to work late, a lot, and I was hurt, angry, and lonely. And Rolf started calling. He was very persistent.

"At first, we met at nearby motels. Then Frank flew to L.A. on a 'business trip,' taking whasshername. She was essential, he said. So I invited Rolf over. There was a beautiful full moon that night and for quite a while we watched it rise, standing on my deck. Then, well, we got horny and went inside. I think that's when it happened. Must have been. In the morning, there was blood on my sheets and pillow, and I had a sizeable bite on my throat.

"He apologized profusely for the injury. Said he was so moved by my lusciousness that he let his passion run away with him.

"No one had described me as luscious for a damned long time, maybe ever. I forgave him."

"Until the next full moon. Am I right?"

"Actually, I'm ashamed to say it was a few more before I admitted to myself that the two-and-two I was putting together really did add up to four. He really was a werewolf, and now so was I. The symptoms come on more slowly for some and I was in heavy denial. Also in lust."

"Wow. So then?" I gestured with the brandy bottle.

"How about a regular glass? Just a small one?"

"Be back in a flash."

At this point, we'd kicked off our shoes and were each snuggled into opposing corners of my sofa, cradling juice glasses of brandy.

"So," Sheila swallowed and continued, "Frank found out about Rolf and me, of course. I was making too many excuses to be away during the full moon, which meant he'd have to be there for the kids when they got home from school. Wasn't pleased about that. He also was starting to freak out about all the hair he'd find in the shower after I came home.

"In a fragile moment, he confronted me, and I told him—about Rolf and then . . . about what I'd become.

"He didn't believe it at first. Not about the werewolf thing. Of course, he believed the part about Rolf and saw it as pay-back. Which it was. He said he was sorry and that it was all over with Elsa, Tracy, Danielle, whomever. Couldn't we just put the past behind us and start over? It was an emotional night for us both. He still thought I was simply delusional about the lycanthropy, insisting the guy must have slipped me some kind of hallucinogenic . . . until I lost track of the days and he came home to a snarling, barking and astonishingly hairy wife."

I snorted. "Sorry!"

"'S okay. Thankfully, Patty was playing in her all-girls soccer match. It was an away game." (So she *was* a soccer mom.) "And Steve and Ricky, they're my boys, were overnighting at a buddy's doing homework.

"Frank ran out to his car, grabbed his syringe out of his medical kit that he keeps with him, plunged the needle into a vial of some kind of anti-psychotic tranquilizer and rushed back, pinning me to the hall wall before I could lunge at him, and injected me."

"Then he locked you in the basement?"

"Garage. Zip-tied me to the rider mower until he could figure out what to do."

"Didn't the neighbors hear you howling?"

"They were having a party. The music was turned way up.

"Next morning, after I'd changed back, he hugged and kissed me and told me he was so sorry for not believing me. And he asked me what the hell we were going to do."

"What did you tell him?"

She set her glass down. "I told him the only thing that was sensible."

I was expecting to hear that she'd demand that he shoot her with a silver bullet or something. You know, the noble gesture, and Frank's noble refusal. I shouldn't have been surprised by her more practical, self-protecting solution. I'd probably have done the same.

"We'd get a divorce," Sheila said, "and he'd have to take the kids. And move far away."

"That had to be hard."

"The hardest thing I've ever done. I really love my kids and, it turns out, I still love Frank. We just screwed up, both of us, me more than him, though. Way more!"

"So that's when he and your kids moved to L.A.?"

"Right. He'd been working with a group there for years. It made sense. And the boys were still in middle school, so they settled in well. It was Patty who had a hard time of it. She was my first-born and all her childhood friends were here. Her high school social circle was her anchor and validation. So she didn't take the move well at all. And, of course, she demanded better explanations for our split-up than we were giving. But how could we possibly tell her?"

"You couldn't."

"Anyhow, she got a soccer scholarship with Loyola Marymount University in L.A. She really was good. She'd been her team's captain. Then a game was scheduled against Loyola in Maryland. Frank agreed to let her go and forked out the airfare, feeling guilty. And Baltimore was far enough away from me, he figured.

"She asked her dad if she could stay a week longer, see some sights. In a weak moment, he said yes. She never came home, not back to L.A.

"She came up to see me and her old friends, right after the game. They won by a spectacular margin, so she was excited to share the news. When I picked her up at the bus station, she was still jumping up and down with the thrill of it, hugging me and telling me how much she'd missed me, both of us crying.

"I was so overjoyed at the thought of seeing my baby girl again, I'd called Rolf and cancelled our 'date' for that night."

"You were *still* seeing him?!"

"Alice, I was scared and missing my family and *my life*. He knew how it was, I thought. He and I were the same. And I was lonely."

"How did Rolf take it when you cancelled your date?"

"Not well. He was always egocentric. And I knew that. But this was my daughter and I hadn't seen her in over a year. He switched gears and apologized, said he understood.

"Then said he'd love to meet her. Why didn't we all go out on Friday night to Cala's, that posh place in Manchester? I was on speaker phone, multitasking, fixing dinner. Patty overheard and squealed she'd been dying to go there, it was getting such good raves. So what could I say?"

I was beginning to see where this was going and my blood ran cold.

She looked up from her empty glass, tears streaming down her face. "Yes. I led her right to him, or him to her. My own child. I thought I could keep her safe, keep him away from her, but I was wrong."

"She fell for his charm, too?"

"Hook, line and stinker. Just like her stupid mom."

I put an arm around her. "Not stupid, just duped."

Sheila wiped her eyes and pushed her hair out of her face. "She postponed her return to L.A. It was spring break and she had an open ticket. Frank asked where she was saying and she just said 'with friends' and told him not to worry. She knew better than to mention me.

"I saw another full moon was coming up and started panicking. I finally called Frank and told him where she was and who she'd met. We were both panicking by then. I pleaded with him. 'Frank! You've got to bring her home! Even if you have to fly out here to get her.' Patty had started sneaking out her window at night and I was pretty sure where she was going and who with. I'd find her bed unslept in when I got up in the night to pee. We had an awful argument about it and him. Which was stupid. It just drove her toward him more.

"The next day, while I was out at Star Market getting groceries, he came by the house, offering to take her sightseeing since she was stuck at home while I was running errands. Frank and I never saw her again."

I stayed quiet for some minutes. Finally, I asked what I'd been dreading: "What does Patty look like?"

Sheila squeezed her oozing eyes shut. "Like you."

THIRTY-ONE

DOPPELGANGING

I plunked back on my sofa. All I could think to say was, "I'm out of brandy. Sorry."

"I've had more than enough. And I should get going." Sheila started gathering her coat and purse. My phone pinged. And pinged again—Emma and Jared wanting an update. Sheila and I had been talking for quite a while. I held up an index finger. "Hold on. I need some more information. I just need to reply to these first."

She slumped back down too and I walked into the kitchen for some privacy. Texted them both back: "Still w/ Sheila. Get back 2 u soon." While I was on my phone, I heard her go into the bathroom, but there was no sound of flushing.

When I returned to the living room, her new bottle of hair conditioner was on my coffee table. Had to laugh. "You break into my apartment to give me a new bottle, and now you're taking it back?"

"It wasn't fair to you. It wasn't right. I'm sorry."

"What wasn't right? Was it a bad batch?"

"No, it was an extra potent batch." Like that told me anything.

"So what is it with this super-duper conditioner you make?"

She took a deep breath. "It's a lure."

"Allure?"

"Not as in 'alluring,' although it certainly is that. 'Lure' as in bait."

"You mean you were setting me up, like, like . . . prey?!"

"Yes. I'm sorry. He tends to prefer petite brunettes, and you look so much like my daughter, and like Dee Dee Thornton—"

"—who's *dead!* I saw the news clip. From the photo they showed, she could have been my twin."

"Oh God. Alice, I was doing everything I could to find my daughter. I hoped you'd draw Rolf out so I could track him to wherever she is. I'm so sorry. You don't know what it's like." She was sobbing now.

"What's *in* this stuff?"

"Powerful pheromones that wild male canids, mostly, respond to."

Not just male canids, judging by the human male reactions at La Cantina, not to mention Rick's. "What kind of range does it have?"

She was scrabbling in her purse for a tissue. I handed her the Kleenex box from my desk. "Depends on the lunar cycle. The closer the wolf is to the full moon, the longer its range is. Possibly half a mile."

That was certainly farther than the end of the block or the street behind our parking lot. "Well, I think it's been working."

"Why do you say that?"

I told her about the UFV stakeouts in our lot and the notes left. Also told her about Mona's Disney gig Rolf was setting up with her.

Her eyes popped at *that.* "Is she brunette, too?"

I nodded. "Pixie faced."

"Jesus. I've *got* to stop him!" she cried.

I nodded again. "I've been working on that problem." I picked up the bottle of conditioner. "I think I'll hold onto this a while longer."

"No, Alice! I can't jeopardize your life for this! For all I know, Patty might not still be—"

"Human or alive?" I gave her another tissue. The other was shredded.

"Both."

I put my hands on hers and said, "Look, Sheila, we'll find Rolf and put the sonuvabitch down. And we'll find Patty. I promise. I haven't been working on the problem alone. And Kate and I will somehow get Mona away from him before she's lost, too."

"How? And who are you working with?"

I wasn't ready to divulge that quite yet. "Just some awesome friends. I'll have to get back to you with the details, when I know more. Okay?"

"Okay." She sounded dubious. "But we have to act *fast*. We have just over a couple of weeks before the next full moon."

"Just trust me, please. We'll get him." I prayed I wasn't bluffing.

Her left arm jerked up and she checked her watch. "Crap! I have to go. I have another appointment."

"Go, go! I've got stuff to do, too." Besides data entry. It was going to be a long day and my bosses were probably ready to riot. Me, too.

THIRTY-TWO

ENTER, A NINJA

After she left, I realized I'd never interrogated her about my laptop. Might be just as well not to play my entire hand right now. Maybe Dion would be able to tell me if there was any cyber intrusion.

I also didn't find out why she chose that vanity plate. But I now had a good idea why she had. Rolf knew where she lived and what she drove. However, it looked for certain she didn't know where *he* lived. I was betting her plate was a threat she was broadcasting to him in case he followed her: "Watch out! I'm on to you!"

But why, if he was pleasurably boinking the mom, did he take her daughter? Out-of-control machismo or narcissism? Yes, to both, probably. I wondered if Patty could also be leverage, some kind of hold he wanted to keep over Sheila.

I logged back onto my laptop and punched my virtual time card. I'd lost a chunk of time, talking to Sheila. Gotta keep the docs happy, make 'em think I'm doing something worthwhile, meaning for *them*.

Opened my emails and groaned—25 new ones since this morning. Didn't these guys have anything better to do than pepper my inbox with nags? "Coming, Mother!" I snarled at my monitor and started smoothing feathers—sending excuses and apologies. I did them in a batch, pasting in the same message, saved in my draft folder. Then I sent them at the same time, which gave me some time to text my growing posse back.

Now I was just waiting to hear when Emma and Randy would be free so we could meet up with Jared and Dion. Emma bartended at night, so we might have a snag there, but Jared could catch her up if she couldn't make it. And I could do the same for Kate.

Keeping an eye on my cell, I dove back in to my data entries, then did more email triage when I needed a break from that.

Didn't take too long to hear back. Jared texted everyone asking if we could meet Dion at 4:30 p.m. at the Starbucks where we'd met after the W.A. meeting.

There was a flurry of new replies: too close to her shift for Emma, Randy would still be in the ER, Kate couldn't clock out until 5:00 and then hoped to be meeting with Mona. I really should be working until 5:30, though I could probably fudge it. Again. I texted: "Could we make it later?" and "Kate, how long you think you'll be with Mona?"

Kate texted back, "Hour & a little? But can see her afterwards."

"So could we go for 6 p.m.?" Randy suggested changing the venue to his place. Nice and private there.

Jared texted us back, agreeing: "6-ish at R's." He'd fill in Emma later. Nice excuse for the lovebirds to get together.

On the way to Randy's, I filled Kate in about Sheila's daughter and how she could be Rolf's leverage. Kate looked sick. Now, we were once again sitting around Randy's coffee table, waiting for Jared and Dion to arrive. Hearing a car pull up in front, Randy went to the door to check through his peephole. Then stumbled back, hand on his chest, laughing. "Ladies, the ninja cometh!" He added, *sotto voce*, "A rather small ninja."

With a flourish, he opened his door. "Jared! Good to see you again. And I guess you must be Dion," he said to the short Asian guy standing next to him.

Grinning, Dion thrust out a hard, calloused hand and shook Randy's. Randy winced (just a bit). "I guess I must."

Jared hadn't really prepared us for Dion: four-feet something, flowing black hair down past his knees, rock-hard calves, and a Ho Chi Min mustache/beard combo. But what we really weren't prepared for was the gravelly voice, especially in someone that young. Kinda went with the cloud of weed he arrived in, though. Probably what caused the stone-ground vocals. We were getting contact highs off the dude.

"Come in! Come in!" Randy waved them in with a bow. "Refreshments anyone? I've got coffee, tea and gummies for you youngsters."

"Nah, we're good on the THC," Dion rasped. "Already tanked up."

Kate snickered. "I could tell."

"But that's cool!" I assured them.

Randy gestured to the couch and side chairs. "Make yourselves comfortable. Coffee then, or tea?"

"Got any green tea?" Dion asked. I made a face.

"Actually, I do," Randy replied. "Kate, Al, what's your poison? Coffee?" We nodded. "Jared, you sticking with coffee?"

"Sure. That'd be cool, or hot as the case may be," Jared said.

"Four hot coffees coming up and one hot green tea. Back in a moment." Randy whisked off to the kitchen.

"How thick are the walls here?" Jared asked.

Randy called back, "Fairly thick. Old house with horse-hair plaster. But let's settle for small talk until I come back."

Kate and I sat back, checking our phones. Jared and Dion talked animatedly about the newest skateboard park near their school. Apparently, Dion was a ninja at that, too. Jared passed me his iPhone with video of Dion doing tricks on his board.

My eyebrows rose. "Impressive!"

"Thanks, dude. Been ridin' since I was five. Every minute I'm not at school or workin' on a project, I'm ridin' my board."

"You do any competitions?" I asked.

Dion ducked his head. "Couple."

"And?" I tipped my head, waiting for the results.

"I did okay."

Jared slapped his friend on the back. " 'Okay'? *'Okay'?* Dude, you aced it! Made the other guys look like they were slo-mo, like tortoises on rusty wheels."

Dion smiled and shrugged. Clearly not a braggart. I was liking him already.

Randy came back with his butler's tray, loaded with steaming mugs, sugar, honey, and half-and-half. He set it down, then came back with some spoons and napkins. "I miss anything?"

"Only that Dion here is also a *skateboard* ninja. Check this out." I handed Jared's phone to him and replayed the video.

"This is you?" he asked Dion, who was wearing a black, forward-facing baseball cap in the video.

"Yep, it's me. I have to put my hair up in a cap, for obvious reasons."

"Woulda thought it might be better in a helmet."

"Nah. Not cool. None of the board bros wear 'em."

"Yeah, coolness is all. But what's your injury count like?"

"Not too bad. Bashed elbow, sprained wrist and a bashed knee a few times, and a messed up second toe. We're tough and we've all been ridin' since we were kids. Wore helmets back then. Parents, you know. But probably a good call while we were learning."

"Probably," Randy said wryly, sipping his coffee.

Kate and I just shook our heads.

Randy set his coffee down. "So. Jared tells me you'd be a good guy to join our posse. He's told you about the gig we're working on, right?"

Nodding, Dion circled his index finger at Jared's cell and he shut it down. Kate and I did the same.

Randy switched his off, too. "I'm not on call. And I can always get back to Hank later. And you're on board with it, if we need you, Dion? Oh, sorry, that wasn't a pun."

Dion chuckled. "Yeah, man. I'm totally stoked. Wouldn't miss it for the world."

I leaned forward, "You do know how dangerous this guy is, right?"

"Oh yeah. Me and Jared been friends since grade school. I was the first one to spot what was going on with him. So I get what this dude is capable of."

Jared put an arm around his buddy. "Dion's always had my back with the school bullies. Never freaked when he found out about my . . . condition, either."

"Why not?" I asked Dion. "*I* certainly did about mine!"

"Monster legends are common in Asian cultures," he said. "We tend to just take them for granted: werewolves, vampires—spirit stuff. But, yeah, I guess it'd be a whole lot different if it was happening to me."

Jared laughed. "Knowing you, dude, you'd rock it!"

Dion smiled. "Thanks, bro. I'd certainly try to, but I'm not cool with hurting people, unless they're trying to hurt me and mine. And Jared's my friend. I know he feels the same. Plus, you always had *my* back, too, J, when kids called me a pipsqueak gook."

Jared blushed. "Dude, I didn't do much. Just stood by you. Faced those assholes off."

Dion slapped his buddy's back. "Solidarity, bro. Sometimes that's all you need."

"But this guy, Rolf, didn't turn Jared," I persisted.

"Yeah, I know," Dion said. "It's this curse that Jared's family's got, which sucks."

He took a sip, and went on. "But I've seen what Jared's gone through and I wouldn't wish that on *anyone.* I want to help take this fucker down."

"And Dion be da man to do it!" Jared said. They bumped fists.

"Jared also told you how well-connected Rolf is?" I asked. "He's got friends in high places and I doubt they're all good guys. Some might be part of his pack.

"And," I went on, "he's got more money than God, so he's got all the latest and greatest tech, not to mention a buncha henchmen at his beck and call."

"Yep. I know. Jared and I talked about all that." Dion took another sip of his tea, added some honey and stirred.

Jared set his phone down and picked up his coffee. Between swallows, he said, "'S another reason we need Dion. Besides his badass fighting skills, he's a crack hacker."

Kate snorted, spurting a little of her coffee. She blotted it up, laughing, "Now *there's* a spoonerism itching to be free!"

Jared looked puzzled. "Turn it sort of inside out," she said. "You know, switching the first consonants. Works both ways."

"J, you don't know what a *spoonerism* is?" Dion asked, smirking.

Dion's no dumb bunny either. "She's sayin' I'm also a hack cracker!" Dion turned to Kate, "And that would be true, too."

"And I'll bet he's a dead-eyed hack cracking!" I couldn't help but add. Kate and I giggled. We saw the WTF side-eye squints between Jared and Dion. I waved the moment on. "It's a Beatles thing."

There came the eye rolls: *Old people!*

Changing the subject, I turned to Randy. "What did the report Sheila sent back say, about the shredded panty evidence?"

"Pretty much what I expected: traces of unidentified canid DNA combined with human. There was an interesting note on that, or more of a diplomatic conjecture, implying the victim could have been into some kind of kinky sex, which might explain two different types of mammalian DNA."

"And that was it?"

"Not quite. In carefully worded biochemical terms, there was mention of an odd, undocumented strain of some type of virus, as well."

My eyebrows rose, and as one, we turned to Jared.

"By golly, Jared, you may be onto something with that theory you're working on." Jared and Dion snickered at my "By golly."

Then Jared nodded, thoughtfully. "Then, by Jove, I'd assume Sheila's following down the same rabbit hole, Alice."

"As well as her ex-husband, I'd imagine," I added. "Would love to know what they've come up with so far."

"So would I!" Jared said.

"Well, the jury's going to be out a while on that. In the meantime, anybody coming up with a plan?" Randy asked.

"I do have one," Dion said. "Been thinkin' it over a few days. Just need the location where the MF lives or hangs."

"Oh, we can certainly help you with that!" I beamed.

He quirked his mouth. "Cool. Be good to do a drive-by first, check things out, like where his phone and Wi-Fi enter the place. Check the security set-up. Stuff like that."

"No problem," said Randy, smiling widely. "But we have to be extremely stealthy. Guy's got eyes and ears everywhere, even in the sky. He's got a chopper. We might need a drone."

"Got one. I was sorta figuring on that." We nodded our approval.

"So . . . what are you thinking?" I asked.

We'd been talking a good while. Kate looked at her watch. It was 7:45.

"Yikes! I still have to meet up with Mona!" She rose.

"Okay," I said, "then let's wrap this up for tonight. Kate will get back to us with whatever she learns from Mona."

She yawned. "Probably not until tomorrow. Gotta be at work early, making sure the melons don't get bruised."

"But soon as you can, okay?"

"Roger, dodger!" Kate saluted, Vulcan style.

Another eye-roll from the dudes. We set a time and date to do a cruise by Rolf's.

"I'm starving," Dion said. "Let's take a drive and hit Gino's, J. They've got standout eggplant parm there."

"You a vegetarian?" I asked.

He shrugged. "Mostly. Got kinda turned off of red meat a while back." With a buddy like Jared, I could understand.

"Just be on the lookout for the Rolls or the Lexus. Should be easy to spot the Rolls."

Dion had nearly died laughing when we told him the license plate.

"Lexus will be tougher, being one of those hybrid electric thingies."

"Dion's got ears like a bat and the eyes of an eagle," Jared said.

"Good to know."

"Good to have." Dion winked.

This dude definitely deserved the honorary title of ninja, if all that was true.

I was looking forward to seeing him in action, and praying it wasn't all just pride plugs for a bro.

THIRTY-THREE

HERE'S PIE IN YOUR EYE

"You know, another trip down to Gino's sounds really good," I said to Kate. "I could totally go for another large roni and shrooms. Why don't you call Mona and see if she'll meet us there?"

Gino's pizza was so good, people up and down the North Shore and beyond gladly drove the 20 minutes or more to get their food. It attracted all sorts, even posh ones slumming for the sake of a great pie.

"Brilliant!" Kate pronounced, in her British brigadier accent, started dialing and stepped outside to talk. Two minutes later she came back, a smile spread on her face. "It's a go! She said she'd be there."

Outstanding—killing two birds with one pie. "You want to come along, Randy? It's a nice night for a drive."

"Nah. I'm good. Got some lasagna to heat up."

I narrowed my eyes at him. "Lasagna!" Randy's lasagna was magnificent, as were his apple pies. "And you weren't gonna share?"

He held up his hands. "Sorry! I've finished all but one piece. One very *small* piece," he amended.

Kate's bottom lip was out. I seconded that opinion. "Then no leftovers for you! You sure you don't want to join us? Bring back some company for that tiny little piece?" I asked him.

He shook his head, "Actually I was sort of hoping I could hook up with Hank."

I smiled, hands on hips. "Bet you'd share that teensy little piece with *him*."

"Any piece I can."

"Oops! Gotta go! Call me tomorrow, okay?" He saluted us out.

I texted Jared that we'd be joining them, as well as Mona. With Jared and Dion's head start, we expected them to be there already when we arrived, tucking into their pizza. But there was no sign of Jared's old banger in the lot and Gino, when queried, said they hadn't seen the boys.

We put our order in and told Gino to take his time. As I didn't have my Indiana Jones hat this time and Kate didn't have her cloak, we felt a bit exposed, so I asked if it would be okay if we went into the rarely-used "family room," the area they kept for overflow.

"Sure. No one's in there, so it'll be more private for the bunch of you," he said. Gino didn't miss much. Our swivelling heads, checking out the parking lot from the front windows probably gave us away. We grabbed two beers out of the reach-in and headed next door.

This room was like Boston's old North Beach in its heyday: knotty pine paneling, wrap-around red leatherette banquettes, more travel posters from the Old Country, and clusters of plastic grapes festooning the rafters. Unlike the businesslike glare of the fluorescents in the shop, the wagon-wheel chandeliers cast a low-light coziness over the room. There were even raffia-wrapped Chianti bottles with candles in them on each table.

Probably looked kitschy to teens, but it felt like home to us. The bonus was that the café-curtained windows looked out from the side of the building at the street.

Easier to see what was coming while not being seen.

Ten minutes later, Joanne came in and said, "Your pie should be up in about 15 minutes. Is that okay?"

"Perfect." Kate smiled.

"We've got our brews to occupy us." I raised my bottle. As she went back to the kitchen, my phone pinged. Text from Jared: "Took a little detour," followed by an emoji with bouncing eyebrows. Kids! Where the hell do they find *those*? Then, "We're almost there and look what's in front of us."

Kate and I scampered to the windows, crouching down below the curtain rod and peeping through the checkered curtains. We couldn't see Jared's old banger, but we could hear its failing muffler. He must be keeping back from whatever was in front of him.

And he was. Just pulling up to the curb now was a familiar gleaming Rolls, and stepping lightly from it and blowing the driver a kiss was Mona in her trademark black cloak.

The Rolls rolled off, its license plate ostentatiously visible.

Well, well, well.

A few seconds later, we heard Jared's banger rumble into the lot. Gino stuck his head in. "The boys just arrived. You want me to hold up your pie some more?"

"Yes, please, if that won't ruin it."

"*Non preoccuparti.* It'll be just fine. Oh, and you gotta another guest—*una ragazza.*"

Gino held the door open and Mona entered with a cat's smile and a canary-savoring swish of her cloak, followed by a gob-smacked Jared and Dion. Kate and I scooted over and Mona sat down in the center, like a queen in her court. The guys scooted in on the other side.

"You guys order yet?" I asked the boys.

At my question, Jared seemed to come to. "What? Oh! No. I'll go," he offered, a bit reluctantly, I thought.

"No, I'll go," Dion rasped. "You'd just screw up my order of eggplant parm."

He wiggled up-curled fingers for money. Jared fished out his wallet, handed Dion some twenties. Dion trundled back to the counter.

"What about you, Mona?" I asked. "You going to have anything?"

"I thought I'd just share whatever you're having." That was *so* Mona.

"Better grab yourself a beer, then," I said.

"I'd rather have a glass of cabernet, if they have it. Chianti, if they don't. Would you mind ordering it for me?" she asked sweetly. "Oh, and in a glass, please, not plastic." She scrunched up her nose.

"Sure," I said back as sweetly. "I'll just put it on your tab."

I gave Jared a meaningful head toss to join us to help carry stuff. He followed.

While the guys and I were standing at the counter, making our orders, I whispered to Jared, "So how did you end up behind Rich Fucker?"

He held up an index finger to hang on. Made his order, then stepped back, out of earshot. The front of the shop was getting busier, so Dion pointed to the table in the corner Kate and I had sat at on Friday night.

We dragged some chairs out, sat and waited.

"I thought I'd cruise by Emma's bar, see if she wanted us to bring her some pizza," Jared said. "She works at the Pickled Onion, over on Rantoul in Beverly."

"They allow that? Bringing in somebody else's food?"

"Tony, he's the owner, is pretty relaxed about it and so's Bob, the bar manager. And anyway, they don't have pizza on their menu."

"So, you were able to talk to Emma there?"

"Yeah. Just quickly."

"Had she met up with Sheila?"

"No, which was weird, because Sheila had seemed really insistent. So, because it was getting close to her shift, Emma said to just come over to her bar to talk. She told Sheila that, with two bartenders on, she could probably take a break and grab a table away from the bar. Then Sheila no-showed. On the way back we saw Rolf's Rolls and tailed it here."

Hunh. "When's Emma get off work?"

"Mondays, they usually close about 11. They keep shorter hours weekdays ever since COVID."

"You guys are going by, then, after this?"

"That's the plan." And Kate and I would be joining them.

Gino dinged his bell. "Orders are up!"

Joanne slid a glass of red wine over. "It's just the house red, a blend. I'm sorry, but it's all we have right now."

"Don't apologize, Joanne. She'll have to like it." I winked. The boys carried our pizzas in and I grabbed a bunch of napkins and the pepper flakes. Setting the wine down in front of Mona, I said with a bow, "The house's best."

"Oh. In a milk glass. How quaint."

"Hey, it's how families drink it in Italy, in case you didn't know. *Salute!*"

After we'd scarfed down our food, we sat back groaning, packed our leftovers in the boxes Joanne brought in, and finished our drinks. The boys and I had been teasing Mona about her swanky ride, hoping to learn something useful. In front of the guys, she stayed coyly cagey. It was obvious she was bursting to blab, but was laboring under someone's gag order, whether self-imposed or Wolf Man's, couldn't tell. Could be she was just shy about sharing juicy details with two high school kids.

Feeling the guys' frustration, I raised my eyebrows at Kate.

She batted widened blue eyes at me, signaling she'd give me the dirt she'd learned, while the guys and I were up front, later.

As we were going out the front door, Joanne came over with another box—the extra pizza Jared had ordered to take to Emma. "You forget something?" she asked him.

Guess he'd been a tad distracted by Queen Mona. He did a head slap. "Jeez! I totally did! Thanks so much, Joanne." Jared's flaming face as he took the box from her said volumes. He turned stricken, don't-tell-Emma eyes on me. I shook my head and zipped my lips at him.

Carrying our boxes, we stepped out into the parking lot, scanning for scary skulkers. Just our cars there.

"How are you getting home, Mona?" I asked, not so innocently. "Looks like your rich guy's left you high and dry."

"I t-thought I'd just get a ride with you," she stammered, her poise plummeting. Had to smile at her reply.

"Sure." I shrugged, sliding my told-you-so eyes over to Kate.

You can be sure we grilled the hell out of Mona on the way back. The good news was the Disney gig couldn't happen for at least another month. She was really put out about that. Her pout stuck out an inch. "I was just about to give my notice at my job!" she whined.

The bad news was Mona wouldn't hear a word against Rolf, however strongly we hinted. She certainly seemed smitten but, so far, unbitten.

"Good thing you didn't quit your job, then," Kate commented dryly. "You know how unreliable men can be. They're all talk."

"Not *all* talk." Mona gave us a lascivious smile.

"Okay, yes, you said. Great in bed, blah, blah, blah."

"Phenomenal!" Mona corrected.

"Fine. 'Phenomenal'!"

When we'd hinted he might be a real creep, she merely remarked, "Well, at least he's a rich creep."

I tried to weigh in, gently planting the thought that he might be some kind of predator and that she was still just in the crazy monkey sex phase.

"Oh, this guy isn't monkeying around." She winked. I tried not to gag. Mona wrapped a corner of her black cape across her face, peering over it with sly brown eyes. "And he appreciates the dark side of me."

If she only knew.

Giving up, Kate threw her hands upward. I grabbed the pizza box before it slid off her lap.

Mona confronted us. "Look, even if we don't work out, I'll be living the dream in Disney World, and I imagine there'll be a nice selection of male gorgeousity there to sample."

The "sampling" part was exactly what we were afraid of.

"So, you want us to take you straight home? Kate and I were thinking of cruising by the Pickled Onion, since we're up this way." Mona lived in Salem, like Jared.

"Home is fine. Rolf may come over later."

Oh, boy. Yep. Smitten for sure. Good thing he'd still be human.

We dropped Mona off, then chugged on up to Beverly.

It was just as well we didn't have her tagging along. Don't know what I was thinking, inviting her. We would never have been able to speak freely to Emma if Mona had been along.

And as we pulled up to the curb to park, I discovered there was a whole, better reason Mona had *not* come along. Parked at the curb in one of the handicapped spaces in front of the Onion was a silver Rolls with a suggestive vanity plate. Poor Mona. No, make that *lucky* Mona. And lucky neighbors being spared her all-out, screeching fit.

Behind Rolf's Rolls a few spaces was Jared's banger. Kate and I stared at each other in horror. "Jeez. What do you suppose the body count is inside?" I asked her.

"Should we just leave, do you think?" Kate asked, gnawing a lip.

"And miss this show? Hell no!" But I opted for parking at the back of the lot by the side of the building . . . right next to a white SUV with the license plate "I BITE."

"Holy sh- Sherlock!" Kate exclaimed.

"The game is definitely afoot," I replied.

At least the game wasn't apaw. That god awful disaster at least was spared us for another 12 days.

THIRTY-FOUR

ROCK AND ROLLS

The bar was so dark when we skulked in, we could barely make out who was there. But the noise made up for that in liveliness. Over the hard rock blaring from the jukebox, we almost couldn't hear the shouts and curses. And the bodies were just a blur, backlit by the lights on the bar back shining through the tiered rows of bottles.

As my eyes adjusted to the gloom and melee, I saw, in the center of a ring of hard-eyed bikers, with serious hardware, busting to join the fight and staggering regulars trying to bust it up, Dion whirling like a dervish around Rolf, who was bent over double, wheezing, and cupping his manly parts. The bartender yelled over the din that the cops were on their way. Dion was definitely getting the better of Wolf Man. Even the bikers were holding back, impressed by the little dude's fury and efficiency.

I looked around for Emma, Jared and Sheila. Emma and Jared were shrinking back in a dark corner, keeping away from the action. She was white-faced and he had a comforting arm around her. A Gino's pizza box lay on the floor. There was no sign of Sheila.

"Let's check the ladies' room," I shouted to Kate. On the way there, I picked up the Gino's box and placed it on the bar, sighing over the waste of great pizza. Kate opened the lid and pronounced it still probably edible: cold, but only scuffed a bit.

The ladies' john was quiet and looked empty, except for a pair of navy pumps just visible under the door of the last stall. I walked up, tapped on the door. "Sheila? We know you're in there. Come on out."

The stall door opened gingerly. "Are you alone?" she asked.

"I've got a friend with me. A close friend. And she knows." I added.

"Where's Rolf?" she asked. "He doesn't know I'm here."

"In the bar getting the shit kicked out of him."

"Good!" Sheila emerged and I introduced her to Kate.

"Wanna tell us what's going on and why Rolf's here?"

"Don't know for sure. I came over to talk to Emma—"

"We know." I'd decided it was too late in the game to pussyfoot any longer. "You think we don't talk?"

"You and Emma?" she asked.

"And Jared. And the little dude out there customizing Rolf's baby-making equipment."

"And me," Kate added, noting the obvious.

Sheila slumped against a sink. "Any others?"

"Well, there's Randy," I said thoughtfully.

"Can't forget Randy," Kate said.

"No one can," I smirked.

"Christ!" Sheila clapped a hand over her mouth.

"I would bet He also knows and His dad, too," I said. "It's all in your pamphlet, right, the God thing?"

"What am I going to do?" she wailed.

"Maybe it's time to face the music." At this juncture, we heard the final bars of *Born to Be Wild,* punctuated by more crashes, shouts and curses. Kate laughed out loud. Then the music in the bar switched to rap. Over the bass beats, "bitches," and "hos," we heard a distinctive howl.

Emma burst into the bathroom. "Guys, you *gotta* see this!" As one woman, we burst out to check on the howler.

We got back to the bar just in time to see Beverly cops lead away a cuffed and limping Rolf, snarling invective at the bartender, the biker dudes and Dion. Sheila kept back in the shadows, stifling unladylike snorts and guffaws. We tiptoed over to the high windows and peeped out to see a cop push Rolf's head down under the cruiser's headliner and slam the door. A tow truck was already hooked up to the Rolls, a ticket prominently displayed on its window. Apparently, Rolf's presumed entitlement didn't extend to Beverly. At the open door, a bevy of bikers lounged, cheerfully offering busted Rolf the finger.

The most muscular and tattooed of them righted some stools then turned a pierced grin our way, giving his bald head a satisfied rub. I grinned back. "So what happened here?" I asked him.

"He was hassling our Emma here. Me and the boys had to step in."

A ginger-haired dude with a long billy-goat beard and studded, leather bicep bands came over. Billy Goat said, "We don't let no one hassle our girls here. And besides that, he threw her pizza on the floor.

That there's a Gino's pizza. Ain't nobody gonna dis a Gino's and get away with it."

Jared and Emma came over, nodding approval at Billy Goat. "Ginger, here, managed to save the pizza. Mostly." Emma smiled her thanks at Ginger and offered him a piece.

"Why thanks, Emma." Reverently, he picked out one with low damage, dusted it off with a paper napkin, then downed it in three bites. "Great stuff. Just the tiniest bit of grit. Hey, it's good for your gullet."

"Good thing you guys were here," I told him.

"I suppose, but the little dude had it covered," Ginger said.

"Yeah, I saw it, at least some of it. Where is he?" Looking around the room, I found him sitting at the far end of the bar next to Sheila.

Bob, the bartender, sauntered over to them asking what they'd have, saying it'd be on the house. Dion confessed he wasn't old enough to drink. Bob retorted, now that the cops were out of earshot, that if Dion was old enough to kick deserving ass in his bar, he was old enough to be served. "So what would you *like*?" he asked Dion again.

"You got any Narragansett?"

Bob laughed. "Does a bear shit in the woods?" He slid a cold one over to Dion. "And what would the lady like?" he asked Sheila.

"Dewars? On the rocks? I'll pay." She took out her wallet.

"Keep your money, sweetheart. I saw you runnin' into the ladies' to get away from the stylin', hairy bastard. Just glad you got to see him get his come-uppins." He slid over a ten-count rocks glass of Scotch.

"*Thank* you, Bob. So am I!" She turned to Dion and clinked her glass against his beer can. "My name's Sheila."

"I figured," Dion rasped out. "Dion." He extended a hardened fighting hand to her, adding, "I'm a buddy of Jared's. We go way back."

Weakly, she asked, "So . . . you know, too?"

"Yep. Just one big happy family here." Winking, he hoisted his beer.

Sheila downed her Dewars. Emma, Jared, Kate and I settled down next to them. Bob came over. "You have any Rolling Rock?" I asked.

"Sure do. For the four of ya?" Kate shrugged. I nodded. "And another Dewars and a 'Gansett?" We all nodded and reached for the Gino's.

Rock and roll.

THIRTY-FIVE

NOWHERE TO RUN

As the bikers and regulars swarmed the bar again, my phone pinged with a text. I got up and moved into better light to read it. It was Randy saying Hank had come and then had to leave. He'd been called out to a fire.

"Did u get 2 share your L?" I typed. Lasagna was too hard to text.

He texted back, "L no. Had 2 eat it alone."

I felt sorry for Randy and sent my condolences. Between his on-call interruptions at the hospital and Hank's at the station, it looked like Randy's love life was going up in flames.

"So, what's up with u guys?" he sent.

"SO much 2 tell u, but 2 long 2 text!" I sent back.

"Where R U?"

"Pickled Onion. ALL of us."

"All of U??"

Typed a thumbs up emoji, then, "Want 2 join the circus?"

"Should I come armed?"

I pictured him entering with a dart gun at the ready, so nixed that. "Should be safe now. Cops left."

"Oh boy. B there in 10."

I returned to my bar stool, leaned over to Kate and Emma and told them, "Randy's coming over." Their eyes swivelled sideways toward Sheila.

"You think that's a good idea?" Emma asked.

I shrugged. "Might as well add to the hilarity. The cat is so far out of the bag now, it's nursing kittens."

Kate nodded sagely. "The Day of Reckoning hath come."

I was about to correct her with "Shouldn't be 'hath cometh'?" then remembered that Kate was the only person I knew who could properly conjugate Middle English, so merely quipped, "It thertainly hath."

We both studied odd things in college.

"But," she went on, "I reckon we should move our discovery council away from the bar." She pointed to one of the high-top banquette tables in an empty corner along the back.

The jukebox had been turned down a notch, just below ear-bleed level, so we might actually be able to carry on a discussion at the far table. I signaled our relocation to Bob, we picked up our drinks and the remnants of our dusted-off pizza, and shuffled over to the high-top. I finagled the seating plan so that Sheila would be trapped between us on the back seat. Bob brought over fresh drinks, and we mouthed our thanks over the blare. Just as Randy walked in, the music switched to good old Martha & the Vandellas: "Nowhere to Run." 'Gansett spurted out of Dion's nose, just missing Sheila.

"Randy said he could join us, Sheila. Hope you don't mind."

Recognizing Randy, Sheila's eyes were like saucers—flying ones, now orbiting the room for exits. "*That's* the Randy you were referring to?" she squeaked. Six heads nodded.

Randy's own eyebrows shot up. I guess I should have warned him better. "My goodness! Good evening, Dr. Armstrong," Randy addressed her and took a stool. Bob came over again. "I'll have what's she's having," Randy said, pointing to Sheila.

"That would be a heart attack," she replied, pounding her chest, "and I don't recommend it!"

"Make that two!" Randy replied with a nod.

Taking them literally, believing it was a drink name, Bob inquired, "What's in that?" At which we all burst out laughing. Talk about an ice breaker.

"Ingredients too numerous and awful to mention!" Randy chortled. "I'll just have a Stella, thanks." He leaned toward Sheila, "So, what brings you to the illustrious Pickled Onion, doctor? What did I miss?"

Blow by blow, the seven of us went over the amusements of the evening.

Sheila had come in for her chat with Emma, probing for information on Rolf and the rest of us, when the man himself sauntered in. She was thankful she'd parked around the side and happened to be sitting at the end of the bar closest to the ladies'. At the other end, Rolf was leering and leaning across the bar at Emma. Emma's face was white and angry; her back was against the bar back and she was hissing something at him. While Rolf was cajoling Emma, Sheila whipped on sunglasses and a scarf over her hair and booked it to the john.

Even from inside the bathroom, she could easily hear angry voices ramp up, smacks and blows being rained on someone's meat, and furniture getting disassembled like an Ikea production line run backwards without benefit of screwdrivers.

Babbling over each other, the five of us described the scene and sounds we witnessed that Sheila didn't get to enjoy, especially the part where Rolf was dragged away by the cops and his precious Rolls was ticketed and towed from the handicapped spot in front.

"Sweet suffering Jesus on a cross! I believe I'll need another Stella," Randy breathed at last and summoned Bob.

Kate spoke up. "You know, we'll have to tell Mona. She was hoping he'd stop by her place. She'll be crushed."

"And a damned good thing that would be!" I said.

"True. Still, it's hard to find out you've been two-timed."

Returning to the theme of the crime, Emma cried, "The bastard had the effrontery to think he could charm me all over again. After what he did?! Un-fucking-believable!" Then to Sheila, "Oh, sorry!"

Sheila said, "Oh, it's believable, fuckingly so." Kate's eyes widened.

"And then he tried blackmailing me!" Emma went on. "Said he could see to it that I'd lose my job if I didn't cooperate. He even threatened that he'd see to it June and Mike lost theirs, too!"

Dion's face scrunched in puzzlement. "How would he do that? It's not like he could tell everyone what you are now, what he turned you into. Who'd believe it? How could he even blab without implicating himself, saying someone did?"

"It's not that. It's his connections. Says he can pull strings. He's got fingers in *everyone's* pies, if you can believe his bullshit."

"Emma," Jared entreated, "*please* don't tell me you're considering hanging with him again."

"God, no! No way. And anyway, I can always get another bar job. I just don't want him hurting my friends. But I can't help it, I'm scared."

"Well, he's out of commission for tonight, Emma." Jared put a hand on hers. "Maybe a bit longer, thanks to my buddy here and the boys on bikes." He and Dion fist bumped. "Still, why don't we follow you home, Emma?"

"Yeah, okay. Thanks, Jared."

"When do you get off your shift?" he asked her.

Bat-eared Bob came over and said, "Now's fine, sweetheart. It's Monday and slowing down, so I can handle the rest."

Emma hugged him her thanks and we stood. Sheila made another try at settling up, waving her credit card at him.

"That's okay, lady. I'll put it down as entertainment expenses."

Stumbling about boozily by our cars in the parking lot outside, I spoke up, rocking back on my heels. "So, Sheila! Now what? I mean, now that you know that we know that you know . . . ?" I waggled my head.

Randy stretched and cracked his neck. "It's late and I'm buzzed, so I move this session be adjourned. But I do think it's time, since we all know that we know, et cetera, that we schedule a new meeting and pool our resources." He turned to Sheila. "Wouldn't you agree, doctor?"

She hiccupped. (Only once.) "I do agree. Are you on call tomorrow?"

Randy pulled out his cell and checked his cell's calendar. "Yep. But Wednesday is a regular shift for me."

"I'm sure I can switch my Wednesday shift at the bar with June," Emma said. "Should it be the whole group or just the seven of us?"

"Better just us for now," Randy said. "I'm glad to offer my place again if you guys want. Seven thirty-ish work for everyone?"

Something was niggling at my sodden brain about that plan, but we nodded or shrugged as called upon. It was the most we could do.

The aftermath of adrenaline surge and booze finally hit us and we blew out stunned sighs. Randy turned to Sheila. "I'll send you directions to my condo tomorrow. Everyone okay to drive?" he asked the rest. "If not, I'll take you home and you can crash with me."

"I'm good," I said. More careful nods from the others.

Kate smirked. "And I'm not driving."

"Me neither," Dion rasped. "But I'll be keeping watch," meaning over Jared's driving, I assumed.

"It's not like we haven't drunk alcohol before," Jared objected. "You've been a teen yourself once, right Alice?"

"So Mom told me. Had my first beer when I was twelve," I beamed.

Jared waved a "Well, there ya go!" at me. I caught his arm before his gesture toppled him.

Dion clapped an arm around Jared. "I gotcha, buddy," he said. Unlike Jared, the ninja looked sober as a judge. "You want me to drive?"

Jared see-sawed his hand. "If I run any lights, dude, pull me over and we'll switch." A fairly reasonable plan. It was late and a Monday.

With ninja Dion riding shotgun, Jared drove Emma around the corner to the side street where she was parked. The rest of us climbed into our cars, flashed our headlights in goodbyes, and headed off.

Kate punched on the Kia's radio. Martha was back with her Vandellas and they weren't running. They knew it was futile, too.

On the way back to our building, Kate was unusually quiet, just beating her hand on the window sill in time to the radio and looking off searchingly into the dark streets.

"Why so quiet, Kate?" I asked. "Something on your mind?"

"Besides hair, you mean?" she replied. Her lower lip was telescoping in and out.

"Sounds like you're upset and I'm guessing it's not just about the dust-up with Wolf Man."

"What do you think? None of you ever ask for *my* opinion!" she flared. "I'm just the fall guy, the sidekick who's supposed to tag along with the hero."

"Don't you mean heroine? Or don't you do drugs?" I smiled at her, trying to lighten the mood.

She sighed. "Do you really think it was a good idea to risk the whole gang of us being seen by Rolf in a single place? Hmmm? Didn't any of you think of that? 'Cause, if he did ID everyone, now he can identify us *all* and link us in our common purpose, ya know."

Shit. She had a good point. And she had (rather weakly, I thought) suggested that joining the fray might not be so prudent. "Maybe you should have made that point earlier?" I asked.

"I sorta did, you know."

" 'Sorta' didn't really cut it, looks like. You could have been a little more forceful, Katie." But that wasn't her style.

"Would it have made any difference?"

I sighed. "Probably not, in the heat of the moment. But it was fun to watch, right?"

Kate smiled at last. "Yeah. Supercalifragilistic!"

"But . . . ?" She sat silently, chewing the inside of her cheek.

"Oh, Katie, I'm sorry. You're also feeling left out, aren't you?"

Kate shrugged. "Maybe a little. It's just . . . I have a mind, too, and ideas. I'm not just a grocery clerk."

"I know. You also moonlight as Jane Eyre." (And Mary Poppins.)

"*And* I'm the official planetary counsel on *The Enterprise,* don't forget!" The funny Kate I cherished was back.

"Spock couldn't do a thing without you!"

"Damned straight!" She relapsed into silence again and peered back and forth up the side streets. "And you *still* didn't get your print back."

Crap. *Again!*

"Are you worried he'll come after one of us tonight, Kate?"

Her hand stopped its drumming. "I suppose he'll be in a cell for a while, but with his connections, it's possible someone still might. Plus, some mucky-muck could probably bail him out in minutes, if Rolf snapped his fingers and waved his wallet."

That had finally occurred to me, too. Besides being well-connected, Rolf had henchmen and multiple vehicles.

As usual, Kate had read my mind: "Just because his Rolls got towed doesn't mean he wouldn't use one of his alternate rides or those henchmen." Our two brains went way back with sharesies.

"And we have no way of knowing which of us he'd target first."

"Don't we?" Kate's tense baby blues turned my way. "I think we do, Alice, and it's you. That's why I'm so worried."

"Not following you."

"Al, now he knows the gal he's been stalking the most is in league with at least two others like him, one of them with a ninja bodyguard."

"Maybe we're worrying for nothing, Katie. Rolf was pretty busy when we came in," I giggled, "and anyway it was really dark and loud." "I'm not sure he'll have connected Dion with us. Hell, he probably didn't even see us come in, with all that was going on. We hung back in the corner of the bar behind a bunch of bodies, remember."

"Correct me if I'm wrong . . . ," she began.

Oh, here we go. I braced myself: Kate was seldom wrong.

"Weren't you the one who told me what heightened senses werewolves have?"

"Well, yeah, but under the moon's influence."

"But," she held up a finger, "what if you came from a long line of werewolves? Mightn't that give you an evolutionary edge, give you super sight or something, whether or not the moon was full?"

I thought about that. And remembered the hair conditioner. One of those heightened senses had to be smell.

"It only makes sense that he comes after you first, Al."

"Why me? Why not go after Sheila?"

She harrumphed. "Maybe it's good you've got a sidekick, after all. Somebody needs to keep track."

"Okay, I know I'm being dense. What have I missed, Watson?"

"Well, Sherlock, since you've asked. One, Sheila arrived before Rolf did, but it was dark inside, as you said, and, seeing him enter, she disguised herself *toute de suite* and made for the john. So, being occupied with Miss Emma, he probably, *hopefully* missed Sheila's arrival."

"Hey, that's actually a good thing! I had forgotten that, Watson. So he might not link Sheila with us after all."

Kate gave me "the look." "Beside the fact that you're both his victims and you were possibly noticed with another of them? He definitely would have seen Jared, who he knows through Jared's dad. Even if Rolf missed IDing us at the bar, he'd connect the dots eventually, don't you think?"

"Well, maybe a lot later rather than sooner," I said, wistfully.

"Let's hope. Two," she continued, "you told me Rolf's got Sheila's daughter as leverage, so he'll want to keep Mama thrashing at the end of his hook."

I had told Kate about that, I remembered now. But I hadn't gotten around to telling the others, events had zipped by so fast.

I opened my mouth but was stopped by her stern, Watsonian finger.

"And three, I'm just not happy about all of us meeting at Randy's house."

I bridled. “Why? Randy’s a great host!”

“He is.”

“And I’d *really* like to get my print from him. I suppose, though, after all the booze, it’s just as well we didn’t do the transfer tonight.”

“True. But do you really think it’s a good thing to risk having *all* of our addresses discovered and shared? Think: sneaky plus henchmen.”

Ah. *That’s* what was niggling at my beer-soaked brain a moment ago. “I wonder if Jared would mind playing host this time, Kate. Sheila knows where he lives and it’s close for all of us.”

“Splendid idea, Sherlock. Text him tomorrow first thing and see.”

“Bless you, Watson, I shall.”

But I was still getting the shivers over something else I knew I was missing. “What did you do with that thingy you found under my car?” I asked her.

“Shoot! We forgot to show it to Randy!” Kate rummaged in her handbag. “I’ve got it right here.” She drew it out and handed it to me. For the first time I noticed it had something embedded on the inside.

“Hold onto it, Katie. My gut says it’s just as well we didn’t bring it up tonight with everyone there. It could be an ace in the hole, so make sure you don’t lose it. And let’s plan on meeting somewhere with Randy first, early tomorrow night. I want to show it to him before the others join us, especially Sheila.”

If that thing was what I was thinking it was, Martha’s lyrics seemed to be turning back in my direction: there was nowhere to run now and nowhere to hide.

THIRTY-SIX

"MONDAY, MONDAY"– THE LONGEST DAY *EVER*

Kate and I got back to our building without further drama and slid into our apartments, after brief walk-throughs, followed by relieved hugs.

Still, I couldn't quite settle down. I was beginning to feel the pull of the fattening moon. Today had been one helluva day. With all the recent craziness, it had been easier to shove my monthly dread to one side and feel like a normal, merely observing human. Having loyal friends with good brains and senses of humor helped. But now, with only 12 days to go before I'd be forced to lope on four legs, sprout fur and snap at folks simply for being warm-blooded and theoretically edible, I could feel the tension building, along with my depression and helplessness. And my spidey sense (only for me, I guess it's fangy) told me that a whole lot of awfulness could come down in the meantime. And probably would.

I found myself whipping my head around at the slightest sound, kept the light off in the kitchen when I tiptoed in for a drink of water, took a flashlight with me into the bathroom to avoid being spied on from outside. What a way to live. I thought of Freddie Mercury's song, "Who Wants to Live Forever?" and agreed, at least for sad monsters like me.

It had been a while since I'd been into Boston, prowling among the homeless, and I was grateful that I'd given it a pass, even if my reaping was a mercy. And I hadn't gotten any calls from homeless folk I knew on the streets notifying me of anyone new lingering on death's doorstep.

Yeah, the homeless have cell phones. They can get them courtesy of SafeLink. There's irony for you: their calls to me sure don't ensure safety. Still, people like to stay connected, come what may.

If it weren't for the urgency of stopping Rolf, I'd sit this moon out.

I dragged off my clothes and dropped them on my bedroom chair, then pulled on flannel PJs, drawing comfort where I could. Squirming down under the bedclothes, although the full moon was still a ways away I checked to see if the fine hairs on my arms were starting to thicken. So far, normal! With a dissolving lump in my throat, I turned out the light.

And in the next instant sat bolt upright in my bed. "Christ!"

My dog-tired, overstimulated brain was finally processing clues like the begrudged dropping of a ten-year-old's quarters into his piggy bank. The thingy! And it was in Kate's bag. And Kate was right next door and we had *no* idea what, if anything, was inside it. Would have given myself a head slap, if it hadn't been aslosh with booze and exhausted adrenalin. I couldn't afford to be nursing a hangover tomorrow.

I switched on my bedside lamp again, drew my princess phone over and dialed Randy. Preparing for the response I was sure would come, I cringed and waited for him to pick up.

His tired, patient voice answered. "Ye-e-s, Alice?"

"Are you up?" I whispered foolishly.

"I am now. Why are you whispering?" His voice changed to alert status. "Is there someone there? Do you have an intruder?"

I hadn't realized I was whispering. "Sorry," I said at a more normal volume. "I'm okay, I guess. Just sorta wound up."

"Then what's up that couldn't wait?"

I hesitated, wondering how much I could safely say over the phone. My fangy sense was barking at me not to let my guard down; there could be enemy ears trained in my direction. I dropped back to a whisper.

"There was something odd we found I meant to show you when we were over at your place. I was going to just call you tomorrow and arrange a time to meet up with you before our . . . get together." I was going to say "pow-wow," but decided in time that might be too revealing, saying someone *was* listening in.

"So . . . let's do that. Take two aspirin and call me in the morning."

"Wait! Don't hang up! I'm sorry it's so late and I'm sorry I forgot about it, but I think it could be really important. And, maybe kinda urgent. And I need you to tell me what to do with it, like now."

"What is it?"

"I don't want to go over it on the phone."

"Little pitchers?" he suggested.

"Possibly elephant-eared ones. I could leave in a few minutes and drive it over to you. But first I have to get it back."

"Get it back?"

"Yes." The kitchen clock ticked.

I heard a sigh and the resigned flair of a match. "When you get 'it' back, can't you just send me a photo?"

"I don't know if my Nikon's battery is charged. If it isn't, it would take at least 45 minutes to charge it."

An exhalation of smoky exasperation came through the line. "Alice, you have a cell phone, am I right?"

"You know I do! But I'm on my landline right now."

"Still, your cell is charged and operable?" he pressed. I grunted a yes. "Excellent! Now, listen carefully. There's a camera on your cell phone. You know how to use it, right?"

I groaned. I never thought of those things, just like it never occurred to me to Google directions to a store I needed to visit or even call them first to see if they were open. "Yes," I answered, in a teensy voice.

"Great!" he said, his sarcasm hitting its stride. "Then get the thing, snap some photos of it, then text them to me on my personal line, okay?"

"Okay." I felt so beyond stupid I was ready to cry. "Give me five minutes."

"Might as well," he replied, heavily. "I'll give you ten."

"Thanks."

"Take a deep breath, Al. It'll be okay. We'll figure this out." He must have heard the wobble in my voice.

As I hung up, I heard a knock on my door and about jumped out of my skin. If only it were that easy, I thought, come a full moon. Then I could just leave my pelt behind and charge home in the altogether. And wouldn't someone be surprised when they found it? Or me, without it?

I tiptoed to my front door and peeped through the peephole. Kate's voice answered, "It's me, Al." She was whispering, too. "I couldn't sleep."

Lotta that goin' around. I opened the door to Spock in flannel carrying a handbag.

"I got to thinking," she began, pushing her handbag toward me like it contained the Black Death. "That thingy . . ." I drew her in with a hug. Once again, our wavelengths had mingled.

"Yeah, me too. We need to find a new home for it, somewhere safe and where we aren't." She nodded. After bolting my door again, she pulled the thing out and set it on my coffee table. I powered on my cell.

I know! Don't say it. Everyone else just leaves their cells on, and charges them nightly. After my dispatch days, I guess I'm a tad technophobic.

In a moment tiny clapping hands appeared, applauding my imbecilic success in starting up my own phone. Even Androids insulted me. I thrust my phone at Kate. "Can you take some pictures of it for me?"

Her kitten smile pulled up in triumph. Kate wasn't much better with technology than I am, but her smirk said, loud and clear, "Even *I* know how to do this!" She drawled, "You really don't know how to take a photo with your cell?" I hadn't wanted to admit it to Randy, but no, I didn't, at least not successfully. My few pitiful attempts had resulted only in unintended, huge-nosed selfies and jerky, three-second videos of subject matter I swear I wasn't aiming at.

I shook my head in shame. "You do it. Please." At least I'd mastered texting and calling on the evil thing. "I need to send them to R."

"'R'?" she asked, eyebrows twisted. I slid slitty eyes sideways toward the potentially eavesdropping walls.

"As in Rochester," I prompted, whispering, to her inner Jane Eyre.

She raised her voice. "Ah. Mr. Rochester. I was not aware that the master was open to digital visitations at this tardy time of an evening."

If that gibberish didn't throw someone listening in off, I don't know what would. Sometimes, it helps to talk crazy. She swiped to the photo app and turned on the thing's camera and took several shots, in *pro* mode, both with and without the flash. (Show off.)

"There!" she, murmured, opening the photo library's app and flourishing my phone at me. "Will they do?"

"Very clear. Thanks!" I whispered, and enlarged the best one of the thingy's underside. Kate had shown me how to do that at least. My stomach flipped. "Very clear, indeed." I looked up at Kate, mauling her lip at me, and mauled my own with a wince.

"Oh, boy." She backed away from the thing on my coffee table as if it were a fast-creeping fungus. "You need help attaching them?"

"Yes, please." I started a text to Randy: "Found under car. What is & where put?" I was too shaken to make grammatical sense. Then I handed my phone back.

Kate took one look and burst out in quiet laughter. "Jeez! 'What we do with moose, Natasha?' Shall I add, 'Look out, here comes Mr. Big!'?"

I rolled my eyes and shrugged a smile. "Just send the damned thing."

Kate saluted, attached the pix (but inserted "to" before "put"). "Sent!"

In two minutes, I saw the little dots, showing that Randy was typing. His response came back: "Sh*t! How long you had that?"

I looked at Kate. "Sunday?"

"That's just when we found it. Coulda been there longer."

Not what I wanted to hear. It could have been there since Friday . . . (the 13th). I thought back to where I'd been in my Kia. Not Manchester, Essex or Ipswich—Randy was driving. But definitely Gino's and the Pickled Onion. And Randy's . . . And, after Sunday, anywhere with Kate. I typed back, "Is it what it looks like?"

"Think so."

"So it really is a 'fiendish thingy'?" whispered Kate in shock.

"Too right, Ringo." The "sh*t" was rising fast. "Found Sunday," I typed. "Infection could have started earlier, like Friday." I waited.

"Remove ASAP but retain."

"Where?" I waited, watching for the typing dots.

"Got a P.O. Box?"

"No," I typed back.

"Know anyone who's deaf or leaves their TV on all day?"

Kate and I looked at each other. "Chang and Kazinsky!" we shouted, then clapped hands over our mouths (as if either would hear).

"Think we have a solution, but have 2 wait until a.m.," I sent back. No way could we roust either of them this late to plant the thing.

"No. Do now, somewhere. Mailbox?"

I thought he meant mail it to myself, which wasn't a bad idea, but texted, "Don't have the postage."

"Not mail, mailbox."

"OK. Whose?" Kate and I only had keys to our own and I wouldn't want to put it in either box.

Randy must have been coming to the same conclusion. He texted back, "Or laundry room?"

Kate peered over my shoulder. We straightened up and grinned. "Perfect!" I typed back. "On it now. Bye."

We did a happy dance, I grabbed the fiendish thingy and a flashlight, and we repaired to the dungeon.

Our building's laundry room would have given Dr. Frankenstein the shakes. Black mold bloomed between the bricks, spiderwebs festooned the low ceiling in luxurious swags, unknown things with way too many legs skittered into the baseboards, and the place was lit by a single, grimy lightbulb. You only climbed down there in desperation, when you were down to your last clean pair of undies. And the air-locked heating pipes clanked so loud, you were nearly deaf by the time you left.

The only good thing was that the two of us had discovered (through penurious trial and error) that Kate's old bicycle lock key opened the coin box for the washer, so we could get our quarters back. It would make a perfect hidey hole for the "bug." And it would be a long, long time before it was discovered: Kate and I were the only ones who used the laundry room. Chang and Kazinsky sent their laundry out.

So, between the clanking pipes and laundry noises, I figured any bastard listening in would get one helluva headache.

Back in bed, after I'd plucked spider fluff out of my hair, I sent up a prayer to whatever god might be tuning in on the woes of stupid humans. I was non-partisan when it came to religion. In the doldrums of despair, I'd Googled different gods and discovered one of the oldest: Wepwawet, the Egyptian god with a head like a wolf. They called him "Opener of the Ways." That really worked for me.

People got him mixed up all the time with Anubis, the god of the dead. Easy mistake to make: both had doggy heads of one sort or another. But Wepwawet's other title was "One with sharp arrows more powerful than the gods." I liked that in a god. Like Anubis, Weppie did a few death gigs on the side, some funerary rites and stuff, but mostly he was into leading armies and kicking ass. So I really hoped he was my guy and was paying attention. "Great Wepwawet," I whispered, praying I hadn't totally mangled his name and pissed him off, "please show me how to kick Rolf's ass and send him back to whatever hell he crawled out of. But most of all, please protect my friends. That goes for the rest of you guys," I added, covering my bets. "I can use all the help I can get. Amen."

THIRTY-SEVEN

CONTROLLING PESTILENCE

Wednesday morning I awoke with a start. I'd enjoyed a quiet day off from all the angst on Tuesday, just doing mundane shit like work. But now my hideous dream of fangs and slavering jaws was still chasing around in my head, making me disoriented. Trembling, I shoved back my pajama sleeves, believing I'd see fur and claws, then collapsed back on my pillow when there was nothing more than the usual arm fuzz.

My bedside calendar confirmed I still had 10 more days before I went through my personal monthly hell. On the other paw, less than two little weeks to go before showdown wasn't exactly reassuring. How in unholy hell were we going to take Wolf Dude down in that short time?

I unplugged my cell from the charger (yes, I do remember to charge it sometimes), and took it with me to the bathroom. Powering it on, its smug face told me it had 100% charge. Wish *I* had. Finishing up, I checked my texts.

From Randy, referring to the "bug": "Did move go OK?"

"Yep," I texted back, adding a smiley face. "But DON'T contact SA yet, OK?! Will call u later & splain."

"OK."

From Jared: "What time will u be @ R's? D&I want 2 meet u earlier." Interesting. More wavelengths were amingling.

I texted back: "Change of plans. Will M&D be home tonight?"

"No. Out tonight. Got a thing to go to. Why?"

"Could we use ur place instead?"

"Don't c why not. Was thinking same."

"Thanks! I'll tell the others, but want 2 meet w/ R 1st & u2, if u want, b4 others arrive."

"Can we change time to 8 & R & U guys come around 7?"

"Sounds OK. Send directions, etc."

"Will do. Later."

Next text was from Emma: "Something 2 show U K&R re last nt!"

Jeez, everyone was into initials now, a regular spy ring. “Can U say over fone?” I typed.

“No. Want 2 meet w/ u before others 2nite.”

I felt laughter bubbling up. *You and the whole damned rest of the party, except Sheila.* Looks like none of us were totally trusting her.

I texted Emma back our change of venue and time.

Next, I called Kate at work on the store’s phone. She sounded harassed. As she picked up the phone, I heard her saying to some customer, “No ma’am, the sale on the honeydew is 89 cents per *pound*, not each.”

“Can you talk, Kate?”

“Yeah, I guess so, now that the crazy old bag has left. She does this every week!”

I explained the change of plans and I heard her relief. “You’ll be home by 6:00 at the latest, right?” I asked.

“Yeah. Don’t forget what we have to bring with us.” Ack! I almost *had* forgotten the thingy. But Kate hadn’t, and she’d had the presence of mind to code her message; though it was unlikely the grocery store line would be bugged, my phones certainly could be. It is good to have a smart sidekick to keep you on track.

“If I do, I know you’ll remind me,” I smiled into the phone. “See ya!”

Then I cranked up my laptop and started the coffee. Ignoring my bursting inbox, I emailed the same info, except with a later meeting time, to Sheila. I pointed out, “You already know where Jared lives. BTW, his parents will be away tonight.”

She sent back a cryptic reply: “Works for me.”

Finally, I called Randy and ’splained. “You know,” he said, drawing in smoke, “I started worrying about that same thing last night, but I wasn’t thinking the clearest at the time, I guess.”

“None of us were,” I said.

“This works out so much better, Al. Sheila already knows the place and it’s close for everyone. You’ll bring that ‘item’ with you, right? If Dion is as good a nerd as Jared says he is, he should know what to do with it. If he doesn’t, Hank or one of the guys at the fire station might.”

Good to have fallback choices.

“I should be able to make it by 7:00,” he went on. “Send me his address. My GPS will get me there.”

I sighed in envy. The GPS app that friends swore came installed on my cell never spoke to me. At least I knew my way around Google Maps.

I checked for a new text from Jared and found it. I Googled a street view of his address. His home was one of the beautiful, old, red-brick Federal homes on Chestnut Street. Must be nice for some. Then I remembered what woes we shared. Money wasn't everything.

I texted Randy only the address and he sent back a "Thanks!"

So far, so good.

I was itching to know more about the new development, but I got myself a cup of coffee and hunkered down to the job I was paid to do. Who's a good girl?

By 5 o'clock, I'd logged off, showered, washed and conditioned my hair. But I used my old conditioner, not Sheila's. I felt enough eyes and ears had been trained on me for a while. My spikes did look a bit limp without it, but I'd just add more gel. At 5:50, I heard Kate's door being unlocked. I screwed my eye to the peephole to make sure it was Kate. She knew I'd be lurking, turned and gave me a wink and a thumbs up. I was already dressed and ready to go and was dithering at the thumb-twiddling phase. I'd wait for Kate, however, to go down to the laundry room, in case of ambush. She could scream bloody murder and I was revving up for some shit-kicking. Twenty-five minutes later, she knocked on my door.

First thing out of her mouth was, "You didn't use the special conditioner, did you?"

I smiled. "No, I didn't as a matter of fact. You?"

She grinned. "Nope!" She pulled up the hood of her grey cloak.

"That's my girl! Ready?" She held up her handbag and a Ziploc.

"Then let's away, dear Jane, to the dungeon and seize the demon!"

We tromped downstairs and retrieved the bug. I peered into the jumbled contents of her purse. "Ziploc was a good idea, I have to say. Where'd you have it before?"

"Um. In my tampon case, but I think this looks more professional."

I howled. "Not bad! That kept it safe from prying male eyes."

She simpered and dipped a thanks.

We were just going out my door, when I remembered I'd forgotten to shut off my computer's power strip.

Yes, I do know that's another thing most people just leave on, but I'm conscientious that way. Save the whales, forests and national grid. As I bent down under my desk to turn it off, I saw the power light wasn't on. I felt sure I hadn't turned it off. I toggled the switch and it was still off. Then toggled it back and the light flickered. *Great, another thing to fix!*

So I dragged it out and when I did, it fell apart like a clam shell. I'd never seen the innards of a surge protector bar before, but mine looked like it had taken on a stowaway. Lying neatly in a channel on one side were some looping black wires and connections, and they sure didn't look connected to anything in the bar itself.

I rose slowly and showed it to Kate. "Remember when we came in after Sheila had been here and found my surge protector on?"

"I do."

"Well, does this look normal to you?"

She shook her head. "I mean, I'm no electrician, but that stuff there," she pointed to the loopy bits, "looks alien. I think you've got a Klingon."

"Spock, I think you're right." I got a plastic bag from the kitchen, unplugged the power strip and stowed it inside. "I'd better bring this along, too, and show it to Dion." I grabbed some Tums from the john. My stomach was churning.

Downstairs, at the parking lot door I donned my jean jacket and shades and took a sweep of the lot. After seeing that it was clear, we foxtrotted to my Kia.

THIRTY-EIGHT

SHOW AND TELL

Jared's family home was one of the nicest on the block, set well back behind spreading maples now turning that amazing Mercurochrome color they do in fall, getting ready to drop their lovely petticoats on the lawn. There was a party going on down the block, a baby shower from the looks of it—pink and blue balloons bobbing in the breeze. Either twins or the couple preferred a surprise. Because of all the guests' cars, we had to drive quite a way up the street to park, then walk back.

Jared answered the door and herded us in. Antiques everywhere and the good smell of wood polish.

When we reached our meeting place, Emma was practically squirming in her seat like a first grader trying to grab the teacher's attention. "I've got something to show you."

The rest of us were still in awe, ogling Jared's home and temporarily ignoring everything else.

Being a "mature woman" of 18 (old enough to serve but not to drink . . . in public), Emma resisted the predictable pout and finally turned her head to crane with ours. "Holy shit!" She was that caught up in her discovery, she'd blocked out the grandeur around her.

I jerked my head toward Jared. "You haven't been here before?"

She reddened. "Only outside."

Jared was cruising in from the kitchen, playing butler with a tray of . . . let's say, entertainment. As if we all hadn't had a bunch of that! He set the tray down. "You like the old homestead?"

My flabbers were aghasting. I hoped I wasn't drooling. I'd only seen places like this in movies and museums. We were in the library and it had all the accoutrements you'd dream of: walls of polished cherry raised panelling, bookstacks that soared to the second-storey galleries, French windows with a view of the luscious gardens beyond that let in light on acres of Moroccan book bindings with gilt titles, and the gold Rococo frames of lovely Old Masters' paintings. I'd pinch myself except that would be too clichéd and I knew, with my thick hide, I'd never feel it. I mean, have you ever tried to tickle yourself? Doesn't work.

Jared grinned. "Pretty cool, right?"

"Coolest place *I've* ever hung," Dion gravelled.

All I could say was a limp "Wow."

"Help yourselves." Jared gestured to the tray he'd set on the low Duncan Phyfe table by the crackling fireplace. Like, with real logs. The pointed-arch stone surround mimicked those of Tudor England. Classy.

We dug into the array of drinks and edibles.

"So, Emma, I guess you have the floor," Jared said.

I shot up my hand (like a kid in class). So embarrassing. "Actually, I'd like you all to see what I brought first. Sorry, Emma. Don't want to rain on your parade but I think it may have, I don't know, stuff with far-reaching consequences," I ended. *So* eloquently said. (Not.) "Okay? And I need a techie's take on these ASAP."

Emma seemed mollified, and simmered in her chair with a gummy.

I overheard Jared's whisper to her, "Babe, this way might be better. You know, save your thing for the big reveal."

She smiled, poured a Scotch, and settled back, kicking off her shoes.

I brought out the Kia's "fiendish thingy" as Kate and I now called it. Randy and the guys leaned forward to examine it.

"Looks like one of those rubber plugs that keep falling off of cars," said Jared.

"That's what I thought. At first."

Dion lifted it up and turned it over. I slid a smile at Randy. He nodded. Dion looked up and rasped, "Where'd ya find it?"

Drum roll. "Under my car."

He shook his head slowly. "When?"

"Found it Sunday." He nodded.

His eyebrows knit. "But it coulda been there longer?"

I sighed. "Probably."

Dion pursed his mouth, nodded again. "Somebody fuckin' with you."

"That's what I was afraid of. Any idea who?"

He looked up at me under those black eyebrows. "You kiddin'?"

I slumped. "Yeah. Pretty sure I know who."

He laughed and lit up a joint and blew out a lungful of skunk.

Emma turned to Jared. "Your folks cool with pot?"

He smiled at her. "They're pretty mellow about it. Dad tokes once in a while, too. Says it takes the edge off of, you know—looney stuff."

I thought I'd been imagining things when I was toking, but that seemed to track with my own looney experience. Logged that item.

Randy leaned back, absently fondling his G&T. "That's exactly my take on the situation," he said, referring back to Rolf as the fucker doing the fucking. Kate gave me a confirming thumbs up.

"What do you think we should do about it and with it?" I asked Dion.

"Depends on what you been doing with it and where it's been."

Kate and I told him where all we thought the thing had accompanied us. Then we told him about the laundry room. He had a coughing fit.

"That's fucking brilliant! Except for one thing."

"What's that?" Emma asked.

"It's not a bug. It's just a tracker. Somebody just wants to know where Alice is. They can't listen in on it."

Kate gestured to my plastic bag. "Okay, but . . . Alice just found this. Show him."

I took out my mutilated power strip and shoved it over. "I only discovered this tonight because the strip's light was already out when I went to shut it off. I always shut it off when I'm done with my computer."

Dion grunted, "Same."

I felt somewhat vindicated. "So, does this look normal?"

"Nope. Now *there's* your 'fiendish thingy.' This one's got ears." He pushed it back toward me.

We told him about Chang and Kazinsky.

"Planting it with them could work, too, for this bad boy. But I'd feel better if you got the fucker totally away from you and all of us." He laughed again, "But man, that laundry room! Genius!"

His eyes watered and it wasn't just from the pot.

That felt good.

"Thinking about it, the laundry room probably is the safest choice for right now," Dion said. "Put some big-ass tennis shoes in the dryer and confuse the hell out of the dudes." He started cough-laughing again.

"The only problem is, the power strip is too big to fit into the coin box," Kate pointed out.

"Just scoot it behind the dryer on the floor. No one ever looks there."

Duh. "Not the washer?" I asked.

"Nah. Washers walk. Dryers just thump."

Got it.

"But I still need a surge protector," I said.

Dion shrugged. "Stuff's cheap. Go to Job Lot."

"What if I can't find a twin of this one? It'll look different."

"You think whoever planted it might come back?" Emma asked.

I nodded.

"But you know it was Sheila," Kate said. "She confessed—the new bottle of conditioner and everything."

I turned to her. "I know—about the conditioner part—but she might not have had anything to do with the bug. I mean, what if I or *we've* had other visitors we don't know about?"

"Oh, gimme here," Dion said, reaching for the power strip. He dug into his back pocket for the long tweezers he used as a roach clip. With surgical precision, he removed the Klingon and laid it on the table. "Got a zippy, J?" he asked Jared. "Oh, and some tin foil."

"Coming right up!" Jared left and came back a moment later with a Ziploc bag and about a yard of foil.

Dion wrapped the thing in the foil, stuffed it in the bag and handed it back to me. "Now it'll fit. Pretty much anywhere."

"What's the aluminum foil for?"

He shrugged. "Supposed to block some of the EMF."

"'EMF'?" I was working out a translation. I scrinched my nose. "Like, Electric Mother Fu—?"

Everyone howled. Emma choked on her Scotch. "She's good!"

"Stands for electromagnetic frequencies," Dion explained. "The foil's supposed to block some of the signals. But if it doesn't, the crackling of the foil if it's moved about should mess with them plenty."

"Thanks." I stowed it in my purse.

A horrifying thought then hit me. "Wait a second! Do you think it's been listening in to me, to *us* here, this whole time?" Then I shook my head sheepishly. "No, sorry. That's stupid. It couldn't. The strip wasn't plugged in or turned on. And at home I've turned it off every night, so I must have been okay at least part of the time, right?"

Dion sat back, blew a smoke ring and growled out, "Doesn't have to be on. Works off Wi-Fi."

"Holy crap!" I paused, thinking. "Well, I shut my laptop down every night, too."

"You shut down your router every night?"

I put my face in my hands. "No." I wasn't *that* OCD.

Kate was lip worrying again. "In that case," she began, "won't they be listening to us right now? Everyone's got Wi-Fi."

Jared leaned over with a wink. "Not in here. This is Dad's 'safe zone.' It's Wi-Fi free. That's why I brought us in here."

Dion hoisted his joint in salute: "The 'Cone of Silence!' " he crowed. Everyone cracked up.

I blew a puff of relief up my bangs. "Thank God for that, then!"

I turned back to Dion. "So, you don't think we should disarm it?" I asked him.

He sat back, inhaling more weed. "Maybe. Lemme think about it. Gotta work out the consequences." I was trying to do the same.

"Emma?" Jared asked. "Your turn."

She took a big breath, well, after inhaling a slug of 15-year-old single malt. Kids these days! We never had those perks in my day. We were lucky if we got passed a lukewarm Pabst in a paper bag.

"Okay. So after we all left the Pickled Onion, and Jared and Dion followed me home . . ."

She turned her head toward the boys with a fond crimp to her mouth. "Thanks so much, guys!"

Dion hugged her. "No prob, babe."

"Anyhow, when I got home, I got a call from Bob. You know, the bartender you met? He's also the bar manager." We nodded.

"He said two guys, white hulk with tats and a long-haired Asian, had been in about an hour later, about something a buddy of theirs lost in the bar, and asked him to check the floor and all. Bob said the muscle guy stayed by the door while the Asian did the 'negotiations'—Bob's word for it. He pulled out a wad of money and told Bob it'd be worth his while if he found it. Then the Asian dude described what had been lost."

Breathlessly, we all leaned forward. Okay, maybe it was just Kate and me. I had a woo-woo moment. Pretty sure I knew what it was.

"Well, Bob had watched the fight and seen something fall from Rolf's neck. After the cops hauled Rolf's ass off, Bob went over and picked it up, then stowed it in the cash register. Called me up and said he was holding it there for me. But he wasn't about to let on to the two tough guys. He just brought out a flashlight, turned up the bar lights and said, 'Can't leave the bar, but help yourselves.'

"So the dudes got on their hands and knees and searched everywhere, pulling the stools out, crawling under tables. Then they went into the johns and checked those. Bob said he had to turn away to keep from laughing. He told me he felt certain they were connected to the asshole the cops had dragged away. And he figured the thing might come in handy. Bob's a sweetie and has always had my back. And he's way smarter than he may look. Very little gets past him.

"When the guys gave up, Bob said to leave him a phone number and he'd call them if it did show up."

I perked up. "Did they do that?"

"Yes, but it's probably not Rolf's phone number."

Still, it might give us another lead.

"So . . . ? What *was* it?!" we chorused.

She looked straight at me. "I'll bet Alice would have a good guess."

With a sly smile, Emma pulled out her prize and spread it on its chain on the Duncan Phyfe.

It was Rolf's pendant.

"Well, I'll be damned!" I exclaimed. "Rolf must be desperate to get it back. Did Bob see what car they came in?"

She smirked. "He did. Followed them outside and saw a silver hybrid Lexus pulling away."

Good news: we got a 95% connection to Rolf. Bad news: that meant Rolf could have been sprung that night. Or soon after.

Dion pulled the pendant over and examined it. He looked up at us, sucking on his mustache. "You know, I thought I felt a chain snap when I grabbed his hair. Dude shouldn't wear his long hair down in a dive bar he doesn't know."

I'd noticed that Dion had his own rubber banded up in the bar. "And," he said, "unless I'm totally fucked up about this, the dude will be way more damned than any of you ever will be."

"How so?" I asked. I imagined the pendant would have huge ancestral clout and familial sentimentality, but the ability to damn, I mean more than we sort already were? I couldn't grasp it.

"Like I told you, us Asians got a lotta background with monster mythologies. Way more than you guys. So, the legends say that if such a monster—werewolf, vampire, fucking Godzilla or whatever, has a powerful talisman, one that's been passed on by papas and mamas since the first days, if that dude loses it, he's screwed."

"Screwed? Like how? Does he lose all his powers?"

"Nah, not all. He's still a damned werewolf or whatever. He's stuck with that." Dion laughed at the karma. "But his, or her, ability to prevail is righteously diminished."

"Diminished? How?" I asked.

"Oh, you know. His brain is fucked up. Can't think straight or smell or see straight. He's messed up. Gets confused. Makes bad judgements. Shit like that."

"So you're saying he's more vulnerable?" I suggested.

Dion hollered and took another toke. "One way to put it. His ass be grass and ready for reaping."

"Like, right away?" I hoped.

"If I'm right, it'll take a little time. His senses will erode little by little. Which will make him even meaner," he cautioned. Made sense.

"What should we do in the meantime?" Randy asked.

"First thing *I* would do is hack into his systems. Mess with the accesses he relies on, but so he doesn't notice it."

"And you can do that?" Randy pursued.

Dion shrugged. "Don't see why not, long as you show me where he hangs his hide. Done it to a bunch of other muthas who deserved it."

Jared panned us with a proud smile that shouted, "See?!"

"Then we'll be happy to take you there," Randy declared with a grin.

"God damn!" Dion clapped his hands in the air. "You know where the dude lives?"

Randy nodded owlishly. "We do. When can you go?"

Dion was pounding his chest and coughing after the last toke. "Shit! Any time you fucking say! This is gonna be SO awesome!"

"What about your classes?" Mother Alice had to weigh in.

Dion tsked me, amused. "Alice, dontcha think if I can hack into a sophisticated system, I can manufacture an excuse from my parents?"

Jared laughed until he snorted out overpriced Scotch through his nose. Flagrant alcohol abuse.

But, okay. Point taken. And noted.

I raised my B&T in salute. (Bombay and tonic.) See, I can too do acronyms.

The doorbell rang. Correction: it gonged.

"Damn! I lost track of the time. That'll be Sheila," Jared said. "Time to tidy!"

In a communal flurry, we began gathering the evidence, stowing weed and thingies away. Emma held the pendant out to us, a question in her raised eyes.

"I'd hide that for now," Randy advised. "Need some help?" he offered to Jared's back.

I called out my endorsement, "He buttles very well."

"I know!" Jared called back. "Thanks, Randy. I'll get the door while you take the tray to the kitchen. It's straight back. I think there are some ginger ales and cokes in the fridge. Maybe grab some of those and some fresh glasses? Dion, you want to get out the scent neutralizer?"

"Yes, Mother," he grumbled, taking a canister from a cabinet and spraying the air.

A couple of minutes later, as we heard the tapping approach of Sheila's heels on the hall parquet, Randy returned with the tray freshly laden with iced glasses, a crystal dish of lime slices, sodas for the kids, and Waterford decanters of gin and vodka for us adults, along with an antique siphon of tonic and linen napkins.

"Well, you certainly made yourself at home!" Kate chuckled.

"I always do," Randy replied, setting the tray down.

"My, we are quite a party!" says Lady Sheila, flinging down her coat upon the davenport.

Jared stammered, "I guess I should have hung it up in the hall."

Sheila flung him a gracious "Think nothing of it" wave.

She gazed around the room taking in the opulence. "It's been a while. Your home looks just as beautiful as I'd remembered it."

"Thanks." Jared blushed. "Gin and tonic? Or vodka? We've got both." I noticed he didn't mention the top-shelf Scotch.

"I'll take a vodka and tonic, I guess," she replied. "And you have limes! What a sweet little dish." He poured her one, stirred, garnished and handed it over.

She took a sip and smiled tightly. It hadn't escaped her that she was the last to arrive. "So! What did I miss?"

We kept our eyes straight forward and blank. "Nothing much," Emma said. "Just catching up."

"Catching up?" she asked, gazing over the rim of her highball.

"You know, just yakking generally," Kate amended. Sheila nodded, lids lowered.

"How much time do we have to yak? When will your parents be back?" she asked Jared.

"They're staying in town tonight, at the Harbor Hotel." Sheila grimaced in remembrance. "Some big teachers' gala, soirée or whatever you call it. The association holds it every year."

"Your dad teaches?" I asked him. "You never said."

"Mom and Dad both. Dad's at Salem State—Professor Stan Butler—and Mom teaches at the high school."

"Butler, huh? Thought your family was originally from Poland."

"They were. Butler's an old Polish nobility name. Goes back to the 1650s."

"So buttling well comes naturally, then," Randy quipped, gesturing to the nicely displayed refreshments. Jared smiled and shrugged.

"Somehow I got the impression your dad was a business man," I said.

"He sort of is. He teaches economics, the science and history of it and how it's affected civilizations. Dad also has some small business ventures on the side."

"What subjects does your mom teach?" Kate asked.

"Science and mythology, with a little history mixed in."

Now there was a curious combination.

"It's why they got hitched. They're both history *and* science nuts." Reading my mind, he smiled. "It's not as odd a combination as you'd think. Mom tries to demonstrate how they can reasonably coexist together, what they each contribute to the world."

"I remember what avid scholars your parents were, and are, I presume," Sheila said. "Stan is quite well known in his fields."

"Yep, Mom and Dad are still bitten with the bugs."

I stifled my wince at his turn of phrase, having suffered from both bites and bugs.

Emma and Dion stayed mute, watching the interchange. I raised a cold can at her. "Ginger ale?"

"Why not? Go big or go home!" she joked. Poor kid. Looked like despite last night, she was expected to revert to dull sobriety while Sheila was here.

It suddenly struck me as odd that I was learning people's last names so piecemeal. Guess they hadn't been important at the time. And Sheila hadn't demanded last names in the group, for privacy's sake. I turned to Emma. "What's your last name?"

"Everett." Aha! So, at the W.A. meeting, my crystal ball had only a slight malfunction. Not *from* Everett, *an* Everett. I grinned into my drink.

Randy leaned forward, changing the subject. "So, Dr. Armstrong, I got your report on the samples I sent you. Do you want to share what you found, now that we all know . . . ?"

"As Emma said, 'Why not?' " She set her V&T down. "I apologize if it was a bit ambiguous, but I hope you understand now why I felt I had to take that approach."

"I'd probably have done the same in your position," he said.

"My position . . ." she murmured, raising her glass again. "Yes, I think you probably would have." Then, all business now, "Your suspicions were well-founded, Randy, especially after attending to Alice and then becoming such close friends. The DNA samples do show canid traces from the saliva residue. A very specific type of canid."

"Anything else?" Jared pressed.

"Yes, in fact. The presence of a most unusual virus."

His eyes widened with hope as he took that in.

"I'm aware of the research your dad is doing in that line. My ex keeps in touch with him, as you probably know. But don't get your hopes up quite yet on an antiviral. The R and D—"

" 'Research and development,' " Randy translated.

"Thanks," I murmured.

"—Sorry. Yes, 'research and development.' That normally is not only costly and time-consuming, but would be tricky, given the extraordinary subject matter."

Jared's shoulders slumped in despair. "How much time do you estimate?"

"Normally? Four years? Three at the least."

He sat up. "But what if you had help? I mean, there might be someone out there we could trust, besides my dad, of course—someone working in the same field."

She smiled. "There is: Frank, my ex. We've already been working from previous samples of the same organism for over two years.

"So, all is not lost. When I got Randy's samples, I compared them with those we already had archived. They *appeared* to be identical. So I took the liberty of sending Frank a portion by Express Mail."

Well, that would save us the cost of postage, not to mention some awkward explanations. And we'd be a few more days ahead of the game. Assuming she was telling the truth, of course.

"I know my dad has reached out to Frank a few times. Can I tell Dad about this?" Jared asked.

Sheila lowered her eyes. "Let's wait a bit regarding your parents. The situation is messy enough as it is. But I will ask Frank to call you personally to let you know when he's reprocessed the samples I sent him. Will that help?"

"Yes. Thanks, Sheila. How long do you think that will take?"

"No more than a couple of days, five at most, unless there's a hiccup in transport. I'll follow up, too, with all of you."

I could see the wheels turning in Jared's head. He'd be logging those dates on his calendar and doing a follow-up, just in case.

I would, too.

"In the meantime, what do we do about Rolf?" she asked the room.

The rest of us eyeballed each other. I got "why not?" shrugs back from Emma and Dion, head tilts from Kate and Randy. I guess that was a "go ahead."

I put my shoulders back, bracing for objections. "As I mentioned before, we've been working a plan, actually."

Sheila narrowed her eyes at me. "*You guys* have?"

"Yes. But, before we get into that, I think there are some things that you shared with me that you really need to share with the rest of us, don't you? Especially about your daughter?"

She looked like a cornered mouse, the fear and shame were so huge in her eyes. I reached out a hand to hers and gave it a "there-there" pat.

Eyes closed, staring through the lids at the ceiling, she came to a decision. "You're right. The more we all know, and *understand*," she added, "the more we might be able to find a way forward."

"And get your daughter back."

I could see Sheila was tearing up. "Yes. And then get the bastard!"

Emma's eyes were huge. "Wait! Rolf's got your daughter?!" I turned to her and nodded a confirmation. "Oh, Jesus. As if there wasn't reason enough . . ."

"You need a refill?" I reached for Sheila's highball glass.

"No. I can do this, but the rest of you might . . . maybe want something stronger?"

The kids' eyes slid sideways like the typing dots—connecting with gleeful shock.

Sheila rolled her eyes. "What? You think I wasn't young once? Just don't go crazy. I don't want to have to explain to Jared's parents."

Jared stood. "I'll be right back with the ice bucket and more limes."

THIRTY-NINE

A TALE TWICE TOLD

So Sheila told her tale, part of it: about her affair with Rolf and losing her husband and sons, and about the discovery of Dee Dee Thornton's torn-up body.

I leaned forward. "You never told any of the W.A. group?"

She shook her head. "I'm sorry. I wasn't sure who I could trust and who might be a plant or mole or whatever you call it—someone working with Rolf."

"Well, Sheila, we know the feeling," Emma spoke up. "Alice told us about the hair conditioner and its purpose."

Sheila reddened again. "I was really, really desperate. I still am.

"And it's only so I might be able to track him to his lair by following one of you following him. I thought maybe I could somehow find my daughter. It was just a lure. I didn't think it could hurt any of you, as you'd already been changed. At least not until Dee Dee. I *know* Rolf killed her. But now . . . I really felt I had a shot at him."

"I think we still do, Sheila," I told her. "We have to try."

"I'm afraid—for *you*, for you all. He's so cunning and vicious. Dee Dee tried and got killed. I can't face any more blood on my conscience. Unless it's his."

"Dee Dee Thornton was your first buddy partner?" Kate asked.

Sheila nodded. "She wasn't a werewolf, though I introduced her to the group that way. She was my lab assistant and a good friend, working in secret on the lycanthropic research Frank and I both are working on—trying to find a cure or at least mitigate the mutation."

Looking at me, Randy spoke up, "Then she went missing."

Sheila looked down. "Yes. Somehow, Rolf had got word of the research we were doing. His network is pretty extensive, I guess. Ears everywhere. We had a showdown. He demanded that we abandon the research. Said I'd be made a laughing stock and was wasting my time and money on what couldn't be fixed. I told him we wouldn't back down and he shouldn't expect me to if there was even the slightest hope of success. Two nights later, after finishing a long shift, Dee Dee went missing. Her car was still in the hospital parking lot."

"This was five years ago?" Randy asked.

"Yes."

Kate and I looked at each other. I fished out the thingies. "The hair conditioner wasn't the only way you were tracking us, or at least not me, was it, Sheila?" Her questioning eyes looked troubled. "This look familiar?" I shoved over the car thingy.

"What is it?" she asked.

"I thought you'd tell us that."

She picked it up. "Looks like those rubber plugs that keep popping off cars on the road."

"Turn it over," I said. She did and her brows knit.

"Is that some kind of, I don't know, bug or tracer?" Her fingernail was prodding the innards of the gizmo. Then she snatched her hand back like it was on fire. "Jesus, I probably shouldn't be messing with it! Where'd you find it, Alice?"

"Underneath my car on my building's parking lot. You didn't put it there?"

"What? No! I don't even have the skill set," meaning knowing how to set it up, I assumed. "*Is* it a bug?"

Dion weighed in, "No actually. It's just a tracker. Shows where the tagged vehicle is and where it's traveling when it's on the streets."

Sheila threw up her hands. "So simple! I wish I did have that skill set or knew someone who did. Would have saved me a whole lot of money on conditioner."

"But you do know someone, don't you?" Randy asked.

She nodded fast, lips pulled in. "I guess I do."

"So, you honestly didn't plant this?" Kate asked her. Sheila shook her head no. "But you have an idea who did?" Another head shake, this time an up-shake: a yes.

"It's got to be Rolf or someone working for him," she said.

"That would be my guess, if it wasn't you," Emma said. "Unless the two of you were working together?"

"Never in a million, billion years! How could you even think that?"

Emma softened. "You can't blame us for wondering, Sheila."

Sheila's voice was small. "I guess I can't. Sorry."

I held up a stalling palm at Emma and the rest. "You haven't heard the whole story," I told them. I slid my compromised surge protector strip over to her. "What about *this* little gizmo?" Her face went purply-red and blotchy.

Sheila's voice was shrinking by the moment. We had to lean forward to hear her reply, another tiny "Sorry."

I settled back and stowed the evidence again in the Ziploc. "Well, I suppose it's good it was you who left it in my place, not yet another stalker, and thankfully, not Rolf. Kate and I did wonder why someone would break in just to leave more hair product."

Kate muttered, chuckling, "Now *there's* a new business concept! Burgling hair product vendors!" The perfect tension-release remark. Kate excelled at that. "Well, at least it makes you look not quite so manic, Sheila, finding out you were just 'multi-tasking.' " She smirked the finger quotes.

I'd earned the right to play bad cop to Kate's good. "It still chaps my butt, Sheila," I said, "to find out that you were listening in to everything we said." Or did.

"I didn't hear all that much, actually. I didn't know how to set it up that well. The sound was pretty bad and the range was miniscule."

Well, that was some relief. No one wants to think somebody's listening in while they're in the john.

"I just needed to see if you could be trusted, Alice, and more importantly, I was so hoping you'd lead me to Rolf, one way or another. What a total ass I've been!" Sheila's nose and mascara were running. I handed her a tissue and waited a bit.

"Sheila, tell them about your daughter. It's time. You're safe with us," I said.

Fishing another tissue from her own purse and mopping away snot and black smears, she drew out a long sigh.

She told—simply, baldly, heartbreakingly. From the squirms, fidgets, and hand clasping around me, I could see the others were just as moved and horrified as I was at the first telling.

Emma slammed down her drink and shot off her seat. "I just cannot *believe* he took your own daughter!" she exploded. "The sick bastard!" Turning to me, she demanded, "Why didn't you mention this before, Alice?"

My mouth twisted as I considered the best answer. "There was so much other scary stuff going on, I guess it got sidelined. And maybe I didn't feel it was really my story to tell," I said, looking at Sheila.

I also wasn't totally sure before that her story was completely legitimate. But I didn't want to say that.

Emma turned back to Sheila and the rest. "Well, it's all the more reason we've got to shut him down!"

"Not until we find my daughter," Sheila insisted. "But right damned after! If we can."

We all agreed.

Jared took Emma's hand in his. "And the sooner the damned better."

"But, hang on!" Emma went on. "When your daughter was visiting, you said you cancelled your date with Rolf. How could you possibly have still been seeing him after that?"

Now it was Sheila squirming in her seat, like she was trying to work out a wedgie. "It wasn't an actual date, although he was trying to get back in my good graces. After Dee Dee's abduction, I broke it off with him, although I had no solid proof he was responsible for that. But just before Patty arrived, he called, suggesting that we bury the hatchet and have a civil discussion, compare notes. He told me he'd been doing his own research, too. So maybe we should join forces."

"You *believed* him?" Emma's mouth was agape.

"I did not," Sheila answered, lips firmly pressed. "But I wanted to find out what he was up to."

"And then your daughter just happened to be there and he charmed her. . . ." That was Kate stepping in. And there was Rolf's leverage.

Sheila's next words confirmed it: "I think Rolf grabbed her so he could have a hold over me and keep us from completing our research."

Jared kept his eyes down, focused on his drink.

Dion sucked in some smoke. "That's messed up."

She pounded the heels of her hands against her eyes. "If I could only find out where that son of a bitch lived!"

I gulped. "Um, about that . . ."

"We know, Sheila," Randy said, in his soothing ER voice. She panned our faces in confusion.

"You *know* where he lives? And you didn't tell me? You heartless b-b-b beasts!" she finished.

She was so angry she was spitting stutters or maybe merely choosing the most appropriate term. I guess "beast" was appropriate for us, except for Kate and Randy. And Dion.

Sheila popped up, yanked up her purse and coat, dragged an uncaring cashmere sleeve across her nose, and said, "You. Will. Tell. Me. This *instant*, where that mother fucker lives, God damn you! I'll go over there and TEAR OUT HIS STILL-BEATING HEART!"

I winced at her apt, if unfortunate, choice of insult.

Randy stood. "Sheila— Dr. Armstrong, please. Sit down before you detonate. They didn't know about your daughter until now. I didn't either. And it won't help Patty if you go charging off unbriefed. It might even make things more dangerous for her. Let us tell you what we know about where he lives and how it's set up. Please." He patted the cushions.

Sheila sagged back onto the couch. "Any delay . . ." she moaned, turning beseeching eyes to us. "We might be too late! I've *got* to get her out of there." She began to weep in earnest, rocking herself forward and back. "It might be too late already!"

"From what you've told us, I don't think it is, Dr. Armstrong. She's too precious as leverage. Rolf's going to keep her alive to keep you dangling on his hook, so he can keep you from ruining his little game."

"How long have you known?" Sheila's tone was as dull as her eyes.

"Well, technically, since last Wednesday." I cringed, waiting for her to do the Jack-in-the-Box thing again. "But we didn't—" I began again.

Randy looked steadily at her, the Voice of Reason. "—but we weren't able to check out the premises until Saturday morning. And none of us knew about your daughter then. In any case, we needed to see the layout, exits, security, numbers of vehicles to account for. That sort of thing."

"So we could plan our attack," Kate finished. "You really don't want another flubbed attempt, right? Like following him in Essex?"

"You saw that?" We nodded. Sheila drew out a long sigh. "No, you're right, Kate. So how did you get his address?"

Randy smirked. "I have a friend who's a first responder."

I didn't dare look at him, knowing his penchant for naughty double-entendre. But he was playing it straight now (as straight as he ever got).

Randy went on, "He ran the plate and got it off their database."

"As in police?" Sheila asked, clearly miffed.

"Like that." Randy didn't want to implicate himself or Hank any more than he had.

"Hunh! Didn't work for *me*. I dated a cop for a while. Steve. He was between separations with his wife. I was the third." Her mouth twisted in disgust. "Good ol' Stevie. I made up some story, claiming Rolf had ripped me off, and worked on Steve to run Rolf's plate for his address. Thought I'd convinced him. But Steve got up on his high horse and said he wouldn't help me. Couldn't betray his brothers' code of honor. Guess his marriage vows weren't included in that code. Typical. It's all about the old-boy network."

"Then thank God, for low horses," Randy murmured. And there went the straight man.

After Sheila's well-justified meltdown when she learned we knew where Rolf lived, I no longer had any doubts about the truthfulness of her story. But something still wasn't adding up for me.

In silence, I watched the others fiddling with their drinks, pushing stuff around on the coffee table, crossing and recrossing their legs, and could practically see lightbulbs flashing off over their heads as they came to much the same conclusion.

Kate and I leaned forward and started talking at the same time: "About Steve . . ." I waved sideways at Kate. "Go ahead."

"No, you go." Kate sat back.

"All right. So, Sheila, why did you have to make up a story for Steve? I get it that you couldn't say, 'I want you to go after the werewolf who kidnapped my daughter.' But why didn't you file a missing persons report and get an APB going as anyone would for their child? And what was Frank doing all this time, once he learned about Patty's abduction?"

"My thing with Steve was after Dee Dee disappeared, before Patty was taken," Sheila explained. "The story I made up was because I didn't have enough evidence, that I could share, to link Dee Dee with Rolf. And I wasn't her next of kin. Plus, Steve was such a dick, I didn't trust him."

"Was Frank doing nothing to help? And what about later with Patty? What about Patty's school?"

"Frank wasn't completely convinced that Rolf was involved in Dee Dee's abduction. For that matter, he wasn't entirely sure Rolf was behind Patty's disappearance, although it did seem too strong a connection to consider mere coincidence."

"But *you* were sure, right?" I pressed.

Sheila hesitated. "I was, and I still am."

"But?"

"Rolf was devious and careful. He never hinted at taking Patty, any more than he let on about any connection to Dee Dee."

"Wait. You said he left a note that he'd taken Patty sightseeing or something while you were out, right?"

"Yes. And after I hadn't heard from her for hours, I called him and he acted surprised that she wasn't home again. He said that after their little jaunt, Patty had asked him to drop her off at some friends' place nearby."

Kate leaned in again. "Didn't you call her friends to verify?"

"Rolf said he couldn't remember their names," she said.

Well, of *course* he did.

"But he thought he remembered the street. It took me a while to figure out who they were. But I did and called them."

"And?" Kate was more patient than I at teeth pulling.

"They said they hadn't seen her."

Kate frowned. "But he said he'd dropped her off! Her friends would have seen both of them when they opened the door."

"And they would have seen his car," Emma added to Kate's point.

"Rolf just dropped her off at the curb, then drove off. He said."

"Such a gentleman!" Jared snarled.

"Total douche," coughed Dion.

Randy was quiet, letting his slot machine wheels tumble to see what came up. He tilted his head to one side. "Alice asked about Patty's school. Her friends there must have missed her and made inquiries. And what *has* Frank been doing all this time to locate his daughter?"

"Frank and I decided we'd better just tell the school that Patty had decided she wanted to stay in New England and wouldn't be coming back. Her friends there were disappointed, naturally, but really sweet about it and retrieved her things from her dorm. Frank has them now."

"Frank didn't go to the police out there either?" Randy's frown lines were deepening.

"He was working quietly, behind the scene, with connections he could trust on the force, but we didn't dare go official and public. We'd received an anonymous, typed letter, postmarked from Boston, warning us not to get police involved if we ever wanted to see our girl again."

"Any luck with that, with Frank's connections?"

"Blind alleys all the way. Which is why I've been trailing Rolf any chance I could get. And, yes, doing some surveillance on the rest of you."

"Is that why you formed the group?" Jared asked. "Just to spy on us to find Rolf?"

"No!" Sheila looked genuinely hurt. "Or not entirely. That idea came to me much later. When I started meeting more and more like us, I don't know, I was so heartbroken and angry with him, even *before* he took Patty, I wanted to protect his victims from further harm. And keep them from becoming like him, like I was afraid *I* would be if I didn't find another way. A better way."

"How did you find them, well, us?" I asked, with a sweep of my hand toward Emma and Jared. "It can't have been from that dinky card in the deli. You had to know about at least one when you put that up."

She nodded. "The first one was Connie O'Mara. We go to the same church. It's one of the old-school Catholic churches. Back then it kept its doors open all day until after the last mass. One night, the moon was rising and it was full. I was sick with dread but couldn't stay home; I felt like I was jumping out of my skin. So I went inside to pray, get some solace."

I rocked back and forth, eyes closed. I knew that feeling.

"Connie was kneeling in the front pew, rosary beads in hand. I heard her voice, quaking, rasping out the words. I thought she was weeping and my heart went out to her, so I walked up to give her comfort.

"As I sat down beside her, the full moon rose behind the altar. There's a lovely stained-glass window with the dove of peace shining its light down on the saints, and the moon behind it gave it a supernatural glow. It felt like an answer of hope, like a benediction." Her eyes moistened.

"And in the next moment its light flared out through the glass to a blinding glare and I heard her gasp, 'Sweet Jesus! Dear Lord and Father, what have I done that this should be brought upon me?'

"I was startled and the next thing I saw was the hair on her arms and face thickening, her nails and her nose extending, and her teeth lengthening. I looked down at my own arms and they were doing the same!

"She turned to me with a snarl, 'So, have you come for me at last, you devil's spawn? Has himself down there sent you to finish me off? Well, I'm ready. Father, forgive me! But I'll not be one of them. I'd rather die than live with such wickedness!' And she closed her eyes and bared her throat at me.

"I backed away and said to her, 'And I won't either. I came in here for comfort myself. We're the same, you and I. But not wicked. Never, ever wicked. I didn't ask for this—this thing. It seems you didn't either. And I've been searching for another way to live. I guess I came here looking for an answer, a way to make sense of this. Maybe you're my answer. Maybe God sent you to me, or me to you to, I don't know, join forces I guess, against the one who did this to us. And who may be, for all I know, creating more like him at this very moment.'

"Connie noticed my own miserable transformation, nodded at me and smiled at last. As well as she could, anyway, over her fangs. 'Ye just may be the angel I was asking after,' she replied. 'But for now, lass, I think us two better take a runner!' I heard the front doors bang closed and footsteps. 'That'll be the blessed father closing up. Quick! Out here!'

"We scampered out the side door onto the street, panting like—"

I snorted, nodding my head fast. "—like dogs. But not wolves?"

"It shouldn't be funny, but if you'd seen Connie, you'd know the answer to that. God knows what scary thing I'd look like to an outside observer, but Connie was sort of cute, all curly, white and fluffy with a yap like a squeaky toy." She covered her snicker with her hand.

"Did she look like a Bitchin' Frisbee?" Jared asked.

Sheila turned to him. "A *what*?"

Deadpan, I translated: "*Bichon Frisé*."

"Oh, my dear Lord! She did!" Sheila snorted and clapped a hand over her mouth. Her head waggled back and forth, struggling for contrition.

Jared turned to me, arms crossed, a "See?" smirk on his face.

"I'm sorry," she whimpered, heaving. "I'm so, so sorry! Not funny!"

We all busted up.

After we'd shaken ourselves free of hilarity, some of us trotting to the kitchen for refills, others trotting to the closest bathroom (for obvious reasons), Sheila filled in more blanks, telling us about how she and Connie teamed up after that, cruising the bars, as the moon waxed, looking for Rolf, how they eventually found Salem Sally, one brightly lit full-moon night, sprinting in fright out of a bar on Derby Street . . . on all fours, just after closing time.

Then it was putting up the index cards—not just in the deli (I had wondered how a single card could do the job)—some on bar bulletin boards too, then on to Sheila's going over the bite cases at the ER, getting the victims' addresses and sending out flyers, developing the special hair conditioner, and finally forming the group and making an attempt at group therapy and guidance.

Most of the victims had answered her ad, as I had. Others were bar rescues, like Sally. It all synced up.

She shrugged. "I guess that's it."

"It" was certainly a helluva lot for any one person to take on. "I *am* sorry if I sort of used you all," she said. "But I also did want to protect you too and brainstorm with you all how we could track down Rolf and my daughter, and maybe, just maybe, get some of our old lives back. And do no harm."

The doctors' creed. Randy gave her a collegial thumbs up. "So, you ready to listen to what we've come up with?" he asked.

Sheila flopped back, freshened glass in hand. "Okay. Shoot."

Randy smiled. "Well, that's only part of it." Kate chuckled.

So we fleshed out our plan we'd been developing, going over the layout of Rolf's place, brainstorming about how we'd get in, where we believed Patty was and why, the hacks Dion proposed, the guard dog, guards and vehicles, the dart gun and Kate's pistol and silver bullets.

"Dion's going over with us tomorrow to case the joint, as they say, see where the Wi-Fi server is so he can hack into his account info, and see if he can plant any devices."

Sheila sat forward, mouth compressed. "I want to go with you."

Randy shook his head. "My car will be full as it is, and if you drove your own car, Rolf would recognize it. Then he'd probably move Patty so none of us would find her again."

She nodded at the sense of it, but her shoulders were back up to her earlobes, with the fear and stress.

"We really don't want to do anything to tip him off," I told her. "It may take a few days to set things up, so we want him to think everything's turning up roses—"

"—Instead of noses," Kate put in, getting Sheila's shoulders to descend a notch.

"What if you can't get inside to plant a bug?" Sheila asked Dion.

"Buddy of mine, another techie nerd like me, makes these really wide-range ones that you can just stick onto an outside window. They can listen through super thick walls—brick, stone, even iron, whatever. But if it doesn't look that's possible, you know, without making it noticeable, I can just work off Rolf's Wi-Fi connections and providers, once I have them.

"It would be really cool," he went on, "if you could give me his email address, if you have it, as well as the cell number he's used to text you. Whatever you've got."

"It will be my pleasure," Sheila purred, with a slit-eyed grin. "Got a pen and paper?" she asked, pulling up her contacts on her cell.

I frowned at Sheila's old-fashioned methods. "Or he could just store these on his phone," I suggested. "Right, Dion?"

Dion tipped his head, looking at her under lowered, black eyelashes. "I could, but I think 'old-school' is the way to go with the intel," he answered, smiling his approval at Sheila, and pulling out said implements.

"Ohhh!" I got it. "One-way connection, intake, no outtake, cutting off a traceable link to you?" I asked him.

He see-sawed his hand. "More or less. In case the dude's got his own tech nerds too, be a good thing not to leave breadcrumbs leading to us."

"If you *can* plant the bug, and Patty is . . ." Her voice trembled.

"We will definitely be listening for her, as well as the activity in the house. But with or without it, I think I should be able to pinpoint where she is just through text, phone and email activity."

"God, I hope so," Sheila breathed out. "And thank you, *thank you,* Dion, for taking this on."

He grinned. "You're welcome. Man, this is like the Holy Grail to us techies. Plus, the asshole righteously deserves getting fucked over."

Shoulders forced back and down, Sheila gathered her bag and coat, preparing to leave. "Please let me know, the second you know it, what you've found out. Will you do that? *Please*?"

Jared put out a stalling palm. "Wait a second, Sheila. Don't go just yet. Emma's got another ace up our collective sleeve to show you."

Sheila tilted her head to one side and sat back down.

"Show her, Emma," Jared said.

Emma silently produced the pendant Bob had snagged for her. No drum roll. Sheila's eyes bugged out.

"But that's, that's Rolf's! That's his pendant. I'd know it anywhere, with that wolf's head and the old German letters." She looked up at us, jaw agape. "How? Where?"

Emma and the boys told her, the rest of us perched like a clowder of Cheshire cats grinning away in glee.

There's another great word, like "guffaw," to stash in the old memory bank: "clowder." Sometimes the old words are the funnest. You may have to look it up. I did. But that's what Google is for, right?

Then Dion gave her his theories of what that will mean to Rolf and what he's likely to do and how he's likely to behave. "This should draw the mutha out. Best bait we could have wished for!" he cawed.

Sheila held up a palm towards him, aiming carefully, with one eye closed against the vodka. Dion caught on and they high-fived.

"I've always wanted to do that, but was too afraid I'd miss!" she giggled.

She almost had, but I'd caught Dion moving his palm in time to contact with hers. I smiled to myself. Gee, what a *nice* ninja.

FORTY

Texts to Try and Test Us

Near the witching hour, the party broke up. Randy and Kate helped Jared clean up and the rest of us set the library back to its former non-party state, so all denials would hold up in parent court.

The baby shower down the street was breaking up at the same time so there was the usual tug-of-war confusion as guests staggered into their cars and jockeyed for first position of departure. The pink and blue balloons sagged from their strings like the strung-out guests. We had to duck a couple of times to avoid getting bludgeoned by bobbing rubber.

I walked Sheila back to her SUV as Kate and Randy walked ahead. As we reached her car, I told her, "I know that took a lot of trust and courage to tell us what you did, Sheila." She made a sharp head shrug. "You're not sorry you did, are you?" I asked. She slowly shook her head. "Are you worried we'll blow it?" Her arms flapped helplessly up like penguin flippers.

"I'm used to having control, I guess. It's hard for me to accept help and even harder to let others do what I feel *I* should be doing," she said.

"I totally get that," I replied. "But none of us, not one, is capable of doing everything, every single task we need to handle in order to win. We all are bringing different skills to the chase. We've become a team. We *are* a team, right? And aren't we lucky we have the specific brains and talents necessary and the heart to join up?"

My pre-game pep talk gained me a hug. "It's just . . ." she began, "I want to be there!" She was wringing the long strap of her handbag, like it was a garrotte.

"And you *will* be! I gar-on-tee it!' " I added, in a Southern twang and giving her shoulder a timid pat. "Just not tomorrow. Once our ninja figures out how to—" I whipped my head around, checking for eavesdroppers, and decided on caution "—do what he needs to and we figure out the best approach, then we can summon the cavalry. . . ."

Her mouth mustered a thin smile. "The girls."

"Yep. Circle the wagons and bring on the womenfolk. Menfolk, too. Then we can move ahead."

"It's just so hard—the wait and worry. You have no idea."

I wanted to say I did, but honestly, I didn't. I couldn't begin to imagine how tortuous this situation would be to a parent. "You're right. And maybe that's a good thing. Maybe it will give us clearer heads being more emotionally distant?" She beeped open her driver's door.

"There is one thing you could be doing while you're chewing your nails off, Sheila."

Sheila turned back to me. "What's that?"

"I don't suppose you happen to have her phone, do you?" I was still being careful not to use anyone's names now that we weren't inside the "Cone of Silence."

She looked at me raised brows, like "Seriously?"

"Yeah. It was just a long shot. But you have texts from her, right? At least from before . . ."

Sheila must have been worrying about invisible ears, too. She motioned to get in her car. I called up the street to Kate and Randy, "Be there in a sec!" and got in.

She pulled out her cell and started scrolling. "I have a few. And I also have other texts I've gotten from unknown numbers. And photos."

My brows knit. "You do? Like from . . . um, whomever?"

"It must be. Here." She held up her cell to show me, tapping on one text after another. None were from stored or recognizable contacts. Each was from a different phone number, probably unlisted. The area codes varied. They were clearly threatening and ugly and about her daughter. Some had photos attached. Preparing for the worst, I cringed, expecting gore or amputation. I was relieved to be spared that horror, but there was distress aplenty without it.

They were sick and subtle. One of the shots was of the dress Patty was wearing the day she was abducted, Sheila said. Blue and flowered, sweetly feminine, a small blood stain high on one sleeve. Another was of Patty standing at the overlook by Tom Shea's looking out at the Essex River, her laughing face of study of delight. It was taken the last day Sheila saw her daughter. Tom Shea's must be one of Rolf's favorite date stops. It's where we saw him with Mona. No text with this one.

She was watching for my reaction and got it. The sickness I felt for her was visceral, sicker even than I had been. The photos and stark, ugly texts made it more real than any story could have done.

"I've gotten things in the mail, too."

"Like?" I winced, thinking, *Oh God, here come the severed fingers.*

Reading my face, she reassured me, "Nothing too awful. Snips of her hair once. Postcards other times, in her handwriting. Well, printing. You know kids these days—they don't do cursive much. It's not cool."

"Postcards? From where?" My brows were knitting a second sleeve.

"All over."

"The U.S. or the world?"

"Both. Several from Europe, mostly Germany or maybe Austria. The messages were very stilted as if scripted, not her usually chatty self. A sort of forced, stereotyped 'Having a ball, wish you were here' thing."

There was a tap on my window, and we both jumped. It was Randy. Sheila started her car and I pressed the window button down.

He stuck his head in. "You guys okay? 'Cause I need to get going and Kate looks ready to drop. And I wanted to give you your print."

"Sorry! Here, take my keys. Let her into my Kia, put the print in the trunk, then get yourself home. I'll be there in a minute or two. Thanks!"

He did a two-finger salute and walked back to our cars.

As I turned back to Sheila, she said quietly, putting her phone on speaker, "There's also this." She confirmed the voice mail was Patty's voice, slurred and slow—not drunk, more drugged—the struggling words drawn out almost singly: "Hi Mom. It's . . . me. I'm . . . okay. Just . . . wanted you . . . to . . . know." Then a cut-off, hiccupped sob. Sheila's eyes were wet. Mine too, and I had a hard fist of despair in my throat.

"You see why every single extra second of delay kills me inside?" she asked. I did a slow nod, ashamed, wordless.

Finally, I snuffled, "You need to get these to Dion, Sheila, as soon as you can. He might be able to track the phone numbers."

"They're probably from, what do they call them? 'Burner phones'?"

"They might be, but no stone unturned, right?"

She turned away. "Right."

"You'll get her back," I insisted, blowing my nose. "It *will* be okay."

It *had* to be.

FORTY-ONE

SCOPING OUT

It was almost dark Thursday evening when we got to Rolf's mansion. Kate, Jared, Dion and I were huddled in the back of Randy's Bronco, now devoid of artwork. Watchers would merely have seen a clean-cut white man in a respectable, black Ford cruising past. As before, he parked far down the street, away from any view from Rolf's windows.

Emma had to work, but that suited our plans, too. If Rolf's goons came back to the bar, checking up on the pendant, her presence, rather than absence, wouldn't be a tip-off that something was going down.

Silently we emerged from Randy's SUV, holding unlit flashlights and taking care not to slam doors. Randy locked his car from the armrest console, so the key fob wouldn't beep. His infrared binocs were around his neck and Dion carried his geek goodies in a black nylon daypack. Walking up to Rolf's, our sneakered feet kept to the grass as much as possible, minimizing any advance warning to unseen ears.

Randy, Kate and I sidled up to the same back door on the cellar level we'd been to. All quiet. Not even the dog in sight. Kate went over to the garage to count cars. She tiptoed back. All present except for the Rolls, which, as we knew now, was Rolf's babe trap.

Excellent! We only had to worry about his guard goons.

Dion and Jared had crouched by some bushes. Randy motioned them over and shown his flashlight through the door's glass panel. We went over the layout with Dion and Jared. I pointed down the hall. "Those last two doors on the left go to the 'gym,' " I whispered, using finger quotes, "and his temperature-controlled wine cellar. It's huge." The hall alone was about 30 feet long. A set of granite steps led down to the door well.

"Wine cellar's the last door, next to the stairs?" Dion whispered.

"Right. They go upstairs to the kitchen directly above."

"What about the two doors closest to us? The iron ones with vents in them. You know what he used them for?"

I shook my head. I didn't, not back then.

"But you have an idea, don't you?" Jared asked us. Solemnly we nodded yes.

"Any windows to the rooms on the outside?" We led Dion around the side and pointed to two low windows behind bushes near our end. Farther back, corresponding to where the gym/lock-up and the wine cellar were, the brick wall was blank. No reason for windows there.

As we looked, a light came on in the second room back from the door. Randy instantly switched off his flashlight. We ducked, although we couldn't have been seen from a window unless someone inside pulled over a chair or a bench to look out. And we'd been silent as spiders.

Dion quietly unzipped his daypack and drew out something long that telescoped and had an eyepiece at one end and some mirrors at the other. Randy's eyes enlarged in surprise and admiration. "Periscope"? he mouthed. Dion gave him a thumbs up.

Jared breathed, "He made it himself. Has an infrared lens."

I breathed back, "Wow! But he's lying on the ground, so . . . ?"

"Watch," Jared whispered.

Dion slid the periscope sideways onto the glass from the window's near, vertical frame, slowly rotated it and put his eye to the eyepiece at the bottom end. None of us breathed. After almost a full minute, he lowered it. Five breaths eased out like slow-leaking tires.

Kate and I opened our mouths, but Dion put a finger across his lips. Rummaging in his pack, he pulled out a small note pad and a pen and wrote. We all leaned in to read it, the lighted window making his message clear: "Found her."

I took the pen and pad from him and wrote, "Sheila's daughter?"

"Think so," he scribbled back. "She look a lot like you?"

I nodded, then wrote, "Is she alone?" He nodded. "And—" God. How do you succinctly phrase your grisliest dread?

"—whole and reasonably healthy," he wrote, finishing my question.

She was alive! I covered my face with my hands and slid down the wall into the shrubbery. She wasn't even my kid, but my relief that she was alive *and* well hit me like a ton of the bumpy bricks I'd just slid down. I could feel hysteria and hope rising like twin fountains, but managed to turn off the water main. *Thank God* Sheila wasn't with us. We'd be busted for sure. Breaking glass makes quite a racket.

I massaged my back and Randy dragged me upward on my wobbly legs and pointed questioningly to the window closest to the door, which was dark. I shook my head fast, too afraid of what I might see. I wasn't up for another potential horror show. I flapped Randy onward. The guys were made of tougher stuff and stepped carefully beneath the dark window. Dion's periscope peered in again, swivelling its cyclops eye.

Apparently, Kate felt the same as I did. Her trembling hand was gripping my arm so hard it was cutting off circulation. At this point, all five of us could get jobs as deep sea divers, we were getting so adept at breath holding.

The periscope collapsed down. Dion slid it back into his pack, turned and circled an "OK" with his right hand. Next, he drew out two small discs. After cleaning the glass, he stuck them in a lower corner of each window. They must have had suction cups. Dion wiggled them, to make sure they were well stuck, and gave us a thumbs up. He pulled out some ear buds, plugged in, and fiddled with some gizmo in his pack. Another thumbs up, this one with a grin. Now *we* had "ears" with which to hear.

Kate and I were about to move off, when he held out a palm: "Wait."

We tensed. What had he heard? I hadn't heard a thing, but I didn't have the ear buds. And then I heard it. It was the jingle of a dog chain. Yikes! One of the guards must be out walking the dog! Frantically, I waved to the others to beat it, but Dion put his palm out again. He waggled his index finger back and forth, then hooked a thumb toward the house's interior. Dog and walker: inside, not outside. Kate was patting her heaving chest. I hoped my drawers weren't noticeably damp.

The guys came back towards us and curled an arm to follow. The Rolls' bay being conveniently vacant, we stepped inside the open garage door for a regroup. As we shook with silent mirth, Dion stuck the tracker off my Kia underneath the Lexus, rasping, "*Touché,* assholes!"

Then he murmured, "Okay, now I need to scope out where his electrics and Wi-Fi go into the house. I'm hoping, with a house this old, there'll be something like a main phone box with all the connections on the outside, instead of some central station inside." He scanned the side of the building for wires. "You remember seeing anything like that when you were here before?"

I screwed up my face. "What does a main phone box look like?"

Randy glanced toward me and beamed. "Even if Alice doesn't know, I do. This way, please. Watch your step," he added, shining his flashlight on a pile of dog turds we'd somehow managed to avoid. *Eeeuuw*. Must be beneath Rolf's guards to poop scoop and bag. (The poor gardeners.) If we'd stepped in it, they wouldn't even need electronics to track us.

Leading us around the side of the building, Randy took us to the far back corner nearest the street and pointed to a large, black plastic box with snap tabs on two ends and its own plastic awning to keep out rain. Last Saturday, when we'd been walking around the back side of the house, checking out the upper storeys, we'd walked right past it. And I had failed to register it. But Randy hadn't. His guy recall had pulled that smirking rabbit right out of his neuronal hat.

Peering upward we saw multiple wires and cables set into the bricks, neatly hugging one side of a black downspout, then spanning across to a pole on the street, camouflaged tastefully by the embrace of an elm.

"Would this be what you're looking for?" Randy asked Dion.

"That be the one!" Dion was all grins and went to work. The rest of us hung out as lookouts, but the neighborhood seemed peacefully tucked in for the night. And the deep shade of the elm allowed Dion to work in better light. He'd strapped on an LED headlamp and laid out a small tool case of extremely specialized tools. Looked like the kid really did know his stuff.

Five minutes later, he stood up fully and stretched, packed his tools and switched off his light. "All set."

I hadn't realized how high my shoulders were this whole time until we climbed back into Randy's Bronco and I felt my twin deltoid knots dissolving. Mutually drained, Kate and I traded massages.

"Did Sheila send you those texts she got about her daughter?" I asked Dion. He was busy lighting a joint and jerked his head up and down in a yes. Normally, Randy doesn't like anyone smoking anything in his car, but now his free hand was curled upward, fingers jiggling a "gimme" to Dion after he'd taken his first toke. After a long, releasing exhale, he passed the doobie to Randy. Then he plugged in the ear buds again.

"Hear anything?" I asked. He passed the ear buds to me. I heard singing. A lullaby. A young girl comforting herself. Tearing up, I put my hand over my heart. Dion put his hand over mine and patted.

FORTY-TWO

Counting Down

Next morning, after showering and caffeinating, I threw myself into my much-neglected job, the one that was paying my bills. Friday: eight days to go before the next lunar blast. I was getting serious jitters at the countdown, so mindless work helped me thrust my inner calendar to my brain's back burner. I'd even turned my cell off, to concentrate on less scary things. Randy volunteered to update Sheila. And after our late night, I didn't expect I'd hear from anyone until much later.

Kate seemed to be doing the same. I'd heard her leave early for her job. Surprised, I checked my peephole to see if it was really her. She was usually running late. Who could blame her? Replenishing the rutabagas and arugula probably kept her mind off impending terror, too.

About 1:00 p.m., I took a break and turned my cell on. For once it was silent. I texted Emma: "Do u know if D's making any headway? Or is it 2 early to ask?"

From Emma: "2 early. Just got up. Worked late last nite. Let u know."

"Sorry. Just counting down the days."

"Gotcha. Ditto. Bye."

Jared and Dion were probably in class, so that was a no-go. I thought of texting Randy, but decided I'd better not nag. That would be neither prudent nor productive. Randy would let me know the second he knew anything. He was good about that. But it felt like there was a big, loud clock in my head, like the one in the gym, ticking down the minutes and days before the big game.

Might as well go down the street to the deli to grab lunch. I knew my cupboards were pretty damned bare. I clocked out, thrust my feet into loafers and grabbed my jean jacket, locked up and headed out the front door. Peeped into my mailbox: junk and bills, so I left them there. I'd figured if I waited until 1 p.m., I'd miss the lunch rush, but when I got there, it looked like everyone else had the same thought. The line was out the door. At least it was a pleasant fall day, not pissing down rain.

After 10 minutes, people started standing on tiptoes and craning their heads to see what the holdup was. I was almost to the door, but had been there for a while, so I asked the tall guy in front of me if he could see what was going on. With teeth clamped, he told me that some woman in a fur coat was ordering catering for a party of 40 for the weekend. We commiserated with groans. "And she couldn't have waited until *after* the lunch rush?" I humphed.

He answered my rhetorical question: "Right?" then looked at his watch and started tapping his foot. It was nice that I didn't have a boss ready to kick my butt when I got back to work for being five minutes late. Still, I should have phoned in my order. Right on cue, he cursed and said, "I *knew* I should have phoned in!"

"Yeah, me, too."

Finally, I got to the counter. "Hey, Paula. What's the fastest today? Reuben, grilled cheese, BLT?" A slitty gaze and silence. "*Dill pickle*?"

She finally laughed. "I'd go with the pickle at this rate! Honestly, some people have no sense of courtesy or just don't give a damn." Paula was Bud Kazinsky's granddaughter. The Kazinskys had been running the deli for generations. Her eyes were now shooting daggers at the woman in mink who'd ordered the catering, a smirk on her self-entitled face. "I mean, don't get me wrong, we can always use the business, but that woman's attitude sure got my goat."

"I hear ya. So maybe I'll just take one of the pre-made subs."

"Turkey and bacon or ham and cheese?"

"They got lettuce and tomato?"

"Always. And I can add some onion if you want."

"Turkey and bacon then, with the onion. Thanks, Paula."

By the time I got back, it was 1:36 p.m. I'd have to gobble at my desk after I logged back in. I thought of how well a beer would go with my sub, not to mention lessen the stress from my inner clock, but I resisted the temptation. My job was so mind-numbing at times, alcohol wouldn't help my concentration any.

Just in the time I was at the deli, my inbox had exploded again. *Don't these guys ever eat?* I fumed. I wondered if Mink Mama was one of their wives and was at this moment spoon-feeding her hubby lox and caviar.

I clocked back in, but snuck a peek at my cell, preparing to shut it off again.

The text pings reminded me of my nagging microwave, beep after unremitting beep. I checked Sheila's first. Her group text began with "URGENT!" so people wouldn't bat it away until later. She was notifying the whole W.A. gang that she wanted to hold an emergency meeting at her house, tentatively on Saturday night, Sunday at the latest. Looks like she'd heard back from Dion, at least enough to start organizing a meeting.

The pings volleyed back and forth as everyone checked in about the time, directions, their availability, etc.

I responded that I'd be available and was sure Kate would be, too, if it could be after work. Kate sometimes worked the weekends and I didn't know if this was one of them. Emma and Jared were in, whenever. She could always switch shifts with June. Dion texted the same.

Then Martha, Sally, and Ruby said they'd come. Ruby! *That's China Doll's name!* Went with the burgundy hair. (But my OCD still asked whether she was from Rockport or Revere.) *Never mind! It's just the jitters skittering your mind to into silly back alleys.*

Randy replied last. He'd be there if we could wait until after 6:30. He was filling in for a nurse on sick leave both weekend day shifts.

The time at last was settled for 7:30 p.m. at Sheila's, but she'd have to get back to us about which day. She warned us *not* to park in front of her house but scatter our cars around the neighborhood and rideshare where we could. "And NO HAIR PRODUCT!" she added. I would let Kate know when she got home. Her market was snarky about employees using cell phones at work. (Like management didn't.)

Well, there went my concentration.

As behind as I'd gotten in my data-entries, I decided that I'd really better not attack that backlog right now. I could well imagine the furious complaints as patients discovered I'd linked someone else's life- or genitally-threatening disease to the wrong person. I could also imagine the headlines and malpractice suits . . . and my pink slip.

So I focused instead on the *prima donnas'* precious papers, correcting their misspelled biochemical terms and making grammatical sense, when they made a hash of it, of what should have been a simple, clear statement instead of gobbledygook that resulted in utter confusion. But that's academics for you. At least it's less taxing than data entry.

By 5:30 p.m., my brain cells were playing bumper cars with recombinant DNA, glycoproteins, angiogenesis and their other play pals. I caught myself typing Myrna when it should have been mRNA, Fizzer for Pfizer, and Murk for Merck. I suspected my neurotransmitters of seditious commentary and gave it up for the day.

Even after the sub, I was starving again. Heebie-jeebies will do that to you. I decided it was time for an archeological excavation and opened my fridge. Not much there, except for a six-pack of beer, the penicillin-thriving end of a bread loaf, a green-tinged chunk of cheddar, and some leftover pizza. I went with the obvious choice, grabbed a Rolling Rock and extracted the Gino's pizza box, setting them on my kitchen table. As I reached for my landline to call Kate to see if she wanted to share in the feast, a chill—not one related to refrigeration—marched up my spine with great big crampons on.

There had been no *leftover pizza*, not at my place. Like the box I'd bestowed upon Kate after she and I returned from Gino's the night we found the receipt notes, on Monday, the night of the bar fight, I'd given her our box, too. She was the one earning minimum wage. Jared's pizza he'd brought to the bar for Emma was hoovered down to the last crust.

I backed away from the table, doused the kitchen light, scanned the parking lot. Nothing out of place that I could see. Couldn't see any new notes under the wipers of Kate's Honda or my Kia. I checked my *Joy of Cooking*; the notes were still there. I felt a bit miffed. Jeez, did everyone know I was a hopeless cook? Back in the living room, facing my desk, I picked up my landline to call Kate, then set it down carefully.

On autopilot, I'd turned off my surge protector, not noticing that it looked different and totally forgetting that I hadn't yet gotten out to buy a new one. I also hadn't reinstalled my old, de-bugged one. I had read somewhere that laptops weren't as vulnerable to power surges as desktop computers, so I'd put it off a day to make up work hours.

Grabbing my door keys, I dashed out over to Kate's, deadbolting my door behind me. Locking might be futile, but at least it would slow down whoever the SOBs were who kept waltzing into my apartment. Looked like Sheila wasn't the only one.

I pounded on Kate's front door. "Hang on a sec!" she called out. "I just got home." She twisted her deadbolt, opened the door and took a step back. "What? What *is* it?"

"In! In, *in!*" I demanded. I rushed through the gap, closed and re-bolted her door, and peeped out her peephole. Standing stock still, she looked at me like Bambi in the headlights.

"Kate, honey, did you bring back the leftover pizza to me from Monday night? Please God, say you did."

She gave me a hurt frown. "I thought you said you didn't want it."

"I didn't. Want it, I mean. So, *did* you? Bring it back?"

"No. I grabbed it before I left for work and ate it for breakfast this morning. We had an early staff meeting and I was warned not to be late."

I slumped into one her kitchen chairs. "So, just to be clear, you have no pizza in a Gino's box in your apartment?"

"Well, I have the box in the trash." She rummaged beneath her kitchen sink and brought it out. "Here."

I opened it. Empty except for leathery crusts and grease spots, neither fresh. My thoughts were racing like my heart.

"I could heat up some soup if you're hungry," she offered. "I've got tomato or alphabet." I chuckled weakly. Only Kate at her ripe old age would still be eating alphabet soup. But then only Kate liked to play scrabble with her soup.

"No, thanks, sweetie. As it happens, I have my own pizza to gnaw."

"The kind you thaw?" she asked.

"Pshaw!" I replied. "But no. It arrived on its own, burgled into my home, and into the fridge, ha, ha!" Okay, we were Dr. Seuss fans, too.

"Don't tell me. Gino's?"

"Yep."

"Full or partial?"

Made me think of dentures. I screwed my face up in confusion.

"You know," she clarified, "a whole pizza or just some slices, to make it seem like it was someone's leftovers."

I'd only peeped under the box lid a second so couldn't be sure. But that would be a damned good way to go if you were hoping to convince someone their memory was failing regarding the number of pizzas recently consumed and the status of leftovers.

"And," I went on, "it seems to have come with a side order of surge protector."

Kate screwed up her face now. "Eh? It's usually crusty rolls."

"And we didn't put the tampered surge bar back in the basement because we knew that Sheila's the one who planted it."

"True. Would she have planted a new one?"

I waggled my head. "I doubt it, now that we know what she was up to. And this looks nothing like the old one. Whoever's done this must think I'm a total airhead who'd never notice the switch." I noted her cocked eyebrow. "Eventually."

"So maybe we should relocate this one to the basement? If the new burglars tune in, they'll get their auditory nerves scrambled and blasted."

I considered Kate's suggestion. But what prompted them to put in their own bug now? I was finally convinced Sheila wasn't working with Rolf and his men. But she could also be bugged and tracked, with them following her every move and text, the same as I.

"Here's a thought, Kate: Could the new listeners have tapped into Sheila's home-made bug? 'Cause, if they did, when they got no signal, they'd have been tipped off that it had been removed, so they'd need to replace it ASAP. In which case, they'd have been in too much of a rush to care about matching it."

Kate nodded. "Something to have Dion check."

"Right." I stood. "Let's go check out that box."

After securing her premises, we cat-footed over to my place, eased ourselves in. First, the pizza box: slices, not whole. The gaslighting bastards. Next, I dragged the surge protector out from under the desk, but couldn't see how you could pry its tan casing apart. Pulling it out all the way, I saw that its cord didn't match and had an AC adapter thingy in the middle of its black, two-part cord, like the one that powered my laptop. I'd never seen one of those on a surge bar. Then I spied black electrical tape around the end going into the protector's power strip. Hidden under my old desk, the mis-matched cord would have gone unnoticed, without pulling it out. The adapter had been adapted, too, and sported its own light. I turned the assembly on; it lit up in two places.

I was pretty sure the set-up was way beyond Sheila's skills. With a finger across my lips, I took out a notepad and wrote, "Need to tell Dion."

Kate nodded. “And no texting or calling using Wi-Fi,” I printed. I was trying to remember if I’d texted that day through Wi-Fi or LTE. Assuming the bug’s technology was similar to the first, I really hoped I was not on Wi-Fi at the time, so, with luck, any calls or texts on my cell weren’t tapped into. I snatched my cell up and checked the settings.

Whew! Sometimes it paid to be a little scatterbrained. I’d never set it back to Wi-Fi after last night. It was still set to LTE.

“Let’s take this thing to the basement,” I wrote, unplugged the surge bar, and grabbed my keys again, along with my copy of the bicycle key.

Down in the basement with a flashlight, we left the new bug on the floor behind the dryer, as Dion had suggested. Kate pulled out a single Spock sock and laid it on top, her James Bond equivalent of leaving a spittle-coated hair across the door jamb to alert you to intruders.

“What a noble sacrifice!” I hugged her.

“His contribution to the enterprise. He would have insisted.”

“I’ll get you another pair if he gets beamed up,” I vowed.

I plugged the bug into a low outlet then threw some dryer balls and old tennies I’d brought with me into the dryer. We grinned, relishing the ensuing scene: henchmen cursing and ripping off headphones, shaking their heads violently, pounding on ears to stop their ringing. It would serve them right.

I was about to feed in a quarter (then retrieve it), then stopped myself. The tracker from my Kia was still inside, which was good. But thinking it over more, I felt that the cacophony would be worse than silence from my apartment, a definite give away that the new bug had been removed. So I pulled the tennies and dryer balls back out.

“What’s up with that?” Kate asked.

I made a “shtum” slash across my lips and motioned upstairs.

In the downstairs hall, when we were well out of earshot, I whispered, “It’s just a gut thing. Whoever left it still has a lot of time to replace it with something before . . .”

I gave her a raised-eyebrow stare, making sure she got it.

Kate did and nodded. “Silence is golden?”

“For now, I think. Plus, it might be a lot more *diverting* later.”

“And a lot more fun!”

I nodded back, gave her a thumbs up.

As we were walking up to our floor, Kate turned to me. "Something else is bugging *me* now. Did you happen to open your fridge last night after we came back?"

"You know, I *did,*" I said, remembering at last. "I ate a hunk of cheese, the part that wasn't green yet, and some stale Triscuits."

"So, you'd have noticed if the pizza box was there then, wouldn't you? I mean, we were dog-tired, but a Gino's box is pretty hard to miss."

"I damn well would have!"

"Okay, but weren't you home working all day?"

I groaned. "Not every minute. I went down the street to the deli to get something for lunch. I *really* have to do more grocery shopping."

"Well, but the deli's just at the end of the block. You couldn't have been gone that long."

"I was out over half an hour." I told her about the epic catering order.

"Bud and Mrs. Chang home?"

"Sure to be." *There* was a slam dunk for easy access. "But I really felt, we *both* did, I was insect-free at last." I rubbed my upper arms to take away the shivers. "It just keeps on getting worser and worser."

"Darkest hour before the dawn," Kate reminded me. "And right now, it's dawning on me that *neither* of us have eaten dinner."

"And it's time for *Jeopardy.*"

We both could do with the brain stimulation, not to mention the distraction.

"So, pizza?" I asked, raising my shoulders. But she made a face.

"I don't think so. We don't know where it's been. *Or what's in it.*"

"True." We shared a quiet moment mourning a wasted Gino's. "Well, there's still alphabet soup. I'll crank open a can and rummage up some crackers. You bring over the beer."

"Will do."

As we were opening our doors, she turned back. "Hey, I know! If we go out later, let's take the pizza along and if we see a really annoying yap-a-doodle or similar, toss him a slice and see if he keels over." (An inspired twist on mine canaries.)

We're both huge animal lovers, but there's a limit to everything. Spoiled, shrieking doodle dogs were ours.

"You got it!"

After soup and *Jeopardy*, we decided to stay in, so yap-a-doodles were safe for the time being. Both of us were too drained to face strangers and too afraid to leave the fort unguarded. I could hear the screech of Mrs. Chang's Chinese game shows from the floor beneath. Might be one reason Bud was so deaf (or chose to be). With the two of them, we might as well just leave the door wide open, a mat on the step with "Welcome Burglars!" Nevertheless, I was determined once again to have "the talk" with them in the morning, stressing that we'd already had two recent cases of intrusion. They weren't mean people, just old and forgetful. Surely, they'd be more vigilant.

Right. Like in a perfect world.

Kate went back to her place and I opted for an early night, earlier than those we'd lately been enjoying. *Not.*

But about 9:30 p.m., there was another flurry of texts. Sheila texted there was a hold-up with something so we'd have to have the "party" on Sunday, instead of tomorrow night. "Same time, same place." Another bubble popped up: "Same requirements," she added. (Same warnings.)

My inner lunar clock was ticking so loud now I could have mistaken it for my heartbeat, except it was slower. Like the ticking swing of a pendulum.

I hoped to hell we'd be able to organize our posse well and fast. But I had a suspicion the round-up could be more like herding cats, or in our case, keeping an unruly kennel focused and squirrel-free.

On the other hand, Kate and I both could use another fright-free day off and some time to organize our own lives. Stuff like grocery shopping came to mind. I'd make up a list to give her in the morning and give her some money. I figured we could *all* use a one-day free pass on fright. And Emma wouldn't have to juggle her shifts.

If I couldn't get my old surge protector to work again, when Kate got off work maybe I could head out to Job Lot and pick up a new one. That way, one of us would be here to watch out for creeps and stalkers.

Popularity is such a burden.

FORTY-THREE

SLEEPLESS IN SUSPENSE

Even though I'd turned in early, I didn't get much sleep. Every little sound in the building and outside, every headlight cruising the back street and the parking lot kept launching me wide awake, enforcing my tiptoeing around, peering out dark windows. So as it got light, I was a hollow-eyed zombie. But it was Saturday so I *should* have been able to turn over and go back to sleep, or try to.

Andy Android had other ideas, however. When I crawled in bed last night, I'd been too tired and stressed to remember to manually schedule my Do Not Disturb. Its default settings were still on, making it come back to life at an inhumane 7:00 a.m. I stabbed in a re-set, but finally deep into REM, I was shocked awake again by a barrage of pings, bloops, and tootles. *Oh, why don't you just throw in the* entire *woodwind section?* I growled. When I'd set up the all the fun, personalized notification tones, I'd thought they were hilarious.

Only a week to go before all hell broke loose. Scrolling tensely through the blue bubbles, I checked out Dion's first. And smiled. If I had to be wakened this damned early, at least his was worth it.

It was now 8:30 a.m. Might as well get my java perking. I'd need more of my brain functioning to digest the other texts. While waiting in my kitchen for Mr. Coffee to get a move on, there was a polite tap on my front door. It sounded like a Kate tap, and as I was about to peer through the peephole to be sure, I heard her raspy croak, "I smell coffee!"

"Come on in. I figured you'd be around. I'll get your mug. You sleep at all last night?"

"Nary a wink. Well, maybe one or two. You?"

"Same. And then I forgot to set my Do Not Disturb, so I was treated to the *1812 Overture* on my cell."

"No cannons, surely?" she asked. I laughed, knowing "Andy" would have been thrown right out the damned window if *those* had gone off.

"Thankfully, no. Just most of the brass and woodwind sections."

I handed Kate her mug of coffee, set the sugar bowl on the table and morosely eyed the dairy creamer. "I've really got to get some real cream. Which reminds me . . . Could I give you a list of groceries and some money so you could pick up some things at your market for me? I'm disinclined to leave, especially with you out on a Saturday. Or will that make you late for work?"

"Sure, no problem. I don't start until 9:30 today."

"Fantastic! *Thanks.*" I stirred sugar and powdered, pretend cream into my mug, then handed her the spoon.

"So, lots of texts and calls, I take it?" she asked.

"Texts, anyway. I'm just starting to go through them now. So far, I've only looked at Dion's, but you're gonna love it!" I slid my cell over and waited while she read. It was cryptic but said plenty. She looked up, a "Whoopee!" grin on her face.

I nodded. "Yeah. The ninja dude came through." I felt like I'd been holding my breath for days, like maybe since the new moon. But I was breathing just fine now.

Dion had more than come through. He'd hacked into Rolf's security system and was able to dismantle it anytime, on call.

I texted Dion back a thumbs-up emoji, then alluded to a new pest—the second surge-protector bug I'd found.

"U on Wi-Fi?" he shot back.

"Nope."

"Pest controlled?"

"Yep. Soon to be deafened."

I got back a LMAO emoji.

"Singer still in good tune?" I texted him, worrying about Patty.

"Yep. All good. Talk at ya later. Need some Zs."

"Looks like everything's going well and Patty's still safe and sound. Well, reasonably sound," I told Kate.

"Thank God!" Kate yawned, downed the rest of her coffee and put her mug in the sink. "Well, gotta go! The melons, they are a-callin'. Let me know what Sheila says, okay?"

"Sure thing. I may go back to bed for a bit, first."

She looked daggers at me. "Oh, go right ahead and gloat, why don't you?" and flounced out, as well as you can in a Spock bathrobe.

I raced to the door and caught her by Spock's dangling belt. "Wait! I nearly forgot. Here's my grocery list. And some cash."

Taking my envelope of $20s, she scanned down the list (it *was* a tad long), and slid slitty eyes back to me.

"Sorry, Katie! I was way overdue."

"Ya think?" She sighed and stuffed the list and my dough in Spock's pocket. "I'll have to add 'HRM's personal shopper' to my résumé."

I winced. From the landing's window, I'd also seen it had started to rain. "I'll make it up to you!" I called to her back, then locked my door.

From his laughing emoji, I knew Dion assumed I'd stuck with the original plan re the new bug. I felt bad for misleading him, but this wasn't the time and place to get into a discussion of why I'd switched tactics, if only slightly. I'd tell him about that and the planted pizza later.

Shuffling back to the kitchen, I drained the rest of my coffee and set my mug by Kate's in the sink. I had every intention of making good on my gloat, but now guilt forced me back to my texts.

Next up was Sheila's. For her, it was short and terse. Being careful. "Project going well. Making good time. Will know more tomorrow."

Talk about leaving you on tenterhooks!

But that sounded promising. I wondered if I should just pick up the phone and call her to get more info. Or drive over. My next jaw-shattering yawn decided me against it. She was probably zombie-eyed, too. I felt sure we all were.

The next texts were from Emma and Jared, and confirmed it. "Glad party 2morrow. Dead on feet 2day. No work Sun," she sent.

Jared typed, "Sun def better 4 me 2," followed by three zombi emojis—🧟 🧟 🧟. "Will party then."

Seems "party" was our preferred code word for "meeting" now, although I can't imagine any of us were in a festive mood.

Glancing at the remaining texts (most were from work, yep, even on a Saturday), I decided they could twiddle their thumbs a few hours, so churned back to bed.

At 5:30 p.m., I woke up starving and wondering if that planted pizza might actually be safe to eat. I know—a stupid risk, right? But I was ravenous.

So I padded into the kitchen, opened my fridge and pried open the box lid. I knew to look for signs of spoilage—you know, discoloration, mold, stink—and check for foreign objects like insects, hair (*eeeuuw*), even metal fragments.

I took a teensy, cautious taste of a bit of crust with only a smear of sauce. It didn't taste bitter, sour, or unusual or I would have spit it out and given up. I held it up to my face and took a deep sniff. Nothing unusual or pungent there either.

Just as I was about to drag it over to the microwave and possibly commit accidental poisoning, my landline rang. It was Sheila.

"Hi, buddy. I thought this number might be best since your Wi-Fi is . . . acting up." She was still being careful with her words, but switching to a landline at least *should* be less traceable, given the last two insectoid examples. Unless someone else had come up with a more multi-functional type of "ears." I turned my phone set over to inspect it. Looked factory pristine, but you never know.

She must have had the same worry. "I have so much to tell you!" she gushed, deceptively girly-girly, "but I'm getting a lot of static on my end. Is there somewhere close by you could call back from?"

The deli had a pay phone, one of the last, probably, in the state. It was in the back hall past the bathrooms. "Yeah. Give me twenty minutes?"

"Sure. You know the number, right?"

"Of course. Talk to you soon."

I rushed to my bedroom, threw off my pjs and yanked on my cleanest sweats and a red knit hat. As I grabbed my purse, making sure I had some phone change as well as Sheila's number, I remembered Kate wasn't back from work yet and I was about to leave our apartments unguarded. Shit. Well, my Kia in the lot should make stalkers think I was home, right? And this had to be super important, or Sheila wouldn't have called, right? Right? Unless this was a ruse or an ambush.

I shook that thought away once more. Why would she double-cross us? Sheila needed us, her posse, to rescue Patty, if not also to take Rolf down for good.

At the bottom of the stairs, I pounded on Bud's door and shouted, "Bud! Open up!" I heard soft, leather soles scuffing over the carpet to the door. "Please! It's me, Alice," I added.

He opened his door and peered out, smoothing his thinning, white hair and removing earbuds from both ears. "No need to shout, Alice. I can hear you."

I *knew it!* Not hearing aids after all. Pointedly, I eyeballed the earbuds he was cupping in his hand.

"Oh, these? Guess I'm busted." Bud pulled his Steelers bathrobe closed, but I'd already gotten a glimpse, beneath his grey T-shirt, of his Patriots boxers—his subtle comment on Brady's defection.

I laughed. "You certainly are!" *On* both *scores.*

"It's them damned Chinese soaps. Sound like knives and forks thrown at a window. Sends me right up the wall." I had to agree.

"Your secret's safe with me! But, look, I've got to make this quick: I have to go out for a bit, and I'm relying on *you* to stand guard for Kate and me and not let anyone in we don't know, okay? It's *super* important."

"Not even the pizza delivery guy?"

"That was you who let him in?"

"He said he'd get in trouble if it wasn't hot when you got it."

Ah *ha.* "Yeah, well, the guy wasn't what he seemed, Bud, but I'll have to tell you about that later. For now, just don't buzz *anyone* in who doesn't live here. Okay?"

He saluted. "Sure thing, Alice. I'll keep the plugs out so I can make sure Chang doesn't either."

I gave him a one-armed hug. "You're the best, Bud. Kate should be home soon from work. And when I get back, we'll have that talk."

He looked longingly at his earbuds and sighed. "Okay."

Couldn't really blame the guy, but we had to tighten up security in a big way and fast.

The deli was just getting into its after-work rush when I got there, so I put my order in for a meatball sub for dinner and went back to the pay phone in the back while I waited. Sheila answered on the second ring.

"Hi, Sheila. It's Alice."

"What phone are you calling from?"

"Deli's. At the end of my street. Phone's way at the back by the johns, so we're cool."

"Good." From her end, I heard voices going past and rubber-soled shoes squeaking, then her door closing firmly. "Thanks for doing this, Alice. I'm still at work, calling from my office. There's a lot of new stuff I wanted to tell you, given your work background, and I didn't want us to be overheard. I'll tell the others, but I wanted to tell you first."

"Okay."

Sheila had gotten Frank's results from her samples at last, confirming the virus was exactly the same as the one she'd found on bite victims. She went on, saying that he was working day and night on an antiviral. Looked like Dion wasn't the only one burning the midnight oil.

I was glad the pay phone was in the back, away from the clatter and customers of the deli, because then she talked about identifying viral markers, immunofluorescence techniques, serotype-specific monoclonal anti-dengue antibodies.

If I didn't wrestle with terms like these on a daily basis at my job, my eyes would have glazed over. As it was, I got a lot of it and felt excited and . . . maybe a little hopeful.

"Any update on a possible timeline for success?" I asked her.

"I'm not sure yet, but should know more tomorrow at our meeting. But I doubt an antiviral drug will be ready in time. However, what I think will be doable, in the time Frank has, is making a temporary antidote that would lessen or at least stall immune reactions to the virus and possibly even the effects of the lunar pull."

"Just 'possibly'?" I had to ask.

"Yes, but he sounded really hopeful."

Okay, so excited, yes, but I'd put hope on hold. "So, how's he going to get this to us, assuming it works?"

I could feel a drum roll coming from the excitement in her voice. "He hopes to be flying in with it in a few days. So keep your fingers crossed!"

"Believe me, they already are! Oh! Before I forget, I need to ask you something, Sheila."

"Go ahead."

"You didn't by any chance pay me a visit while I was out earlier today and leave me some leftover pizza, did you?"

"No. . . . But it's curious that you asked. Was it in a Gino's box by any chance?"

"Yes." I waited.

"Whole pie or slices? And where was it left? On your doormat?"

"Slices. And *in my fridge.* Found it yesterday evening."

"Friday evening," she mused. "And Kate hadn't left it for you?"

"That's what I wondered at first. On Monday, after the five of us left Gino's, Jared and I each had boxes of leftover pizza, and he had a whole one to take to Emma. I let Kate take my leftovers when we got home. I did ask her, though, thinking maybe she'd decided she didn't want it. But she said she'd eaten ours for breakfast yesterday morning before work."

"Shit." That was probably only the second time I'd heard Sheila cuss. "I got one, too. But on my doorstep on Friday. Just slices inside."

"Double shit."

At least Sheila's home was better fortified than mine, obviously. Or the pizza guy was being more subtle with her.

"Well, here's something else strange, Alice. You know those little, plastic table things they put in pizza boxes? Did yours have one? Because mine did. People normally toss them out after they open the box for the first time. They're just there to keep the box lid from settling on top of the pizza and adhering to the hot cheese."

"I always wondered what those were for. Could it be that leaving it in is just a personal quirk of whoever's left it?"

"Maybe. But why would someone break into your place to leave it?"

I gave it a beat. "Well . . . ahem."

"Oh. Yeah."

"I hope you can see that's why I thought maybe it was you who left the pizza. But, wait, you weren't even at Gino's Monday, so that doesn't make much sense, you know, that you'd leave me leftovers on Friday."

"I don't blame you thinking it was me. I would have, in your shoes."

Then I told her about the new surge protector bug that was planted.

"Damn! But that wasn't me either, Alice. Not this time," she added. "And anyway, I had to give back that thing that opens deadbolt locks. It was just on loan."

"You said your ex had gotten it for you, to help with Patty."

"Actually, he borrowed it from a hotel manager friend who owed him a favor. If guests croak with the deadbolt shot, it comes in handy. So, did you get rid of it?" she asked. "The bug?"

"In a manner of speaking. At least it's away from my Wi-Fi."

"Well, that's good, I suppose. . . . It's just," she paused, "I've always heard there are different types of bugs, ones that don't use Wi-Fi."

I'd heard that too. "Old tech, like in those James Bond films?"

"Yes. And I think they can be really small, hence the name. I just don't have a clue how they work."

"In the films, they were stuck to just about anything. Like that tracker that was stuck to my Kia." And Maxwell Smart's shoe phone. "Are you thinking what I'm thinking? About those black tripod things?"

"Yours was black, too? Aren't they usually white?" she asked.

"Most I've seen were. But I can't say for sure if Gino's uses them. Doubt it. They're pretty old-school and they don't deliver. Anyway, if they do use them, suckers'd get tossed pronto while the pizza's hot. And the one in my box seemed thicker, clunkier than, say, Dominos'."

"Mine, too. Then I think I *am* thinking the same—that we need to check those ASAP."

"Jeez, I was so famished I almost tried a bite, but decided to order a sub here instead. I don't suppose it *might* be all right? To eat?" I asked.

"I wouldn't try it, not without testing it first."

"No idea how to do that. But what a waste of great pizza."

"If you can bring it tomorrow, I have a test kit we can use. I may just use it myself tonight and see if it's harboring anything nasty."

"You don't mind being the guinea pig?"

"Like it's going to kill me, Alice?"

I sighed. "Oh." I kept forgetting about that—the immortality part.

"I know, Alice. We can still get plenty sick, though."

"Order's up, Al!" I heard hollered from the front counter.

"Gotta go, Sheila. I don't want to keep my meatball sub waiting. We'll talk more tomorrow, okay?"

"Yes. We will. Enjoy. But . . . be careful, Alice."

We were silent a few counts. "Right," I said, and hung up.

That last bit, about the pizza thingies, left me feeling shaken, not stirred. I wasn't sure how much enjoyment I'd be getting out of my sub now, but as long as I could keep it down, at least I'd get fed.

Just wish I were going back to my own "Cone of Silence" instead of Grand Central Station for Burglars.

FORTY-FOUR

DOOR DASH, NO WONTONS

As I was coming in our building's front door, Kate was staggering in the back with sacks of groceries. I ran over to her. "Here, let me help with that!"

She scowled. "Thought you'd never ask. Been hollering up the stairwell for like five minutes. Thought you were home. You *said* you wanted to stay and mind the fort. Otherwise, . . ."

"Yes, otherwise I could have gotten my own damned groceries."

"Gosh, you're bright, Alice."

"I'm sorry. Something completely unexpected came up and I didn't have any choice but go out."

Kate eyed my meatball sub in its paper bag meaningfully. "I can see that. Care to share?"

"Of *course* I'll share. It's why I ordered the extra-large. But it's not why I had to go out." I grabbed two of the bags and threw the sub in one. "Is that it?" I gestured to the two remaining bags on the floor.

"Yeah, that's it."

"Come on, I'll tell you upstairs. And keep the change if there's any."

Still grumpy, she picked them up, and tromped after me up the stairs.

"I got a new six-pack," I wheedled, sing-song.

"You'd better have!"

When we got to our landing, I unlocked my door and swivelled my head around my living room for a quick reconnoiter. "So far, so good. Which are mine?" I asked, pointing to the bags. She shoved over three.

"Not all of them? I mean, the way you sounded . . ."

"Hey, I have to eat, too."

"You do, and I'll join you." I shoved the perishables inside my fridge, locked up again, and stuck the sub into her bag.

Her head was cocked in puzzlement. I put a finger across my lips, and motioned for her to unlock her place and go in. I followed.

I set her bag down on her table. "Oh. Be right back. Beer run!"

Back in Kate's place, after nabbing the six-pack and relocking my place (fat lot of good that would do, apparently), we settled down at her kitchen table. She plopped paper napkins, two paper plates and a knife next to the sub. "Shall I cut or you?"

"You go ahead, Kate. You earned the honor." I still watched to see how even the division would be. Mostly in the middle. She put my "half" on my plate, and started in on hers.

"Beer?" She nodded, mouth full. I opened one and slid it over. "Better?"

"Yes, thanks. Sorry, Al, it's been a bitch of a day, but that's nothing new. So, what's your update?"

I took a bite of sub and swallowed some Rolling Rock. Much better, if only temporary.

I brought her up-to-date with Sheila's call, requiring me to leave our "fort" unguarded, and all that our conversation revealed.

Kate gulped down a big bite. "We *really* have to have that conversation with Bud and Mrs. Chang."

"I told him that. Did you know his hearing aids are actually earbuds?"

"No! Really?" She almost choked on a meatball. I motioned for her to drink her beer. Recovered, she said, "Well, that makes sense, with the constant racket from Mrs. Chang's TV. Can't much blame him. After we're finished with din-din, why don't we go down and have that chat with the two of them?"

I was about to agree, then put down my sub and stared at my plate.

"What? Someone sneak in an anchovy or something?" she asked.

I looked off. "No. Sub's fine. But today, when I went down to ask Bud not let anybody in we didn't know, Mrs. C's was silent."

"Like completely silent?" I nodded. "But it's never silent, well, not until she knocks off to bed at 9:00 o'clock or so."

"I know."

Kate put her sub down. "We need to do a wellness visit, like *right now.*"

"We haven't finished our subs," I pointed out. "Or beers." I was not looking forward to this.

"Microwaved meatball subs and stale beer aren't the worst things to happen. Come on!"

As we were racing out the door, I called back to Kate, "Grab your phone. Keys, too!"

When we got to the bottom, Mrs. Chang's door was standing wide open, no sound coming from inside. I sucked in my lips and shot a worried glance at Kate. I mean, Mrs. C could be a pain sometimes, with her loud Chinese programs and loud Chinese family, when they visited. And letting in all and sundry from sheer laziness.

Nah, I should cut her some slack. I knew her hips were shot and killing her, and she was terrified of hospitals, having seen the worst in her youth in her poor backwater back in China. But she'd brought us egg rolls and pot stickers every Chinese New Year and had happily dog sat Kate's beloved Reggie, before he went over the rainbow. He adored her wontons. And, anyhow . . .

As we were about to tiptoe in, Bud came out!

"What are you doing in Mrs. Chang's, Bud?" We burst inside. She was bound and gagged, trussed up expertly to her Barcalounger, eyes wide in terror and thrashing her hardest. He had a rope end in his hand.

"More importantly, Bud, what were you doing *to* Mrs. Chang?" Kate asked, dialing 911 furiously.

"Untying her," he said. "And I've already called the medics. Should be here any moment." He calmly continued unravelling her trusses, laconic as usual. Kate ended her emergency call.

"I know you're a man of few words, Bud, but jeez, you wanna catch us up?" He held up a palm. One thing at a time. Priorities.

When she was freed at last, he started massaging Mrs. C's poor bruised arms and hands, getting her circulation flowing again. She was sobbing. He wrapped her up in a blanket. "Ask her yourself."

I knelt down. "Mrs. Chang, who did this to you?"

She shook her head. "Not know him. Thought it was Yu."

"Me? Why me, Mrs. Chang?"

"Not you, *Yu*. Nephew, my Louie. He always come see me Sundays, bring Chinese treats. I make him wontons."

The fēn dropped. I turned to Bud and explained, "Louie is her nephew's Americanized name, but it's Yu—'Y-U'—in Chinese."

"Oh! I wondered what she was going on about. Before I came in, she'd been shouting 'you,' or it could have been 'not you!' "

"Why did you think to check on her, Bud?"

"Well, since you made me take out my earbuds, I realized for once I couldn't hear her TV, so I thought I'd better see if she was alright. With us getting on in years and all. As I was making myself presentable, I heard her shouting at someone inside her place, only it was mostly in Chinese. Thought maybe it was a family argument, so backed off."

"Yes, he talk Chinese, this man. He stranger, not Yu," she piped up.

Bud went on. "After it sounded like her visitor left, I went over and found her—just like you saw."

"So, you never got a look at the guy?" I turned to him.

"No. Sorry, Alice."

"But you didn't hear the buzzer, either?"

"I did, but I was in my—" he nudged his head in his apartment's direction, blushing. "The 'you know.' "

Aww. Chivalry was alive and well among the old folks.

"In toilet," Mrs. C clarified, recovering her composure.

"Um, yes. In there. By the time I was finished, she'd already buzzed him in."

We heard the wail of sirens, tires screeching, then her buzzer went. "Paramedics! For Apartment One?" Chang's buzzer number was stickered over with the Chinese symbol so you couldn't match it with the mailbox.

We buzzed them in. Police followed. As they were strapping Mrs. C to the gurney, I asked her, "Do you remember what the guy looked like?"

She shrugged. "Chinese." I almost snorted, but decided I'd better *not* go there. "Also long hair. Very long."

What was it with Asian dudes and long hair? Too many kung fu movies?

"Anything else? Clothes?"

"Yes. He clothed." Well, *that* was a relief. Not to mention an image I'd never unsee: a bare-assed, long-haired Asian burglar into bondage.

She poked me in the ribs. "Got you going!" Then she wheezed a laugh. "He wearing black."

"All over?"

"What I can see." Then she winked. Mrs. Chang actually winked!

The EMTs and cops whisked her away. We goggled at each other, then busted up. "Mrs. *Chang?!* Bud, maybe you been missing out!"

FORTY-FIVE

TALKIN' THE TALK

Bud shook his head, but he was laughing. As the ambulance and cop cars' taillights disappeared, he shut the building's front door, then Mrs. Chang's, making sure it was locked, then walked toward his own.

Kate spoke up, "It's nice you're looking after her stuff, but if she needs something from the hospital, how are you going to get in, Bud?"

He shrugged. "Gotta spare key. She gave it to me a while back."

"Oh, you do, do you?" Kate winked at me.

Bud turned red. "No! It's not like that!"

"You sure you really *were* missing out?" I threw in.

He sighed. "I'm sure. She's not my type. But there've been a lot of odd people coming and going lately, well, over the last year or so, really. And we both thought it might be safer if we exchanged keys, in case of . . . I don't know. You see all sorts on the news."

"About that . . . " I began. "We need to talk. Can we go inside?"

His eyebrows went up. "My place? It's kind of a mess."

"Don't worry. Mine is too."

"Okay. Just don't pull on your white gloves!"

We trooped in and I shut and bolted his door. His eyebrows rose again at that. "This looks serious, Alice."

"It is. It's time we had that chat I mentioned earlier."

He tossed some newspapers and a football scoresheet off a sagging, leather sofa and motioned for us to sit.

We filled him in on the intrusions and UFVs in the lot.

He was a good listener. Never interrupted, until we got to the bugs and the tracker on my Kia. His Barcalounger shot upright. "In your apartment, Alice? Right above me?"

I nodded grimly.

"Not one but *two* of the suckers? Plus that thing they'd stuck to your car?"

I nodded again.

"Well, I'm gonna put a stop to that!" Bud slammed his fist on his armchair, dislodging a blue, diamond-shaped pill from the crease. He caught it like an outfielder as it shot up. "Wondered where the damned thing went to," he muttered, red-faced. He stuffed it in a robe pocket, but not before we'd clearly seen the incised "V" on its side.

Kate snorted. I studied the photos on his desk.

"You *positive* safety's the only reason you and Mrs. Chang exchanged keys?" Kate couldn't resist poking that bear.

"I told you no! I mean, yes, it was the only reason."

Lips pooched out, head tilted, Kate nodded slowly.

"Don't get me wrong," he said. "Penelope's okay."

"*Penelope*?"

"Sure, why not?" (*Welcome to America!*) "Penelope Jane. But with her, I could never get past the stink of that stuff she cooks."

"You don't like Chinese food?!"

"Can't stand it. Had enough gook food while I was in Korea to last me a lifetime."

"You shouldn't say 'gook,' Bud. And Korean isn't really the same," I said.

"Close enough!" We waited.

"Sorry. *Asian* food. But regarding, *you* know . . ." Another head nudge, toward the contents of his pocket. "Hey, I'm a regular guy, and I'm not dead yet."

"So," I ahemed, moving on, "do you see why it's super crucial that we all stay vigilant and not just let anybody in because we're too lazy to see who it is first?"

"All the years I've been living here there hasn't been any problem," he grumbled.

"Until there was, Bud."

"Girls, what in Sam Hill is going on?" he demanded.

We couldn't exactly tell him about the werewolf thing, so I said I hadn't a clue. "But my last boyfriend and I didn't part on exactly the friendliest of terms."

Bud growled, "That idiot was a loser. You're well rid of him."

"*Thank* you, Bud. But maybe he's angrier than I knew, or jealous? Or both? You know how some exes can be, if you believe the news."

"Well, he or whoever the hell it is, won't get past me!" Kate and I looked at him under our eyebrows. "Anymore," he finished.

Kate sat forward. "When Penelope comes home—or do you call her Penny?—we need to tell her, too."

"She prefers Penelope, actually. Says Penny Jane Chang sounds too much like tumbling silverware."

We all guffawed. "It does!" I was beginning to really like Mrs. C.

"So you'll go over it with her, when she's back?" I pressed.

"Sure. But with them gimpy hips of hers, it's hard for her to get up and down all the time. 'S why she just pokes the thing with her cane."

"But it's *got* to stop. I'm sure she'll agree after this."

"You're right, there. She was pretty cut up about it. Can't blame her."

He rubbed his greying stubble. "You know, buddy of mine is kind of a homemade genius, real good at rigging up stuff to make life easier. Done a lot of clever stuff for his late wife, who was in a wheelchair, even specialized remote controls. Maybe I can get him to make up something like that for Penelope, so she don't have to hit the buzzer physically. Maybe put in a little camera so's she can see who's there first."

"That's a terrific idea! When can you reach him?"

"Tonight probably. Saturday's the Elks' bingo and potluck night."

That reminded me. "Hold that thought!"

I raced upstairs to my place, let myself in and ran to the kitchen. Pulled the mystery pizza box out and lifted up the black plastic thing. And was very, very glad I'd put the box back in the fridge, what with its dense, soundproof casing. Because when I turned the plastic gizmo upside down, there was indeed a pestilent Klingon.

I looked around, wondering where to put it, spied my crockpot, then oh so gingerly settled the Klingon inside and banged the glass lid on.

Take that, you assholes!

Back in Bud's living room, I handed him the crockpot. "Lift the lid up and tell me what you think." I put my finger across my lips. He lifted the lid. "Just a dish I thought you might like to take to your potluck."

"Mmmm *hmmh*. Somebody went to a lot of trouble!" Putting on his readers, he examined the bug. "Pretty fancy recipe, I'd say. Thanks! I'll just take this to the kitchen." I heard his oven door open and close. When he returned, we grinned at each other and high-fived.

He plonked back down on his chair. "That should take care of the little bugger, for now anyway. I'll show it to Jimmy tonight. He's the one who had the disabled wife. We served in Korea together. Used to see stuff like this over there."

Bud might have been pushing 90, but his mind was sharp as a tack.

"Can you get back to me about it tomorrow some time?"

"Don't see why not. Jimmy'll know right away how it works. He'll give me a full report."

I sat back against his sofa. "So, hopefully, our plans should help keep intruders from our door."

Kate sat forward. "The front door, maybe, but what about the back door?" Its keypad had no buzzer, because strangers came in the front.

I slumped. "You're right. Not to mention our apartment doors."

Bud frowned, looking at Kate. "*Both* your apartment doors?"

"I don't think mine got compromised, but I kept worrying. I never got on with Al's ex," Kate fabricated. "He always had it in for me, jealous of our friendship, Alice's and mine. And both our cars got tagged."

Bud squinted at me. "Seems like going to a lot of trouble, over-and-above, if you ask me. You forget to give him back the ring, Alice?"

I laughed out loud. "What ring? He was way too cheap for that!"

"True to form," he commented. "Looks like someone's desperate to get something or find something out."

All I could safely say was, "Yeah, and it's driving us crazy."

I could see he was still puzzled about something. "But why would someone attack poor Penelope? Your ex have connections with an Asian gang or something?"

That had been bothering me, too: why Mrs. Chang? I shook my head. "Not as far as I knew. He was too stodgy. But ya never know."

"Like maybe they thought you had something that belonged to them that the ex left behind but they mixed up the apartment numbers?"

I scrunched my face—the picture of innocence. "Doug left his ratty bathrobe and some boxers behind. Oh, and a lot of dental floss."

"Don't forget the CDs," Kate added, turning to me. "They're mostly classic jazz," she said to Bud.

Now his face scrunched. "There some kind a black market for those things? I mean, what do I know?"

“Doubt it,” I answered. “These aren’t all that collectible, too mass-produced.”

“Well, it’s gotta be *something* to go to all that trouble.”

I agreed. Thinking of Rolf’s missing pendant, it did look like a foiled search to me now. But Rolf’s goons had never been uncertain about where I lived before. I shivered in remembrance. So why mug Mrs. C?

Aha! Maybe they’d noticed the bugs had been moved, didn’t know where to, and wondered if the pendant was hidden in the same place. Then, figuring my little old lady neighbor downstairs might know or have overheard something (though how *that* would have happened, I don’t know), roughed her up. Maybe they even thought the pendant was hidden with her. Hey, *we’d* thought about hiding the bugs there.

Interesting that the goon they sent for Mrs. C was Chinese. How would they know her race? Would the bugs’ range go that far—downstairs—and pick up her soaps? Were they listening in now to her phone calls with her family like they were listening in to mine?

Oh, duh. I did a mental head slap.

Mrs. C was their usual entry point and anyone would have noticed the Chinese characters for her apartment number next to her buzzer, even if they weren’t deafened by the soaps.

And I recalled that one of Rolf’s heavies searching the bar was Asian.

“Maybe it really was a mix-up in apartment numbers, like you said, Bud,” Kate said. Good deflection. *Thanks, Katie.*

Bud sighed. “Maybe. What a world. Just hope Penelope’s okay.”

“Me, too.”

“You poor girls. Lemme have a think about the back door situation. You say you seen some, whadya call ’em—UFVs—in back?”

“Couple of times, maybe more.”

He ran a liver-spotted hand through what was left of his hair. “Well, I’m taking Queenie out tonight, and I’ll take a gander.” It was how he referred to his 1984 Lincoln Town Car. She was his pride and joy, white-walled, gold, and in show-room condition. “Shame we have to share our lot with the other buildings. We could narrow it down easier if it was just for our four apartments.”

“I’m pretty sure I know everyone’s vehicles now, Bud,” I said.

“Residents, maybe, unless they trade up, but what about visitors?”

"Visitors do seem to present a problem," Kate agreed.

Except for the handicapped spots for each building, two per, there were only six visitor spaces and they were next to the lighted street behind the lot. The rest were assigned by apartment number. But that didn't keep someone from poaching a closer resident spot if it were vacant.

Queenie and Mrs. C's ancient Ford had pride of place next to the building in the handicapped spots. Bud was perfectly hale but used the war wounds card—veteran privileges. Kept a cane in the front seat.

"Well, anyhow, let us know what you find out. And thanks again, Bud." I walked to his door, peeped out and gave a thumbs up.

"Katie, we have subs to nuke and beer to finish."

FORTY-SIX

SERMON ON THE COUNT

Dee-eee-eee-eet! Dee-eee-eee-eet! Dee-eee-eee-eet!

Damn it! I'd forgotten to turn my stupid alarm off. Groaning, I whapped the snooze button and rolled over and stuffed my head under my pillow. That should give me twenty minutes of peace.

Then I heard texts pinging on my cell. I grabbed it and stabbed the Do Not Disturb on. I'd forgotten to do that, too. Then I heard something slither under my front door.

"Jesus Christ! It's freakin' Sunday morning, folks! Leave me alone!"

A few minutes later, I heard a timid tap on my door. Guess someone heard my complaint. If so, they were persistent.

I gave up, threw back the covers, threw on my robe and shuffled over to the door.

"It's me, Al."

"I can see that, Kate. Do you know what time it is?"

"Sorry." She looked around then whispered. "Can I come in?"

"Might as well." I opened my door. "Come on in. No sense in waking everyone else."

Inside, she said, "It's just that I thought maybe you'd like to go to the late mass with me." She was already dressed.

I gave her a stare. "For this you woke me up?" I almost never went to church, especially now. I mean, how would I word my confession?

"Remember how you said you wanted to hook up with Connie at mass last Sunday?"

"Shit. That's right, I did. But we never made it."

"Well, I was thinking, that since this is the last Sunday before . . . you know." Yeah, I knew: six measly days to go. "Maybe we should go," she went on. "It might do us good, in case things go very wrong."

She patted my arm. I locked my door.

I hung my head. "I suppose you're right. Sorry I snapped. I'm just so dead tired and jittery, the closer I get to the full moon."

"I can only imagine, Alice. But maybe you also could catch up with Connie, like you wanted."

"Two birds, one stone?"

She winked. "Or even two birds, *two* stones. I've got a couple of joints I can bring, little girl," she drawled, in gangster *sotto voce*. "Think of it as after-church communion."

Kate was always good at lightening up a tense situation.

"I'm not going to confession, though!"

Kate nodded. "I'm with you on that!"

I groaned again. "What time is mass?"

"Eleven."

I glanced at my kitchen clock and went into overdrive. It was 10:15 and St. Peevy (St. Pius V) was at least 20 minutes away.

St. Peevy's was an old-fashioned, rather stern appearing, red-brick landmark near Flax Pond in Lynn. Homey area, busy church, busy street. The lot filled up if you were late. "Start the coffee, okay?"

Kate gave me a salute, then turned back. "Oh, this was under your door." She held up a hand-written note. I froze. "It's just from Bud about Mrs. C. Nothing bad. You can read it in the car."

"Right you are, Watson!" I dashed into the bathroom.

Kate and I crept into St. Peevy's only 13 minutes late, genuflected, then scooted into an empty pew toward the back on the left. Sheila was up front on the right. Only a few pews ahead of us, I spotted Connie's cloud of white hair. Guess she wasn't anxious to partake in communion or confession either; like us, she was positioned to make a quick, guilty exit.

Someone's perfume made me sneeze, and she looked back, then smiled at me in surprise. Gave me a tiddling finger wave and gestured at me and then herself, mouthing, "After service?" I nodded.

I don't remember much of the service, I was too busy going over everything we knew about Rolf and his mansion, as well as Sheila and her daughter, and what were our actual odds at taking him down. Kate put a hand on my jiggling knee. Like Sheila's pamphlet, the father's sermon could have been at least a partial cut-and-paste from the AA's 12 steps, leaning heavily on turning our wills and our lives over to the care of God and He'd make it all better.

Maybe the priest was running out of ideas or running late writing this week's sermon. I wondered if Sheila had loaned her pamphlet to him. She was staring at the ceiling, *not* smiling.

When the service was over, I introduced Connie to Kate, then the three of us made a beeline for the door. We looked back for Sheila. She was paying her respects in the benediction line at the door. She looked grimly patient, but smiled at the priest as he grasped her hand. Keeping up appearances, obviously. And covering her bases. Weren't we all?

"Should we wait for her, do ye think?" Connie whispered to us.

"Apparently not. She just high-tailed it to her car," I said, watching I BITE pull quickly into the street. Wonder what tale she told the parish about her plate.

"Well, herself has other fish to fry, it seems," Connie remarked. "Now then, I don't know about you girls, but I'm perishin' for a pint."

"Connie, you shock me!" I said, smirking.

"Well, seein' as how I've tithed, I'm believe I'm due for a tipple."

Kate laughed. "Where to?"

"Tony's is my usual now. It's close by. Used to be the Porthole until that bitin' bastard started showin' up. If any nosy parkers ask where I'm off to after church, I tell 'em I'm off to commune with St. Anthony."

"Lead the way, then!" Kate said.

We followed Connie's teal Saturn to Tony's, a sports bar institution since the 70s, dark and rowdy inside, if there was a game on. And Sundays, there usually was. Good place to convene and not be overheard.

Kate seized one of the corner high-tops for us next to the back wall. Connie and I came back with our brews, Harpoons for Kate and me, and a Switchback for Connie.

"Thought you'd be having a Guiness, Connie."

"Ah, no. 'Tis not the same as back home. Was thinkin' of tryin' a Devil's Purse, but I thought that might just be temptin' the Fella Downstairs." She crossed herself and lifted her Switchback. "I suppose ye might say this here is a bit of wishful thinkin', but it's quite tasty, all the same."

After a long swallow, Connie leaned forward and whispered to me, "So, is this one here, yer Katie, comin' to the meetin' tonight, too?"

"Yes. She knows everything and is unbudgeable in keeping secrets."

Connie smiled at Kate and turned back. "She one of us, is she?"

"No. Just a very good friend. My lifeline, you might say."

"Good on ye!" Connie beamed at Kate. "'Tis grand to have true friends. Cheers!" She turned back to me. "So then, Alice, what have ye learnt since I last saw ye?"

"Well, you'll hear most of it tonight at the meeting. Sheila did say she'll give us an up-to-the-minute update."

"Ah, go on! Give ol' Connie the juicy details, love."

So I got her up to speed with the bugs and break-ins, including Mrs. C. She tutted. "And how's that lady doing, yer Mrs. Chang?"

"Oh, jeez! I'll tell you in a second." I'd completely forgotten Bud's note in our hurry to get to the church. I rummaged frantically through my purse. "Do you remember where I put Bud's note, Kate?"

Kate rolled her eyes over to Connie. "It's in your right pocket, Al."

Laughing, I gestured to Kate: "My handler."

"And a good thing it is, too," said Connie.

Unfolding his note, I read down quickly. "She's gonna be okay! Just a little banged-up and bruised. Should be home in a day or so."

"Well that's grand. But the poor woman. Honestly!"

"He also confirms that thing from the mystery pizza box was another bug, military-grade, according to his war buddy, Jimmy."

"Dear me! That's makes three now, does it? Plus the whatchamacallit stuck to yer car?" I nodded. "My, sucks to be popular these days!"

"Yep. So what about you, Connie? Have you heard anything new?"

She sighed. "No, as it happens, and I'm surprised. Several of the girls in our group go to the bingo and potluck at the Elks'. We usually have a gab after, but no one's reported any new action. Well, not like yours."

She smiled into her beer.

"Our neighbor downstairs, Bud Kazinsky, goes to those," I told her.

"He went last night, in fact," Kate added. "After he helped Mrs. C."

"Ah, now there's a handsome man." *Bud??* "Don't reckon I'd kick *him* outa bed." Kate and I banked shocked eyeballs off of each other.

"But it's strange like, with no new developments here at all. 'Tis like the world is holdin' its breath."

I couldn't disagree.

"But there have been *some* new developments," I said. I told her about the techie work that Dion was helping us with and Frank's work on the virus.

"I remember Frank, Sheila's ex, but I don't recall this Dion chap at all," she mused. "I don't suppose he's Catholic?"

I smirked. "Wouldn't think so. And if you'd ever met him, you'd certainly recall him!" I gave her a description.

"Sounds like just the fella we need!" She raised her pint and we tapped ours to it. "Lookin' forward to meetin' this—ninja, did ye say?"

We nodded.

She scooched her stool closer. "But here, now. This virus work you say Frank's doin'—that sounds promisin', doesn't it?"

"It does, but . . . well, don't get your hopes up for any time soon, Connie."

"I see. So not by Saturday, then." She looked crestfallen. "What was I thinkin'? How could it be, with the posts the way they are."

"Actually, Sheila said he's flying in soon with something he's cooked up that might help. But it's unlikely to be an antiviral drug, at this point."

"I suppose those do take time to concoct. Well, we'll just have to leave it in the hands of the Man Upstairs, then. But, sure, I'll be tellin' Him to get a move on!"

Kate belched. "Excuse me!"

Connie chuckled and patted her on the back. "Better out than in!"

We'd been sitting in Tony's for several rounds and the football fans were starting to pour in, grabbing the best stools before the game.

Meaghan, one of the bartenders, had started her shift and came over. "I always know it's Sunday if Connie's here. Good to see you, Connie, as always!"

"Same here, love. You know I'm devoted to yer man, St. Anthony. And 'tis always best to be seen than viewed."

Meaghan laughed. "Anything else for you ladies?"

We shook our heads and settled up. Outside, as we tottered to our cars, I asked Connie, "You okay to drive?"

"Oh, I'm grand, love. I only live a short way away, and my nephew, Timothy, is on the force. He and the boys look after me." She yawned. "I'll be glad for a nap before the meetin'. See you later!"

We waved her off, walked down the street and climbed in my Kia.

"Kate, we gotta beat it home and sober up!"

Those three pints were going to my head, and Kate was looking mighty sleepy.

"Katie, love, you gotta stay awake and make sure I don't get a ticket. I feel well Harpooned." Good thing we never smoked those joints.

I lowered my passenger window, letting in a brisk breeze to wash over us.

She nodded owlishly, scooched down and pulled her coat tight.

FORTY-SEVEN

CAN YOU HEAR ME NOW?

When we got in, we'd sobered up and were met at the back door by Bud. "Aww, Bud, you didn't have to wait up for us!"

"Was wondering when you two'd be back."

"We just came from church." He looked at his watch, an eyebrow raised. "Well, and a session afterwards. We met up with Connie, an Irish lady I think you know. Goes to the Elks, like you."

He smiled. "Now *there's* a fine woman, and a good cook. She was there last night but she was huddling with some women last night, so I couldn't get a word in, and I missed out on her cock-a-leekie."

"Her *what*?"

"It's a traditional Scottish soup," Kate translated.

"Oh. But I thought she was Irish."

"She is, but she puts her own spin on it. Personally, I just think she likes making it because of the name."

I was beginning to think that blue pill would see use soon.

He closed the door firmly behind us. "You get my note?"

"Yes, thanks. I'm glad Penelope's okay. And thanks for having your friend check out my 'potluck' offering." Bud picked up on my speaking in code and followed suit.

"You're welcome, Alice. It was quite an impressive recipe." *I'll bet.* "I'll bring your crockpot to you in a bit."

"I can just wait for it down here. Save you the steps."

"No, no. It's no problem. I'll bring it up." He stuck his head out the back door and grunted. "Got something else for you. I'll be up in a tick."

Five minutes later, as Kate and I were sitting in my kitchen with beers, we heard a tap on my door. I looked through my peephole to make sure it was Bud.

He came in holding my crockpot and we trooped to the kitchen. "Can I get you a beer, Bud?"

"Won't say no." He set the crockpot down and pulled up a chair.

I lifted the lid. "Any leftovers?" Kate asked.

I smirked at her. "Nope."

"Jimmy kinda cleaned up. Did you want any back?" Bud asked.

"No. That's fine."

"Probably for the best," Kate agreed.

I handed him a cold one from the fridge. "What was the other thing you said you had for me?"

He took a swig, got up and motioned me over to the sink, as if we were doing dishes together. His head lowered toward the faucet, he murmured, "See that van out there?"

I'd noticed he kept peeping up at the lot, so I took a look. There was a maroon van with some business's logo on its side parked on the edge of the lot, near the street.

"I think that's one of your UFVs, Alice. You're not having any plumbing work done here, are you?"

I'd certainly never seen it before. "No. Is that what it is, a plumber's van?" I asked quietly.

"So it says. But I started seeing it, mostly at night, not when you'd think any normal plumber would be on the job."

"Could it be something ongoing in one of the other apartments next to us?" Kate asked, voice low. "Or a new tenant, and that's his company vehicle?"

He shook his head. "Don't think so. I've been asking around."

I stood. "Why don't we take our beers into the living room?" I suggested at a normal volume.

"Good idea, Al!" Kate picked up hers and walked toward the kitchen door, pretending to head off. Bud jerked his head at the light switch. I switched it off and we all stood in the dark, crouched and watching.

"See? There's a light on in the van and the motor's running. Was that way when I looked out when you two came back," he said softly.

"And there are two guys in the front seat," Kate whispered.

I squinted my eyes. "Isn't that a headset one of them's wearing?"

Bud nodded. "And you see that fancy antenna in the back? That's not something any normal plumber would need."

Shit. If they were still here and listening in, then there must be a new bug planted somewhere. Well, at least I knew where one of them was. I beckoned them to the living room, rooted through my purse for a quarter. Grabbed the tennies and dryer balls from the bedroom, along with the bike key. “Sorry, guys! I’ll be right back. Left something in the dryer.”

Kate grinned evilly at me and turned on the TV. “We’ll be watching the show while you’re gone.”

As I dashed back in, five minutes later, I was just in time to catch the last act. The van was peeling away, burning rubber. We could hear expletives hollered all the way across the lot.

Kate and Bud had tears in their eyes, cough-laughing and pounding each other on the back. “Funniest goddamned thing you’ve ever seen!” Bud wheezed. “Jesus!”

Kate handed him his beer and he took a swallow. “You should have seen it, Alice!” she hooted. “I told Bud what you were up to. When the dryer started up, they both jumped about three feet. The guy with the headphones hit his head on the roof. We could *hear the bang* all the way across the lot through the driver’s open window! Then Mr. Ears yanked off his headphones and dashed to the back. Through their back, side window, it looked like some kind of light show, all these panels of colored lights flashing erratically then going dark.”

Wiping her eyes, Kate shook her head and took a deep swallow.

“Yeah, and the driver musta been smoking one of them marijuana cigarettes,” Bud said, “hence the open window. Looked like he dropped it and set his lap on fire. He was flailing his arms and hopping up and down in his seat, batting it out, and cussing like a sailor! Man, I gotta tell Jimmy about this!”

I lifted my Rolling Rock and took a long, satisfied swig. “Well, that was certainly worth the price of admission. A quarter, anyhow.”

“You got it back, right? The quarter?” Kate asked.

“’Course I did.”

Bud and Kate toasted me. “Atta girl!”

FORTY-EIGHT

SUMMIT MEETING

On our way that evening to Sheila's house in Lynn, I got a ping from Randy. "U on UR way?"

"Yep. U update S on D?"

A thumbs up emoji was sent back. Great. Now Sheila was up to speed with Dion's discoveries at Rolf's.

"B there soon," I texted.

"Meet me @ St PV B4, OK? You can ride with me."

"OK." A black Bronco would be less noticeable than my red Kia.

Sheila's street was dark and quiet when we arrived. The moon was just past the first quarter. Randy parked far down the block on the other side, then we walked back, passing Jared's banger and Connie's Saturn. Didn't see Emma's car; she and Dion probably rideshared with Jared. I didn't remember the other ladies' cars, but there were several late-model SUVs along the street, not parked in driveways, and an old brown Saab with some Wiccan stickers on the rear window: a Tree of Life surrounded by two crescent moons; another that said, "Don't Preach to Me and I Won't Put a Spell on You!"; and a third, with a witch riding a broom and "I'm Sailin' in Salem!"

Kate nudged me and whispered, "That's got to be Sally's."

I snorted. "Ya think?" I whispered back.

Sheila met us at the door. "Come on in. You can hang your coats on the hall tree."

As we filed in, she pulled me aside in the foyer. "Did you check that pizza gizmo out?"

"I did, with expert help. It's just as we thought." She groaned. I'd remembered to bring the spy pizza box with me, and handed it to her. "Was yours edible?"

"Yes. Just a decoy. I'll test yours, too, and tell you if it's the same."

"Thanks, Sheila."

She had brought in her dining room chairs to her living room to join her large, oatmeal sectional couch, matching armchairs, and end tables. The kitchen was just off the open-plan living room and had a bar and four, swivelling stools at its counter. The kids were already seated there, glumly nursing herbal teas.

Arranged along the sectional were Ruby (China Doll), Maddie's Martha, and Salem Sally. Sheila was presiding from a desk chair she'd pulled over, Connie took an armchair, and Randy grabbed the other. Kate and I scooted in next to the womenfolk on the sectional.

"Help yourselves," Sheila said, gesturing to the trays of nibbles on the coffee table. "There's also a drinks set-up on the bar for the adults."

I caught the resigned side-glances from the kids at the bar. (So close, and yet so far . . .)

When people got resettled with their drinks, Sheila sat forward. "I have some encouraging news for you all."

She filled us all in on the progress Frank was making on the antiviral for the virus. Several sets of ears perked up at that.

"Oh my God! I mean, the Goddess be blessed! That's wonderful!" Sally's excitement shook the sofa.

"How soon will it be ready, Sheila?" Martha asked.

"I know it's exciting, but developing a drug takes time, even when circumventing the FDA, as we must. He still has to be extremely careful to get it right and not cause harm."

If they'd been in werewolf form, their ears would have flattened and there would have been whimpering.

She held up an index finger (Pavlov ringing a bell). "But!"

Ears perked up again. "He's also been working on an antidote to mitigate the lunar effects."

"How long will *that* take?" Ruby asked.

Sheila smiled. "I believe it's ready now."

"Great, but it'll never get here in time," Jared pointed out.

"Actually, it will. Frank's flying in Tuesday with the latest results from the viral samples and the antidote."

Applause broke out. "Praise the Blessed Savior!" Connie said.

Sheila held up a palm. "So that's the good news."

And now for the bad.

"The bad news is that he's only had time to prepare enough to inoculate a few of us."

They slumped. I'd already heard it from Sheila, so turned to the others. "It's only temporary, guys."

"You knew about it already?" Martha asked.

"Sheila just told me yesterday." Martha harrumphed.

"How temporary is it?" Jared asked Sheila.

"He said it *should* be good for 12 hours. Hopefully, anyway."

"So who gets it?" Ruby demanded.

"It wasn't an easy decision, but I'll get a shot—"

"Of course you will." Martha muttered.

"Look, it's my daughter in there and I need to be clear headed when things go down and not be running off in all directions!" Sheila fired back.

"And right ye are, love," Connie spoke up. "We'd all of us feel the same if we were in Sheila's shoes. Now then, who else?"

"Well, I thought Alice probably should have a shot too, if she's willing. She seems to be Rolf's biggest target and she knows the layout of his mansion."

I didn't want to mutate into a six-legged dog or something, so I asked, "He's tested this stuff, right?" She nodded. "Then I'm game, I guess."

Sheila went on. "And I thought Jared, also, if there's enough. With his family connections to Rolf and brainstorming with Dion on the technical side, it would probably be best if the two of them could communicate." Other than in barks. Lassie's entreaties only went so far. Subtext: he'd probably also be better at herding a crazed wolf pack.

"Okay?" Sheila asked us.

We nodded, some, unhappily.

"So how are we going to do this?" That was Emma.

"Randy was kind enough to fill me in on your foray on Thursday, for which I'm eternally grateful." For the benefit of the others, she gave a re-cap. "Have I got that right?" she asked the Snoop Troupe Five.

Randy, Jared, Kate and I nodded. Dion see-sawed his hand.

"Maybe you can fill us in with anything I missed, Dion?"

He swivelled toward us. "Sure, Sheila." When he finished, he added, "I hope that wasn't too technical for some of you."

"I think we've got it, dear, or most of it," Connie assured him, glancing at the other women, who nodded their agreement. "Pretty slick work there, lad."

"Thanks," he rasped back.

"So now you've got to come up with a solid plan, a foolproof one," Randy pointed out.

"You sayin' we fools, bro'?" Jared asked. Dion snickered.

"Not right *now* . . ."

"Any thoughts, people?" Sheila asked.

"Actually, we fools have thought up a lotta stuff." Jared again.

Sheila motioned to him to continue.

"Dion and I have been thinking. On Saturday, it being the full moon and Rolf not having his precious pendant, he'll be a little wacko, more than usual, anyway. Won't be thinking straight.

"So after we all get there and we scope out the place, Dion will knock on his door and lure him out with the pendant, draw him out of the place."

"Good so far, but how will we get there without being noticed by the neighbors?" Sally asked.

Jared looked at her under his brows. "Sally, *you're* asking me that? On that date, so close to . . .?"

She slapped her head. "Halloween party?"

"Bingo! We'll park on the side street, naturally. And if we start to turn, any neighbors who see us will just think it's a themed costume party. Wolf Man throws all kinds of parties, so they won't be surprised."

Brilliant. We all grinned.

"Okay, but how will we get there? Driving's a bitch with claws," Martha pointed out.

It was Randy's turn. "I've got my Bronco that's already set up for transporting wildlife—" Emma snickered. "—so I can put four of you in the back to keep you safe."

"Sounds a little crowded," Ruby commented.

"Assuming Alice's antidote works, she can ride up front with Kate."

"And I can drive Jared's car with him and Emma in the back," Dion said. "Pretty sure I can handle them. Done it before with Jared."

"That just leaves you, Sheila," Sally said.

"Frank can drive us in my SUV."

"Ye might want to cover that vanity plate of yours, Sheila, at least when you get near," Connie mentioned. "Talk about yer tip-off!"

"Good point, Connie." Sheila said. "What about Rolf's guards and that dog?" she asked the room.

"We're working on that. Dion's monitoring everything at Rolf's place and we'll also be armed," Randy told her. "I'll have a tranquilizer gun and Kate here has a pistol with actual silver bullets. My cop buddy, Hank, is taking her to the shooting range tomorrow to make sure she doesn't shoot one of us."

"Hey!" Kate objected. "I've been told I'm a crack shot!"

"Sure that wasn't crack*pot*?" Randy quipped back, winking.

"And Dion here is a ninja master at throwing stars." Jared grinned.

Sheila looked puzzled. "Throwing *stars*?"

"You never seen the movie, *Predator*?" Dion asked her.

Sheila shook her head.

"I've made some myself, in shop class, when the teacher was out. They're lethal. Fly just like a frisbee. But these will have to be custom."

She shuddered. "And you've practiced with them, Dion? With, um, results?"

He shrugged. "Just on inanimate objects. Don't want to hurt animals, outside of this badass wolf dude, of course."

Jared sat forward. "But you should see him, Sheila. I've never seen such speed and accuracy. No one would see it coming, he's so fast."

Waterworks were threatening. "I have to tell you all again how grateful I am for your help. It's looking like a real plan, a good one, is shaping up." She sniffed in and turned to Dion. "But I still have to ask again, is there no way to bring this forward? Might it not be better if we're *not* in transition? Every day might be Patty's last!"

Ruby piped up. "I've been wondering the same. Now that we know Patty's being held there, why can't we just give the cops an anonymous tip-off and let them liberate her and clap Rolf and his goons in jail?"

"Won't happen there," Dion coughed out. Heads swung his way.

"Why the hell not?" Martha, again.

"Town cops are hooked and crooked. Rolf's bought 'em. I've been listening to some crazy shit outa that house. Sorry, I mean 'poop.' "

"'Tis all right, Dion. Sure and I've heard worse," said Connie.

Dion added some honey to his tea. "The fu— sucker is connected beyond your wildest dreams, all the way up to the White House."

Jared spoke up. "Rolf has to be terminated. He won't stop until he is. Even if he did get jailed, he'd get sprung almost immediately and that would make it all the harder to hunt him down again."

Dion held up helpless palms. "Sorry, Sheila. And anyhow, I'm still waiting for the smithy to deliver the new stars. A buddy at my school who's also into military stuff, swords and whatnot, is making them up to spec. His dad runs a forge for the local stables. Makes custom horseshoes for special events to give them better traction. He's made me some of the regular stars, but these need to be silver and they have to be special-ordered. It's not something that farriers have lying around."

Sheila flopped back, studying her hands.

"But maybe if I get those stars sooner, we can give it a try."

"Couldn't we try without the stars?" she asked. "If Randy has the tranquilizer gun and Kate has *her* gun and silver bullets . . ."

"Rolf's guards have guns, too, don't forget, plus a Doberman. For multiple targets, we'll need all the firepower we can muster. But, like I said, I'll keep listening, and if I see an earlier window of opportunity and have all the gear, I'll let you know. Just need to keep *everyone* safe."

Dion got up, walked over to her and took her hand. "I know it's hard, but I'm listening in virtually all day and night, checking on Patty."

"You are? How? Aren't you at school weekdays?"

Dion and Jared laughed. Emma, too. "High school's changed a lot since you were a kid. Teachers yack at us, pass out the laptops, and go off on extended breaks."

"Plus, Dion's kind of a teacher's pet, he's so smart," Jared put in. "He basically runs the classes while they're out. The computer tech teachers are always bugging him to catch them up on software innovations so they don't make asses of themselves with IT."

"I'll let you know ASAP if anything changes with Patty, Sheila," Dion said. Sheila nodded, still looking down. "Patty's tougher stuff than you know. Must take after her mom."

That got a smile. "Thank you, Dion. Oh, before I forget, Alice and I each got another bug, planted in Gino's boxes. So be vigilant, everyone, and perhaps stay off their pizza for a while."

FORTY-NINE

JUMPIN' AND JIVIN'

You know that movie, *Cat on a Hot Tin Roof*? Well, that was me, only not a cat. Obviously. It was Tuesday. With four days to go, I was just that jumpy. I'd started closing my front curtains to shut out the reminder.

Monday had been quiet, a lull before the storm, waiting for more news from Dion and Sheila. So I hunkered down and applied myself to my job. But as the moon increased its pull, it was getting harder to type. I kept having to file my nails down. In a couple of days, normally I'd have to use wire cutters. But this cycle, I'd be letting them grow.

All the better to scratch Rolf's eyes out.

I'd noticed, when I went into the office, lots of gals in the typing pool typed with those girly, long paste-ons. I'd have to learn, too.

Hadn't heard a peep from the guys in the van since our laundry serenade. Didn't mean they hadn't infested the building with something else, though. I do have to sleep sometime.

Mrs. C was due home today, so yesterday Bud and I'd gone to her place and tidied up, put new sheets on, and scoured the place on our hands and knees looking for unauthorized insectoid listeners. I was glad that Bud was ex-military. He had a far better eye for this stuff than I do. Wish I'd known before. You really need to get to know your neighbors.

Anyhow, bug-wise her apartment was clean, as far as we could see. And we hadn't seen any more UFVs in the lot. So he went back to his TV and Barcalounger, and I trudged back upstairs to my laptop. Had to spellcheck everything three times. My mind just wasn't on the job.

Around noon, I got a cryptic text from Sheila. "Pizza very edible. I'll keep it for you, if you want."

My stomach growled. I wished I had it right now. I sent back, "No, you keep it. Enjoy!" I guess I'd have to cook something, now that I had stuff to cook. "What time does F get here?"

"ETA 3:40 p.m. Text you later."

"I'll be here." I got a smiling emoji back.

About 4:30 Sheila pinged again, this time to the group. "F's here and has the goods, enough for 4."

There was a barrage of excited emojis pinging back and forth.

"And D says he's got the supplies now!"

Our phones were peppered with clapping hands, thumbs ups, and one of two raised hands from Emma. I had to look that one up.

Sheila responded: "So the big question is, is everyone available to party tonight? And meet first at my place, 7-ish?"

There was a lull while everyone checked their work schedules and plans. One by one, the replies came in, all but Randy and Kate. The consensus was: "Let's do it!"

"Fantastic! We're just waiting on R and K. So stay tuned."

Adrenaline was pulsing through me now. I honestly didn't know if I felt ready. I wondered if anyone else did. And I'd been kinda counting on that extra wolf strength to help. But this might be best. We'd probably be better at organizing ourselves, although there is much to be said for the mind of the pack.

We got a new text from Sheila: "Please do come smelling nice." That meant we should wear her special conditioner so we'd be irresistible at the "party." A thought came to me that made me laugh: anyone hacking into our texts would think we were the Great Unwashed. Which, for remote workers like me, *could* be true.

I checked the clock—4:52. Close enough. I couldn't have typed another character. I saved the file I'd been working on, waited eight minutes, and clocked out. Time to shower and wash my hair.

At 5:40 I heard the key turn in Kate's door, and stuck my head out. "Did you see the texts?" I whispered.

"Yes, I just texted her back. Give me a sec." She dumped her purse, phone and coat inside, locked back up and came over.

"Did you tell her you'll be able to make it tonight?" I asked.

"Like my dance card is that full?" she quipped.

"Just checking. I've been on pins and needles waiting for the details."

Kate nodded, drawing in her lips. "God, I hope this works, Al. And I hope I don't somehow screw up."

"Same," I sighed, and locked the door behind her.

I held up my carafe of stale coffee. "Coffee? I can nuke it."

Kate shook her head. "Had four cups of the hideous brew at work and it's given me the shakes. And this switch isn't helping. Was counting on more time, to sort of ramp up the ol' courage."

"Me, too. Maybe it's best? Us wolf people will be saner, I suppose."

"I suppose. Beer?"

"Coming right up! My nerves can use it." I pulled out two R&Rs.

She glanced at the time. "Frick! I'd better jump in the shower first and do my hair. Keep my beer cold!"

Kate came back 20 minutes later, damp and smelling sweetly earthy.

Her fingers curled toward me. "Come to Mama!" I slid her beer across the table and she gulped, burped and shuddered. "I may need two of those babies."

"No problemo. Got a new six-pack."

Watching our cells like cats for koi, we drank in silence.

I finally got up and poked my nose into my fridge, perusing the new additions. "You eat anything yet? I guess I could rustle up something."

"I couldn't eat a thing," Kate said.

"Me neither," I said and flopped back down. I'd been starving earlier. Not so much now.

At last, there were new group pings. We grabbed our cells and read.

Randy: "Can't make it. Stuck on call today. 2morrow? Thurs. better."

A long pause. My wolfie sense could feel the combined relief and frustration coming through from the others.

Sheila: "What do you think, guys? Tomorrow work?"

As the replies were dribbling in, there was a new text from Dion, marked "Urgent!" (And no, I didn't have a clue how he did that, either.)

"HOLD UP! No party 2morrow. Host many miles away on plane."

"How long gone?" I texted back.

"Yes. When be back?" Emma chimed in. We were beginning to sound like Injuns in an old Western. I hoped it wasn't also many moons.

"Friday. Late. Hearing lots of activity."

"Send smoke signals later, Tonto?" I texted.

He got it: we got back a laughing emoji and a thumbs up with "Soon."

Dion followed with a sobering reply just to me: "Where smoke is fire follows, Pale Face."

FIFTY

Tick-Tock, on the Clock

Wednesday morning. Tick, tick, tick. Three days before the full moon. I felt its pull yanking on me; I'd been dreaming of steak tartare. Kate and I had polished off the six-pack last night and were feeling the effects of Rolling Rock on empty stomachs. I'd need to make a beer run later.

She came dragging in cradling a loaf of artisan bread from work and a jar of raspberry jam. "Trade ya breakfast for some java?"

"For you, always." I brought over Mr. Coffee, two mugs, spoons, a knife and a couple of plates. She sliced some bread and handed it over. Great aroma! I inhaled appreciatively. Ain't nothin' like the real thing. I popped the bread into my toaster.

"Sugar?" I slid the bowl her way.

"Yes, darling?" It felt good to laugh, considering. . . .

Dion's last remark the previous evening was still worrying me. As we ate, we checked our cells for new texts, but all was quiet on the Wolfen front. Took a sip of coffee then texted him again directly.

"Any update on our singer?"

"All good, but I think she's getting company."

Uh oh. That didn't sound good.

I texted back "??"

"Can't talk now."

"OK." As I ended the text, my stomach roiled from pondering how and why Rolf could act that fast, turning and imprisoning new victims, especially now he was out of town. At least that's what I assumed the "company" meant. Ah, but maybe that was *why* he was away—he was out shanghaiing more of his harem.

As I was ruminating, Kate's cell pinged. She frowned, reading it.

"It's from Mona's office. They're wondering if I'd seen her and how recently."

I took a brave breath. "How long's she been missing from work?"

"Since Tuesday morning."

"After she met up with us at Gino's Monday night?" She nodded, face crumpling. So maybe Rolf *had* gotten bailed out that night.

I had a bad feeling who Patty's "company" was going to be. But I'd keep that to myself until I talked to Dion. For now, I'd offer her some hope. "You suppose Rolf flew her to Disney World, Katie? You know, to get things set up then catch up with her later when he flies back down?"

"Maybe." Kate's voice was faint, a subscript I had to lean in to hear.

Kate looked up as I glanced at my kitchen clock.

"Time to go rustle them rutabagas, Katie love." She nodded again and handed me her empty mug. I reached out for her hands. "Mona'll be okay, honey. She's good at landing on her feet."

My front door closed quietly behind Kate.

After lunch, I got a new text from Sheila. Frank had arrived safely and had the antidote. And Dion had texted that Rolf was flying back on Friday, so she was rescheduling a planning meeting for Thursday night. Good so far. But later, we got a new update from Dion. Not so good.

After it got dark, Randy had driven Jared and Dion back over to Rolf's while he was away to make sure everything was in place for rescuing Patty. But they ran into a snag: too much henchmen activity. Headset on, Dion overheard that Rolf was in the process of major refurbishments. The place was teaming with contractors' vans.

So our "party" was off again for now. Talk about a nail biter. Good thing we had strong teeth. Thursday's meet-up should soothe some.

Then Dion sent a second text, just to me. "Call me. Landline."

Wasn't it a very good thing a bunch of us still relied on landlines? In my case, it's partly because I'm crap at texting, even when human.

He picked up right away.

While he was listening in, he'd heard more activity in the cell next to Patty's. "Looks like I was right, Alice. Rolf's setting up that cell next to Patty's for someone new."

"Fuck! Any idea who?"

"Not yet. But don't mention it to the others until I know more, okay?"

I was chewing on that information. "Damnit, maybe it *is* time to call the cops. But from another jurisdiction? The feds maybe? They can't all be crooked, can they?"

"Al, every damned thing I've heard has shown me clearly how far politicians on every level are in Rolf's pockets. Any anonymous tip-off would be first seen as a pissy pay-back from the opposing party."

"Which party is that?"

"I'm pretty sure you know the answer to that." I did.

"Look, Rolf is a big name in politics, like Musk; he just keeps a lower profile. Keeps his mouth shut. Rolf's given beaucoup bucks to these guys. Feds would likely check with his party's bigwig benefactors first before embarrassing themselves."

"Hang on, Dion. I gotta take some Rolaids." This was giving me a major case of heartburn. "Okay, I'm back."

"You all right, Al?"

"No. But at least I didn't throw up. So what about Hank, that fireman friend of Randy's? Could he maybe round up some firemen to respond to a fire we could anonymously call in and, I don't know, they could somehow manage to bash in the basement doors?"

"So we'd set fire to the downstairs?"

"Maybe just the bushes?"

"And what if it caught more than the bushes, Al? And burned the people down there? Plus, you'd be bringing in another non-believer."

"But would adding Hank be so bad? He's a good guy, from what Randy's said. He knows how to work the Jaws of Life, so he's strong, and he's good with wildlife relocation. He's got a tranquilizer gun, too."

"The members we have will be hard enough to manage without adding a new one. We need to stay on a 'need to know' basis, for everybody's safety, trust me."

"I guess you're right."

"On the bright side, with the full moon so close, Rolf will want all civilians out of the way when he gets back Friday."

"I would *hope* so. Speaking of flying back, do you know where he flew to?"

"No. Sorry, Al. Mighta had someone make his reservations for him. Well, I'd better get back to my head-set. Talk at ya tomorrow."

"Get some sleep if you can, guy."

He laughed. "Hey, that's why God made Red Bull."

I hoped it gave him wings. He deserved them.

FIFTY-ONE

POSSE PREP

Before work on Thursday Kate came in, relief all over her face. "Mona's work called. They found an email from her, sent Tuesday, saying something had suddenly come up and she needed some days off!"

"Well, that's good. But what the hell took them so long to read the email?"

She rolled her eyes upward. "Got stuck in someone's spam folder."

"Dopes! So maybe she did go to Disney World, Kate?"

"Maybe. And she's only asked for a few days off, which means she'll be back."

"We'll have to keep her away from Rolf," I reminded her.

"True. But he'll probably want to keep his distance on Saturday. He always has in the past, during full moons."

Unless she was turned by now . . . Then he'd be just fine with staying up close and personal. "Just to be safe, so she doesn't stumble into a situation she's not expecting, let's think up some way to keep her occupied."

"Ooh! Maybe with one of those gorgeous guys from La Cantina?"

"Oh, I think that idea is *muy bueno!* I thought she'd sprain an eyelid making goo-goo eyes at them."

"Well, I'm off!"

"Only sometimes," I said, getting a laugh. "Have fun at work and don't let anyone fondle your melons."

When we were all assembled again at Sheila's and soothing ourselves with nibbles and drinks, she introduced us to Frank. I wasn't prepared for how handsome he was: tall; thick salt-and-pepper hair, cut expertly; tweed jacket over a black T-shirt and black jeans; kind, quirky smile that reached his blue eyes, eyes that didn't miss a thing. I was expecting the nerdy doctor stereotype, I guess. Easy to see why female patients would find him irresistible. I was betting he had one helluva bedside manner.

Yep, he did. Frank went around the room, greeting us all with a smile and firm handshake, slightly more lingering on the women. He repeated our names, cementing them in his memory, his eyes looking straight in yours, reading you. I caught Ruby fanning off a hot flash. Martha cocked her head and crossed her long legs. Both Randy and Sheila were smirking. Other than the momentary distraction of Frank hotness, the meeting went smoothly, though pretty tense.

"So! It looks like the party's back to Saturday," Sheila announced.

Kate raised her hand (like we were in class). Frank acknowledged her, "Kate, right?"

She bobbed her head. "Sheila said you brought some kind of antidote. Is it really safe? I'm sorry but I can't help but feel a little worried, for the others, not myself. I won't need it. Please don't take any offence, it's just that you developed it so fast."

Annoyed, Sheila rolled her eyes. Nobody sucked up to *her* like that!

Frank took Kate's hand. "I know it was quick, but the research behind it was something we've both been working on for quite a while."

"And you've tested it?" Emma asked him.

"Yes, I have."

"On what? A mouse?" Ruby demanded. "Not a human, I'll bet."

He smiled. "No, not on a human. I didn't have the right sort of test subjects in L.A., despite the proximity to Universal Studios."

This got a grudging laugh, even from Ruby. "I used a pair of male possums," Frank explained. "And it's safe."

"So the possums made it?" Kate, like me, worried about the critters.

"Aside from significant, *temporary,* hair loss and a reduced tendency to fight, they survived just fine."

Kate shot me a silent *Whew!* "Sheila said it should last about twelve hours. Is that right?"

"Possibly a little longer. I'll be administering a somewhat bigger dose because of the increased body mass."

"What if you got it wrong? What if the dose is too strong?" Kate still worried.

"Or it isn't strong enough and wears off too soon?" Sally joined in. "They could be sitting ducks!" I didn't dare look at Kate. I knew she'd be processing the image of ducks with fangs and claws the same as I.

Martha reached across to Sally. "Sally! Girl, where's that Wiccan power you're supposed to be drawing on?" Sally ducked her chin in.

"Even if I doubled the dosage, no one would come to harm," Frank assured us.

"Except maybe going bald as coots," I muttered.

"No, not even that. The dose I gave the possums was triple the human dose, for their body mass compared to ours. And their fur grew back in a week."

Martha sat forward and gave me a hard stare. "Look, it's better than nothing." She turned to the others. "And remember, it's not *us* who'll be getting it. It's *those* guys." She pointed an aggrieved finger at Jared, Sheila and me, then crossed her arms and slumped back on the sofa. "Personally, as I was *not* selected as a test subject, I'm happy knowing I'll be drawing on my wolf power so I can rip off his ba—"

"Ball bearings?" Connie suggested.

"Yeah, those, with my teeth."

Connie smirked. "Good girl!" Martha threw her back a low "Woof!"

"Wait! Sheila, you'd said there was enough antidote for four," Martha said, "but you only mentioned three of us getting the shot. Who gets the fourth, Frank?" So much for her ballsy, ball-biting speech.

Frank hesitated. A look passed between him and Sheila. She sat forward. "We're assuming there'll be enough for four, but we may have to play it by ear and possibly increase someone's dosage."

Frank stepped back in. "It's okay, Sheila. The likelihood of that is very low. But I am worried that Patty, our *daughter*, has also been turned. We were hoping to save the last dose for her, if the need arises."

Martha shut her eyes tight. "I keep forgetting. I'm sorry."

Sheila let it pass, then handed out print-outs to each of us with the layout of Rolf's place, including aerial shots of the mansion and surrounding streets and neighborhoods. "We've marked the best places to park out of sight and the exit roads for quick getaways. There's also a map of the town and environs, along with Google Maps' street and terrain views." Ruby pinched the bridge of her nose.

"And here's the complete list I've updated with all of our contacts. Be sure to store the phone numbers in each of your phones, okay?"

"Yes, ma'am," Jared saluted.

"Very thorough," Randy commented, pursing his lips.

Sheila smiled modestly. "Most of this you can thank Dion for." She explained that Sunday afternoon before our last meeting Dion had gone with Jared to Rolf's and flown a drone over the place and the area. Martha mimed an approving clap.

"Not your usual neck of the woods, I'd think," said Ruby to Dion.

Dion shrugged and vaped. "Town's got a sweet set of tennis courts on Summer Street. Good skateboarding. No one seems to use it."

"And, if people do show up?" Ruby asked.

He shrugged again. "What can I say? It's fun to piss off the natives."

"So how'd you manage the drone in broad daylight, Dion, without alerting the guards and annoying the neighbors?" Emma asked.

Exhaling vape, Dion croaked, "Oh, there's gonna be one neighbor who'll be super annoyed." Jared was cracking up but staying mum.

We turned to Jared, heads cocked like puzzled pooches.

"You wanna 'splain, Lucy?" Kate prodded.

"It was brilliant! D attached a long, sparkly streamer to his drone with 'Marry me, Stephanie!' on it." Jared was slapping his thigh, actually slapping it.

Emma grinned. "Great fake-out, dude! But what if there's no Stephanie in the neighborhood? Wouldn't the neighbors get suspicious?"

"That's the great part: there is!" Jared, said. There went the thigh slap again. Great way to tone up your muscles. Or tenderize.

"You know that, how?" Kate asked.

Jared punched Dion's bicep. "Tell them, D."

"She lives just down the street. One of the guards is hot on her and sneaks over to her house when Rolf's back is turned, allegedly walking the dog. I told you, I hear *everything*," Dion answered.

"So she's the one who's going to be super annoyed? Like when she finds out he doesn't really want to marry her?" I asked.

"Exactly!"

Emma scowled. "That's kinda mean, Dion."

"Not really. Guy's got a record of assault and B&E. I'm just helping her dodge a bullet."

"Dion da man! He be savin' the world one hack at a time," Jared crowed.

That broke the tension. Even Sheila laughed. Then she got back to the business at hand. She referred to her clipboard, checking stuff off.

"Randy, are Alice, Connie, Martha, Ruby and Sally still riding with you?"

"And me," Kate corrected, with a hurt frown. She was always getting left out, not being of the wolf persuasion.

Sheila looked up from her clipboard. "Quite a full house."

"Kate and Alice can ride up front with me, and the cargo area is very roomy," Randy replied, syphoning off some G&T.

Jared spoke up, "Dad'll be in lockdown so Dion and I can use his wagon and can bring Sally. We live in the same town, after all."

"That's helpful, Jared." Sheila checked off some boxes. "And you'll have Emma with you, too, right?" He nodded. Check. "Everyone okay with this?"

"Randy's car still sounds a bit close for comfort. Couldn't I ride with you and Frank?" Martha asked, always the *prima donna.*

Sheila looked to Frank. He sighed. "I guess so, going over, but don't forget we'll need extra room coming back, God willing. So you'll have to squeeze in Randy's car on the return."

Martha shrank down. "That's fine."

The elephant in the room had gotten so large it was practically trumpeting.

"Thank you, Martha," Sheila said, lips tight.

Ruby asked, "What time again will the moon be full?"

Sheila checked her notes. "Not until 9:03, they're predicting."

Sally checked her witches' almanac. "Says here that there's also going to be pe— penumbr—," she stumbled "—some kind of eclipse Saturday afternoon."

"Got that from your witchy almanac, didn't you?" Martha teased.

Sally blushed. Emma came to her defense. "It was also all over the news and weather. Maybe you missed it, Martha?"

"It's called a penumbral lunar eclipse," Sheila explained, smiling at Sally, "and is supposed to begin about 4:24 p.m. and last four hours and another 40 minutes or so."

"Looks like those witches had their shit together," Dion rasped.

"I heard it's going to make the moon look red, too," Kate put in.

Connie crossed herself. The kids chorused, "Cool!" Randy and the rest just rolled their eyes.

"So by 9:05 p.m.," Sheila went on, "the moon should be full and fully visible again. We'll need to be in place well before that, because I don't know what affect the eclipse will have on our rate of transformation."

"I'd think it might slow things down," I offered.

"That would be my guess, too, but I just don't know, so we can't count on it.

"And we also don't know what additional affect it will have on Rolf and any people inside. Neighbors will likely be outside watching it, so my thinking is that we shouldn't spring into action until 9:15 or so, after everyone's gone in if they've been outside. It's going to be unusually warm, too. They're predicting temps in the low 60s with passing clouds."

Randy sat forward. "I understand your thinking, Sheila, but might not having the neighborhood outside watching the eclipse provide a great cover for what we have planned? Kids will probably be running all over the place, neighbors drinking cocktails together. When Dion knocks on the door to lure Rolf out, he'll probably come out smiling, thinking it's a neighbor inviting him in on the fun."

Jared spoke up. "Rolf'll be on the point of change like most of us."

"Right, right." Randy tipped his head, nodding.

"Dude's more likely to come out grinning, thinking a neighbor's unwittingly delivered a new victim," Dion rasped.

"Whichever it is, eclipse partying would probably cover up a lot of chaos," Randy said.

Sheila looked thoughtful. "That's not a bad thought, Randy. I guess we'll have to play it by ear. Frank and I will have our dog whistles with us, so be alert to the signals. Do you all remember them?"

"Two short bursts then a long one is 'charge!' right?" Emma said.

"Yes. And one long whistle is 'stay in place.' "

Ruby piped up, "What's the signal for 'Hide or we'll all be killed'?"

Jared snorted. "Since I've been appointed pack herder, I think if it comes to that I'll just yell, 'Run away!' "

"And if that doesn't work, Randy and I'll grab your asses and haul you away," says Dion.

"Don't you just love it when he talks like that?" Randy, who else?

"All right, youse. Sure and that was hilarious, but it's going to be mighty serious business out there. And we don't want any of us gettin' hurt, including herself that's in the lock-up."

"Yes, Connie," we mumbled. She was right, of course.

"So should we meet first at my house, so we can go over any last-minute questions or problems?" Sheila asked the room.

Randy looked skeptical. "I really don't think we want to go in a big convoy. It would attract too much attention, whereas arriving one by one would look like normal neighborhood activity. We can confer there."

"Randy's right, Sheila," Frank said. "So could you swing by earlier with Alice, Randy? And Dion, can you bring Jared, so we can give them their injections?"

"If you gave me their two doses, I could do the shots at my place," Randy said. "Would save a lot of backtracking."

Frank raised his eyebrows at Sheila. "That makes sense," she said. "He *is* a nurse practitioner, Frank."

"That's right! So, is it okay if I send the doses over to Sheila's office? You could pick them up there tomorrow."

"Works for me. What time do we administer the doses on Saturday?" Randy asked. "How long before it takes effect?"

"It should take effect within 30 minutes, but just to be on the safe side, we should dose them by 5:30 p.m. at the very latest, before it gets dark. And the moon will be an hour into its eclipse."

So it was settled: Dion would drive Jared, Emma and Sally over to Randy's where I'd be waiting with Kate. Randy'd give Jared and me our shots, and we'd all hang out at Randy's until showtime. Sheila would get hers, of course, from Frank.

"What do you think, Dion? We'll want give ourselves plenty of time to case the grounds and take note of the last of the red eclipse activity before we take our places. Say, get there by 8:30 p.m.?"

"Man, I'm thinking earlier than that. Set-up takes some time, when you're hiding in the dark."

"8:00 p.m., then?"

Dion squinted his eyes against the vape smoke. "I think I can work with that. It'd be a whole lot easier, though, if somebody had a panel van. I could sort out my stuff there, unseen, before I set up."

"Actually, I think I can probably get one for the night," Frank said. "Buddy of mine here has one he could loan me. If not, I'll just rent one."

"Great! Send me the description of the van with the license number, Frank, when you have it."

"Will do, Dion."

"So, is everyone clear now where we meet on Saturday, who we're riding with, the places we can hide and all?" Sheila asked us. "And you'll make sure your phones are charged and on?"

We gave her worried nods.

Connie spoke up, "Ah, no. Don't be so hang-dog. We can do this, dear hearts. I feel it, truly I do."

The reality was hitting us and all we could do was nod again.

Sheila rose, hands cupped at her waist. "I know we're all nervous, but we really have a good plan, thanks to all your brainstorming, and we have good back-up, as well as the advantage of surprise and numbers. So try to not get too stressed. At least not any more than I am!" She looked at Frank, then back at us.

"Rest up while you can, wear comfortable clothes—"

"—expandable" Kate put in. She'd seen my wardrobe malfunctions.

"Yes, expandable clothing and, for you *non*-wolves, your most reliable running shoes—"

"With bloody good grip and laces, mind you," Connie added. "Don't want any of youse slippin' on the grass and goin' arse over tea kettle."

"Right. As Connie said." Sheila inhaled shakily and smiled at us. "We *will* do it. Oh, come on, anyone for a group hug?"

"Yes, coach!" We all piled in, even Jared and Randy.

Leaving Sheila's, I checked the moon as I had every night for the past week. Nearly there. I quaked. I could feel slow changes already.

"You're getting twitchy again," Kate said.

"Yeah. Sorry." I reminded myself to stop by the 7-Eleven and grab a new six-pack and more Rolaids on the way home.

Kate read my mind. "Didn't you say you were out of beer?"

"On it! A six-pack's comin' right up."

She fished out a twenty for me from her wallet. "Make that two!"

FIFTY-TWO

FROM HEARTBURN TO HEARTACHE

Popping Rolaids and pounding my keyboard all day, by 5:00 p.m. on Friday I was more than ready to clock out. As I grabbed a cold, hoppy sedative from one of the six-packs, I got a cryptic text from Dion: "Landline!"

This couldn't be good. Dion didn't use exclamation marks.

I yanked the curtains closed and dialed. "Hey, D, it's Al."

"Sorry, man, but I thought you'd want to know before our gig."

"Okay . . ." I took a big swallow to keep my hackles down.

"You're not gonna like it."

"Isn't Rolf back?" I heard him taking a long, slow suck off his vaper.

"Yeah, he's back. And all the vans have come and gone."

"Then *what*??" My left leg started dancing all on its own.

"I heard voices just now in that cell next to Patty's. One of them was a woman's."

"Oh dear God. You know who it is?"

"Think so. Take a listen." He'd recorded it and played it for me.

My heart sank. "It's Mona."

"That's the dark-haired woman who joined us at Gino's, right? The one who's got the hots for Rolf?"

"Yep. Kate's friend. The one who thinks she's got a ticket to a job at Disney World, thanks to him."

"That sucks. Looks like she's got a ticket for something else."

"She sounded coherent, at least," I threw out, tentatively. Also righteously pissed. "Why do you think he's chosen now to abduct her?"

"No fuckin' idea."

"You think maybe Rolf et al. somehow know what we're planning?"

"I don't see how. I've hacked into to all his texts and listened to his conversations, as well as his goons' and their stupid jokes, not to mention their farts. Man, those dudes seriously need to cut back on the red meat!"

I let that remark slide. "Rolf probably encourages that, the red meat part. But this is really scaring me. He's already so furious about losing his pendant, could he be so pissed off he'd kill Patty just for spite and abduct someone else in her place?"

"There's been absolutely no hint of that, no repeated code words or evil guffaws. And I'm still picking up Patty's voice."

"Then why'd he snatch Mona? Seems like he was cutting off his, *you know*, to spite his face. No more poontang."

"'Poontang'?" Dion cackled. "But why would locking her up cut *that* off? She's a captive audience."

Damn. "Like Patty."

"Yeah." We both went quiet.

He went on, "And I know where he flew off to now. Disney World."

"Wait, he went to Disney World and didn't take Mona?"

"He took her, but he brought her back. Heard them fighting last night, upstairs in the boom-boom room. I think maybe the Disney deal went sideways."

"I remember the boom-boom room is at the top, attic level, off-limits to the servants and probably the guards. I think it even has its own lock."

"So the staff probably doesn't know about her yet. Rolf could move her to the cell himself and lock her in after everyone's crashed."

"You suppose she finally figured it out, what he is?"

"Could be. Or could be Mona got to be too much of a pain in the poontang to deal with. She seemed pretty bossy."

"She can be."

"Either way, locking her up would be one way to keep her in line."

"And silent." I heard another inhale—smoking agreement.

Yesterday I could not imagine this getting worse. Guess I just didn't have that good of an imagination.

"You know, D, I've always wondered what the guards and staff think about all this. First Patty, and now Mona, who they'll discover pretty soon and have to feed."

"Same." He coughed. "But I think I've pieced it together from all the chatter I've listened to. Most of the staff have only been with him a year or so and don't know his secret. All they know is that there's a crazy girl installed in the basement, *for her own good*—some family member, like a niece, with schizophrenic psychotic episodes."

The rat bastard. No crystal ball needed to see where this was going.

"And because he's so fond of her," I sneered, "out of the kindness of his heart he's taking care of her instead of letting her be institutionalized?"

"Yep. They think he's some kind of mucky-muck physician, seeing as how he has such easy access to prescription drugs for this 'niece.' "

"Jesus!" Now I was wishing *I* had something to toke on. "We *have* to take him out. Before he blows a fuse and kills everyone."

"Preachin' to the choir, Al. But here's a little bit of silver lining: Rolf's planning to stay in on Saturday and Sunday and do some private entertaining, so he's let his guards and goons have the weekend off."

"Well, that will lower the body count. And it seems to confirm that his goons who've been bugging and tracking us, don't realize what he is any more than the guards and servants. But how is that possible?"

"Seems crazy, but that's what it looks like. They're just in it for the money anyway, and he pays well, so why ask questions? I overheard another conversation. Sounded like it could have been an overseas call, you know those two-burp ring tones."

"Who was it with, Dr. Mengele?" I snarked.

"Couldn't make that out. But you could be close, it was mostly in what sounded like German. A man answered in English, then switched."

"Rolf's from Germany. His family's still over there. Did you record that conversation, too?"

"Of course. It's my auto-pilot setting."

"Good. Because I'm betting that Jared could translate it."

"Fuck! Why I didn't think of that? I'll run it past him right now."

"Don't beat yourself up. You've gotta be a little sleep deprived."

"No excuse, but thanks, Al."

"Should I tell Kate about Mona? I don't want her blindsided."

"There's nothing we can do for Mona or Patty right now. Give Kate another day of hope, Al. She'll find out soon enough."

He was right. "You think we're really ready for this showdown?"

"As ready as we'll ever be. And we've got a bunch of good and determined people on our side, not to mention some unusual weaponry."

I smiled into the phone. "Thanks for the pep talk, Dion. You'll get back to me about that German recording?"

"*Jawohl*, tomorrow. Sweet dreams."

I wasn't counting on those.

FIFTY-THREE

THUS SPAKE ZARATHUSTRA

D**-day**. I was up way before dawn. Couldn't stay asleep. Even with the curtains closed, the moon had been so bright it had snuck in anyway, especially the kitchen, where I'd never bothered to put up anything but a valance. When I'd gotten up about 2:00 a.m. for a glass of water, I'd jumped back in alarm to see the parking lot lit up like a stadium by the moon. Seems stupid, but it always came as a shock to me, a physical one. Normally, at this point, I'd be pounding down espressos and readying myself for lockdown. But I didn't have that option this time.

The watch on my wrist showed me that the deli had just opened. It also showed me a whole lot more hair on my arm than yesterday. Yeah, I know, not many people wear watches these days. They just check their phones. But you try operating a smartphone with big, ol' honkin' claws. For us wolves, as the moon goes full we have to revert to old tech.

I was already jumping out of my skin. Might as well jump down the street to grab a bagel and an espresso or five. I threw on my poncho and hat, pulled on long-fingered gloves and grabbed my keys and wallet.

Eight a.m. and a gorgeous Saturday, sunny and warm—Indian Summer. Good to be outside, away from the voices in my head for a while. Except for the nail problem, wouldn't have needed gloves.

I got there early enough to beat the breakfast crowd and order my toasted bagel and espressos without standing in line. When I paid, I made a pretense of fighting with the poncho so I could turn away from the guy at the cash register and extract the right money, gloveless, without raising eyebrows at my lack of manicure. He'd already raised them when I ordered three doubles. "Exact change!" He smiled, shutting the drawer.

"I do my best!" I smiled back, and skedaddled, sucking in high-test caffeine and taking my time walking back to what waited ahead.

For now, a new text from Dion was waiting. I picked up my cell from my desk where I'd left it and gingerly flat-fingered it alive. Jared had come through with the German translation. I called back on my landline.

"Well," Dion began, "it wasn't Dr. Mengele, but close enough."

I sat down and started slugging back my second espresso. "Don't tell me. It was his brother." I'd been thinking about this most of last night. Rolf's brother was the head of his clan, the top dog, so to speak. "Klaus?"

"That's the one."

"What'd they talk about?"

"Rolf was begging Klaus to fly over and loan him Klaus's pendant, since Rolf's was lost."

"Oh, Jesus. Just what we need, another evil werewolf! So, is he coming over?"

"Said 'No way!' he wasn't letting it out of his sight. And anyhow, he had something important going on there." Tough karma for the Germans. "Klaus told Rolf sorry, but he needed to chill at the *schloss.* That's his castle, right?"

"Right." So Klaus was staying home and pulling up the drawbridge, away from the torches and pitchforks. Probably had a portcullis, too, to skewer the peasants with.

My shoulders scooted down a notch. "That's a bit of luck, then. So much for brotherly love."

"Yeah. Doesn't seem like they're exactly close. Anyhow, if Klaus shows up later, it'll be for Rolf's funeral."

God bless the ninja! I brightened a little, then groaned. "I just had a thought: when Klaus gets the news, he probably *is* going fly over. I mean it's only right that he gives his respects to his dead brother. Then we will have a new evil werewolf to exterminate!"

I heard his sigh. "One catastrophe at a time, Al, one at a time. I guess I'd better go back to my headphones."

"Wait. Is everyone still okay in the cellar?"

"Yeah, though a little quieter than I'd like, but still vocal. So, what are you doing the rest of the day, until we meet up at Randy's?"

"Oh, I thought I'd go to a mall, do some shopping, maybe get my nails done for tonight. You?" I drawled, with more snark.

"You worried about that antidote?" he asked me.

"Wouldn't you be?"

"Maybe a little. But don't forget, you guys can't be killed except by extremely special means. And I've got your backs."

"I know you do, Dion. And I do keep forgetting about the immortal part. Hey, call it a lifetime habit. But we can still get sick."

"With all that wolfie adrenaline pumping through you, I doubt you'd feel it if you did. And I have some new secret weapons."

"You do? Besides the throwing stars?"

"I do." I could hear the smirk in his voice.

"Okay. Spill it, Dion."

"Nope. Only Jared knows. It's crucial it's a surprise for it to work."

"You gonna throw out doggie treats as a distraction?"

He laughed. "Better than that. See ya later!"

Just after 4:30 p.m., Kate, Dion, Jared, Emma, and I were once again arranged around Randy's coffee table. He'd wrangled an early shift at the hospital so he could get off early. Even though Randy'd set his stove's timer for 5:00 for our injections, Jared and I were eyeing the minute hands on our watches, like cats clocking goldfish. When the timer went off, we both nearly jumped off the sofa.

Randy went in and turned it off, then came back with his black bag. "Okay, roll up your sleeves, you two." His eyebrows shot up at the pelts on our arms.

"*What?*" I asked, heart thudding.

"Nothing. I was just wondering if I should shave your arms first."

"Just get on with it, Randy! Think of us as wildlife."

"Well, that's no stretch," Randy said. He swabbed a patch on my arm with alcohol, and inserted the hypodermic needle. The doses came pre-measured, so it was fast. Which was just as well. I couldn't have stood a long, drawn-out production. I looked at Jared and heard him gulp. "Not so bad," I reassured him.

"Yet," Jared muttered.

"See? Another satisfied customer," Randy joked. "I always aim to be painless. Next!"

Jared offered his arm and looked away. He jumped a bit after the pinch, then let out a breath. I checked my watch again: 5:15 p.m. And now we'd wait.

The others' eyeballs were bouncing back and forth between Jared and me like ping pong balls, waiting for the big reaction.

Randy took his bag away and went back to the kitchen, coming back in with a round of coffee and bottles of water. "No alcohol, tonight. Sorry. Doctors' orders. And you'll probably want to hydrate well."

Damn. I was already panting for a drink and it wasn't water.

"So . . . ," Kate began. "How do you feel, Al?"

"I feel like throwing up," I mumbled.

Randy looked concerned. "That's not a side effect Frank mentioned."

"I don't think it's the antidote. It's my fright and flight kicking in."

"Don't you mean 'fight or flight'?" Kate asked.

"Nope. How about you, Jared?"

He considered a moment. "I guess I feel okay, maybe even a little calmer than when I got here. You're looking smoother, I notice, Alice."

I looked down at my arms and saw he was right. My nails were still long, but that was a good thing. I shot Jared a tight smile. "Maybe I'm calming down a little, too. You're looking more clean-cut yourself."

"Oh, the slur! Like that would ever be the case." We laughed.

Emma looked morosely at her own arms growing hairier.

It was such an unseasonably warm day, Randy had fired up the grill in back and was cooking burgers for us. "How do you want yours?" he asked us.

Emma rolled her eyes. "Seriously? Rare, I'm assuming for us three," she said, motioning to Jared and me. "Right?"

We shrugged an embarrassed yes.

"Kate? Dion?"

"Medium well, please, with everything, if you've got it," Kate said.

"You got anything less meaty, Randy?" Dion asked him.

"I could grill up some tofurkey for you," Randy offered.

"Super! And with everything, also."

"I've put the fixings on a plate so you can choose for yourselves. And there's a tossed salad, with my homemade vinaigrette."

Randy headed back to the patio. Twenty minutes later, he came back with a platter of five perfectly cooked moo burgers and one soy, no feathers. We gathered around his long, oval kitchen table and helped ourselves.

"Chow down, guys. Gotta keep up your strength."

"And hopefully keep *down* any misdirected blood lust," Kate muttered.

Randy gave her a thumbs up, we filled our plates and filed back into the living room. “So, what’s on TV?” Dion asked.

Randy pointed his remote at the TV. As it blinked alive, he scrolled down the guide. “News, news, news, *America's Funniest Home Videos*, and *Wheel of Fortune*, but it’s a *Celebrity Wheel* re-run right now.”

“*Wheel!*” we sang out.

I turned to Jared. “*You* like *Wheel*, too?”

Emma snickered. “Hidden depths!”

“Hey, it’s good brain exercise,” Jared defended.

Dion laughed. “Dude, ’fess up. You just like seeing airheads ask for a vowel when there’s only one letter left!”

Jared laughed back. “Okay, yeah. That, too.”

Emma’s chest was heaving. “Oh my god, do you remember that one where the puzzle was some lyrics from a song in *Moana*? What was it?” she asked, turning to Jared.

“ ‘How Far I’ll Go,’ ” Kate provided. She owned the DVD.

“Yes! How’d it go again?”

I’d even seen *that* episode, but Kate beat me to it: “ ‘See the line where the S-blank-Y meets the sea, it calls me.’ ”

Emma was pounding the coffee table, making the bottles jump. “And that poor woman asked for an ‘o,’ making it ‘soy’ instead of ‘sky’!”

“Ryan even *reminded* her there were no more vowels!” Jared crowed.

Kate’s dry wit got the better of us: “It was a Japanese shipping disaster, obviously.” I nearly choked on my water.

“*Wheel of Fortune* it is then,” Randy laughed, switching channels.

At the third commercial break, Randy checked his phone as the rest of us got up, stretched, and took a pee break. Plopping back down, I checked my watch. Only 6:22 p.m. Still a ways to go. I could see Emma was getting pretty jumpy. Actually, I was surprised I wasn’t, not as much as I usually would be, anyway. Looked like the antidote was helping. Poor Emma would be needing Nair and a manicure tomorrow.

Dion went out Randy’s back door. “Hey, guys, check this out!” he called through the open door. “The eclipse is awesome!”

Randy and Kate got up. “You coming?” he asked Jared.

Jared looked at me, undecidedly. “What do you think?”

I really wanted to see it, but was still worrying it would trigger the change; it was much too early for that, if the antidote didn't work right.

"You go," I shooed him off. "See what you think. If you don't come back barking, maybe I'll join you."

"Okay. Emma? You wanna check it out?" he asked.

She shook her head, massaging her foliating jaw. "I'm good."

When they came back in, seeing there wasn't any noticeable change in Jared, I got up. Took a breath. "Maybe I will go. You look like you survived, Jared."

"It is really something, Alice. And later, we'll probably be too busy to appreciate it."

Emma sighed and stood, too. "Oh, okay. But I might just peek through the kitchen window. See how it goes."

It *was* awesome: a huge, red, balloon rising with pomp and a cup of shadow. You know that famous music at the end of *2001: A Space Odyssey,* "Zarathustra"? It was like that. We all stood on Randy's patio with mouths dropped, going Wow! like it was the Fourth of July. Even Emma was drawn outside. I hugged her (carefully). "Glad you didn't miss it now, aren't you?" She nodded, speechless.

When we went back in, there was a text waiting from Sheila for Dion. They'd be heading over around 7:00 p.m., bringing Connie, Martha, Sally and Ruby in the van. She gave him the van's description and license plate.

As luck would have it, the van was an extra-long plumber's van Frank's buddy had just bought, with a heavy cargo screen behind the rear seat to keep hot water heaters and the like from crashing forward when you stomped on the brakes. There'd be room for Dion to set up his gear in the back seat and plenty of room for the girls in the cargo area where they'd thrown in a pile of blankets, pillows and humane tie-ups. And it had the business's logo on its black sides.

When Randy heard that, he'd told Dion, Jared, and Emma that they could ride with us in his car. "The fewer vehicles we bring the better."

So here we were, the six of us, Jared cozy in the back with Emma.

"If they're heading over at 7:00, when should we head out?" Dion asked Randy. "I wouldn't mind getting there earlier, so I'll have plenty of time to set up in the van."

Randy considered. “Normally, it should take them about 35 minutes to get to Manchester, but I’m guessing they’re giving themselves some extra time because there’ll probably be extra traffic with moon watchers along the way, especially through Beverly Farms by West Beach. I can get there most days in 15-20 minutes. But today . . .” He scratched his chin. “I think we should probably leave by 7:15 at the latest.”

Dion nodded. “Sounds good.”

“You got all the stuff?” Jared asked him.

“Of course.”

“I mean, the extra, surprise stuff?”

Dion winked. “What do *you* think?”

“You’re still not gonna tell us?” I asked.

“Nope,” they chorused.

I seemed to recall that Zarathustra was some kind of major, hairy prophet back in B.C. and that he’d preached some good things—good thoughts, good words and good deeds, wasn’t it? Something like that. Basic “play nice with others” stuff.

Well, we were certainly here to do some good deeds. I didn’t want to count my plots before they hatched, but this red moon eclipse thing was beginning to feel like a good omen. We could sure use one. A *good* moon on the rise.

Cue the kettle drums: bum! . . . , bum! . . . , bum! . . . , *Bah Dum!*

FIFTY-FOUR

JUST A SHOT AWAY

Randy was right: Route 127, the coastal route from Beverly up to Manchester, was pretty clogged—across from Endicott College and any place there was a peek at the ocean. After Prides Crossing, cars were pulled over in thicker groups, a bunch turning in the gate at West Beach, then more, farther along, looking over the tracks by Boardman Avenue.

It was a good thing we'd left earlier. The crowds were also a great cover for us. No one would notice yet another unfamiliar vehicle.

Years back, Kate and I'd watched Fourth of July fireworks displays near Boardman, sitting on the slope of the Rockport commuter rail's gravel embankment. It had been a double thrill: the train thundering past, mere feet behind you, as the rockets burst in the air.

Now we were treated to a different display. Randy was finding it hard to keep his eyes on the twisting road. "Good thing we didn't toke up before we left!" he commented to Dion.

"Who's this 'we,' white man?" Dion replied. We'd gotten so used to the cloud of skunk following him, we hadn't noticed he'd recharged his vaper with something more . . . soothing.

"You gonna be okay with that?" Kate asked, worried.

He gave her a grin and blew a smoke ring. "Babe. I do some of my best work this way." (O ye of little faith, just follow the ninja.)

When we got to Rolf's neighborhood, it looked like one big block party, just as predicted. Everyone was outside, oohing and aahing and trying to capture photos on their iPhones of the red orb slowly rising; kids were running around with sparklers and shooting off fireworks, left over from the Fourth; parents were outside barbequing and keeping an eye on the eclipse and their kids.

After we parked far down the street from Rolf's place, Randy withdrew his dart gun from the Bronco and a box of darts. It was quite a long rifle, so he'd stowed it in the drawstring sleeve of one of those folding canvas chairs and slung it over his shoulder by the strap. The boy's definitely got smarts.

We set off down the street, keeping mostly to the shadows. Everyone we saw as we passed, though, was focused on the eclipse from their own backyards, with some neighborly cocktail exchanges. A few waved as we sauntered past. We waved back, anonymous in the dark.

The only house that wasn't lit up like a Halloween lantern was Rolf's.

As we got to Rolf's drive, we stopped and peered around. Kate stopped me with a hand on my arm. "How are you doing?"

I shrugged. "Okay so far." She was standing so close I could feel her shivering and put an arm around her. "You cold?"

She shook her head. "No, just terrified."

It finally hit me that she'd never seen us all in wolf mode. Hell, for that matter, neither had I. But at least I was one of them. Kate wasn't. No wonder she was terrified. There were so many ways this could go gruesomely wrong. I gave her shoulder a squeeze. "*¡Ándale!*"

Below her breath she sang the refrain of *La Marseillaise.*

As we walked up Rolf's dark drive, we saw Frank's van pass us on the road and park farther on. Dion padded over to the van and slid inside with his backpack to sort out his surveillance and weaponry.

Randy motioned us to our stations: Kate by the garage, him and me by the outside cellar door. Jared went over to the van to check on the others. The only lights we could see in Rolf's were upstairs, in what I remembered as his library, and the basement hall. In the basement's light, I kept checking my limbs for sprouting fur, but it looked like I was still human. So far, the antidote seemed to be doing its thing. I did some slow Zen breathing to calm my pounding heart.

It was still pounding so loud in my ears I never heard Dion sneak up next to me, several minutes later, carrying a large duffel bag. I don't know how I managed to stifle a yelp when he startled me, but I did, then gave him a glare and socked his bicep. He just grinned back.

Randy and Dion went along the outside of the house, underneath the basement cells' windows, consulting in whispers, as Dion set up. Jared tiptoed over and pointed to the moon which was just then shedding a long skein of cloud. He hadn't turned Airedale yet, so the antidote seemed to working for him, too.

Randy looked at the illuminated dial of his watch, then spelled out the time to us on his fingers. He looked like a TV announcer counting down to live air time. It was 8:30 now; it had taken us 40 minutes or so to get there, and another few to get organized and start setting up. Pretty decent timing so far.

I beckoned Jared over and he stooped next to my ear so we could whisper. "Where's Emma and the others? They doin' okay?"

He see-sawed his hand and breathed, "They're gettin' pretty hairy and antsy in the van, except for Sheila and Frank, of course, but I think their spirits are still up." To Randy he whispered, "Let me know when everything's set, and I'll go get them."

Randy gave him a thumbs up. "Just don't forget the 'props.' I've got mine ready." He propped his tranquilizer rifle against the brick wall.

Five minutes later, Dion donned his headset beneath Patty's window and signaled he was all set. Jared trotted silently back to the van as Dion dialed in his audio and zipped open the duffel, hauling stuff out.

"How are you doing, Alice?" Randy murmured.

"Okay, I guess, except . . ."

Randy clutched my shoulder. "You'll do fine, Al."

"It's not that. Um. I need to pee."

He flapped his arms in the air and did a half-turn, then hissed back in amused annoyance, "Why didn't you go before we left home?"

I winced. "I know. And I did, but . . ."

He pointed sternly to the far shrubs and mouthed, "Go! *Quick!*"

The others were coming over now, so I made a dash into the shadows.

I was just pulling up my drawers when Dion gave us a frantic *psssst,* pointing upward and hissing, "Incoming!" The light in the kitchen above came on and his headphones had picked up movement in the hall.

I heard the click of toenails and jingling of dog tags, a chain and a leash.

Everyone scattered like cockroaches and were safely hidden as the cellar door opened. A guard came out with the dog.

Looked like Rolf had changed his mind about keeping a guard there tonight. It made sense, with another mouth to feed and monitor and a dog that needed feeding and walking, too. Rolf wouldn't be able to take care of it once he was under the change.

The dog took one sniff and started barking. The guard swivelled his Maglite around the drive and wrinkled his nose. “Shut up, you stupid mutt, it’s just a skunk.” Then the dog lunged toward Dion, still hidden in the dark.

Hiding in the shadows nearby, Randy was ready.

The guy only got out, “This is private property! Who the fu—,” before Randy got him with the dart gun. The guard went down like a slab of juiced beef, twitching and fading out. Must have been a good-sized dose. The dog dodged a second dart and, yipping, ran off in fright, the two of them leaving the door to the cellar left wide open.

Dion was ready, too. Rolf, hearing the noise, had come downstairs to investigate. His aging-rock-star mane was back-lit by the hall light; the cellar’s outside light revealed an elongated set of choppers and glowing amber eyes.

I shrank back farther under a bush, cursing myself for wearing my snaggable Mexican poncho. My heart was in my mouth and I was praying it wouldn’t be in someone else’s soon.

When Rolf ventured outside, Dion gave him a little “yoo-hoo” wave. Rolf, still mostly human, bared his teeth and grinned. “I don’t remember ordering anyzing vom Door Dash, but *you* vill do!” (Accent was back.)

Rolf shot out a paw to snag Dion, who summersaulted backwards then held up a white frisbee. On its topside were the famous mouse ears.

“Thought you might enjoy a little souvenir,” the ninja rasped.

“What ze fuck I vant viz a Mickey Mouse frisbee?” Rolf growled. “Got plenty of ze rodent’s souvenirs. And it’s vay past my dinner time.”

Standing under the halogen light, Dion swivelled the frisbee over to the concave side. In its dead center was Rolf’s pendant in a jewelry-sized Ziploc, Gorilla-glued to the disc. “You sonuvabitch!” Rolf bellowed.

Dion hopped out of the way as Rolf made a grab.

“Lose something, Rolfie?” Dion taunted, then took off running across the field, shouting over his shoulder, “Here boy! Fetch!”

Rolf had already started the change, but took one look at the giant, unoccluded red moon and went full wolf like he was on warp drive.

At least the kitchen light threw a little more light on the field. As I heard two short bursts then a long one from one of the dog whistles, the girls burst out of the van yapping and snarling.

And they're off!

Randy goes down on one knee, watching for an open shot at Rolf, but the girls are too fast and too committed, practically on Rolf's heels (or another part of his anatomy).

"Shit!" I exclaim and start running toward them, trying to catch up. I don't want them to be accidentally shot.

But Jared's got this: he streaks forward with a bucket of frisbees. Dion shouts "Pull!" directing Jared to start throwing them and dances away from Rolf. As Jared begins flinging out the frisbees, I stumble to a stop, amazed and impressed. Dion's secret weapon is *way* better than doggie treats.

I notice they're coated with something fluorescent that picks up the light in pool-toy colors: orange, red, lime green, and Zonkers' screaming yellow . . . and one other white one.

With a sleight of hand so fast you'd miss it in broad daylight (if you didn't have wolf sight), I see the exchange. Sailing the pendant frisbee to Jared, Dion catches its duplicate deftly.

I also see him snatch something shiny with five points out of his black vest.

Randy sprints forward to get in closer firing range and drops again to a knee, steadying his aim, rifle butted against his shoulder. I can see his breaths puffing out in the night air as he concentrates on his target. The other frisbees have successfully broken up the pack, keeping the girls safe and opening up Randy's line of sight, likewise Dion's.

Kate is ready, though trembling, with her pistol and silver bullets.

I don't know what to do, so I'm just dodging back and forth like a linebacker, revving up for a tackle if need be. I feel absolutely helpless and wonder if I wouldn't have been more useful without the antidote. I certainly would have been braver.

But I needn't have stressed. The frisbee ploy is working out just fine.

It's sheer, hilarious chaos and brilliant—all those weredoggies of various breeds, jumping and yipping in the game, because that's how we're wired. I see Connie's white ball-of-fur snatch a red frisbee right out of Ruby's (red setter) maw in triumph. Lynn 1: Rockport? 0.

Then Martha (standard poodle) breaks off and tears after Rolf, bites into his butt, managing to pants him. While she's snapping at his "ball bearings," with a tremendous heave he escapes emasculation, splitting the remains of his trousers right down the middle seam. They flap pathetically around his ankles like frenzied flags in a game of flag football. After a few yards, they shred off.

Now Emma (black lab mix) takes up Martha's chase. I hear another shout of "Pull!" and a bright yellow frisbee sails off toward the woods, Emma and Sally, diverted, racing neck-and-neck toward the prize.

My wiseass brain is playing a soundtrack that sounds like part of a Strauss waltz—the she-wolves' galloping eighth notes ascending, the leap (2,3), snatch (2,3), the thudding landing (2 measures), the phrase repeated in 3/4 time with each frisbeed leap.

Jerking my head back to the Dion/Rolf chase, it's more like the theme song from *Benny Hill*.

Sheila, Kate and Frank join me, sharing a mutual jaw drop and "WTF?" cartoon bubble. Despite our white knuckles, we all nearly piss ourselves laughing. (I was *really* thankful I'd gotten that pee in.)

Then Kate comes to and vaults forward with her pistol.

Just as she's closing in and Rolf is about to spring on Dion, slavering jaws agape and lethal claws fanned wide, we see the ghostly outline of a black lab springing into the air. Kate calls over to me, hand over her heart. "It's Reggie, Alice! Oh, my big old love!" She's jumping up and down, tears in her eyes. "Sic 'im, Reggie! *Sic* the bastard!"

Reggie responds with a ferocious growl, headbutts Kate out of danger and shoulder slams Rolf away from Dion, then runs interference between the two.

Dion staggers, then hurls the white frisbee forward, toward the ocean's edge. When Rolf gains some distance from Dion, Randy gets off a clean shot into Rolf's left shoulder, but the dart only wings him.

It's going to take a *lot* more than a tranquilizer; Rolf barely stumbles. And I feel certain Rolf's chilling howl can be heard through the whole neighborhood. We stiffen like statues, expecting neighborly interference.

But the kids down the street think it's all part of a game, a spooky Halloween stunt, and start howling themselves in giggling glee, pointing to the really big, pointy-eared dog racing off after the white frisbee.

Dion stands rock steady, gauging his aim and distance, then whips up one of his silver throwing stars and zings it in a blur at Rolf.

It's a thing of beauty.

Like it's in slo-mo, we watch breathless as Rolf's rippling form arcs up, clearly visible now against the dark sky, under the light of the red, rising moon, snapping the frisbee victoriously in his jaws. . . .

Followed by the lightning flash of a silver star point ramming into Rolf's jugular.

His spurting blood matches the color of the moon. And the night becomes still.

Over my shoulder, I see Frank lowering the dog whistle he was about to blow. There's no need for one long whistle to stay in place.

We stand stunned.

Twenty or so glacial seconds pass, then, with a mental head shake, we reanimate and move *en masse* toward Rolf's body.

The girls have beat us there and are chowing down, ripping off pieces. Even mild little Sally (golden spaniel) is delicately lapping up the pool of his blood.

Ruby's growling and gnawing a severed hind foot while Connie runs in circles yapping out instructions to the others in wolf-speak. My inner wolf catches something that translates as: "Girls! Leave them fingers for the coppers!"

It's handy to have a clean-up crew—one so forensically inclined.

And true to her promise, Martha, not to be deprived of her "trophies," is worrying at Rolf's naughty bits. There's a pop as they come free.

Randy winces and turns away, shrugging. "Mountain Oysters."

I hear a wolf-like *Ptooey!* and catch Martha spitting them out. "Guess they're an acquired taste," he adds.

Eyes squeezed shut, I fake gag. But not before noticing their size.

I nudge Randy and whisper, "They *are* kinda like ball bearings."

He snorts. "Serious shrinkage. I wonder if those chromosomes act like steroids." Frank, who's overheard us, guffaws and fist-pumps the air.

Sheila mutters to me, "Men! They love finding out the competition is lacking." Then louder, "Randy, cover that," she circles her hand, "up."

Dion stoops over Rolf's body and extracts the star, cleans it off with a wet-wipe, stows it back in his vest. Randy pulls Rolf's shirttail down.

"Jared!" Dion calls, "Grab the frisbee with the pendant, before anybody gets any ideas."

"On it, buddy!" And off he trots. A moment later, he trots back with the frisbee bucket. "All accounted for, sir!" He salutes Dion and hands him the white pendant frisbee for safekeeping. Dion salutes back.

By the edge of the woods, I see Kate bending down and hugging a black ghost dog and murmuring sweet nothings in its ear. Rolf's runaway Doberman crawls out from the trees, belly dragging the ground, front shoulders and paws bowed in submission to his alpha dog. Reggie nuzzles him back. Kate pats the dobie, too, and he whimpers an apology, wagging his tail. Reggie takes one last look at Kate, she makes a heart with her hands and blows him a kiss, and he vaporizes into the woods.

She rejoins us, wiping her nose on her sleeve. "What a good doggy Reggie was. And *is*, as it turns out. God, I miss him."

"I know. He obviously misses you, too. Honey, you've got yourself an angel dog there."

"I do. He saved my life, Al." She straightens up. "So . . . is the bastard really dead?"

Dion rasps an amused huff, "I'd say so."

"So, what do we do now?" she asks, still panting.

My chest's still heaving, too, but with a sly smirk I manage to drawl in a Downeast accent, "First, make sure he's dead."

With an answering wink, Kate plants both feet and with both hands fires a silver bullet straight into Rolf's chest. One final firework.

And right out of *Men from Maine!*

As we high-five, our palms connect with a resounding smack.

Jared points up to the sky. "Check it out, guys!"

The moon has risen free of its penumbra and is now snowy white and gleaming serenely over the field, as if it were choreographed by some cosmic intelligence. We hear the neighbors applauding the *finis* and start heading back inside.

I glance back down. "Check *that* out, guys."

Rolf is morphing back to human form on the grass, right on cue. Pants-less and neutered, it is *not* a good sight. A *castrato* without a tune left, not even a howl.

FIFTY-FIVE

OFF TO THE RESCUE!

Clearing his throat, Randy brings us back to earth. "So, Ephus, what's the second thing?" He points to the open cellar door.

Sheila shoots upward, shrieks and grabs Frank, "Patty!" They bolt off toward the basement.

Randy tosses his dart gun to Dion. "Keep an eye on the girls. Make sure they don't wander off!" The others still don't know about Patty.

Dion snatches it one-handed out of the air. "Got it!"

Jared gives the girls a sharp bark, then loud, two-finger whistles for them to come back. And, amazingly, they all do and follow him like happy puppies to the van. Hunh. *Our* alpha dog, I guess.

Randy races off after Frank and Sheila. I cup my hands and yell after him, "What do *I* do?"

"You come, too. You know the room plans. But first, grab my bag from the car and bring it."

"Mine too," Frank shouts. "It's in the back of the van. It's open."

I see Frank stoop over the prone body of the guard then hear the jingle of keys. I run for the van and the Bronco. No time to explain to the girls.

When I get back, panting and lugging the two medical bags, Frank's hands are trembling as he fumbles with the big ring of keys, trying to find the right one. Sheila's tap dancing in place, yelling at him to hurry.

A light goes on in Patty's cell. A woozy voice cries out, "Mom?"

"Patty! Yes, I'm here, honey," she sobs. "Your dad's here, too. We're getting you out of this hell hole! Are you okay?"

"I'm okay." Then she starts blubbering too, great gulping sobs.

"Found it!" Frank shouts, turning the key in the lock. Before opening the cell door, he says to Randy, quietly, "Got any more of those darts?"

"Sure, but at this range, I'd prefer to use the hypodermic needles. If you need them."

Frank crosses his fingers. "Maybe we won't." Randy pulls a primed needle out of his bag and flicks his finger against the tube.

Swatting away their hands, Sheila yanks open the cell door and Patty collapses into her arms. They're both bawling their hearts out and hugging fiercely. Kate and I join in on the weepy group hug.

Randy approaches cautiously sideways, shielding a hypodermic needle on his off side. But she's okay. Patty's scarily thin but furless. Unlike Sheila and me, and probably Jared by now. We were slowly approaching plush status, but we'd made it through the worst. Noticing it, Sheila passes Patty gently off to Frank.

"Thank God!" Randy exhales slowly. "I'd better go check on the others," and he takes off with his bag.

There's a still moment where Patty and I stare at each other in shock. Sheila sees it and nods. "You see what I mean? You could be sisters."

"Hell, practically identical twins," I murmur. Even in her unkempt, emaciated, traumatized condition—let's be real, Patty looked like an Auschwitz survivor, minus the striped PJs—there is no mistaking the resemblance. Shivers rattle my spine, like a rough-running engine.

Patty reaches a hand toward my face, then pulls it back.

Solemnly, I nod too. " 'Mirror, mirror on the wall . . .' "

Then the moment is broken. Patty croaks out an ironic laugh. "Well, the 'fairest of them all' sure isn't me!" I swallow hard and hold her hand.

Jared lopes inside and confirms my guess: he's half Airedale but still intelligible. "Before I lose my communication channels, I thought you guys ought to know the frisbee with the pendant has gone missing. Man, I swear I just turned my head a second!"

Dion's come back and is packing up his gear, Randy following, and gives Jared's withers a pat. "'S'okay, dude. I'll 'splain later."

"What about the girls?" Kate asks Randy.

"They're all fine," Randy says. "Dosed and docile, sleeping it off in the van, except for Martha and Sally. They're in the back of my Bronco. Jared's riding back with Frank and Sheila and the others in the van to keep an eye on them, as long as he can anyway."

I smile. *And to keep a paw on Emma.*

I hear a toilet flushing. Must be a shared bathroom. Then a light in the next cell goes on. Someone's pounding on the iron door and calling out. "Kate, is that you out there? Can you get me out of this damned place?"

Kate's been leaning against the cell door and jumps. The doors have eye-height louvered vents and as she turns around, her shoulder hits a tab on the side of the vent frame and it swivels open like a mini-blind.

They peer at each other through the door. "Oh my God! Mona?" She grabs the key ring from Frank, locates the correct key, and lets Mona out.

"God almighty, Mona, what the *hell* were you thinking? You just never listen!" Then Kate grabs her and rocks her until Mona's mascara streaks down like Pagliaccio's.

Dion finally admits he'd seen another bed in the other cell, the other night when he peeped in, but it was empty. Then later picked up what sounded like Mona's voice but didn't want to confirm until he was sure.

I feel it's best to keep mum about *that*. Kate would never forgive me if she knew I already knew. I'm encouraged to see that, otherwise, Mona's in considerably better shape. She turns to Patty, who's still gibbering in Frank's embrace. "I guess I don't have a right to bitch, compared to you, Patty. I'm so glad you made it out at last."

Patty reaches out her hand and squeezes Mona's. "We both lucked out, thanks to these guys."

As we all scrabble for Kleenex or dry sleeves, Mona relates how she and Rolf had flown to Disney World, then had a flaming shout down.

"What about?" Kate asks.

"Something bad he was planning, really bad, I'd overheard. Not about . . . this. About the Disney corporation, I think. And the manatees!" Now, tough-as-nails Mona starts sobbing.

We bounce befuddled glances off each other.

"The manatees, Mona?" Kate prompts, brows lifted.

Mona puts a palm over her diaphragm to still the hiccups. "It's bad enough I find out he's a fucking werewolf. With Rolf's generous funding, Disney and its affiliates, or maybe one of its competitors, are apparently planning to bulldoze the Everglades—a huge swathe of what's left of them—to build another goddamned theme park! The *Everglades*—mangroves, manatees, sea turtles, wood storks, *all* of it!"

And the fast-disappearing panthers. "Jesus," I breathe, fists clinched.

"As if theme parks haven't already raped half of Florida," Dion spits.

Mona goes on, "I'd overheard him laughing about it, har, har, har, with his buddies in the hallway outside our hotel room when he thought

I was soaking in the jacuzzi. I'd stepped back out to grab another towel. I could *not* believe my ears. They all have a cut in it. There were *congressmen* with him! I could see the 'old boys' through the peep hole. Even that new dickhead from the EPA!"

"Not surprised. I know about that dude." Dion risks a little arm pat.

She sobs, "I really wanted that gig, but not at *that* cost!"

"The mother fucker," Kate mutters.

I turn to her, goggle-eyed.

"What?" she bridles. "Sometimes an expletive is simply necessary."

"When Rolf came back inside," Mona says, "I screamed at him, 'The manatees? Seriously, you don't even give a shit about the *manatees*?' He just smirked and said, 'Sure, I like manatees. Zey taste great broiled.' That's when I smacked him."

Dion's lip curls. "That explains what little I picked up from the fight upstairs. Beyond all the yelling and shrieking, I just caught the words 'manatees' 'sea turtles' and 'mangroves.' Now it makes sense."

"Oh, he tried to make up to me. Told me I was overreacting. It wasn't so much Everglades, as such, mostly old, dead or dying orange groves, trees that had succumbed to some blight, just like the first parks."

"I beg to differ with him on *that,"* Frank says through gritted teeth.

"Next morning, he told me the gig was off. Disney had had to lay off some of the characters they already had, so couldn't take on new."

"On account of diverting funds to the new venture?" Randy mutters.

"I know I was an idiot to confront him," Mona goes on. "It just gave him an excuse to haul me home like a naughty child . . . and add me to his pack."

Or silence her for sure.

"What a dope I was! You were so right about him, Katie. I actually believed the Disney World gig was going to work out," she wails. Then her lips push out in a pout. "Though it might have been helpful, Kate, if you'd told me a bit more."

Kate gasps, affronted. "Would you have believed me? *Any* of this? You know how obstinate you are."

Mona sighs and shakes her head. "No, you're right. It's way too Gothic, even for me. And the rest is just . . . unthinkable."

"So, are you okay, Mona? I mean . . . *you* know," Kate asks.

"Am I about to sprout fur and fangs? No, he didn't 'turn' me. The prick didn't have the chance, I'd kicked him so hard in the balls while he was trying to inject me with some drug. He backed off after that, big time! I'm just still spitting nails about it."

She shrugs. "I did get a little nick, but you know how I've always been drug insensitive. It takes a lot to put me down."

Mona reaches across and takes Patty's wrist. "What about you, Patty? Did the bastard get to you?"

"It's a miracle, but I think I'm okay," Patty says. "I just got a little nip but I managed to fend off a major attack." She chuckles and winks at Mona. "My own damage to his do-dads might have had something to do with that, too."

It was probably the adrenalin ebbing, but I feel a fit of the giggles coming on. I glance over at Sheila, hold up an imaginary Groucho cigar to a corner of my mouth, bouncing my eyebrows. "So, doctor, would you say repeated pummeling to the testes might result in . . ."

She howls. " 'Ball bearings'?" she shoots back. "The data is still out, but current findings would suggest that might well be the case."

"Look, can we just get the hell out of here?" Mona asks, jerking her head toward the open back door. "Before Rolf gets back?"

"God, yes, Mom! Let's get out of here *fast!*"

When we don't move, she cries, "Why aren't we moving?!"

Sheila's voice shakes, but she's smiling. We're all beaming now. "Honey, Rolf's dead."

For a moment I think both Patty and Mona are going to faint. Randy dives for Patty and Dion lunges for Mona as they sag, shuddering in relief. "Are you sure?" Mona snaps.

Dion nods. "Yep, we got the asshole."

Mimicking John Cleese, Kate chimes in, "'E's bereft of life, 'e's kicked the bucket, shuffled off 'is mortal coil, rung down the curtain and joined the bleedin' choir invisible."

I grin at my fellow Python fanatic. "You missed the bit ''E rests in peace,' only in Rolf's case, it's in pieces." Everyone breaks up.

Frank puts his arms around his daughter and his somewhat shaggy ex. "Let's get you girls home and safe." They lean their heads against his shoulders.

"Sounds good to me!" Sheila gives him a smooch. "You did well, tonight, Frank. *Thank* you, honey." She sniffles phlegmily. "Thank you so very much! Patty, sweetheart, I'll help you gather your things."

"There's not a lot. Rolf took pretty much everything."

Looking around the cell, we see she's right. Besides the spartan hospital bed with steel side rails (convenient for attaching restraints), there's a gaping shopping bag, revealing a value pack of Depends, and the party dress she was nabbed in hanging on a hook.

A cruel reminder of her stolen life.

Patty's shivering in her thin johnny. Sheila grabs the cleanest blanket and wraps Patty up, dumps out the Depends then folds the dress tenderly and places it in the bag. She turns to Frank. "Let's all go home!"

Randy tugs on Frank's elbow. "Just a sec. The good doctor might need a special cocktail on her way back." He holds up a loaded hypo. "It's veterinarian-approved."

Frank gives him a bro hug and takes it. "Just the thing."

Jared ducks his head and mumbles, "I think I'll go and check on Emma and the others." He starts to leave then turns back. "But I should probably get a jab, too." Randy digs in his bag again and passes Frank another hypo. Jared says, "Thanks, dude. See ya! What a night, huh?"

Kate asks Mona, "Why don't I help you with your stuff, honey? And what about your purse?"

Mona sighs. "Rolf took mine, too. But it might be upstairs, maybe Patty's, too."

"We'll keep an eye out and nab them if we see them, when we do a run-through," I tell her.

"And I want my damned cloak back!" Mona adds.

"They'll find it, honey," Kate says. Biting a lip, she looks over at us. "Time for beddy-bye? I'm sure Mona could use a decent night's sleep."

I'd noticed Dion and Kate fidgeting.

Randy has, too. And I'm pretty sure they've noticed my poncho's filling out. Looked like the antidote was wearing off a little faster.

"Change of plans. You guys go on to the Bronco," Randy says to Kate, Mona and me. "Dion and I will do a last sweep here."

"Right behind you," Dion says, then, donning latex gloves and pulling out wet-wipes, suggests, "Maybe a little wipe-down?"

Reaching for my arm, Kate turns to go. I shrug it off. I still feel solid.

"You said you needed me, too," I say, "knowing the room plans."

"You still doin' okay?" Randy asks, running his hands over my arms, prying open my mouth to peer at my teeth.

I growl back in annoyance. "So far, so good. If I get frisky, just jab me in the ass."

"What? *Again?*"

Dion hands us gloves and we snap them on. We go through the whole house, leaving the top storey's boom-boom room for last.

So far, we've found no surprises, except for a hold-all stuffed with banded stacks of $100s, a ticket to Munich courtesy of Disney Vacations, and Rolf's passport left on the library's desk. His wall safe was still ajar.

We left the passport.

But I'm dreading what, or who, we still might find upstairs.

It turns out okay, even when I ride to the top in the dumbwaiter. Just a big king-sized bed with rumpled, gummy sheets, a black garter belt, and some implements of bondage. As you might expect.

No smears of blood in the bathroom. Nothing gory in the trash.

I spy Mona's cloak and find two cell phones and a couple of purses in a closet and bundle them inside the cloak. Randy's got the hold-all.

Downstairs, in the kitchen, I fish out a Hefty bag from under the sink and put Mona's cloak, the phones, and the purses inside.

"Speaking of trash . . . ," Randy begins, jerking his head toward outside. "Dion, wanna give me a hand taking it out?"

I frown, looking at my bag with the girls' things, then the penny drops. *Eeeeeuuuw.* "Something we left on the lawn?" Like a shredded corpse.

Randy gives me a nod and a wink. "Mustn't be litterbugs!" He grabs more Hefty bags and starts off downstairs with Dion.

"Wait!" I call. "Where are you taking . . . it?"

"I figure the woods would be the most logical."

Unsure, I grimace, thinking "toxic waste dump." "Um, what about the environment? And the critters?"

Dion pats my shoulder. "It's all biodegradable."

Back in the basement, we haul the guard back in, dump him on Mona's bed, and turn off the light. Besides his gun holster, I see a set of restraints attached to his belt. "I think we should lock him in," I say. *Payback time.*

We hear dog-tags jingling outside by the cellar door.

"Nah, someone's got to feed the poor doggy," Randy says. The Doberman trots in with a mouse-eared white frisbee in his mouth, head down, contrite.

Randy crouches, takes the gift from him, hands it off to Dion, and fondles the dobie's ears. "Good boy! It's not your fault. You just got put in a rotten home. Let's get you some dinner."

He stands. "You guys go on. I'll lock the house up. And I have a phone call to make." Randy tosses the dungeon's keys to Dion. "Catch! Put those somewhere safe." Then he heads up to the kitchen, whistling to the dog.

I'm starting to feel funny again, the ancient biological pull of the moon. And my poncho's definitely bloating fast.

Randy's left his bag behind and I rummage for another vial and a needle. "You any good with these things?" I ask Dion.

"Have you met my best buddy, Jared? What do *you* think?"

"Thank God. I feel a howl coming on."

We speed walk back to Randy's Bronco.

Dion's steering me gingerly by my elbow.

I nuzzle his neck. "You know, you're an outstanding ninja, Dion. Besides everything else, you probably managed to save some manatees."

"I sure as hell hope so, Alice. Let's *all* hope so!"

I sigh. "I guess we lost the pendant."

Not that *I'd* wanted it, but in case any of Rolf's wolf pack buddies were around, I'd really hoped they wouldn't find it and put it to use.

Dion grins and holds it up. "The dobie brought it back, remember? The mouse-eared frisbee in his mouth? In any case, it was just a decoy. I'd never have risked the real one. I had my buddy, the guy who made the throwing stars, make up a duplicate."

Dion's friend had painted the same wolf's head and Rolf's family motto on it and had done a very convincing job. Quite the artist.

"Randy's going to lock the real one up in his safe deposit box, along with the cellar keys."

"Jared will be happy to hear that! Did you ever find out what that family motto meant?"

Dion fires up his vaper, sucks in, nodding. "Immortal wolves, united in nobility, purity, and blood." Jeez. *Sieg Heil!*

He blows an expert smoke ring. "Oh, I found out what his brother's up to. He's been trying to work a deal with Disney to build a park in Germany, give Europa World a run for their money."

Wolves expanding their turf. I quake thinking about it. "Aren't you glad you nailed the sonuvabitch?"

"Fuckin' A!" His teeth gleam wide under his Fu Manchu and he gives me smooch on my fuzzy jaw.

"When are we gonna fill the rest of the girls in about Patty?" I whisper to him.

"Not tonight, dear!" Dion jerks his head toward the cargo area.

Mona's up front in the passenger's seat. Dion slides in next to Kate in the back seat; Kate peers anxiously at me over her shoulder.

I hop into the cargo area next to a snoring Martha and Sally and curl up, shivering, pulling my poncho and a dog blanket around me. "Okay. Hit me, Ninja!"

"One vet-approved cocktail comin' up, ma'am!"

Bliss. Fade to black.

FIFTY-SIX

COUNTING OUR BLESSINGS

Almost Thanksgiving—an appropriate time, I'd say, for our posse to get together and give thanks, now that our hair-raising Halloween crisis has passed. We'd reserved La Cantina's back function room for a Saturday night and were seated in a couple of spacious, side-by-side banquettes, with extra tables and chairs pulled over.

After Rolf's take-down, Frank and Sheila flew back to L.A. with Patty for a joyful family reunion with their boys. They returned two weeks later bringing more of the antidote. Frank said his team is manufacturing it as fast as possible. We'd all be getting some this time—all of us wolf types—enough to take us into the first part of the new year.

We all breathed sighs of relief, looking forward to holidays that would finally be merry, not scary.

"Hallelujah!" Ruby raised her glass to him.

Sheila hugged her daughter and raised her glass, also. "Amen!" We all joined in, echoing heartfelt gratitude.

Jared asked Frank if there'd be enough to share with his dad. Frank patted his shoulder and said, "I've already planned on it."

Emma and I beamed and raised our glasses in salute to Jared.

Leaning over my margarita, I asked Frank, "Is Patty really okay?"

"Thankfully, yes. That little 'nip' Rolf gave her finally did take, but her immune system's so strong, she was largely resistant to the virus." He smiled at her. "Patty's worst symptoms from the change were having to shave her legs three times as often and, well, growing a slight mustache. But we fixed that easily enough."

Patty leaned over. "It really wasn't so bad and I think that helped put Rolf off me. He was such a vain asshole."

Sheila frowned and cleared her throat at Patty.

Patty slid her eyes over to Sheila. "Mom! I'm just calling it like I see it. You know I'm right."

Jared proposed a toast to Frank and Sheila, Patty and Mona.

As one, we all stood and raised our glasses to the reunited family and the rescued abductees, then settled in, reaching for the chips and salsa.

We were also there to celebrate in an even bigger way. The anonymous call Randy had made, via trustworthy Hank, had done its job. The *Globe's* first-page headline was spectacular the day after, the story bursting with the sensational scoop they'd been handed:

MOGUL'S EMPIRE ECLIPSED BY MAULING

Mutilated Body Found in Manchester Woods. No Shred of Clues.

As the weeks went by, every paper and tabloid vied for exclusive updates on the gruesome discovery. Several reporters cycled back, with pointed conjecture, to the Dee Dee Thornton case, when details about the cellar cells and their obvious recent occupancy, along with the curiously furnished "gym," were divulged and detectives found a purse containing Dee Dee's ID inside Rolf's safe—an arrogant souvenir. Sheila confirmed to police the purse was Dee Dee's as well. Dee Dee's fingerprints and DNA from a hairbrush were also found in Patty's cell.

Rolf's staff and guards were questioned, but denied knowledge of Rolf's activities. But the guards couldn't keep their stories straight. One said he sorta thought he'd heard female voices in the cellar, but pointed out, with a shrug, that the rich boss man did a lot of entertaining. It was nothing to do with him.

Another said he'd been told Rolf was a doctor, taking care of a schizo relative or two instead of leaving them to the nuthouse. "I mean, the dude musta been some kinda doc, he got drugs by the buttload. Had to be writing the scrips himself. Me, I don't mess with no drugs, man." This, from the guy Dion recognized from his recordings as Mr. Needle, the guy in charge of sedating the victims.

There was so much we could add to the testimonies. But with our "conditions," we didn't dare.

Investigative reporters at *The Miami Herald* discovered Rolf's links to the Disney conglomerate and an affiliate theme-park developer, well-known Republican politicians and members of Congress, and ran with it. Reporters all over the country were having a field day.

The exposé had caused a serious stink among even the most loyal constituents. Disney had to do some major backpedaling to thwart the furor. Their last press release stated that environmental studies had proved such projects untenable; neither they nor any affiliate or known competitor were planning on further development, here or abroad.

There was talk on the news of diverted funds, Rolf's offshore accounts, and the courts' likely freezing his estate's assets.

I dinged my glass with a spoon and stood, holding aloft my margarita. "I propose another toast!" I looked down at my glass: two lime slices floating in ice sludge. "Oops! Hang on a second."

Ricardo glided over and topped up everyone's glasses. He winked at me. "*¿Mejor?*"

I dipped my head and winked back. "*Sí, gracias, mucho mejor*."

"As I was saying," I started again, louder, "I'd like to propose a toast to our amazing ninja, theme-park-defying champion of manatees, and warrior for justice, Dion! May his skateboard forever keep on rollin'!"

The responding chorus was deafening. "Keep on rollin', bro!" Jared called out, starting up a chant: "Roll on! Roll on! Roll on!"

I'd have never have thought that anyone with such a deep olive complexion could blush, but Dion was disproving that assumption.

The food arrived at last and hot plates were set down with the usual warnings. Our tables were heaped with enchiladas, chiles rellenos, tacos, fajitas, *y todas las cobinaciones. Guacamole* was passed around with the salsa, both hot and mild. Predictably, Connie stuck to the mild. But I'm proud to report that not one of them, not even Connie, pronounced the *g* in *guacamole*.

Randy was digging into his fajitas and recounting a new bizarre episode in ER. Prepping a seriously obese woman for surgery, a whole slice of toast had fallen out from under her boobs. Sheila and Frank were laughing their heads off.

In gustatory heaven, I moaned over my rellenos. They were perfect and covered in one of the best *moles* I'd ever tasted. Coming up for air and a cooling swallow of lime-laced tequila, I scanned the group fondly, feeling so grateful to know these people and call them friends.

I caught Mona making eyes at Chuy, but he only had eyes for Kate, and she for him; they were locked in conversation, eyes dancing. Randy leaned over to my ear, mourning that Chuy was only chewable to women. I spared him no sympathy; he had Hank to fall back (or forward) on.

Frank and Sheila, still beside themselves for getting Patty back, discussed the possibility of becoming a family again in California with their boys, if they can find a cure.

Jared and Emma were sharing a bathtub margarita through a single straw; they're still in the young, snuggling, giggling stage. And speaking of getting cozy and giggling, Dion and Sally had their heads together and seemed to be really hitting if off. He'd set Sally off laughing with some tale and his arm was spread across the back of the banquette, a couple of his fingers casually circling her shoulder.

I turned away and asked Ruby, "So, where *is* it you're from? I never did hear."

She answered, "Rockport. Why?"

Kate heard and gave me an amused thumbs up. "You still got it, girl!" She knew my game.

But Rockport's not a town bursting with fun hang-outs. Perplexed, I asked Ruby, "Then where was it you got bitten?"

She shrugged. "Gloucester. Despite the welcome blue-law changes, Rockport's still pretty sedate. Gloucester has better places to party."

Martha was hoovering up her *camarones de Veracruz* and getting flirty with the waiters, not at all bothered about being a single at the table. Conspiratorially, she'd whispered earlier that even if she went home alone, there was always a good selection at Maddie's when she got back.

Mona, polishing off her *tacos al pastor* and on her third margarita, was dauntlessly back on the market and getting chummy with the gorgeous male waitstaff. Ruby mentioned she had a date later, as did Randy, with hunky Hank.

Everyone seemed to be pairing up except me. Well, and Connie. But after she'd buried her husband years ago, she divulged she very much doubted she'd be takin' on another.

"What about Bud?" I asked her. "Last I saw, seemed like you had a twinkle in your eye for him." I noticed she'd laid by a man-sized portion of her *tacos de pollo grande* in a take-away carton.

She lowered her eyes and sucked primly on her straw. "Sure, we'll have to see. There's always the bingo."

So things were looking up even for Connie in the love department. I moped over my margarita, thinking of Manny and missing him again.

After the dishes were carried off, we paid our bill, sent our enthusiastic thanks to the kitchen, and lounged back finishing our drinks.

Then, one by one, folks started gathering coats, saying their goodbyes and making promises to meet again soon. I thought at least Kate and I'd be leaving together, but I saw her blush prettily, then, after sending me a little wave, flit off with Chuy who'd just gone off shift.

Checking his phone, Randy made his excuses, gave me a peck on the cheek, and left.

I sucked on my melting margarita through my straw, happy we'd accomplished so much—putting that sick monster down and maybe even saving the Everglades—but wishing I had someone of my own to canoodle and celebrate with.

When I started to heave myself up to leave, Ricardo came over, waylaying me.

"I brought you this." He slid over a magnificent flan, the size of a personal pizza. "I was waiting for the rest to leave," he said, "because it would not feed all of jou. Such a large party! It must have been a grand celebration. *¿Una fiesta grande, verdad*?"

I smiled into his gorgeous dark eyes. "I couldn't possibly eat this all by myself. Won't you join me?"

Ricardo smiled back from under his long lashes. "I was hoping jou would say that." He checked his watch. "*¡Bueno!* My shift is over." He circled his index finger at my defunct margarita. "*¿Otra vez*?"

I inclined my head with a wide smile. "*Sí, otra vez*."

He motioned to the bartender and held up two fingers. "*¡Dos mas, por favor!*"

"*Muchas gracias*," I replied when our refills arrived.

He gave me a little bow. "My pleasure."

And mine, I foresaw.

I tipped my salted rim to his and found myself wondering how he felt about hairy women. And decided I might be ready to find out.

What would I need with Manny when I had "*otra vez*"—a new start?

FIFTY-SEVEN

EPILOGUE

February 12th, Precedent's Day

In February, as Valentine's Day approached, we each got texts from Frank and Sheila saying they'd cracked it!

They'd successfully developed and tested an all-round werewolf cure. Building upon mRNA engineering, the same research that discovered interferon and later developed the SARS and COVID-19 vaccines, it worked on both viral and hereditary lycanthropy. Patty and Sheila both were virus free!

Frank was sending out vials via Express Mail to all the WA members and Jared's dad. Ditto the poor woman from the ER with the shredded Pilates pants. Sheila had discreetly contacted her a while ago before she could go on the rampage.

It was such a tremendous step in medical science, and it would set such a precedent. I mourned, on their behalf, the need for keeping it secret. If only they could publish their triumph without incurring a Big Pharma witch hunt, they'd be the next Nobel prize winners.

I knew my bosses' biotech clients would be practically salivating over the breakthrough, if they ever learned of it. Either that, or having a hissing cat-fight free-for-all debunking it.

The hold-all of banded $100s we'd taken from Rolf's study totalled a whopping $100 grand (and our booty had grown slightly fatter after helping ourselves to some of the contents of the safe). By common consent, we gave $50K to Frank to help defray his costs in developing the antidote and the antiviral drug. Then we divvied up the rest.

Randy donated a few grand to a local wildlife rescue organization and an animal shelter. I sent several grand to homeless shelters locally and in Boston. Randy and I would cash in Rolf's baubles we'd purloined from the safe and put them in a savings account to dip into whenever I learned that someone in my homeless group needed urgent medical aid or he heard of a threat of euthanizing animals, so we could save them.

I still checked, from time to time, on the homeless folk I knew and told them if I wasn't around as often, they could still contact me if anyone needed urgent assistance. I'd given several of them (the sober ones) my cell number for emergencies.

The Everglades theme park swindle was finally kaput and multiple lawsuits were erupting like toadstools, pleasing a circling shark pool of prosecuting attorneys. Implications of corruption—money laundering, racketeering, extortion, bribery—were flying like Death Frisbees at government officials, not just in Florida, with major players coming under scrutiny, even at the highest level. And they were hitting bulls' eyes. I was praying that the chief fungus would hit the compost pile, too.

Somewhere in Florida, beneath the sun-dappled banyans and mangroves, dolphins were smiling.

Mona ditched her job at Disney Vacations and has teamed up with Sally, working for the City of Salem organizing special events (many of which, predictably, encourage costumes).

Though the investigation into Dee Dee Thornton's savage murder was still ongoing, enough evidence has been put together to definitely connect Rolf and identify him as her assailant. The courts would make sure that reparations in the millions will be awarded from his estate to her grieving family.

Kate and Chuy (real name Chuck, no actual Mexican accent) have been going strong. And it wasn't just her melons he was fond of. In any event, she'd aced a job as a social worker in training at the welfare office, so had given notice at the market. She's finally using her anthropology degree for something worthwhile, and will be funding her M.A. with her share of the loot so she can be licensed.

Connie was battling bingo cards with Bud at the Elks (when he wasn't testing Mrs. Chang's *mu shu* pork). Jimmy'd talked him into it. Said she was cutting back on the garlic. Jimmy had installed the remote buzzer and camera for her, and he and Mrs. C were a regular item now. She'd even started up a mahjong group at the Elks.

Speaking of items, Randy and Hank were becoming one; when their shifts coincided, they were rarely apart. And we finally got to meet him! (Hank really is a hunk: tall, dark, ripped, with a sunny smile. Also wise.) Randy had confided in secrecy most of the details about D-Day to him and, maybe not so surprisingly, Hank, bless him, though astonished, was cool about it. Hey, he'd already handled a lot of weird wildlife.

Which worked out in more ways than one. Through Hank's P.D. pals and the database fire and police shared, he'd put in a quiet word to watch arriving European flights for Klaus who'd be coming over to identify his brother's body and set his solicitors in action to sort out Rolf's estate. Hank had given only the details they needed. Klaus was apprehended at Logan and now they had his vital information, DNA, and fingerprints.

We now knew where Klaus lived.

So Hank and Randy are looking forward to a romantic European vacation soon. With Hank's EMT status and Randy's being an NP, they'll both have clearance to transport "necessary" drugs. AAA had happily given them maps of the regions of interest, even highlighting in yellow the village where Klaus holes up in his *schloss*.

Mike and June have pooled their resources and are buying out their landlord on their duplex. So Emma's losing her current roomie, but it's easy to guess who her new one will be. And Dion and Sally are tight.

Ricardo (Rick now, sometimes Ricky) and I have also been a steady thing. Friends love teasing us about the weirdness of Ricky Ricardo hooking up with Alice Cooper. (If they only knew!) I'd managed so far to find credible excuses about not meeting up during the change. But soon Rick would never have to see how hairy I could get. Otherwise, everything was the same old boring routine (minus the fright nights). But sometimes boring routine isn't all that bad, especially when you've got someone you can count on to snuggle up with.

And I finally hung my Rockport print. Ricardo says it looks *muy* classy over the bookshelves by my desk.

Happy Valentine's Day to us!

Best of all is knowing that Team Saints soundly trounced the Sinners and their wicked plots (without enlisting New Orleans' help).

You're welcome.

So . . . looks like this Alice will be coming back up the rabbit hole, getting her life, her old one, back.

And it's looking very, very good.

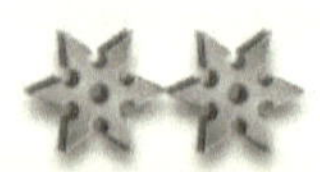

Acknowledgements

Once again, I'd like to thank the funny, smart women of Wise Women Write. Besides being terrific writers, you've kept me rational, thinking, and laughing throughout the depressing and shockingly putrid political disasters of the past several years.

My terrific, sweet sister, Kathleen O'Shell, still remains my Number 1 Cheerleader. Thanks, Kit! You can't imagine how much that means to me.

As always, I have to give a shout out to my personal Grammar Girl Guide, Ruth Haber, to whom I'm forever grateful for striving to keep me on the straight-and-narrow and informing me on the most arcane aspects of English grammar. Forgive me, Ruth, for the times I've put my fingers in my ears.

And a shout out to Tim Lynch and his students for their design help and input, as well as to Jac, Christina and the gang at the BBC in Plymouth, Massachusetts, the first and last remaining British Beer Company pub. Thanks, guys, for not rolling your eyes every time I gave you an update on the book (over the years)—at least not in front of me.

I'd also like to give my eternal gratitude to author and native Floridian, Carl Hiaasen, whose laser wit and political insight have offered such hope to the sane, and probably kept Canada's borders from being flooded by defecting U.S. citizens. Laughter really is the best weapon. May you always poke the bear who deserves it, Carl.

I'll always be grateful for the Stokers, my mother's wonderful family, now mostly upstairs with the Big Guy, who taught us kindness, fairness, and tolerance—and to still recognize a crook when we see one—and how to tell a really funny story (even on themselves).

And, last, my everlasting thanks go up to Billie Stoker Hall, my incomparable mom now dancing in heaven, for giving me a sense of wonder, a huge sense of humor, and an abiding love of language. I really lucked out. Save me a bar stool up there, Mama.

Facts Among the Fiction

o The license plate "RCH FKR" was spotted by an old boyfriend of mine on a Rolls-Royce in Mill Valley, California.

o The Massachusetts license plate "I BITE" (red letters on a white plate) was on a late-model white SUV I happened to be behind on Samoset Street in Plymouth, Massachusetts.

o The story timeline begins July, 2022, the main action taking place the autumn of 2023. "D-Day" was Saturday, October 28th, three days before Halloween. That evening was unseasonably warm with passing clouds that cleared, and there was a penumbral lunar eclipse of the full moon, beginning at 4:24 p.m. and lasting 4 hrs. and 39 minutes. After dark, the moon was red as it rose; the eclipse was past and the moon white and shining fully at 9:03 p.m. The phases of the moon follow those of 2023.

o The Choate Bridge Pub in Ipswich and Tom Shea's on the Essex River were favorite hang-outs when I lived in the North Shore, but, sadly, Tom Shea's closed its doors on October 16, 2023. Which is why, if you check the 2023 calendar, you'll see that the gang spies Sheila stalking Rolf outside it on October 14, 2023.

o My real-life, skateboarding ninja buddy from the BBC, Tommy Ready (Dion in the story), really does make throwing stars. Thankfully, the only wounds you might sustain from them would be paper cuts.

o The refrain from *La Marseillaise* Kate sang during the take-down is "*Marchons!* Marchons*! Qu'un sang impur abreuve nos sillons!*" ("March! March! May impure blood water our fields!") I learned it as a child from my mom. It was a stimulating motivator for doing chores.

o Rolf von Wildlebend Herunterschlingen's red-brick mansion was modelled on a stupendous, mock-Tudor manor on Dexter Lane in Manchester, Massachusetts. It even has the brick-walled basement with black iron doors and an impressive wine cellar. There are no werewolves in residence, however. We hope.

And finally . . .

The Underwear

o The "Bite Me" panties are real; I own two pair. Surgeries being an extreme, nail-biting, acid-reflux event for me,[1] I've enjoyed wearing them, as comic relief, during two bunionectomies and a meniscal arthroscopy, to the amusement of the surgical staff.

o I also have both the pink paisley and purple tropical fish boxers—mementos of a dear, deceased gay friend. Girls, take note: Boxers are much more comfortable in bed on a hot and sticky summer night than panty briefs.

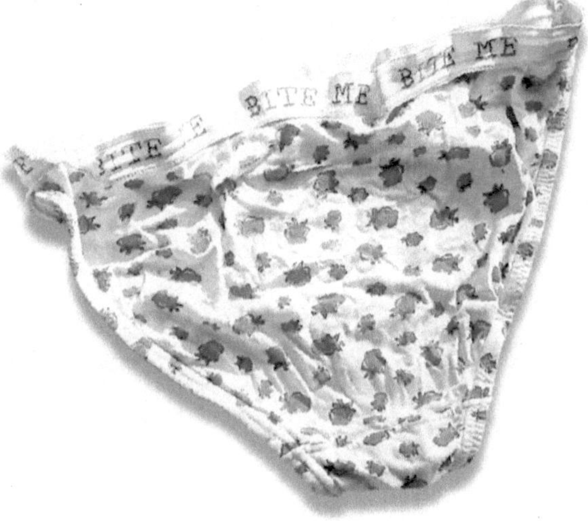

---

[1] It's a real thing, called tomophobia. (I had to look it up, too.)
See also: nosocomephobia. Those Greeks had a word for *everything*.

In Memoriam

Thanks for so many great memories!

KATE

Kathryn Anne Robinson
July 10, 1949 – December 21, 2023

I wish you could have seen Kate in her grey cloak. She was magnificent!

GENE

Eugene J. Cavatorta
June 2, 1941 – July 26, 2021

And Gene would have had you laughing your ass off.

About the Author

Native Californian **LAUREN STOKER** moved to New England for the thrill of skiing on ice and owning a snow blower, and lives with her cat (and Chief Shreditor), Sam.

Among her checkered careers, she was employed briefly by two law enforcement agencies (think, *The Choirboys*), toiled as a travel agent, practiced therapy as a bartender, and most recently worked for over 22 years as a legal assistant in the biotech field.

A confirmed tree-hugger and Anglophile, Lauren enjoys ranting about anti–environmentalists, shouting at newscasts, and hanging out in pubs while drinking fine British ales or their non-tariffed facsimiles.

Since the tender age of 15, she has struggled with the written word (and sometimes won). In addition to her books and some memorable Op-Eds, her short stories and non-fiction have been published in the U.S., Canada, the U.K., and Australia.

The author makes no apologies for the darlings that went unmurdered.

Follow her at: **LaurenHStoker.com.**

www.ingramcontent.com/pod-product-compliance
Lightning Source LLC
LaVergne TN
LVHW090554110826
845146LV00001B/119

* 9 7 9 8 2 3 4 0 1 2 3 8 8 *